# PRAISE FOR MASTER OF THE ABYSS

"*Master of the Abyss* is the riveting conclusion to the Painted Souls trilogy, the ultimate conspiracy thriller series. The novel is infused with heart and drama. The action comes at warp speed and the writing is cinematic. This is masterful world building combined with an elegantly woven plot and characters that come alive on the page."

**- Jayne Ann Krentz, *New York Times* bestselling author**

"Rob Samborn is an effortless storyteller. I slipped right into this story like a warm jacket on a cold day. With characters you'll fall in love with and a plot that will keep you turning the pages, never sure what twist or turn is coming next, it's utterly enchanting, totally unique, and simply unputdownable. I've never read anything quite like this, which meant I had no clue what was coming and I was here for it. My advice: crack open this book and prepare to devour it!"

**- Kiersten Modglin, bestselling author of The Arrangement Trilogy**

"An electrifying finale that masterfully ties together the intricate threads of fate, belief, and cosmic destiny. This isn't just the close of a series; it's the capstone on a narrative masterpiece that challenges the very notions of good and evil. A pulse-pounding quest from Venice to Asia, replete with ancient artifacts, dark villains, and heroes who never lose their moral compass. The Painted Souls series ends not with a whimper, but a universe-altering bang!"

**- Gary McAvoy, bestselling author of The Magdalene Chronicles and Vatican Secret Archive Thrillers**

"*Master of the Abyss* is a high concept and action-packed thriller that captivates from start to finish. With engrossing historical details and polished descriptive writing, Samborn has a unique way of transporting not just his characters around the globe, but his readers as well. The stakes are high, the plot threads brilliantly woven, and the twists and turns riveting in this stunning conclusion to a truly masterfully crafted series. Samborn saved the best for last."

- **Shanessa Gluhm, author of *Enemies of Doves* and *A River of Crows***

"Rob Samborn raises the stakes, the tension, and the conflict to a tantalizing crescendo in this masterful, multinational, multi-timeline finale to the Painted Souls series. Unputdownable, with an ever-twisting plot populated by a diverse cast of true-to-life characters. A winner in many ways."

- **Mike Krentz, award-winning author of the Dr. Zack Winston series**

"Rob Samborn's *Master of the Abyss* marks the thrilling and satisfying conclusion to his Painted Souls series, bringing to an end the captivating adventure of Nick and Julia that was first introduced to readers in *The Prisoner of Paradise*. With his exceptional storytelling and encyclopedic knowledge of historical periods and locations, Samborn once again proves himself a masterful author, weaving a tale that is both fantastical and grounded in reality."

- **Ty Keenum, author of The Little Church series and *The Coincidence of Birth***

## SELECT PRAISE FOR PAINTER OF THE DAMNED (book 2)

"From 16th century Venice to modern Madrid, Painter of the Damned splashes bright history, dark arts, crimson action, and shape-shifting twists onto an epic canvas to create a genre-bending masterwork."

- **David L. Robbins, *New York Times* bestselling author**

"A truly unique thriller blending elements of mystery, suspense and loads of action, *Painter of the Damned* takes readers on a journey unlike any other. Strap in for a heady adventure that delivers on all levels."

- **Andrew Clawson, author of *The Arthurian Relic* and the Harry Fox series**

"Rob Samborn delivers with his latest thriller that whips you from Tintoretto's famous painting which holds captive a 16th century soul, to a present-day race against the leader of an ancient order to gain control of a hidden book that can unlock unimaginable power, to a wife on a mission to save her husband from the grips of his past. You will want to read *Painter of the Damned*. Period!"

**- Yasmin Angoe, bestselling author of *Her Name is Knight***

## SELECT PRAISE FOR THE PRISONER OF PARADISE (book 1)

"The city of Venice soaks into your bones in Rob Samborn's *The Prisoner of Paradise*. As the painting comes alive, so does every word on the page in this gripping and transportive read."

**- EJ Mellow, bestselling author of *Song of the Forever Rains***

"A truly evocative and finely-woven tale reminiscent of Dan Brown and Gwendolyn Womack. Filled with stunning writing, the Venetian art world, and well-researched and vivid historical detail, this thrilling story captivates until the very last page."

**- Charissa Weaks, author of *The Witch Collector***

"*The Da Vinci Code* meets *The Time Traveler's Wife*. In this imaginative thrill ride, Samborn transports the reader between modern day and Renaissance Venice unraveling conspiracy in the pursuit of destiny. I was dazzled from beginning to end. This ambitious debut does not disappoint."

**- Robert Gwaltney, author of *The Cicada Tree***

# MASTER OF THE ABYSS

## PAINTED SOULS BOOK III

ROB SAMBORN

Lost Meridian Press

MASTER OF THE ABYSS (Painted Souls, Book 3)
By Rob Samborn
Published by Lost Meridian Press
www.lostmeridianpress.com

Softcover ISBN: 978-1-959194-47-7

This book is a work of fiction. References to real people, events, establishments, organizations, brands, or locales are intended only to provide a sense of authenticity and are used fictitiously. All other characters, and all incidents and dialogue, are drawn from the author's imagination and are not to be construed as real.

Editor: L.A. Mitchell
Cover Design: David Ter-Avanesysan @ter33design

Connect with the author online at www.robsamborn.com.

First Edition

Printed in the United States of America.

# BOOKS BY ROB SAMBORN

*The Prisoner of Paradise*
*The Swordsman of Venice*
*Painter of the Damned*

# CONTENT WARNING

MASTER OF THE ABYSS is a work of fiction about realistic characters in realistic settings. The content is written to evoke maximum visceral emotion within an entertaining and informative context. The story includes elements that might not be suitable for some readers, including graphic violence, adult language, and sexual situations. Readers who are sensitive to these elements should please take note.

For Cameron.
You embraced the light the moment it hit your beautiful eyes.

*Time,*
*You've gifted me.*
*Time,*
*You've betrayed me.*
*Time,*
*My unrelenting master.*
-- Isabella Scalfini, the day of her trial, 1589


*You will find the spirit of Caesar in this soul of a woman.*
-- Artemisia Gentileschi, 1649


*Without light, we are nothing but pilgrims to the Abyss.*
-- decree no. 1, Ancient Order of the Seventh Sun

# 1702 A.D.

# REPUBLIC OF VENICE

S HADOWS FLICKERED OFF DAMP walls. A single oil lamp clenched in a sweaty fist illuminated the dark corridor. Emanuele Quattrone tightened his grip on a wheellock pistol to steady his nerves.

Behind him, three men matched his pace. Each wielded two primed flintlocks and a sheathed rapier. Moments prior, they'd used their swords to dispatch six Protectors patrolling the Palazzo Ducale, inside and out. The blades enabled silent deaths for a stealth entry; the firearms were required for the bullets' speed. A flintlock was also holstered on Emanuele's hip. He prayed one of their weapons would find its target.

"This way, friends," Emanuele whispered in Venetian. "We're almost there."

The narrow underground passageway necessitated that they travel in single file, and the corridor's curvature limited visibility to a mere ten paces. All four men had trained their bodies for this moment. Rank air and mildew stifled Emanuele's breathing, but his thin, muscular frame flew past the rough ashlar stone walls.

He paused at a T-junction. Relying on memory, he recalled the map passed down to him from his great-great-grandfather. That illustrious man was the first Exalted Master of the Ancient Order of the Seventh Sun—before he was betrayed by his own and sentenced to *Paradiso* in 1614.

The eastward path led to a stairwell to the Great Council Room, home to *Paradiso* and the souls within. If they turned west, the passageway would've reached the warden of the souls, the Painter, Jacopo Tintoretto. It led to vengeance... and an end to the madness.

Emanuele went west, guiding his meager squadron through the Palazzo's bowels. The Order needed to be demolished. He'd been waiting all of his forty-two years for this moment. So far, everything had gone to plan, yet his heart rattled. Perspiration drenched his shirt.

As members of the Order, he and his colleagues had beheld the fantastic. They were privy to truths of this world few would believe. Each person on Earth was gifted a single soul that traveled through seven lives. Upon conclusion of the seventh, one's soul faced final judgment: ascension or eradication.

Except the Painters.

Emanuele also witnessed corruption—crimes against nobility and commoners alike. None epitomized the venality like Jacopo Tintoretto. Imbued with the power of the Sun Crystal, he was one of three who'd been gifted an extended lifespan. Tintoretto had been a Renaissance giant, but that did not justify his continued being. He was an abomination. A curse on Christ himself. Only the Lord should live beyond the lifespan of a mortal man. At 184 years of age, Tintoretto should've been worm food.

His most grievous sin was taking hundreds of lives—souls now confined for eternity in his duplicitous masterpiece.

Emanuele made the sign of the cross with his pistol hand.

*Wrongs would be righted.*

A rustle on the ground prompted him to halt. His compatriots followed suit. A rat scurried by—demon spawn fleeing from the mouth of Hell.

Releasing a breath, Emanuele soldiered on for twenty more paces until an oak door blocked the passageway, like the goal of Daedalus's labyrinth. Who was more dangerous—the Minotaur... or the Painter?

Emanuele beckoned his men closer to the door. He was told the Painter's living quarters would be locked from the outside, but that was not the case. Apparently, Tintoretto was free to come and go. That posed a new problem. Should the door be sealed from the *inside*, they'd have no means of entry. Emanuele raised the lantern. Shadow and tricorne hats shrouded his companions' features, but concern glazed their eyes.

"We've come too far to fail, my friends," Emanuele whispered. "We've lost too many."

They nodded their agreement.

After setting the lantern on the ground, Emanuele wrapped his free hand around the door handle.

Footsteps and angry voices reverberated from the far end of the corridor.

"We're discovered," his comrade whispered.

Emanuele's bones quivered with the unmistakable, gnawing ache of desperation. It wasn't a labyrinth; it was a deathtrap. With a silent prayer, he pressed the thumb latch and cracked the door. All exhaled relief.

He threw the door open. His friends squeezed past and rushed in, pistols at the ready. Slipping inside, Emanuele slammed the door shut and slid the bolt across the frame.

"Welcome, brethren." Tintoretto's spry, deep voice belied his years. He stood at an easel in the far corner, with his back to the entrance. Lush, silvery hair cascaded over a white linen robe on a petite frame, but the Painter was anything but diminutive—his presence dominated the space.

"We should talk," he said.

The men froze, unsure of what to do.

Emanuele took stock of his environs. The room was smaller than he'd imagined, especially for a man not only central to the Order but worshipped by them. A dozen candles cast golden light on cluttered living conditions. Fetid, stale air forced him to pant through his mouth so he didn't gag on the stench. A stained mattress and chamber pot were tucked into a corner. Stacks of leather-bound books lay strewn about on a writing desk and Oriental rug. Three other easels stood on the floor. Paint jars, brushes, and paintings, either loose or framed, overwhelmed the space. The artworks were masterpieces of all types—landscapes, portraits, still life, and somber depictions of the abyss.

"Who is the leader of your delegation?" The Painter dabbed his brush on his palette and applied strokes of gray to the canvas.

The men moved aside for their captain. Emanuele took a tentative step forward, despising himself. Why was he indulging this monster? The wheellock weighed heavy. He couldn't will himself to use it, either unable to kill an almost-mythical being or incapable of shooting someone in the back. "Face us," he said.

Tintoretto continued painting. Ominous storm clouds loomed at the top of his canvas. "What is your name?"

"Emanuele Quattrone. Face us. I demand it!"

"Quattrone?" The Painter grunted without turning.

"Descendant of Senator Marco Niccolò Quattrone, first Exalted—"

"I know who the traitor was."

The insult to his forefather incensed Emanuele. He aimed his weapon at the Painter's head.

"End him," his compatriot whispered. "Do it now."

Someone pounded on the door. Frantic yelling seeped through the wood.

With a shaking hand, Emanuele squeezed the trigger.

As if hearing the pistol's wheel, Tintoretto shifted. The weapon discharged, emitting a cloud of smoke. The bullet flew through the canvas and struck the wall.

Tintoretto dropped his artist's tools and spun. With unholy speed, he launched himself at Emanuele. A glimpse of a thick white beard whooshed through the gun smoke. The Painter clutched Emanuele's throat and shoved him into his comrade, slamming both against the wall. Emanuele's head whiplashed into his friend's nose. Warm blood splattered Emanuele's neck. The man slumped to the floor.

Emanuele steadied himself and drew his flintlock. Tintoretto knocked it from his hand. The other men raised their pistols, but Tintoretto stole Emanuele's rapier from its scabbard. In a flash, the Painter twisted and sliced through both men's wrists. They cried out and dropped their weapons.

Their reactions were short-lived—*as were they*. Tintoretto severed their throats before doing the same to the third man in as many seconds. All three collapsed. Arterial spray gushed from their lacerations. Emanuele's friend clamped his neck, choking and writhing, until the Painter lodged his rapier in the man's heart.

"I told you we should talk," said Tintoretto, without a hitch in his breathing, undisturbed by the blood painting his robe and floor.

Emanuele met the gaze of the man standing victoriously before him. "You—you're a monstrosity. Offspring of Satan himself."

"A curious observation. Since it is *I* who shall grant you Paradise."

# I

# MADRID, PRESENT DAY

C ARLO ZUCCARO'S EYES SNAPPED open. His chest heaved. Sweat drenched his forehead and neck.

The flashbacks had been coming more frequently and vividly. This recent one was a new development. He'd had visions of Tintoretto but hadn't witnessed the man's brutality outside of a Convocation. Carlo once believed the Renaissance master was a tool of the Order—as they expected Carlo to be. To the contrary, Tintoretto was the group's beating heart. If the Order assumed Carlo would bow to their commands—to kill and sentence innocent souls to *Paradiso*—they had instated the wrong person. He was the new Painter, but he had a choice. Simply living in obscurity for the remainder of his unnatural life would prevent additional souls from being imprisoned.

He shuddered. Everyone dreamed of more time; he was only twenty-six and had already learned how quickly dreams became curses.

Adjusting to his present surroundings, he slowed his breathing, wiped his brow, and scanned his new hotel room. The blinds veiled the city's lights. He sat on the carpet, his back against the bed. A lit cigarette dangled between his fingers.

It had been a long twenty-four hours.

Five mini bottles of vodka, four mindless comedy movies, three room service meals, two showers, one hour of sleep, and zero daylight had done nothing to appease his nerves. Sketches of Julia O'Connor on hotel stationery lay scattered about the room, an activity that gave him equal parts solace and distress. He gazed at the black-ink drawing, a decent likeness, but he wished he had color to capture her true beauty. How he longed to see those green eyes and honey-blonde hair.

He sighed. She was lost to him forever. Ironic, since she was never his.

Incredibly, losing Julia wasn't the worst thing to happen to him.

Beyond his regressions to the assassination attempt on Tintoretto, Senator Quattrone's torture, and a half-dozen souls who'd been beaten, raped, and had their life essence sucked from them, every thought imaginable swam in Carlo's head. The strongest was a voracious barracuda.

His life was over.

More than once, he cried like the day his father died in a still-unexplained fire. His eyes again clouded at the memory, but he wiped his face with the back of his hand, determined not to let emotions get the better of him. He still yearned to learn the truth about his father's death, but he didn't give a shit anymore about the Order or being the Painter. He had to consider his life, his future. How could he return to Venice? How could he continue his art career? How could he reconcile with Julia?

A mere two weeks prior, he was Venice's rising-star artist. But it was all a sham. His benefactor and supposed father figure, Salvatore della Porta, Exalted Master of the Ancient Order of the Seventh Sun, had been grooming Carlo his whole life to be Tintoretto's replacement—a position forced upon Carlo when Nick O'Connor extinguished the first Painter's long life. Della Porta had withheld so much from Carlo, not the least of which was the ability to hear *Paradiso*'s furious prisoners—including his father.

Carlo stood and paced the room, careful to sidestep any drawings of Julia and people from his flashbacks. He puffed on his cigarette like an asthma inhaler.

Would things have been different had he not met Nick and Julia? *How a fleeting moment could alter a life.* Nick was also able to hear a soul in *Paradiso*, but only one—Isabella Scalfini, Nick's beloved from his past life. Carlo had truly wanted to help, but as the American tourist regressed to Angelo Mascari, a swordsman from the sixteenth century, everything went to literal hell.

A long drag from his cigarette served to only fuel his nicotine addiction. He snuffed the butt in the overflowing glass ashtray on the dresser and caught himself in the mirror. Bloodshot hazel eyes stared back at him beneath a mop of dark brown. He looked as miserable as he felt.

The tiny room and putrid air suffocated him. The walls tightened by the hour, threatening to squeeze him like a grape in a vise. If he stayed in this room, he'd end up slitting his wrists in the bathtub. The Order be damned; he needed to breathe.

He snatched his key card, wallet, and passport off the nightstand.

People streamed by Carlo in the bustling nightlife of the Malasaña neighborhood. Couples dined and drank. Groups of friends filed into bars with varying types of music, backdropping his cacophonous soundscape.

While the fresh air and activity lifted his spirit, Carlo ambled in slow motion, sticking to the walls and shadows. He lowered the brim of his newly purchased Real Madrid hat to enshroud his face. He'd always admired the football club and their aggressive tactics on and off the field, though he was currently very much on defense.

Other than being landlocked, from what he'd seen, Madrid seemed to be his ideal city. If only the Order didn't have a base of operations there. Not to mention its proximity to Venice. Nowhere in Europe was safe.

He chugged his Coke.

America seemed to be a good choice for his career. Maybe New York. No, farther. Los Angeles. Hell, why not Hawaii? He could change his name. Would a vacationing Order member recognize him? Argentina was a better option. Or maybe Thailand. Julia would become a memory, but he could paint landscapes and sell them on the beach. His friend had spent two months traveling Southeast Asia and raved about the joys of lounging in a hammock by day and dancing with girls at quarter, half, and full-moon parties by night.

The moon brought him back to the Order and their ceremonies based on lunar phases. Knowing the group had sentenced Senator Quattrone, as well as his descendant, sent waves of agitation and anger through Carlo. Was history repeating itself?

He rubbed his tatted forearms. Was it a parallel situation? Or had *he* betrayed della Porta?

A group of drunk college-aged kids headed straight for him, not even acknowledging his presence. Carlo shimmied out of their way like the ghost he was.

'They are liars, free us.'

Senator Quattrone's soul had uttered the words from *Paradiso* in the Thyssen-Bornemisza Museum the night before. Was it a plea or a warning? Perhaps there was a history of double-crossed souls.

If there were a possibility of freeing his father, Nick, and the other souls, Carlo would need to return to the Palazzo Ducale to complete the task. But he was ostracized from Venice, and now, *hunted*.

His phone chimed with an SMS. A number he didn't recognize. A text in English. *'Kapital Club. Third Floor. 2:00.'*

It was 1:08 AM. Carlo searched Google Maps and found the club was a thirty-minute walk away. It could've been a ruse, but would della Porta set a trap in a public place, especially a nightclub? Possibly, but he'd play the odds.

There was a 0.001% chance it was Julia.

# II

C OLD EMANATED FROM THE concrete floor, penetrating the thin fabric of the black halter-neck dress clinging to Julia O'Connor's body. She had borrowed it from Fosca for the ceremony, and though she loved it when she put it on, now—curled in a fetal position and picking her fingernails in the corner of her cell beneath the Thyssen-Bornemisza—a worse clothing option didn't exist. She'd drifted off, finally succumbing to physical and mental exhaustion, but discomfort—and fear—prevented sleep for more than a minute.

Earlier, Salvatore della Porta and Detective Lacasse had interrogated her, demanding to know how she obtained one of the ancient Spanish coins the Order used for passkeys. As if the idiots thought she'd give up Fosca. Lying to them came so easily. She took pride in fabricating stories on the spot.

They also wanted Carlo's current location, which was a baffling request. She'd gone to the ceremony to *kill* Carlo, not only to avenge Nick, but to save the world. Well, at least to back up Fosca, Diego, and Karim. That was before everything went to hell. The event turned out to be *for* Diego. The lanky guy was about to become the Spanish Order's next Painter. With Fosca and her team nowhere in sight, Julia launched into action. She killed El Greco—an icon of art who should've died centuries earlier. Taking any life, even one that should not have been alive, repulsed her, but she had no choice.

As life seeped from El Greco, everything Nick had claimed—everything she couldn't previously believe—presented itself. *Paradise*—no, the hundreds of *souls* in *Paradise*—came alive. Just as Fosca had explained, because the Sun Crystal wasn't destroyed, the souls remained tethered to the painting, unable to free themselves.

"Think of it like two-factor authentication," she'd said. "The Painter needs to be killed, but the Sun Crystal needs to be shattered, too, in a special way."

That special way dated back to ancient Mongolia. *Mongolia?* Julia was still trying to wrap her head around needing a book sealed in a booby-trapped lockbox from the Renaissance.

Meanwhile, she was imprisoned in Madrid while her poor husband was trapped in a new two-dimensional purgatory in Venice.

Della Porta had tantalized her with a letter Nick had written while *he* was in jail. She wished to God she could read it, but no way would she give up Fosca or anyone in the Guild to do so. The Order's world domination plan was terrifying, but for Julia, the odds of just living another day were beyond daunting. She had to accept a hard truth. She, Fosca, the Guild, Nick, *the world*—they lost.

They lost badly.

She released a deep exhale, wincing from the sharp pain squeezing her lungs.

Every breath was a battering ram to the chest. Nick had received the same injury during a hockey practice, so she knew there wasn't a thing she could do about it.

"This was supposed to be a damn vacation," she muttered.

The click of an electronic lock responded to her complaint. Her cell door opened. Without a word, the gargantuan Protector who had pinned her down during the ceremony entered the otherwise empty cell carrying a bundle. A dark-skinned man with a bald head and lambchop sideburns, the man's titanic frame still amazed Julia more than it frightened her, though that frame had cracked her ribs.

Avoiding her eyes, the Protector placed some items on the floor by the door with apologetic mannerisms.

"Qué hora es?" Julia asked, the question sending shards of pain into her lungs. Without a watch or window, she had no clue of the time.

"Noche," he replied before closing the door.

Night. It had to be about twenty-four hours since the ceremony. Not that it mattered. Other than the three men who'd been in her cell, no one knew where she was. No one even knew she was in Spain.

She crawled over to the bundle to find an apple on top of an airline pillow and blanket. Clearly, the Order didn't use this room for long-term prisoners. On one hand, this reassured her. On the other, it was terrifying.

Her body and mind screamed at her to sleep, but rest didn't come easy. Still, what else could she do? She'd gone over her circumstances in her head a million times. She twirled her black hair, dyed the prior night as a disguise.

It got her into the museum, but now, escape seemed impossible. She didn't know where Carlo was and wasn't about to betray Fosca. If she lied about either, would they set her free before verifying her claims? Perhaps she could bargain with them, demand an attorney—or better, that she be brought to the U.S. embassy. Then, she'd reveal critical information, maybe about the doge's black book. The slim chance of freeing Nick from *Paradise* slipped away by the minute. She wanted to bring down the Order and would trade her life for it, but only if success was guaranteed. If anything, the guarantee seemed that they'd keep her silent forever—one way or another.

# III

MORE EXASPERATED THAN EVER, Salvatore della Porta strode the drab hallway with Richard Lacasse at his side. Fluorescent ceiling fixtures lit their way as they passed empty catering carts, which wouldn't be used for some time.

Signora O'Connor played a good game, but it was just that—a game. His gut said she was untruthful, but he'd yet to convince his mind.

"She has specific details," he said to the detective in English.

"It's an age-old technique. Offer breadcrumbs to make someone think you have a loaf."

"The insurance payout cannot be real."

"I'll verify it and check if she contacted the U.S. embassy."

They reached a Protector sitting at the security door. The man buzzed them through.

When the door closed, Lacasse cracked his neck. The larger man's light-brown complexion, prematurely gray hair and gray suit nearly camouflaged him into the walls. He continued in his soothing French accent as they traversed the connecting hallway. "What concerns me is that she used the technique. I've seen it hundreds of times in interrogations. The tell is the breadcrumbs are always peripheral stories, never the issue at hand. They circumvent the question, as she did regarding the Palazzo, her husband, and the urns. But notice, she offered no real specifics about the coin or gaining access to the Convocation."

"She's lying. Why are you concerned?"

"I wonder how she knew the technique in the first place. It's possible it wasn't a technique at all, and she *is* telling the truth about everything other than the insurance policy. Ten thousand isn't much. And she didn't take her husband's letter. Considerable bait, given her situation."

The man had a point. Julia O'Connor may have been a journalist for a brief period, but she wasn't a spy or a hardened criminal.

"His last words to her," della Porta said. "She knows the letter is the closest she'll ever get to speaking to him again."

Lacasse's typically impassive face flashed a look of concern. "Only one person could've told her he's in a new painting."

*A charlatan son*, della Porta thought.

He shook his head, untidying strands of salt-and-pepper hair, which he smoothed back into place. He'd yet to fully deliberate Carlo's actions, but what was there to consider? A self-therapy session was meaningless when he had facts. The man he considered a son was a betrayer, and he'd pay for his treachery. It was that simple.

"Let's look at the evidence," the Interpol detective said. "She came to Madrid with Carlo. He was here all day except when he went to dinner with Vasquez and Lobo—"

"You're using that absurd moniker now, too?" Della Porta pressed the bridge of his Roman nose beneath his eyeglasses, his patience running thin on multiple fronts.

Lacasse raised his hand in apology. "*Diego Blanco-Romasanta*. It's hard to imagine Carlo left Venice with a silver Spanish coin from 1614. Either he managed to steal one and pass it off to Julia in the restaurant—"

"Which isn't out of the realm of possibility." Della Porta stopped at a stairwell door and buttoned his suit jacket.

"Or she got it from someone else."

"I don't believe she bought it. That's a lie." Della Porta opened the access door, and they climbed the stairs.

"Or someone gave it to her." Lacasse rubbed his jaw. "Fosca seems unlikely, given her lineage. There could be another mole here in Madrid. There's Karim, the man they discovered, who has still given us nothing."

Della Porta's lips curled upward. He had watched the video of Karim's interrogation. The filth was dealt with properly by Blanco-Romasanta and José Vasquez, Madrid's Exalted Master. The men had incorporated a tried-and-true technique to coerce information from traitors.

"Perhaps we should use the thumbscrews on Signora O'Connor," he said.

Lacasse swallowed but remained otherwise passive. "Torture offers no guarantee of accurate nor actionable intelligence, as we've seen with Karim. I do not think Carlo gave her the coin. He wasn't even aware of the Madrid chapter's existence before a few days ago. It's even less likely she knows his whereabouts."

What seemed like an avoidance of practical methodology irritated della Porta. "It depends on nothing but a person's ability to withstand pain. Thumbscrews and other devices have been used successfully on thousands of people. Julia O'Connor does not strike me as someone accustomed to discomfort. You like facts, yes? We have two that are indisputable. Carlo and Signora O'Connor left for Madrid together. They were then seen together here in this museum, working in tandem to disrupt the Convocation and kill our revered El Greco. *You* are the detective. Detect."

Lacasse offered della Porta a solemn bow of understanding.

Carlo. *The charlatan son.*

He released a despondent exhale. "My love for Carlo blinded me, but that blindfold has been lifted. I'm not above admitting a mistake. The simplest explanation is the likeliest explanation."

The detective nodded again.

"This is it." Della Porta motioned to the stairwell exit two flights up from the holding rooms, rather than ascending a third that would've brought them to the museum's ground floor.

The two men entered a new corridor, also painted in a subdued gray.

"Question her again. Do what you must. Find Carlo. After you do... kill her."

Lacasse pinched his face. He'd find the tasks repugnant, but they had little choice. Della Porta didn't care that truths had been shown to Julia O'Connor—after all, he planned to reveal them to the whole world. The problem was that she knew too much about *means.* Those means were justified by an end, though some may find them unsavory and seek to thwart a majestic finale. That could not happen. If della Porta was honest with himself, he regretted needing to remove her. She was innocent, and he liked her energy. But they couldn't detain her indefinitely. Lacasse knew this. It had to be done.

A muffled hum grew in volume as the two men proceeded down the hall. At first, the noise appeared mechanical, but as they continued, the sound, comprised of low-, mid-, and high-pitched waves, felt organic. Though della Porta had heard it before, it unsettled him. He stole a look at Lacasse. The detective glanced wide-eyed about and above him, unsure of the sound's origins.

"The souls," della Porta said.

Lacasse swallowed.

The interim Spanish Exalted Master had instructed his Protectors to move *Paradiso* to a storage room in the basement. They'd hoped to bring it to the third-level basement where Signora O'Connor was held, but the large-scale painting wouldn't fit unless they removed the frame, which they weren't ready to do on such short notice.

The wailing grew in volume as they reached a door at the end of the hall. A Spanish Protector wearing noise-canceling headphones handed a pair each to della Porta and Lacasse.

"Nothing can prepare you, señores," the Protector said, nearly yelling. The bearded man, about della Porta's age, in his sixties, appeared far too eager to end his shift.

Della Porta was one of few living people who knew the man spoke the truth—*nothing* could prepare anybody for the scene behind the storage room door. Other than Carlo, della Porta was about to become the only other person to witness a living miracle—no, a living *verity*—twice.

He donned the headphones and motioned for Lacasse to do the same. The nervous expression on the usually stoic detective gave della Porta pause.

As a one-time duke's palace, then offices and a bank vault before it was converted to a museum, with its thick walls, the Thyssen-Bornemisza was the perfect home for the Order. Upon renovation, the walls had been reinforced to insulate sound. That was designed to prevent eavesdroppers on Convocation nights, not hundreds of screaming visible spirits. They had inspected the outside and hadn't heard anything with their naked ears, so they were confident the painting's temporary home in the basement would suffice. But the disturbance radiating from the storage room was so loud, even with the headphones, della Porta worried people would hear something.

Knowing the divine chaos that fumed beyond the door, he expelled three quick breaths to steady his nerves.

With a nod to Lacasse, they entered. The Protector quickly shut the door behind them.

The detective's eyes enlarged. His jaw unhinged at the mesmerizing vision propped against metal shelving.

Though della Porta had seen *Paradiso* in Venice come alive, he could witness this every day for the rest of his life and be entranced every time. Utterly remarkable. Living art. Indisputable proof that people had souls and that everything the Order had done was justified and righteous. If not for the uninterpretable shrieks that sounded like a three-toned dull and the high-pitched vibration that clattered his teeth, he wished he could leave the painting in its animated state.

While awe-inspiring, it also chilled della Porta's bones. His muscles slackened, and he needed every ounce of mental energy to prevent his body from folding in fear.

Irate spirits of every age, gender, and social status clawed and stretched their forms beyond the canvas, screaming, yearning for freedom, unable to break free of their ethereal boundary.

Della Porta took two steps back.

Lacasse took four.

He yelled to della Porta. He couldn't hear Lacasse's words but read his lips: 'Are we safe?'

Della Porta patted his friend's shoulder. Despite the disturbing visual, there was no danger, but keeping the painting in its animated state wasn't possible. For now. It wasn't yet time to introduce the world to Veritism, the one veritable religion. It could be done on any canvas in the future.

The Sun Crystal was safe in Venice, having not been transported to Paris as typically would've happened after a Convocation in Madrid. The situation also necessitated a new Painter. Diego Blanco-Romasanta was della Porta's first choice, and though he could be unpredictable, by all accounts, performed admirably under pressure.

Convincing the Madrid council to move forward would not be an issue. The problem, however, was a technical one. They were in uncharted waters. How could he transfer power to a new Painter if the old Painter was dead? Della Porta had ideas; the original Painters needed to be suffused with the power somehow.

He tensed his muscles and motioned to Lacasse for them to leave the room. The detective made a beeline for the exit, ripped his headphones off, handed them to the Protector, and crossed himself, visibly shaken. Della Porta shut the door.

"No question all that evil is a disturbing sight," della Porta said, handing his headphones over. "Relax, my friend. They're not going anywhere."

He spoke to Lacasse and the Protector. "Keep the museum closed until further notice."

# IV

GIRLS IN SKIMPY DRESSES gyrating to pounding bass beneath a dizzying light show delivered Carlo back to the cusp of his old self—or, more accurately, to a delirious peripheral of his old self. He'd been in Kapital Club for forty minutes, and nobody had approached him. Then again, he wondered how anybody would find him in the vast, darkly lit place. He'd gone to nightclubs in Venice and Milan, but they were nothing like Kapital, a former seven-story theater. Partygoers filled the stage and balconies. Carlo had trashed his baseball hat and slicked back his hair in the bathroom before joining two hundred people on the main dance floor.

A vodka-Red Bull alleviated concerns he had stepped into the Order's snare. After a second cocktail dispersed extant thoughts of Julia, he found himself grinding with a brunette who may or may not have had a name. As the DJ switched up the techno, he jumped up and down with everyone else, his arm raised in sync to the beat as if he were part of a collective heart.

Before he knew it, a different girl displaced the brunette. This vixen had a brown bob with pink tips. A red, knee-high dress with a side slit lured Carlo to her thigh.

Fosca.

He had found her attractive the first time he saw her in della Porta's office. Now, under the lights, with that outfit, a sheet of sweat glistening on her neck, swaying with him, caused an undeniable arousal. He didn't care about the Order or anyone else in the moment. Julia lingered in his head, but he'd never see her again, so why flounder in the gloom of an unachievable outcome? All he wanted to do was grab Fosca and kiss her.

"I need to know something," she yelled over the music, her face and tone all business. "Come on."

Carlo loved her accent. Though Fosca was French-Italian, she had spent so much time in the States, including college, her inflection sounded more like an American who had lived in Europe, rather than the other way around.

His stimulation heightened as he followed her off the dance floor and up the stairs to a standing table near the bar. She glanced around before continuing. It was difficult to hear right next to her, so they didn't need to worry about eavesdroppers. Still, she brought her mouth close to his ear. Her warm breath, mixed with the aroma of her Dolce & Gabbana perfume, caused the hairs on his neck to stand at attention—along with another body part.

"I need to know, Carlo. Were you trying to kill El Greco? Or Lobo?"

Carlo closed his eyes and forced himself back to the reality of his situation. This little slice of heaven—the club, the booze, Fosca—it could never last.

Her question brought it all home for him. Even if Carlo could hide—even if he killed himself, Lobo—Diego Blanco-Romasanta, an artist so pompous, he billed himself as *El Lobo Blanco*, the White Wolf, was still alive. Carlo snickered. *El Mutt Blanco* was more like it. Carlo had met the type in art school. Despite the man-child's outward vanity, his insecurities led him to adopt a moniker. In this case, Blanco-Romasanta appropriated his self-appointed nickname from Renaissance master, El Greco—Tintoretto's Spanish counterpart.

Though he loathed doing it, Carlo intended on dispatching the five-hundred-year-old artistic genius from this Earthly Realm, but a raven-haired woman beat him to it. Fortunately, Carlo wounded Lobo and disabled Madrid's Exalted Master, preventing a power transfer from El Greco to Lobo. But how long would that last? For all he knew, della Porta could've already installed Lobo. Then, the Spanish prick would be on equal footing, with equal strength and *vis vitalis*. There was also the Paris chapter to consider, and he'd yet to learn the French Painter's identity. Should Carlo disappear—willingly or not—the other two Painters could also sentence victims to *Paradiso* in Venice.

Della Porta had many avenues to achieve his plan of Veritism and the prospect terrified Carlo. Della Porta needed to be stopped. The Order needed to be demolished. The souls needed to be liberated.

To do any of that, Carlo had to achieve the impossible: show his face in Venice.

"I'm sorry," he said as loudly as possible without yelling. "I went off script." He stared at the table with dismay. His actions jeopardized everything, but what choice did he have?

A cigarette would've helped, but he preferred dealing with the stress than tarnishing her scent. And Fosca hated when people smoked.

She placed her finger on his chin and tipped his head up.

"You'll need to find the book on your own now," he said.

"But you're a Painter, too." Ignoring his statement, she eyed him with sympathy and curiosity.

It was true. The significance of his new role had been pecking his mind. How could he unbind the souls as a Painter without...? One step at a time. He needed to stop della Porta first. If the man found a book lost to the ages, he'd be able to secure the backing of the Church, and with it, a billion followers. Everyone else would fall in line, and della Porta would be at the helm, banishing anyone who didn't join—or for any other reason. Lobo would gleefully do his bidding. "I couldn't let that psychopath become a Painter, Fosca. Even if we get the book and expose the Order to the world, they'd find a way to turn it around on us. It was my only chance."

"I wanted to do the same thing." Her eyes reflected his angst.

Carlo wasn't sure he heard right. "You did?"

"It was a once-in-a-lifetime opportunity." She reached into her purse hanging from the thin shoulder strap and placed a butterfly knife on the table.

He drew in a sharp breath. He slid the weapon back to her.

"Was that for El Greco?" he asked.

"Either him or... another Painter." Fosca averted her gaze and tucked the knife in her purse. "I realized you're too much of an asset."

The words sunk in. *Another Painter. You're too much of an asset.* Lobo wasn't a Painter yet. Carlo rubbed his forearms, realizing what she implied. Two Painters in the same room. The only way to free the souls.

He couldn't blame Fosca for her original plan. Fortunately, she came to a more favorable conclusion.

Others wouldn't be as judicious. Carlo faced a stark fact: he had a bull's eye on his back. It was yet another piece della Porta had withheld from him—and another reason Tintoretto had been confined to a subterranean room in the Palazzo. As much as the Order needed to sequester him from the public, they also needed to *protect* him. The Guild would hardly be the only people after him. Even if della Porta achieved his goals with Veritism, Carlo would be forced to be the group's primary warden. Millions would want him dead.

"Hey," Fosca said, snapping her fingers in front of his face. "This isn't the time for a self-pity wallow fest. Have you forgotten about Julia?"

Carlo frowned. He was thankful she changed the subject, but thoughts of Julia were equally painful. "I do not think she'll want to see me ever again." The pressure was too much. He retrieved a pack of cigarettes from his pocket.

Fosca scowled at the smokes and backed away. "You're probably right, you idiot, but I mean we need to *save* her."

"What are you talking about?" He reluctantly dropped the unlit cigarette back into the near-empty pack.

"She *did* look like a different person." Fosca grinned. "I don't blame you for not noticing."

It finally hit him. "The woman. The black-haired woman with glasses. I knew her voice sounded familiar. *Julia* killed El Greco?" Then it knocked him in the face. She was in incredible danger. He swallowed. Hard. "I have a good idea where she is."

"I'm guessing locked up in the Thyssen?"

"Exactly. I've been there. They're also holding a guy. A footballer. They tortured him."

Fosca dropped her shoulders and squared her gaze on Carlo. "Karim. He was one of our inside men. At least he's alive. We need to get him out, too."

The news was worse than Carlo could've imagined. He ran his hands through his hair. "This is all my fault. Karim, now Julia."

Fosca reached over and took his hand. This time, she let it linger. Warmth from her skin sent ironic shivers up his arm.

"You know that's not true," she said.

He nodded. She was right. And self-pity would accomplish nothing. "Getting in will be tricky, if not impossible."

"Except it turns out the gatekeeper is a fan of Versace."

Carlo wrinkled his brow. "So?"

"So it's who I'm wearing." She stepped back to show off her dress, instantly rousing him again. "And the Protector is sitting over there chatting up that blonde."

Fosca pointed her head toward the lounge area. Sure enough, on an orange velvet couch sat a man with an anchor tattoo on one of his pronounced cheeks. Foliage ink climbed up his neck from beneath his shirt.

# V

As expected late at night, the hospital was quiet. Earlier in the day, della Porta had checked in on José Vasquez, so he knew the direction to the Spanish Exalted Master's room. Diego Blanco-Romasanta had accompanied him, on crutches with his leg in a cast, along with two Protectors. Since Vasquez was unconscious, the visit was brief. Blanco-Romasanta had inquired about his own status and if he'd still ascend to Painter, but della Porta admonished him. It was hardly the time or place for such a conversation.

Now alone, della Porta needed to pay a visit to Vasquez on his way to the airport.

With a glance up and down the empty hallway, della Porta removed his fedora and overcoat to reveal doctors' scrubs. He folded the coat over his arm, strode past the unoccupied nurses' station, and went directly to Vasquez's room.

If there were ever a shining example of one's decisions leading to dire consequences, it lay on the hospital bed before him. The steady beep of the EKG was the only sound. Bandages wrapped the man's head. The last time della Porta saw him, Vasquez was as smug as ever, chomping on a cigar in his bearded mouth, ridiculing Veritism.

How circumstances change.

Vasquez made the near-fatal mistake of attempting to circumvent della Porta in a power grab. Did fate's hand guide the Spanish Exalted Master's plan to fail with dramatic fanfare? Was it luck? Irony? Or due to the elementary fact that Vasquez failed to think more than one move ahead?

Della Porta often butted heads with his Spanish colleague, but he respected the man. Like della Porta, Vasquez had risen from a modest background. Now, seeing him incapacitated on a hospital bed cut too close to home; any Exalted Master could be similarly assaulted. Della Porta pitied Vasquez. He could've had his share of eminence. Alas, *c'est la vie*—he stood in della Porta's way.

The Uber driver had been paid 100 euro to wait ten minutes. Provided the driver didn't record the stop or rat him out, nobody would know that della Porta was there.

"When you're the house," he whispered into Vasquez's ear, "you make the odds."

It took less than two seconds. Della Porta detached the IV and unplugged the machine to prevent an alarm when Vasquez flatlined.

*Fatal* mistake.

If someone stood in della Porta's way, they stood in the Order's way. Vasquez stood in the way of vision. Of progress. Of *greatness*.

Della Porta donned his hat and overcoat, exited the hospital room, and walked briskly to the elevator.

Nobody saw him—or the grin on his face.

# VI

I N HIS TWENTY-FOUR YEARS on Planet Earth, Diego Blanco-Romasanta had considered himself master of his past, present, and destiny. He never squandered his father's money, nor did he take his artistic talent for granted.

When he adopted the moniker El Lobo Blanco, it was a calculated choice to evoke respect *and* derision. More than anyone, he knew it was ridiculous. It didn't fit his appearance; he looked more militaristic emo vampire than wolf. In part, he chose it in reverence to his predecessor, El Greco. Above all, *Lobo* just sounded cool. It was the rock star name he was destined to embody.

*Was.*

Lobo chugged the remainder of his rioja and flagged the bartender for another. *Sentido Contrario* was a dive bar that served the crappiest red wine in Madrid. The sticky mix of angry drunks and angrier music was the exact vibe he craved. He glanced over his shoulder at the half-full space. The walls and ceiling were plastered with graffiti-covered posters of every band that questioned the establishment since 1975. Most of the wannabe punks and goths that littered the bar wouldn't be caught dead drinking rioja, and that was their problem: a lack of sophistication—or desire to accept a world beyond the gutter—that would forever leave them feeling that life had dealt them a shitty hand.

Even the four Scottish skinheads playing pool, all twice Lobo's size and obviously in Spain on a discount vacation, punching each other's shoulders after each shot, exuded an aura of faux defiance. They were born rotten apples at the bottom of the barrel. Not one had enough brain cells to do anything that would provide a modicum of self-empowerment to step out of the gutter. They didn't even have the mettle to dress outside the mold subscribed to them decades before their time. Looking like they had stepped out of the 1980s, each skinhead wore a Fred Perry polo shirt, suspenders, acid-washed jeans, and black or oxblood Doc Marten boots. For a moment, Lobo wondered if they were quadruplets. He could only tell them apart by their shirt colors. One wearing black—the most boisterous of the bunch—had a cheesy switchblade tattooed on the side of his face.

He glared at those assholes, yearning to utilize the hapkido his father forced him to take for five years as a kid.

"Do you want to have the shit kicked out of you, Diego? Like a little pussy?" his father would say, even when Lobo was nine.

The bartender brought his wine.

"Countless hours in a gym instead of painting," he said to the surprisingly clean-cut server. "Wasted years. Did you know that other than in that gym, I've never thrown a punch?"

The bartender gave him a closed-mouth smile before moving to another patron. Lobo returned his attention to the alcohol. His black hair fell over his eyes as he poured the wine down his throat. Combined with the Percocet he had swallowed an hour earlier, the throbbing in his broken shin had finally subsided.

A Spanish deathrock song pumping through the speakers segued to *Anarchy in the UK* by the Sex Pistols.

Despite his contempt for the crowd, Lobo loved all things punk and goth. The music energized him. The spirit of the subculture fueled his soul. While he aspired for greatness, he didn't believe the two were mutually exclusive. There were hundreds of successful rebels and punks.

Similarly, Lobo refused to flounder in the role of misbegotten radical. He was livid and had every right to be. Carlo Zuccaro attacked him. The *cabrón* broke his shinbone with the Order's candleholder, a priceless relic. There was no way the Venetian prick could've known Lobo double-crossed the Guild. It wasn't even a double-cross. Lobo was loyal to the Order, something Carlo could learn a thing about.

If they had an equal playing field and Carlo hadn't waylaid him, Lobo easily could've taken the little Italian bitch. He could've protected his friend and mentor, José Vasquez. The one time Lobo could've used his martial arts training, he didn't even have a chance.

A clunk resounded on the floor beneath his barstool. A cue ball rested against his crutches.

"Och aye, pal! Could ye gie us a haun?"

Lobo glanced over his shoulder. One of the Scottish skinheads tapped his pool stick on the table felt.

"Whenever yer ready, eh?" he yelled over the music. "Chop chop."

Using his crutch, Lobo whacked the ball back to the table and returned his attention to his wine.

*Disloyalty* was Carlo's worst offense, not disrupting the power transfer. Lobo's ascension to Painter was only a matter of time. Vasquez was recovering in the hospital. The souls needed a master. Lobo had already been chosen.

El Greco lived as an original rebel, subverting the Renaissance and the periods that came before it. Many considered the Old Master to be the forefather of modern art.

Lobo chuckled to himself. He hadn't realized how much he and El Greco had in common. He was truly destined to be the next Painter. Once they transferred the power to him, people would know their place. Especially Carlo.

Of course, with Vasquez in a coma, how or when that would happen was another story. Lobo took another healthy gulp of his wine. Perhaps he needed to turn to Salvatore della Porta. The Venetian Exalted Master seemed to have sway with all three chapters. Endearing himself to della Porta could also lead to a united front against Carlo.

Another clop echoed beneath his stool. This time the cue ball tipped his crutches over, but Lobo caught them.

"Hey," the Scot called. "Be a good boy and toss me ball."

Lobo didn't need to turn to know all four were laughing. Tonight might be a good night, after all.

"Get it yourself," he replied in English.

"Ach, say again, pal? I flat cannae hear ya."

The glass in Lobo's hand offered a powerful vision—smashing it into the loser's eye. He downed his remaining wine and spun on the stool to face the skinheads intruding on his bar, his city, his country, and his personal space.

Blood pumped through Lobo's veins. Intense desire for violence had his brain distributing adrenaline throughout his body. His crutches were at arm's length. His fist still gripped his wineglass. He could get a few shots in, maybe blind the one with the facial tattoo, but with a bum leg and four against one, Lobo would take a beating. Maybe that was okay. Whether he did the pummeling or was the pummeled, it didn't matter, provided it offered a cathartic release.

He was in control. Even if lying on beer stains and cigarette butts, getting kicked in the gut, it would be of his own design.

"You like balls?" he asked. "Kneel and get it yourself."

All four gaped at him and each other before cracking up in unison.

"With a voice like that, laddie," said Tattoo Face, "it sounds like ye already have a cock ticklin' the back of yer throat."

They roared in laughter. Truth be told, Lobo despised his voice. High-pitched but with a coarseness to it, he'd been told it sounded like a bow dragged across the highest string of a cello.

"Ah'm enjoyin' yer spirit, pal," the skinhead said. He slapped Lobo's shoulder, then pointed a thick, tattooed finger between his eyes. The man's expression shifted to deadly serious. "But mouth off to me or my pals again, and you'll be crawlin' outta here on *two* broken stems. Am I clear?"

Lobo swallowed. He knew Tattoo Face wasn't making empty threats. Though Lobo needed catharsis, two broken legs would only set him back. The Order may decline him forever. Adrenaline dissipated.

With the most insincere smile he could muster, Lobo spread his arms wide. "Bienvenidos a España," he said.

"Now that's more like it."

The skinheads slapped and punched each other, laughing raucously, as they returned to the pool table.

Lobo stared them down, resisting the urge to crack a pool stick into the back of their heads.

He remained in control.

# VII

J ULIA SIPPED HER WINE before cutting her salmon, though she wasn't sure if she'd be able to keep her food down. She didn't know why a swarm of butterflies wreaked havoc on her stomach. Or maybe her gut knew—and that's why the rest of her body trembled. It was the expensive restaurant, despite a lack of a special occasion. It was their clothes. It was that she was so insanely in love with her boyfriend, she knew tonight was the night.

She looked up from her plate. Nick gazed at her with a smile that spoke of joy and trepidation. What was *he* nervous about? He had to know her answer.

"How's the salmon?" He'd barely spoken more than those three words.

"Salmony. How's your steak?"

"Steaky. You look incredible in that dress."

"You don't look so bad yourself."

He grinned and knocked his napkin off the table.

"Whoops." He slid off his chair to retrieve it.

*You cheeseball*, she thought. *I love it. This. Is. It.*

She placed her utensils on the table, doing her best not to drop them from her shaking hands. *Why am I so nervous? I know my answer.*

"Jules?"

She turned to Nick, who knelt on the floor. He held a small black box, which he opened to reveal a sparkling diamond ring.

"Julia," he continued. "You may think this is bull, but the moment I saw you in the campus bookstore, I knew. I just knew." He tapped his chest.

Warmth filled Julia. Uncontrollable tears of joy bubbled in her eyes.

"I'm not sure how," he continued, "but I knew we were destined to be together. You are the most amazing person I've ever met, beautiful inside and out. Your intelligence, your—"

A guy tripped over Nick, knocking him over.

"What the fuck?" the guy yelled, recovering his footing. "Why are you on the floor?"

The guy was about Nick's height but stockier, meaner, and with a shaved head that enhanced his menacing appearance. About thirty, he looked ready to boot Nick in the face. If he did, one kick might've knocked Nick out.

Julia swallowed, instinctively shifting backward in her seat.

Nick stood and brushed himself off. He snapped the ring box closed and pocketed it. "You asshole," he said, fuming, his face bright red. "I'm in the middle of proposing to my girlfriend."

"If she says yes," the guy replied, "she's as dumb as you."

Nick narrowed his eyes and clenched both fists.

The guy grinned. "Take a swing."

Julia sent a silent message to Nick for him to let it go. Perhaps he heard her—for in that moment, he glanced at her, and his expression shifted to one of sorrow.

"Go back to your table," Nick said to the guy without looking at him.

Nick took his seat and stared at his plate.

"That's what I thought," said the guy before stalking off. "Pussy."

Nick finally caught Julia's gaze.

"God, I'm so sorry," he said.

"For what?" She reached for his hand and kissed it. Tears streamed from her eyes and formed in his. "Please, babe, continue."

A smile returned to Nick's face. He brought the ring box out again and popped it open.

"I had a whole big speech planned, but I don't wanna risk anything else happening. Jules, I love you more than anything in this world, and I always will. Will you marry me?"

Her mouth opened to give the response she yearned to say, but one question stopped her. "You know my answer, but I want to know why you didn't fight that guy."

He swallowed. "I'll always fight for you. *Always*. But I also love you too much to let that asshole ruin the moment. This is *your* moment. If I fought him, it would be about me. Or worse, him. Could you imagine if I ended up in jail the night I proposed to you?"

Julia couldn't take it anymore. Happiness filled her soul. She could only utter a single word: "Yes."

"You could imagine that?"

"I mean, yes, of course, I'll marry you."

She sat up, reached across the table, grabbed his collar, and locked her lips to his.

In the three weeks since Julia had arrived in Europe, her camera had been stolen, she was kidnapped and brought to a torture room in Venice, a 16th-century swordsman possessing her husband stabbed her, she killed a 500-year-old Renaissance legend, learned one of only two friends in Venice essentially murdered the love of her life, and now she sat a prison cell beneath a museum in Madrid.

Not long ago, it seemed as though she were on a path to the future she'd always imagined: an amazing husband she loved with all her heart, a life that was filled with fun and adventure but inching toward family, and a budding career as a fine-arts photographer.

A single moment had wiped away everything.

The only thing she could do was laugh. Man, did that hurt her ribs. They'd improved slightly over the last day but even breathing was still a chore. The colossal guard continued to show remorse, bringing her a cushioned mat, a plate of eggs, a pair of jeans, and a T-shirt. The clothes were three sizes too large, but it beat wearing a next-to-nothing cocktail dress.

She'd asked him to bring some books, and he seemed amenable. In the meantime, with nothing to do for hours, she replayed everything that had happened. Moments before she attacked El Greco, she realized that it had fallen on her to do so. She had nothing left to lose. The notion depressed her at the ceremony, when she could've gotten up and dashed out the door. Now... now, she had nothing left to lose *or* win.

She traced the rosemary tattoo sprig on her inner wrist—a memento of her Grandma Rosemarie. "At least it can't get any worse," Julia mumbled.

The lock clicked. Detective Lacasse entered, wearing a gray suit, this one a shade darker than his last.

"Bonjour, Madame O'Connor," said the Interpol detective with his calm demeanor.

She wished she could hate that accent, but the man's natural cadence had a relaxing effect that irritated her because it *was* so soothing.

"Where's your headcase boss?"

"Assuming you're referring to Monsieur della Porta," Lacasse said without changing his tone, "he returned to Venice. See how easy it is to reveal information? Have you ever seen one of these?"

He displayed a small black device that looked like two pieces of metal held together with screws.

Julia shook her head. She had no idea what it was. A weird hook?

"It's called a thumbscrew." He twisted the center screw to open the two brackets. "It's also known as the thumbkin or even the pilliwinks."

"Are you going to use it to redecorate my cell?" She pointed to the corners. "I could use shelves and flowers here. Maybe a toilet over there."

"You would not like the way this tiny device can alter things." He took a step closer. "The thumbscrew is very old and very simple, yet *very* effective. There are multiple variations. Some have sharp studs on the inside, others have additional sharp screws, but in its most basic construct, it's a clamp." He slid his thumbs into it. "A clamp that is placed over a prisoner's thumbs." He took a step closer. "Or fingers." He pulled his hand out and eyed Julia through the device as if it were a lens. "Or toes."

A chill bristled Julia's spine. She tried to swallow, but nothing went down.

"It... it's a torture device?" She involuntarily placed her hands behind her back.

"Oui. A rather barbaric one that I'd prefer not to use. Do you think I'll need to use it?"

Julia's body quaked. "I don't know where Carlo is. I swear. He's probably at the Mandarin Oriental. He was staying there."

Lacasse smiled. "I thought you'd be cooperative." He pocketed the thumbscrew and held out his hand. "Please, stand."

Trepidation vibrated her bones. Julia did as instructed, unsure if her wobbly legs would hold her.

"I'm sure you'd like to leave this room, oui? I'd like to show you something."

"What?"

"Come. You'll see." He headed for the door but stopped. "Oh, how silly of me." He removed a black eye mask and blindfold from his other pocket. "You'll need to wear these, of course."

"How will you show me something if I can't see?

Lacasse smirked.

After five seconds, Julia covered her ears in a futile attempt to drown out the screams. After ten seconds, she banged on the door, begging to be let out. When it didn't open, she collapsed, wishing Lacasse had broken her thumbs instead.

She'd heard the souls the night she killed El Greco, and as loud as they were then, now it was as if they'd woken up and demanded their long-lost freedom all at once. The visual was equally disturbing, as if hundreds of diaphanous human maggots, all shrunk proportionately to fit on the canvas, crawled over each other, stretching but incapable of escaping their binds. Not a word was comprehensible, but it didn't matter—they could only want one thing. Julia craved the same.

Freedom.

Standing, she slammed her fists on the door. "Okay," she screamed. "I'll tell you! Anything! Just let me out!"

She wasn't sure if Lacasse heard her, but a moment later, he flung open the door, yanked her into the hall, and sealed the room. He then removed the headphones he'd been wearing and handed them to the guard.

Julia didn't hesitate. Barefoot, she bolted down the cold concrete hallway. She'd been blindfolded when Lacasse had brought her here, but it didn't matter. All she needed to do was reach the door thirty feet away. Ignoring her burning ribs, she collided with the door and yanked the handle. It didn't budge. She tried again, but it was no use.

Light footsteps approached. She didn't need to turn around.

"Where is Carlo Zuccaro?"

Tears rolled down Julia's cheeks. It was pointless. It was all pointless. "I don't know." Her tongue stuck to the roof of her mouth. Her throat closed. The echo of the souls reverberated in her head. She needed to lie down.

"I believe you."

Julia turned. Lacasse stood three feet from her. His response sparked an atom of hope. "You do?"

"Oui. I do not believe anyone knows where he is at this moment. But you do know some things. Where did you get the coin?"

"I told you," Julia said, attempting to conceal her shaking, "I bought it from an Order member."

Lacasse released a somber exhale through his nose. Without a word or warning, he grabbed Julia's arm and dragged her back toward the storage room. Pain pierced her bicep from his squeeze.

"You're hurting me," she said. She tried pulling away, but he was too strong. His intent was clear. She couldn't take those souls again. "Please. I promise. I'll tell you. I'll tell you everything."

"You *will* tell us everything, Madame O'Connor."

He swung open the door, threw Julia in, and slammed it shut behind her.

The souls marauded her.

# VIII

C ARLO CHECKED THE ADDRESS on his phone a second time, then squinted at the building catty-corner from him in the quiet, upscale neighborhood of Almagro. A sprawling elm tree shielded the mid-afternoon sun but offered little comfort from the heat. His black hoodie and hat obscured his features, but he looked like he was about to rob the bank on the street level of the building.

A young-forties woman in a pink summer dress and wide-brimmed hat sauntered by with two poodles. She peered at him over her sunglasses and hurried along.

Lowering his own sunglasses a bit, Carlo studied the building and its surroundings. He'd been standing under the tree for twenty minutes and was the most suspicious person there. Above the glass-windowed bank were flats in the five-story, 1970s-era building. There was nothing like it in Venice, but this type of building populated ritzy areas around the world. Nondescript on the outside, luxurious comfort within. Fosca had given him the address and meeting time, but he still was unsure if he could trust her. It had been two days since he'd seen her at the club. Revealing her butterfly knife—and intent—unnerved him, but not as much as when she left with the Protector with the vine tattoo on his neck.

At first, he wondered if she did it to spite him. Nobody could've been that devoted to their mission. Then again, sex was far easier and more pleasurable than death. Despite numerous texts and calls, worry crept in when he didn't hear from her. Finally, she texted an address and time. Fosca could take care of herself, but under the circumstances, it seemed as though the Order had caught her and took her phone. He shuddered, knowing how they tortured Karim.

Walking into a trap wasn't high on Carlo's bucket list, but now he had Julia *and* Fosca to save. Not to mention Karim—if he was still alive.

The traffic slowed. Carlo crossed the street, weaving between cars. After giving a fake name to the building doorman, who called up to the penthouse and then insisted on escorting him up the elevator, Carlo waited until he was alone before ringing the bell. He flattened himself against the wall to avoid being seen through the peephole.

Muffled voices emanated from the other side.

The door opened a crack.

"Carlito?" a woman's voice whispered.

*Carlito?* Nobody had called him that since his mother. But his mother was in an institution in Italy. *Impossible.*

"Carlito? Is that you?" the woman whispered in English.

If this were a trap, the Order hooked Carlo. His hand trembled. If it wasn't his mother calling him by his childhood name, then who? He had to find out.

Carlo spun off the wall and pressed his hand against the door. A brown eye, similar in shade to his mother's, peered at him through the open crack.

"Who are you?" Carlo asked.

"It is you," replied the woman with a Spanish accent. She opened the door. "Rápido, ven." She wrenched Carlo inside and surveyed the hall before shutting the door again.

An elegantly decorated space greeted him. Brightly colored art, mostly modern but nothing he recognized, adorned the walls. Pink chairs sat on a floral-print rug on parquet floors. Dark wood trim bordered the doors and entries to other rooms, offsetting the femininity of the flat. Wide, two-framed rolling doors sealed off the rest of the apartment from the living area. Natural light streamed in through the large windows overlooking the city. He had no doubt the flat was professionally decorated and based on the cleanliness and lack of personal items, had the vibe of a rental.

The woman scrutinized him from beneath black curly hair that exposed a hint of gray at the roots. Gold earrings dangled over her stout shoulders, framing her early sixties face. She tossed an orange scarf over her khaki pantsuit.

"You are Carlito, sí?" Her singsong voice held an edge of a shrillness, much like an impatient mother—and she was definitely not his.

"Who are you? Why are you calling me that?"

The wooden doors slid open.

"That's your name, isn't it?"

Carlo spun to the new voice asking the question. Fosca entered the living room, striding through two sliding doors as if making a grand entrance. He cocked his head at her remark.

"Carlito," said Fosca with an over-the-top demeanor, "so good to see you. I see you've already met Lucia."

A man about the same age and height as Lucia—both a head shorter than Carlo—followed Fosca into the sitting room.

She approached Carlo with her arms wide. She hugged him, planting a kiss on each cheek. So taken aback by the display and the use of his nickname, Carlo didn't return the gesture. His feet were cemented to the floor.

She motioned to the man. "This is her husband, Hugo," she said of the older one. "And Marcel." She pointed to the younger guy sitting on a floral-print sofa. "Come in, come in, you must be parched."

Carlo studied the two men. Hugo was a male version of Lucia. About the same size, his receding hair was so obviously dyed brown that Carlo suppressed a chuckle. The man looked like he'd shaved every day of adulthood and had his clothes laid out for him by his wife. His smile was warm and inviting, despite Carlo not knowing what it was for.

The polar opposite, Marcel appeared to be about fifteen, but had the air of a college student. With big black eyes and shifty feet in canvas sneakers, he ogled Carlo beneath his unruly mop of brown hair and pimply face. He fidgeted with a Rubik's Cube, blindly rotating the sections.

"What's going on, Fosca?" Carlo asked. "Where are we? And—"

"And *who* are we?" Marcel asked with a whiny French accent infused with suspicion.

"Questions, questions, questions," Fosca replied. "Such weighty concerns. It's like Sartre meeting Voltaire. You know what those guys would do on such a gorgeous day? They'd hit the veranda and chill. You know, since they didn't have Netflix." She headed for the patio door leading off the sitting room. "This pitcher of sangria's not gonna drink itself."

Carlo relented. Though he sensed distrusting eyes on him, he followed Fosca to find a spacious veranda filled with plants on the floor and ledge. She sat on a retro, 1970s-style metal chair clad in four shades of blue vinyl. She crossed her long, silky legs in her jean shorts, giving Carlo ample time to enjoy her exposed midriff below her knotted Pink Floyd T-shirt. He envied the sea monster tattoo slithering up her ankle.

One by one, the others meandered out.

"I get these are somber times," she said, "but for fuck's sake, everyone. Sit down and pour yourselves a drink."

Carlo laughed. "You are so much like your grandmother." He plopped down in the open seat next to her and reached for the white sangria. He found a glass and poured himself a hefty serving.

Lucia, Hugo, and Marcel did the same.

"Mi mariposita," Lucia said. She reached over to caress Fosca's cheek, but Fosca swatted her hand away.

"She doesn't like that name, mi corazón," Hugo said, admonishing his wife.

The exchange amused Carlo. "Are you not a little butterfly?" he asked Fosca.

She scowled at him. "Do I look like I'm four years old? The name is Fosca. Francesca, if you must."

He raised his hand in defense.

"You knew our nonna-mère?" Marcel asked.

"Our?" Carlo asked.

"Marcel is my cousin," Fosca said.

Carlo nodded. "Nice to meet you." He turned to Lucia and Hugo. "Also family?"

"Not by blood," Hugo replied in a thick Spanish accent.

Lucia raised a finger. "Not by *same* blood."

Her statement confirmed the hunch that had been brewing within Carlo. These were three additional members of the Guild. But why 'Carlito,' and why they were okay drinking with the Order's Painter was another story. Unless they weren't aware…

"So my cousin says you want to join us."

"Marcel," Fosca said, "can we get to know each other first? Carlito just arrived in Madrid this morning. He's probably tired, thirsty. Are you hungry, Carlito?"

Truth was, he was famished. He took a sip of his drink with a shrug. Apples and oranges added a tart sweetness to the dry white wine that helped quench his thirst. He could eat later.

"Do we have time for this, mariposita?" Lucia asked, preempting his response.

"No," Fosca replied, narrowing her eyes at the term of endearment. "I suppose we don't."

Lucia turned to Carlo. "Carlito, Fosca has told us very little. Only that you're from Venice. I'd like to hear from you. Who are you, and what do you know about us?"

"More importantly," Marcel said, "why shouldn't we throw you off this veranda?"

Carlo spit a grape back into his glass. He gawked at Marcel, along with the other three people.

"What the hell," Fosca yelled.

"I should say the same to you," her cousin replied. "Lucia's right. We don't have time for this nonsense. Carlito? Really? You couldn't come up with anything more creative? Lucia could create a better nickname in her sleep."

Fosca shrugged. "You're right. We don't have time. Get on with it, then."

Marcel stood and stepped toward Carlo, his skinny frame shielding the sun. "You're Carlo Zuccaro. You're from Venice. An artist. Sure, your family has been burned by the Order—"

"Marcel!" Fosca glared at him.

"Bad choice of words," he said. "The Order has *wronged* your family. But yet... but yet... you chose to become their Painter?"

Rage steamed from Marcel's face. Carlo glanced at Lucia and Hugo. They wore similar expressions.

"Sit down, Marcel," Fosca said. "As if you could even lift him out of that chair."

"The four of us could."

Fosca rolled her eyes. "You're such a child. This is why I didn't tell you who he was. Because you're so short-sighted. Now, sit."

With a huff, Marcel took his seat.

"Explain why he's here," Hugo said to Fosca. "Or we're leaving. Not just this flat, but the Guild."

Fosca nodded to Carlo, indicating for him to answer, then gulped her sangria.

He didn't appreciate the accusations of being the bad guy and didn't need anybody to defend him. He spoke to all three of his accusers. "If you think I *chose* to become Painter, you either know little of the truth or have been misinformed. Or both. The role of Painter was forced on me in the heat of a moment you couldn't possibly understand. I had just been initiated and had about ten seconds to decide. I had no clue of the consequences." He spoke fast. Blood rose to his cheeks as he recounted the tale, defending himself against these judgmental strangers. "Under the circumstances, there wasn't a choice—I had to do it not because I was forced but because I was *there*. I saw what happened and what *could* happen."

He paused to take a drink. He needed to slow down.

"Is this true?" Lucia asked Fosca.

She nodded.

"If I relived the event," Carlo said, "I would do it again."

"Ah, see?" Marcel folded his arms as if proving a point.

"The same thing *did* happen," Fosca said. She turned to Carlo. "You acted differently."

He nodded. "I meant if the same thing had happened to me in the same circumstances. I made the right decision in Venice because I had limited knowledge. Here in Madrid, I knew the truth. I knew more about the Order, about Lobo, and Vasquez's intentions. Della Porta's, too."

"He stopped them," said Fosca. "You all know I witnessed everything."

"Thank you, Fosca," Carlo said, genuinely grateful for her support.

The entire group settled back into their chairs. Tension permeated the air, but it dissipated in the hot Spanish afternoon.

Lucia handed Carlo a napkin. He nodded his appreciation and wiped some sangria that had spilled onto his chin.

"So." Lucia broke the silence with an unabashed throat clearing. "Karim's imprisoned, hopefully alive. Same for Nick O'Connor's wife. Who knows about *his* status? Vasquez is in the hospital, *Paradise* here in Madrid is in... I don't even know the word in Spanish, El Lobo could become Painter any moment, della Porta is more powerful than ever and closer to ruling the world through Veritism." She downed her entire sangria as everyone gaped at her. "It seems we have our work cut out for us."

# IX

M ARCEL'S ROOM WAS THE shade to the rest of the flat's sunshine. A locked door led to what struck Carlo as a teenage tech geek's cave. Only one floor lamp lit the room; four monitors on a desk primarily illuminated the space. Other than an unmade bed with black satin sheets and a guitar with a T-shirt hanging on it, computers, gaming equipment, and Rubik's Cubes crowded the space. K-Pop posters covered the walls.

When they left the veranda, Fosca had explained the flat belonged to their family. They typically rented it out to vacationers, but she'd reserved it for a month as the Guild's base of operations in Madrid.

Fosca leaned over Marcel, who typed away as if competing for the Guinness Book of World Records. Lucia sat in the only other chair, while Hugo and Carlo stood behind Fosca.

The somewhat-welcome atmosphere eased Carlo's concerns, but that didn't stop dominating thoughts in his head. Saving Karim and Julia was critical, but they also needed to focus on the end goal of bringing down the Order. There'd yet to be a mention of it or the means to do so. The last time he saw Fosca in Venice, they had a singular target: the doge's black book. To obtain it, they needed to solve a riddle.

"Fosca," he said. "A moment, please."

Acknowledging the seriousness in his expression, she joined him in the far corner of Marcel's room. He kicked a dirty pair of boxer shorts away.

"Do they know?" Carlo whispered.

"Know what?" she matched his surreptitious volume.

He glanced at the three other people in the room. "After we rescue Karim and Julia, what then?"

"Ah, you mean the book. Yeah, they know." She moved to return to her friends.

Carlo grabbed her wrist, not to hurt her, but so that she wouldn't leave. Her flesh was soft and warm in his hand. She looked at his grip, then him, her face taut. She didn't pull away.

"And the riddle? The Painter's face?"

"Yes," she said in full volume.

The response flabbergasted Carlo. Days earlier, he, Fosca, and Julia had been investigating how to open Isacco Uccello's box and retrieve the book, worried for their lives. How could Fosca reveal secrets so easily? "Is there anything you didn't tell them?"

She again spoke in low tones. "We need this team, Carlo. We need the whole Guild. I trust them with my life. So yeah, they know it all. They *need* to know. They have more invested in this than you." She pried a couple of tightening fingers off her wrist.

He sucked air through his teeth and narrowed his eyes. "*Nobody's* invested as much as me. Nobody."

Fosca laughed. "Over what, a couple of weeks? Get over yourself. We've been fighting the Order for *generations*."

Relenting, Carlo released his hold. She was right. "So we get Julia and Karim, figure out the code to open the box, get the book, and expose della Porta to bring him down?"

"That's the plan."

"What about the souls?"

"Once the Order is abolished, we'll have more time to figure out how to free Nick and the others." Sorrow filled her expression.

Though she didn't spell it out, her words carried a stark implication, just as they did at Kapital Club—to free the souls, Carlo had to die.

"Hey," Marcel said. "Do you two need your own room? Because Fosca has one."

"Definitely not." Fosca stepped back to her cousin.

Her negative response dismayed Carlo; despite everything, he wouldn't have minded a trip to her room. He sighed, scattering his lecherous thoughts, and returned to the desk.

"This, my friends," Marcel said, "is step one." He clicked his mouse. Architectural plans filled his largest monitor.

"What is that?" Carlo asked.

"The Thyssen-Bornemisza Museum," Fosca replied.

"Which my enterprising cousin managed to acquire," said Marcel. "Don't ask her how," he added quickly.

The remark earned him a swat on the shoulder from Fosca.

"It's not just the means of acquisition that make these plans special." Marcel tapped his mouse a few times. The view switched to another section of the building. On a second monitor, they appeared as a 3D rendering. "You're looking at renovations done on the sub-levels."

Carlo peered at the third sub-level. A chill bristled his spine. He pointed at the monitor. "I've been there."

"You have?" asked Lucia.

"That's where they're holding Karim. Vasquez and Lobo took me there."

"So he's alive." Lucia crossed herself and kissed her fingers, then raised them in gratitude.

"Yes. But in bad shape. They tortured him."

Lucia clutched her heart.

"Do you think Julia's there?" asked Fosca.

Carlo prayed she lived but would've preferred her safe at home in America. "It wouldn't surprise me. There were other holding cells."

Fosca leaned over Marcel and tapped the monitor. "That's where we need to go."

Her cousin knocked her hand away. "Now I must wipe your grimy fingerprints off. *Crasseux*. Who knows where that finger's been?"

"Moving on," Fosca said with a prominent eye roll. "Not long ago, the Thyssen was a Duke's palace and later converted to a bank. When the Order bought it, they did so because of these basement levels for vaults. They figured they could store all sorts of things down there."

"Including people," said Hugo.

Lucia choked up and covered her mouth.

Her husband embraced her with a tenderness that made Carlo melt. He treasured being able to chase any girl he wished, but sometimes he had to admit that he saw himself settling down... if he found the *right* girl.

"We'll get Karim out," Fosca said to Lucia. "Now, another reason they purchased the building—"

"Is underground passageways." Marcel tapped his mouse. The view changed again.

Fresh memories of nearly drowning beneath the Palazzo Ducale flooded Carlo's mind, much like the water had done in real life. "Please tell me those aren't sewers."

"Nope," Fosca said with a smile. "Tall enough to stand in. They transported gold bullion."

Carlo cracked his knuckles. "Okay, so that's easier. But the rooms are locked and guarded by Protectors. There are cameras in each one."

"Those tunnels aren't metros," said Hugo. "You can't walk right in."

"You can do both those things if you have the right keys," Fosca replied.

Carlo nodded. "More keys."

"Except in this case," said Marcel, waving his fingers, "we're in the 21st century. My doubly enterprising cousin here acquired the passcodes for the cells. Don't ask how." He again tacked on the last sentence quickly.

Again, Fosca smacked him, this time on the back of the head. "How we get information doesn't matter. What matters is the plan."

"Which is?" Carlo asked.

"If you let me finish, I'd get to it."

Exasperation fueled Fosca's tone. He wondered if it went beyond the situation and was more about how she acquired the information.

"With the museum temporarily closed, it creates a problem. There's less staff, but it's quieter. They'll still have Protectors patrolling the exterior. I'm going to distract them. While that happens, Lucia and Marcel will be in a van. Marcel will monitor everything remotely, including all our comms."

Marcel waved a prideful hand around his room. "Tech habits have their benefits."

"Nice coincidence you have a tech geek in the Guild," Carlo said.

"It's not a coincidence at all," Fosca said. "I could've recruited *any* cousin."

Marcel shrugged with a huge smile. "Benefits. But you only have me for another month. Not even."

"He's going into his senior year of college," Fosca said.

"Fair enough," said Carlo. "I suppose I enter the tunnel with Hugo, we get Karim if he's still alive, and Julia—"

"If she doesn't kill you," said Fosca.

Carlo continued, ignoring her. "Then waltz out as easily as we waltzed in?"

"Pretty much," Fosca said.

"It can't be that easy." Hugo rubbed his jaw.

"Nothing has been easy." Carlo plowed his fingers through his hair. "If we get caught, they'll sentence us to *Paradiso*."

Marcel typed on his computer again. "Sometimes people make things more difficult than they need to be. Or they don't know how to find the path of least resistance." His screen filled with code. "Now, here's the beautiful part. Madrid is earthquake prone. I'm going to trigger one."

"With what, dynamite?" Carlo knew there was a catch. "You want me in that tunnel? Not on your life."

"Don't you worry your Venetian ass. I'm using virtual dynamite." He pointed to his screen. "I've already hacked into the museum. They have no idea I'm in the shadows, waiting. The Thyssen is designed to protect its wares, mostly on the main floors. I'm going to make the system *think* there's an earthquake."

"Like *Trece del Mer*?" Hugo asked.

Marcel dead-eyed the Spaniard. "You mean that old movie when the equipment costs more than what they'll steal? No."

He turned back to his computer. "The doors will seal. The power will switch to a generator, shutting down the basement cameras. The entire system focuses on locking down the upstairs. It doesn't care about a corridor that hasn't been used in decades."

Fosca's phone buzzed. She checked it and typed on it.

Carlo had to admit—the plan wasn't bad. "It won't take them long to figure out they're not having a real earthquake."

"So don't exit through the gift shop," Marcel said. "You'll have an earpiece, and I'll tell you when I trigger the earthquake."

"It'll work underground?"

"Sure. Just leave a booster around the entrance."

"Hm." Carlo crossed his arms. Though Marcel had threatened to kill him, he had to admit—he liked the kid. "When do we go?"

"We'll need to go over every part of the plan," Lucia said. "We'll do it tomorrow or the next night. Once we know we can't fail."

"Crap," Fosca said. "We need to go now."

Carlo turned to her, along with everyone else.

"Vasquez is dead. From his injuries." She leveled her gaze at Carlo. "They're saying you killed him."

The blood drained from Carlo's face. Feeling faint, he braced himself on Marcel's desk. "I—I hurt him, yes. But—but I couldn't have... killed him. I—I just knocked him out. It doesn't seem possible."

Fosca rubbed his arm. Her tenderness soothed some of his consternation, but if he had truly ended another person's life, the guilt would weigh on him for the rest of his life.

"I witnessed the whole thing," she said. "It was a serious hit, but I don't think you killed him. At this point, it won't matter because everyone else will. Della Porta called a meeting. All the councilmembers from the three chapters. In Venice. Tonight. We won't be able to change their minds about Vasquez, but this is our chance to save Karim and Julia. The Order will be distracted. Some Protectors will probably accompany the Spaniards."

"We're not ready, mariposita," Lucia said.

Fosca rolled her eyes.

Hugo nodded. "I agree. It's not worth the risk."

Carlo paced the room. Fosca was right. He had to file thoughts of Vasquez and focus on the immediate priority. This would be the time to go. Another idea percolated in his head. "Can *you* go to that meeting?"

"I'm not on any council. Why?"

Marcel snapped his fingers. "Information. You could go in nonna-mère's place."

"They'll never let me in."

Marcel popped out of his chair. He jostled Carlo and Hugo out of the way and crouched at a filing cabinet in the corner. After rifling through a drawer, he returned to the group. He held a black object in his hand, the size of a small coin. He flipped it over. On the other side was a piece of white tape.

"Just barge in," Marcel said. "You only need to be there for a minute. Less." He held up the device. "Stick this somewhere in his office, and we'll hear every word."

Fosca took it. "It's a bug?"

"This isn't James Bond," Marcel said. "It's a wireless microphone I bought on Amazon. I can remotely connect it to their Wi-Fi."

Carlo smiled. "We won't just hear this meeting. Every conversation della Porta has in his office afterward, too."

"Exactly," Marcel said. He slapped Carlo's back. "I told you I liked this guy from the start." He turned to Hugo. "You wanted to throw him off the balcony."

Hugo chuckled uncomfortably.

"When you get there," Hugo said to Fosca, "make sure your phone is connected to the Wi-Fi."

"Put it on speakerphone so we can hear everything before you set up the bug," Carlo added.

"It's not a bug," Marcel said. "Look how big it is."

"I don't know," Fosca said, staring at the disc. "We need a distraction *here*."

"*I'll* distract the museum guards," Lucia said. "You distract the councilmembers."

"No, mi corazón," Hugo said, concern plastering his face. "It's too dangerous."

Lucia laughed. "Too dangerous for whom? You just don't want me flirting with other men."

"Guilty as charged." Hugo planted a warm kiss on his wife's lips.

Fosca inhaled deeply. She tapped her fingers together and paced the room. Carlo had never seen her nervous before. He wondered if something else was going on. Seeing her so serious again brought back the night at the club—a night he wished he'd taken her home.

Finally, she typed on her phone.

"There's a flight leaving in an hour."

# 1591

THE LONE TIME MARCO Quattrone had visited the Vatican Gardens, he found them to be unlike anything in Venice. Combining natural beauty with spirituality, the layout of winding paths through glorious trees inspired visitors to ponder the Creator.

On this second trip to the gardens, Quattrone regretted it being at night, but neither he nor his companion needed to contemplate the universe. Both knew it well—along with its secrets. Privacy for their conversation was far more important.

"There is nothing quite like Rome in springtime," said Cardinal Philippe de Lénoncourt.

The cardinal's strong nose and pronounced jawline were visible in the muted moonlight, but Quattrone could not discern the man's expression. Though the men were both in their sixth decade, Quattrone couldn't deny a touch of jealousy. Cardinal de Lénoncourt had lived a life of peace and luxury, hailing from an ancient and noble family of France.

"Indeed, Eminence," Quattrone replied. "The air is perfect for an evening stroll."

"I trust all is well in Venice?"

"Better than well, Eminence. It is why I requested an audience with you."

They followed the path into an olive orchard. Trees released an intoxicating aroma of sweet citrus blended with a hint of eucalyptus.

"Some of our Order, myself included," Quattrone said, "believe it is time to expand beyond Venice."

"Some? How many?"

Quattrone cleared his throat. He had hoped the cardinal wouldn't ask this question. "Three."

"Three? Including you?"

"Yes, Eminence."

"That is hardly *some*."

"True," Quattrone replied. "But everything starts with one. I believe you share our thinking that by keeping our Order secret, we are doing a disservice to the world."

The cardinal took a moment before replying. "I do. But I am also of the belief that such a reveal could be dangerous. These are perilous times for dissenters of the Church."

"I—*we*—are not dissenters, Eminence. I believe wholeheartedly in the Lord Jesus Christ and his teachings. As do you."

The cardinal nodded. "I like to think of our knowledge as a book of the Bible that has yet to be shared with the masses."

"As do I. The two can exist concurrently, in harmony. Enlightenment, if you will."

"It would need to be a deliberate, gradual process."

"One that would require influence from the top. Influence from a man such as yourself."

The cardinal stopped walking. He gazed up at the Heavens, then looked squarely at Quattrone. "If I am involved, it needs to be of the utmost secrecy. Only you and I can know."

"Of course, Eminence. Grazie. The world will thank you."

"Let us pray that is how it transpires."

Quattrone nodded. "I believe there is one other issue to which you can lend your expertise."

"What expertise is that?"

"We have a... situation with our Painter."

# XI

"**H**EY, MON AMI!" MARCEL'S squeaky French accent pierced Carlo's ears, followed by an elbow to the ribs. "Did we lose you too?"

As the memory of Quattrone's conversation faded, Carlo adjusted to his present-day confines: a van in a subterranean public parking lot adjacent to the Thyssen-Bornemisza. Like all his visions—other people's *memories*, really—he didn't know if it was random or significant, or if it could help him find the doge's black book. Either way, he needed to focus on the now; saving Julia superseded everything else.

It wasn't difficult to readjust, given the alien nature of where he was. Having lived his whole life in a car-free city, he'd never been in a van, let alone an underground garage. Along with Marcel, he and Hugo crouched in the compact space. Computers, monitors, blinking lights, and the hum of cooling fans surrounded him. A pair of fuzzy dice hung from the ceiling. One of Marcel's screens displayed a three-by-three grid of nine viewpoints from the museum's security system.

"Still no word from Fosca?" Carlo asked in answer to Marcel's question.

"No. Where did *you* go?"

"I'm here, I'm here." Fosca's voice funneled in through Marcel's computer speakers. It was choppy but clear. She sounded short of breath.

"What the hell happened?" Marcel asked into a mic.

"I'm fine, how are you? My damn plane was delayed and the *vaporetto* was packed. I just entered the Palazzo. Give me five minutes to reach della Porta's office."

Marcel turned to Carlo and Hugo. "Okay, it's go-time."

After opening the door and surveilling the vicinity, Carlo and his accomplice hopped out. Clad in all black, they hustled to the wall and found a square steel grating about a meter above the floor. Both had a single AirPod nestled in an ear, connected by Bluetooth to their phones. Marcel had tried to play it off as high tech, but their communication was nothing more than a conference call.

Hugo handed Carlo a crowbar. He wedged it between the wall and a bar and snapped the grating open.

"I love Venice," Carlo said, "but it sure is nice doing this on dry land. Come on, I'll help you in." Carlo cupped his hands together to brace Hugo's foot.

The older man laughed at the offering. "Once a gymnast," he said, "always a gymnast."

Nudging Carlo aside, the Spaniard nimbly vaulted himself into the crawlspace. Carlo followed. While he closed the grating, Hugo removed a signal booster from his bag so their phones would work in the tunnels. He set the device on the floor, turned on his headlamp, and started crawling.

"When were you a gymnast?" Carlo asked.

"In university."

"What was that, forty years ago?"

Lucia answered for Hugo, her voice piping in through the AirPod. "If you're impressed with my love, Carlo, just say it."

"I'm impressed," Carlo replied.

Ten meters later, the crawlspace opened to a rounded tunnel. The two of them hopped out. Compared to the bowels of the Palazzo, it was a slice of Heaven for Carlo. Not only could he stand, but the ground was rat-free. Train tracks ran beneath his feet, presumably for pushing carts to and from the bank vaults.

"We're in the main tunnel," Hugo said. He looked up and down the long shaft. "Which way?"

"Northeast," Marcel said through Carlo's Bluetooth. "Go right."

The two men marched in that direction.

"Fosca, where the hell are you?" Marcel asked. After a moment, he continued. "I don't like this. It's been ten minutes, and she said five. How far is della Porta's office from the entrance?"

"About two minutes," Carlo said.

# XII

$\mathrm{T}$HE GREAT COUNCIL ROOM breathed new life.

Until modern times, this thousand-year-old space had been the grandest chamber in Europe. With three of the walls decorated by Venetian masters commemorating the accomplishments of the Serene Republic of Venice, it had rightfully functioned as the meeting hall for senators and doges. Portraits of the elected leaders graced the tops of the three walls. On the fourth wall was Tintoretto's *Paradiso*, not just the world's largest oil painting, but the centerpiece for the Ancient Order of the Seventh Sun—and home to thousands of souls whose bodily forms had no right walking the Earth.

As he did with the Order's Convocations, della Porta stood on the dais backdropped by *Paradiso*, letting the artistic and existential power of the work encompass him.

He could've held this meeting in his office and didn't need a pulpit, but it felt right. With Vasquez's death and the Madrid *Paradiso* still in a purgatorial state, he'd returned to Venice and called an emergency meeting of the councilmembers of the three chapters. Sans the contessa and Vasquez, twelve men and women sat facing him in folding chairs on the marble floor.

"I am more devastated than anybody about the loss of our friend and colleague, José Vasquez," he said to the group. "When I heard he had died of his injuries—"

"Your hand-picked Painter killed him," yelled a Frenchwoman in her late fifties. "Carlo will be the demise of the Order." Her dyed red pouffe exaggerated her demeanor as if blowing her top. She sat next to Christophe François, the octogenarian Exalted Master of Paris. Della Porta had forgotten the fiery woman's name.

Despite the councilmembers' anger and confusion, della Porta maintained complete inward control, including a repressed smile—he'd never be considered a suspect in

Vasquez's death. He gazed at the others, who shouted in agreement with the woman. Della Porta lifted his hands.

"Let him speak." Zotti's voice echoed in the cavernous room.

The hullabaloo died down. Della Porta signaled his appreciation to Zotti and raised his forefinger to the group.

"While yes," della Porta said, "I chose Carlo to be Painter, remember, I was not present during the calamity in Madrid."

"Is a general not responsible for his soldiers?" François asked.

"You are correct," della Porta replied, "I share responsibility with Vasquez, God rest his soul. I share that responsibility with all of you. What happened was a regrettable and unforeseeable turn of events. A mere bump in the road to greatness."

The door flew open.

"Get the fuck off me," a young woman screamed.

"Signorina, you are not permitted," a Protector said.

Along with everyone else, della Porta turned to the ruckus. Fosca squirmed free from the man's grasp and stormed forth, her pink-tipped bob bouncing over her ears. Another two Protectors chased after her. Della Porta signaled to the large men to halt their pursuit.

"This is a council meeting, Fosca," della Porta said. "We've been over this."

"I have a right to be here in my grandmother's absence." She turned to the group and exaggerated her words. "In Contessa Faustina Baldesseri's absence."

A Spaniard in his late eighties stood, balancing himself with his cane. He raised bushy eyebrows beneath his tan, herringbone ascot cap. A few wisps of white hair hung from behind his ears. "Señorita," he said with a hoarse, high-pitched voice. He enunciated and elongated each syllable. It took him three seconds to utter the single word. His sage-like demeanor soothed Fosca. He continued speaking in slow, deliberate English. "We all pray that your grandmother is found. But her absence does not grant an automatic opening to a family member. If I am sick, does that give my wife, my children, my grandchildren, my great-grandchildren, or any of my twenty-nine heirs the right to take my place?"

"You know he is right, ma chérie," added François.

Instead of answering, Fosca cleared her throat. Her face reddened, and she sat on the dais, as if defeated. She gripped the wooden edge, massaging it, rocking her body back and forth.

"I'm sorry, my dear," della Porta said, "but you must leave."

He nodded at the Protectors, who approached Fosca and helped her stand. She let them, but as she reached the door, she swung her head back with a disarming look that pierced della Porta's core as if to say, 'I know what you did.'

Her expression frazzled della Porta. As she and the Protectors left the room, he took the moment to compose himself. When the door closed, he discharged three quick exhales.

"You are correct, monsieur, madame," he said to François and the fire-headed Frenchwoman. "A general is responsible for his soldiers, wherever they may be. I take full responsibility for Carlo's actions and his *replacement*."

The group uttered their approval.

"Veritism." Della Porta glanced at Zotti, who raised a corner of his mouth.

"Excusez-moi?" Fire Head asked.

François whispered into her ear. She scoffed as if reminded of a joke—and not a good one.

The dissent fueled della Porta's discourse. He caught each person's eye as he spoke. "We don't just need a new Painter for Venice or Madrid. Or Paris, before we know it. We need *many* new Painters."

"What are you saying?" the elder Spaniard asked.

"Veritism," della Porta replied.

"It is his insane plan," the woman said, her head more inflamed than ever. "Did Señor Vasquez not tell you?"

"Tell us what?" replied the eldest of Spaniards.

"Monsieur François," della Porta said to the Parisian Exalted Master, "you applauded when I spoke of it."

The man shrugged. "I am still in favor, but I speak only for myself."

"In favor of what?" asked an impatient Spanish woman in her early sixties.

# XIII

"**Y**OU CALL *THAT* A plan?" Marcel's French accent streamed into Carlo's head through his AirPod as he and Hugo trudged through the tunnel. Traversing the old tracks required careful steps, so it had been slower than they'd anticipated.

"I had to improvise," Fosca replied. Her voice was staticky, but the words came through. Again, she sounded like she'd just gone for a jog.

"Was all that in della Porta's office?" Carlo asked.

Fosca exhaled. "Give me a sec. I'm almost out of the complex."

Moments later, the familiar sounds of St. Mark's Square buzzed in the background. He missed home, even the crowds.

"The Great Council Room," Fosca continued.

Carlo wasn't sure if he heard right. He stopped moving.

"You placed a bug in a room where any tourist can go?" he asked.

"Now it's a bug? It's still in my pocket."

"What?" Carlo asked.

"I thought the meeting would've been in his office," Fosca replied. "I don't know why he needs so much space. I considered fixing it to the stage but didn't want anyone to find it."

Shaking his head, Carlo caught up to Hugo, who reached the tunnel's end.

"Wait," Marcel said from the van. "You're telling me it was a total waste of time for you to go? Lucia's about to risk her life flirting with the guards."

"I can hear you," Lucia said. "If you think I'm too old to flirt, wait until I see *you* again, young man."

Hugo laughed. "Take your vitamins, Marcel."

"Don't tempt me," the kid replied.

"It wasn't a total waste of time," Fosca said. "We know he has all the councils there. He's planning something big."

"Merde," Marcel replied. "Carlo and Hugo, let me know when you're at the prison cells, and I'll set the security feed to a sixty-second loop. The moment you have Karim and Julia, I'll trigger the earthquake."

"How much time does that give us?" Carlo asked.

"How should I know?" said Marcel. "How long does it take to figure out the ground isn't shaking?"

Hugo exchanged a glance with Carlo.

"Are you through the tunnel yet?" Marcel asked.

"You got the plans for the wrong building, Marcel." Carlo examined the cinderblock wall. "There's no way in."

Hugo placed a second signal booster on the ground.

"You're holding the key," he said, pointing to the crowbar in Carlo's hand.

Without responding, Carlo went to work. He jammed the tool between two cinderblocks, scraped the old mortar away, and jerked one out. His newfound strength and speed helped him along. In just a few minutes, he'd removed enough for them to crawl through. Beyond was sheetrock.

Hugo held up his hand. "Do you hear that?"

"Merda." The sound was all too familiar: hundreds of souls desperate to be free. The irony didn't escape Carlo. They were breaking into the room in which the souls were held captive. "This isn't going to be pleasant."

"*What* isn't going to be pleasant?" Hugo asked. "What's beyond this wall?"

"What's going on?" asked Marcel.

"Oh, shit," Fosca said. "Don't tell me."

"It makes sense," Carlo said. "They needed to move it. Just our luck it's in the middle of the path."

"Would *someone* tell me what is beyond this wall?" Agitation fueled Hugo's tone. He removed a stun gun from a belt holster.

Carlo placed a hand on the older man's arm. "You won't need that. On three, I'll break through. We run and hope the door to the room isn't locked from the outside."

"What if it is?"

"It won't be. Ready?"

"No." Hugo's hand shook.

"Three." Carlo used the crowbar to tear a hole in the sheetrock. Dust and gypsum particles coated him, but he powered his way in.

Screams erupted. Carlo and Hugo's headlamps illuminated a storage room. *Paradise* had been propped against rows of metal shelves. When he last saw this version of the masterpiece, he heard Senator Quattrone in his head, the lone soul in painted by Jacopo Tintoretto. The remainder were all enshrined by El Greco, killed by the woman he was there to save. All the other souls screamed in his ears, audible for anyone to hear. The shrill noise was unbearable, but he wondered if he could somehow speak with Quattrone. Maybe the man knew the riddle of the Painter's face.

Hugo dropped to the floor. Carlo surveyed the area. The door appeared in the beam of his headlamp. He helped Hugo up and wrapped the man's arm over his shoulder. They reached the door. Carlo flung it open and slammed it shut.

"Dios mío," cried a startled Protector. He dropped a newspaper and fell off his chair. A pair of headphones slipped off.

Before Carlo inhaled, he slammed the man's head against the wall, knocking him out. Only then did he realize the guard must've been around seventy. Carlo cringed at his heinous action, but there was no choice. He turned to Hugo, who backed away from the storage room, shaking, staring at it. The buzz of souls reverberated through the walls.

"Hugo," Carlo called in a whisper. After no response, Carlo snatched the headphones, popped up, and placed them on Hugo's head.

"I need your help," Carlo mouthed.

Hugo snapped out of it. He removed a zip tie from his cargo pants pocket and secured it around the guard's wrists. Carlo placed a strip of duct tape over the man's mouth and snatched his radio, which he clipped to his belt.

The two of them hustled down the corridor to the only exit. Carlo held up a finger to Hugo, then cracked the door, relieved to find a stairwell. Scanning the area, he recalled when Vasquez and Lobo brought him to Karim's cell. He began descending.

Hugo grabbed his arm. "Do you know how to reach Karim and Julia?"

"It's not up."

The still-frazzled man glanced back at the storage room. "Please tell me there's another way out."

"Not unless your wife can distract everyone between here and the main entrance." Carlo hurried down the stairs.

"She better not be that good." Hugo followed.

At the next landing, Carlo nudged the door open. It led to another hallway that was thankfully clear, without a camera in sight.

After twenty meters, they reached a T-intersection. Carlo held his finger to his lips, then pulled out his mobile phone. He turned the camera on, crouched, and angled the lens around the corner. No guards. Ten meters away stood a door with a small window and a keypad to the side. Vasquez had brought him through that gate, which meant they were inside the prison cell area. Switching to the other corner, he did the same thing—and immediately drew the phone back.

The same dark-skinned Protector who'd been previously guarding the prison cells sat on a steel folding chair, chuckling at something he watched on his tablet. If Julia still breathed, she was held in one of the three cells just past the guard. Carlo was so close. He just had to incapacitate a man twice his size before he could sound the alarm.

Turning to Hugo, he spoke with his eyes: *Be ready.*

Carlo stood at full height, balled his hand into a fist, and planted his foot, ready to burst.

"Um, guys?" Marcel's voice squeaked in through Carlo's AirPod.

He backed away from the corner.

"Can you hurry the fuck up?" The French kid asked.

Hugo took twenty paces back toward the stairwell and answered in a whisper. "We're going as fast as we can. Why?"

"I think we've been spotted. The same SUV has driven by twice."

# XIV

A GAIN, DELLA PORTA CAUGHT each person's gaze as he described a world with Veritism. He paced the dais and animated his hands to hammer his points into his listeners' heads. He found himself speaking more passionately than he had when he previously explained the beauty—no, *purity*—of a single religion. After a few minutes of talking to an audience rapt with attention, he took a deliberate pause and continued with information his allies had yet to hear. "We won't just reveal ourselves to the world as the one veritable religion. We'll expand. We'll have new canvasses all over the world. We shall remake the world. *Reshape* the world into a *purer* form—one without religious oppression, bigotry, or wars because one's god is stronger than his neighbor's."

The irrepressible upward pull of his cheeks della Porta had experienced of late returned. "It's already in the works, my friends. You—everyone in this room—will be at the top."

With those words, the councilmembers' demeanors changed. Even the dissenters seemed to comprehend the reward they'd receive.

"Yes," della Porta continued, "imagine living in the time of Jesus and having a crystal ball."

"You fancy yourself as Jesus?" the elder Spaniard asked, the lone remaining contrarian voice.

Della Porta narrowed his eyes. "Certainly not, and do not spout such nonsense and blasphemies."

The others turned to the Spaniard, their expressions rebuking the insinuation.

"There is but one Supreme Painter," della Porta said. "We know the truth. You know the truth—you saw it with your own eyes. Everyone here knows the truth. Veritism. This is the time. There is one Supreme Painter but *our will* guides his hands. Everyone outside the Order lives in the dark. We know the light, yet we live in the shadows. Now is the time. All can live in the light of Veritism."

"Señor della Porta," said the Spaniard, "this sounds marvelous, but you're forgetting one tiny thing."

"What's that?"

"Billions of people have already accepted their faith as gospel. We are but less than two thousand. The masses will not switch allegiance at the drop of a hat. You don't see Jews, Muslims, and Buddhists converting to Christianity simply because one says it's the right way."

"Ah," della Porta said with a grin, "but it's happened many times in the past. Where do you think Christians came from?"

"It took *centuries* for Christianity to truly take root." A sheen formed on the elderly man's furrowed brow.

Della Porta pulled out his mobile phone. "Now the Bible—a million Bibles—can be sent worldwide in a fraction of a second."

The group murmured amongst themselves. They knew he made a good point.

"Even with modern technology," della Porta added, "I'm not saying we'll succeed overnight. It's better, really, for exactly the reason you said. Veritism needs to take root. And it will. Then, it will grow into a massive, unbreakable tree, with branches canopying the world. For the simple reason that we have proof, and we can show them proof. All other religions are based on faith. Veritism is based on *fact*."

"People take their faith as fact," the Frenchwoman said. "They believe it in their hearts and minds. That's what you're missing."

Fire Head joined the Spaniard at his side. They seemed nervous and resisted the inevitable. That suited della Porta just fine. It would've been foolish for him to expect instant agreement. Just as Vasquez had scoffed at the glory of Veritism, many more would do the same in the years to come. Those without understanding resorted to fear, anger, or conflict. Della Porta needed to hone his responses to all objections. These people served as a sounding board for future malcontents; they were practice for him, nothing more.

"What you're missing is *opportunity*. You look at the Catholic Church and see a billion obstacles. I look at the Church and see a billion opportunities. Once they're converted, all other religions will follow."

"How will you convert them?" a Spanish man with thick black hair asked.

"From the top, of course."

The Spanish and French members broke into laughter. The Venetians, having already heard the plan, stayed silent. "You expect the pope to join us?" the Frenchwoman asked.

Della Porta offered her a sly grin. "He would not be the first."

The amusement switched to gasps.

"Many of you have heard rumors of a book," della Porta continued, their attention glued. "A journal that would hold sway over the Church and prove that popes were more than simply aware of the Order. Many knew our truths and were *secret members*."

"Fantasy!" the elder Spaniard called out. He stood, balancing precariously on his cane. "If not, the book is lost to the ages."

"You are wrong," della Porta said. "The journal will be in my hands shortly. My men are searching for it as we speak. From there, the pope, the Church, and its billion followers."

"How are any of you in favor of this lunacy?" Fire Head asked her colleagues.

"Because," della Porta answered for them, his voice growing in volume and sternness, "you can help lead. Or... if you prefer, you can watch the world change from the sidelines. I believe there's an open spot in the bleachers up there." He pointed to *Paradiso*.

"You have some nerve and no authority," the elder Spaniard called out.

"If you'd like a better seat, my friend, you can join a *new* Paradise. There will be many to choose from. So many."

Della Porta signaled Bernardo, who'd been standing at the rear of the room. The Enforcer of the Charge opened the aft door. Four dozen newly installed Protectors filed in and stood in formation. More than half were also police officers or former soldiers and already familiar with militaristic training.

Councilmembers from all three chapters spun around to watch the procession, then turned back to della Porta. Those already on his side beamed with delight. Aghast, the Frenchwoman gulped in air as if it were her last. Her broiling composure turned ashen. The old Spaniard cleared his throat and took his seat.

Silence descended over the room. All eyes landed on della Porta. He relished the moment. Zotti, the mayor and Trevisan all grinned proudly. Della Porta gazed at his Protectors in the back, then at the other councilmembers. The Spaniards and Frenchmen seemed to be with him for more reasons than just because of the threat of imprisonment. They knew his vision was beyond anything they'd dreamed. He raised his palms to them and spoke as calmly—yet authoritatively—as he could.

"I came to the Order a pilgrim, thirsty for knowledge. I now charge forth as a shepherd, spreading wisdom. I am not alone on this journey. All of us arrived as pilgrims. All of us are shepherds. So, my friends, I repeat. I entered as a pilgrim. I charge forth a shepherd."

Della Porta reiterated the line slower, gesturing for them to join in.

"I entered as a pilgrim. I charge forth a shepherd."

The group remained quiet. He indicated for Zotti, the mayor, and Trevisan to voice the words again. This time, his faithful Venetian acolytes joined him.

"I entered as a pilgrim. I charge forth a shepherd," they all said in unison with della Porta.

They continued stating the line. Bernardo and the Protectors in the back joined in. One by one, the councilmembers from Madrid and Paris uttered the words, even those who had dissented earlier. Whether or not they agreed with della Porta, all knew the ramifications if they didn't conform.

"I entered as a pilgrim. I charge forth a shepherd."

# XV

THE INSTANT MARCEL STOPPED speaking, Carlo snatched Hugo's stun gun and exploded from the corner. By the time the guard looked up at the blur barreling toward him, it was too late. Carlo activated the stun gun and drove it into the Protector's neck. The man's eyes rolled into the back of his head. He slumped over and landed on the concrete floor. Not finished, Carlo jammed the stun gun into Julia's captor's chest. The guard's body buckled from the voltage coursing through him.

"I don't blame you," Hugo said. "But that's enough." He took back the stun gun with an understanding hand, then went to work with zip ties and duct tape.

Carlo hurried to the first cell. He tapped the screen next to the door, waking it up. The camera showed an empty room. At the second cell, he did the same. The monitor revealed a huddled mass in the corner. Carlo prayed Karim still lived.

"Okay," Carlo said into his mic. "What's the code for the second door?"

"Man, you really don't want to know how my cousin got these."

"I swear to God," Fosca yelled into everyone's ears.

"Five-five-seven-seven-two," said Marcel.

Carlo punched in the numbers. The lock disengaged. "Hugo," he called. His partner in crime left the disabled Protector and entered the room. At the third door, Carlo breathed deep, sending a silent prayer to every god and goddess in the history of humanity. He woke up the screen and exhaled when Julia appeared on the monitor. She sat with her back against the wall, reading a book.

"Code for door three?"

"Five-five-seven-seven-three," Marcel replied. "I guess they're not too concerned about security."

"Their cockiness will be their downfall," Fosca said.

Carlo tapped in the numbers. The keypad blinked red. He tried it again, and again, it didn't open. "Are you sure that's the right number?"

"Fosca, is it?"

"It's whatever's on the paper, Marcel," she answered. "Can you read?"

"Wait," Marcel said. "Maybe that's a two. Can you write? Carlo, try five-five-seven-seven-two."

Carlo put his finger on the buttons but hesitated. "That's the same number as the other door. What if we only have three tries?"

Silence.

After a beat, Hugo said, "It makes sense. They're not expecting a breakout, and it's easier to remember. Plus, we don't have a choice."

Gritting his teeth, Carlo entered the code. The pad switched to green, and the lock disengaged. He opened the door.

As an artist in Venice who was no stranger to the opposite sex, Carlo had been surrounded by beauty his entire life. But there, on a thin cot mattress, in baggy jeans and an old T-shirt, with messy black hair and a face that hadn't been washed in days, sat an exquisite image. A smile consumed him. Tears of relief filled his eyes. He stretched his arms wide.

"Julia..."

On seeing him, her pallid complexion twisted into fire-red. She pounced up with more speed than he thought she possessed... and charged. Her fist connected with his jaw. His AirPod went flying. Her hands wrapped around his throat. She slammed him against the door, shutting it.

"Ju—"

Her vise-like grip prevented him from uttering any other syllables. The thought of harming her repulsed him, but she left him no choice. He clenched her wrists and pried them from his throat as gently but firmly as he could. She resisted at first but then relented with a mix of exhaustion and exasperation.

"I should've known." Her voice sounded as if she hadn't drunk anything in days. She rubbed her eyes and scratched her scraggly black hair. "Just get it over with."

"What?" Carlo replied, wholly unsure of what she meant.

"Torture me. Kill me." She gazed at him with pleading eyes. "Or... if you're going to paint me... put me into the canvas with Nick."

Guilt engulfed Carlo, but he had no time to wallow in it. "We need to go." He reached for her hand, but she whipped it away. Figuring she'd walk out the door if he opened it, he reached for the handle, but there wasn't one.

"Merda," Carlo muttered. Locked in.

He tapped on the door, hoping it was loud enough for Hugo to hear but not anybody else. Moments later, the door cracked open. Hugo stuck his head in.

"Who's this?" Julia asked.

"The other guy here to rescue you. *Please.*"

He held the door for Julia, not so much to be a gentleman but to indicate she was free. She hesitated, but to Carlo's relief, she exited. He snatched his AirPod from the floor and followed Julia. She halted and yelped. Carlo stiffened in shock.

Draped over Hugo's shoulder was the naked shell of a man. Gaunt, ragged, unshaven, unkempt hair. Old blood stained the bandages wrapping his hands. The odor of human waste and a body near death accosted Carlo's nostrils.

"He needs a hospital," Hugo said.

Julia raced back into her cell. She returned with a thin blanket, which she wrapped around Karim.

Carlo spoke into his AirPod as he reinserted it. "Do it now, Marcel."

"Done," said the Frenchman. "Sub-levels are sealed."

The guard stirred as they passed. Snot dribbled from his nostrils onto the duct tape covering his mouth. Through widening slits, he caught Carlo's gaze. After a bit of confusion, his eyes popped open. He tried getting to his feet but tripped, the zip ties doing their job.

"Move," Carlo ordered.

His friends reached the T-intersection.

A klaxon alarm rang out, stunning them.

"Is that for the earthquake?" Hugo asked.

"Um, no," Marcel replied.

Julia raised an eyebrow. "Earthquake?"

"Pick up the pace, everyone," Marcel yelled. "Guards are headed your way. Lucia, get to the van."

Her voice piped in. "I'll be there in five."

"Rapido, mi corazón," Hugo said.

Taking the lead, Carlo grabbed Julia's hand and hustled down the hall. He glanced behind, thankful Hugo matched his pace, despite Karim draped over his shoulders.

Julia stopped short and backed up, realizing where they were. "No. No way am I going in there."

"I want to say the same," Hugo said.

The buzz of the souls wasn't audible over the alarm, but Carlo knew that wouldn't be the case inside the storage room.

"You guys have fifteen seconds," Marcel said.

The older guard Carlo had knocked out still lay unconscious at the corner of the door. Carlo scoured his station. He found a bin of headphones and passed them out. "Please, Julia, there's no other way out."

After donning a pair, Hugo placed headphones over Karim's ears. The group exchanged glances and nodded at each other.

Hugo threw the door open. Four Protectors rounded the corner. "¡Alto!" one of them called. Lobo jostled his way to the front of the oncoming group. Upon spotting Carlo, the Spanish Painter's face turned to fury. He shoved a Protector aside and sprinted toward Carlo, even with a bad leg.

"Go, go, go," Carlo called. The group scrambled into the room. The souls went ballistic, howling at the intruders with their indistinguishable demands. As the screaming echoed into the hall, audible over the alarm, the Protectors slowed, unwilling to go further. All but Lobo. He grimaced but continued moving.

"Get them out, Hugo," Carlo shouted. "I'll hold them off." He gritted his teeth at the sonic assault. Though it felt like a knife jabbing his ears, it was far better than hearing those screams in his head, which was like a spoon scooping out his brain.

"What?" Hugo mouthed, his voice too low to be heard.

"Go!" Carlo made sure his new friend brought Julia and Karim to the hole he'd created in the wall, before returning to his approaching nemesis.

"You want me?" Carlo yelled to Lobo, "Come and get me!"

He slammed the door shut.

"Let's go, Carlo," Hugo shouted over the roar.

"I'll meet you at the flat," Carlo yelled back. Mustering every microgram of willpower, he tuned out the screaming souls and approached the Spanish *Paradise*, walking into the ravenous souls.

"Quattrone!" he shouted. "We need to talk."

Unsure of where she headed or who led them on, Julia trudged forth, helping Hugo support Karim. Rocks gnashed the soles of her bare feet, and she had already tripped over two old railroad crossties, but the pain was inconsequential—she needed to escape at any cost. She also needed to help Karim, who was far worse off.

His bandaged fingers hung over Hugo's shoulder. Portions of the bloodied wrap flapped with every bounce. Julia swallowed a wad of bile, recalling Lacasse's threat with the thumbscrew.

Though she'd never met the prisoner in the adjacent cell, Fosca had shown Julia a photo. Karim was unrecognizable compared to the healthy, good-looking soccer player he'd been a short time prior. Julia hadn't seen a mirror in days and wondered how close she was to Karim's state. Still, despite the horrors of the conditions, his presence and Hugo's compassion eased any concerns this was a dream—or something worse.

Hugo brought them to a vent large enough to crawl through. "You go first," he said to Julia. "I'll help Karim."

She did as instructed and crawled thirty feet, arriving at a dank parking garage.

The side door of a white cargo van rolled open, and a skinny teenager with messy hair and a pimply face hopped out. The kid hustled over and helped Julia from the crawlspace.

"I got you," he said with a squeaky French accent. "You're safe. Go into the van."

Julia stayed to help Karim. Hugo shooed her hand away and slunk out with surprising grace.

"Mon Dieu," the French kid exclaimed upon seeing Karim. He rattled his head in anger and guided all three people into the van.

Along with the others, Julia hopped in, surprised the cargo area was filled with tech gear. Hugo slid the door closed. A sixty-something woman in the driver's seat turned to the back.

"¿Dónde está Carlo?" she asked with a thick accent.

"We lost him, Lucia," Hugo replied in English.

"What do you mean 'you lost him?'" Fosca's anxious voice came in through a speaker next to a computer monitor.

"He'll meet us at the flat," Hugo said. Urgency fused his words. "Drive, mi amor."

Lucia threw the shifter into reverse and peeled out of the spot. Julia tumbled backward, along with the stools and everyone else.

"Hang on," called the woman before braking.

Julia crawled to the front and gripped the passenger seat headrest, giving her a vantage point through the windshield. Lucia shifted into drive and floored it. The van sped through the tight garage, narrowly avoiding a car backing out of a spot. She turned, drove to the upper floor, and aimed for the exit ramp.

Out of nowhere, a silver Mercedes SUV skidded to a stop, blocking the van's path. A man in the passenger seat aimed a gun out his window and fired.

Lucia screamed. She spun the wheel. A bullet ricocheted off the side mirror. Lucia headed for another one-way ramp, with Spanish 'no entry' signs emblazoned on what was the garage *entrance*. The van bottomed out as it ascended. Julia bounced up. Her head smacked the vehicle's roof.

At the top of the ramp, a cherry-red convertible waited for the swing arm barrier. Lucia jammed her hand on the horn as she barreled forth, but the convertible didn't budge. She stomped the brakes, inches from hitting the little car. Hugo toppled into Marcel. Julia hung on to the headrest as the three others tumbled backward. A Rubik's Cube flew off a shelf. Hugo protected Karim's head from striking a computer monitor.

The driver of the convertible waved his hands wildly, shouting at Lucia.

"¡Vamanos, cabrón!" Lucia screamed back, still riding the horn. A barrage of uninterpretable Spanish launched from her mouth like bullets, but convertible owner countered, standing and pointing at the various signs.

A crushing impact jammed the van from behind.

Julia's skull whiplashed into the headrest. The van inched forward. Lucia raised her hands off the steering wheel, unsure of what was happening. A lack of a rear window prevented visibility, but Julia knew the SUV had rammed them and was bulldozing them up.

Karim groaned. Hugo and Marcel cradled him, protecting the injured man's body from further damage.

The swing arm barrier finally raised.

Panic filled the angry driver's eyes. He sat and grabbed the steering wheel. Too late. The van collided with the convertible, railroading it backward into oncoming traffic.

"Dios mío." Lucia fumbled with the shifter and pressed harder on the brake, but it was useless. The SUV picked up speed. It forced the van to shove the convertible into the busy street. A speeding sedan smashed into it, knocking it away.

"Go," Julia called out. "Now!"

Lucia seized her chance. She threw it into drive and crushed the gas pedal. The van peeled into oncoming traffic in the Madrid night. Again, the three rolled to the rear of the van. Julia swallowed a scream and watched through her fingers.

A massive crash erupted behind them.

Julia spied the passenger side mirror. "They got hit," she called out. A bus had smashed into the SUV. A pang of guilt smacked her, realizing she had no idea how many people just got injured because of her.

Lucia deftly avoided three cars, then cut down a side street. She turned down a one-way empty alley.

"Did we lose them?" the French kid asked.

"I think so," Lucia replied, checking her mirrors. "But I take no chance."

She drove like a banshee for another ten minutes before settling for another twenty. Finally, she parked on a tree-lined street in an upscale neighborhood.

"We're four blocks from the apartamento," Lucia said, pulling out her cell phone. "We wait here ten minutes."

The group caught their collective breath.

"What's happening?" Fosca asked through the speaker. "Are you guys okay?"

"Thanks to the most amazing driving I've ever seen," Julia replied.

"Julia," Fosca replied, joy filling her voice. "Thank God. I'll see you soon."

"I hope so." Julia's eyes brimmed with moisture.

Lucia smiled as she made a call in Spanish, then turned to the group after hanging up. "The doorman says everything is normal."

"Hell of a way to meet, huh?" the French kid said. "I'm Marcel." He held out his hand.

"Julia O'Connor." She shook it.

"I know." He motioned to everyone else. "You've met Hugo and Karim. That's Lucia. She's practicing for Le Mans."

Karim winced but managed a weak smile. "Gracias, amigos."

Hugo squeezed his friend's shoulder. "Gracias a ti, amigo."

"Yes. Thank you," Julia said, tears welling in her eyes. "Thank you."

# XVI

AN INSUPPRESSIBLE FEELING OF triumph surged through della Porta. He reclined on a bench in the *Giardini Reali*, observing the maritime traffic enter and depart the Grand Canal. The view never ceased to instill comfort and inspire purpose. The vessels symbolized harmonic magnificence in the city's millennium of greatness. He often watched the scene from his office window, but he would come down for an open-air, front-row seat when the mood struck him.

One of the few parks in Venice, the Royal Gardens were a stone's throw from the Doge's Palace and indeed, was once the doge's private outdoor retreats. Minuscule compared to the average European park, the gardens offered a collection of plant life native to Italy. In a city packed with tourist attractions, they were rarely visited, so della Porta always found a free seat. He imagined how grand it must have been for the doge to have his own private park where he could meditate, away from the grueling demands of being the leader of the Venetian Republic.

Veritism brought him one step closer to those rulers of the bygone empire. But he would surpass them in every way. With the other chapters now behind him, all he needed was the doge's journal. From there, he'd solidify the Church's endorsement, and there would be no turning back. Before coming to the gardens, Dante had updated della Porta on the search for that illusive book. Though they'd interviewed almost every surviving descendant of Renzo and Isabella without luck, it was inevitable. A Scalfini or Stefanetti would know the location.

A short foghorn blast followed by angry cursing caught his ears. Two water taxis had nearly collided. It was an uncommon sight in Venice, given the city's strict licensing and testing requirements. On a closer look, della Porta realized a third vessel had caused both taxis to veer off course: an illegal kayaker paddled frantically through the wake.

The scene rippled through della Porta's brain. Renzo and Isabella were a collision of their own, but their demise came about because of a third party—Angelo Mascari. No, he was a mere pawn. The true interlopers were the Bird Brothers—Ivan and Vito Uccello. Della Porta snapped his fingers. How could he have missed that? The Bird Brothers paid Angelo to seduce Isabella and were on the scene, in the house, when the swordsman got caught. They were there when Renzo died, and they detained Isabella themselves. One could've removed Isabella and the servants, while the other had ample time to search the room—maybe the whole house. Della Porta grinned at the obviousness. He didn't fault himself for not thinking of this, nor would he chastise his subordinates. On the contrary, he applauded himself for coming up with the solution. He'd instruct Dante to change tack, interview all Uccello ancestors again, and dig deeper into the family.

But first, he needed a few more minutes to recharge. He closed his eyes and inhaled the salty sea air, letting it coat him internally. Sunlight warmed his face... for a moment.

A shadow fell over him.

"Sior," said the gruff voice, interrupting his peace. "I am sorry to bother you," the man continued in Venetian.

Della Porta didn't need to look to know the owner of that voice. The man had been by della Porta's side for twenty years and deserved respect. Della Porta opened his eyes. The chief Protector shielded the sun, which created a halo effect around the big man's buzzcut.

"Bernardo, life is but a few pleasures interrupting our challenges," della Porta said. "But every challenge can be overcome. I assume this is a pressing one?"

"Sì. Julia O'Connor has escaped from the Thyssen."

An involuntary inhale cut della Porta's lungs. His back snapped to attention. Though Signora O'Connor herself posed little consequence, her escape would reflect poorly on him in the eyes of the Madrid Council. Worse, should she go to the police or media, she could expose many of the Order's secrets. That would be a challenge for Veritism.

He stood and angled himself so that it was the Protector's turn to have the sun in his eyes.

"How?" della Porta asked.

Bernardo reached into his breast pocket and donned a pair of black wraparound sunglasses.

"You're not going to like this."

Della Porta released a sigh that came out as a growl. "Carlo. Let me guess, he's unquestionably working with the Guild."

"I thought you didn't want to validate them by giving them a name."

"*We* have underestimated our foes, Bernardo." Della Porta knew his friend realized the implication of stressing 'we.' While he didn't fault any of his men for failing to realize that the Uccellos took the doge's book, the Guild was another story. The Order paid their Protectors well, and part of that job was to keep all enemies in check. "Do we have any other identities?"

"Only one man on camera. An older man. And some poor angles of a woman driving their getaway van. They also took Karim, the footballer."

"He's of no consequence."

"No, and he needed medical attention. They may have brought him to a hospital. Which would lead to questions."

Della Porta narrowed his eyes. "It will also lead to accomplices. We need to silence the Guild once and for all. It's clear the current lack of leadership in Spain has proven to be a chasm in which important things slip through." He turned for the garden exit. "It's time I sealed that breach. Also, summon Dante to my office. We're taking a new path in finding the book."

# XVII

$\mathbf{V}$ OICES SEEPED INTO JULIA's brain like disembodied aural tentacles.

Her eyes opened to darkness. She had a test in the morning, and, once again, people were partying on a weeknight. *No, impossible.* She was home in her apartment in Boston. Her neighbors were up late. *Rude.* It must've been the middle of the night. She could've used another twelve hours of sleep. Lavender-scented fabric softener lulled her toward a dislocated slumber.

She reached for Nick, but her hand smacked the wall. Rolling over for him on the other side of the bed, she reached too far and toppled off, planting her face in a shag carpet.

*Where's Nick?*

A surge of panic jolted her chest like a thunderclap.

*We don't have shag carpet...*

She crawled to her feet, groping in the dim light seeping through the doorframe. Locating a nightstand, she flicked on the lamp to find herself in a small room coated in floral prints. The lampshade, the drapes, the bedding. In her hazy state, the two-dimensional bouquet heightened her sense of an alien space.

Her heart drummed. Her breath came in short spurts.

She had no clue where she was.

The loudest voice outside her room had a distinct high tone and bizarre American accent infused with hints of French and Italian. Fosca.

Memories flooded Julia's brain, calming her nerves. After the group freed her from the Thyssen-Bornemisza, they brought her to an apartment. She had two sips of water before crashing, fully clothed.

Thankfully, the same glass remained on the nightstand. She chugged it, only half-quenching her parched throat.

Her carry-on sat on the floor at the foot of the bed. She had brought it to Fosca's hotel room the night they went to the museum to kill El Greco. Opening it, Julia was thankful Fosca had been so considerate. She found her passport and two outfits for what was supposed to have been a very short trip to Madrid. But she wanted none of it.

She shut her eyes, wishing, praying, begging that when she opened them again, she'd be back in her home with Nick.

It didn't happen.

She contemplated the flowers surrounding her, thinking how nice it would be to burrow into the bed and stay there forever. But doing so wouldn't stop della Porta. It wouldn't bring the assholes who imprisoned her to justice. It wouldn't free Nick—if such a thing were possible.

With a deep inhale, she composed herself. She changed out of her disgusting captivity clothes into her own shorts and t-shirt, then opened the door. Following Fosca's voice, she found her friend in the living room, chatting with Marcel, Hugo, and Lucia.

"Julia..." Fosca uttered the words with a combination of relief and elation. She jumped off the sofa and rushed over, wrapping warm arms around her.

Julia returned the embrace with watering eyes. She didn't want to let go. Shivers of gratitude—and, more importantly, *security*—fluttered through her body, though she was far from safe. None of them were.

Fosca gave her another squeeze, then released her hold. Julia wiped her eyes.

"I'm gonna kill those fuckers," Fosca said. "All of them. They've taken all this way too far." She brought Julia over to the floral-print roll-arm sofa. A yellow teapot next to an assortment of snacks called to her from the marble coffee table.

Plopping next to Lucia, Julia observed the crew.

"Where's Karim?" she asked.

Hugo and Lucia exchanged a mournful glance.

Julia covered her mouth. It couldn't be.

"The hospital," said Lucia.

Julia exhaled.

"He has a family," said Hugo. "He can't be a part of this."

The comment forced an unwelcome tremble. Julia knew Hugo didn't intend to upset her. He had a family. They all had a family. Of course, Hugo meant Karim had kids. Still, Julia had a family, too. She had a husband—and she'd do anything to get him back.

Seeing her distress, Lucia rubbed her arm. Julia caught Fosca's eye. Fosca—whose family had lost more than anyone's—was in the thick of it. Her expression said it all: *This is bigger than any of us. It needs to end.*

Julia reached for an unused mug and poured herself some tea. An essence of mint wafted into her nostrils, reinvigorating her. She didn't equate mint tea—or any tea—with Spain, but it fit the décor of the apartment and the mood of the group. Unfortunately, it was too hot, so she kept it on the table. "We don't need to kill them all," she said. "But they're going down. Do you have a computer here?"

"And then some." Marcel smiled. "What do you need?"

"The internet."

"You could use my phone for that."

Julia laughed. "One of those would be useful too." She turned to Fosca. "I think I know how to open Isacco's box."

Fosca began to reply, but the doorbell buzzed. The group fell silent as Hugo checked the peephole. He opened it a moment later, yanking in a person who instantly soured Julia's mood.

Carlo.

"Where have you been?" Hugo asked.

Ignoring him, Carlo rushed over to Julia. "Are you okay? Are you hurt?"

She slapped his grasping hands away and glared at him with more rage than she'd ever felt. "Don't pretend to care, Carlo. You got me out. Thank you for that. But don't think for a second that makes up for what you did. Not even close."

Carlo's shoulders sagged. His gaze plunged to the floor. "I know," he said, barely audible. "I know you'll never forgive me. But I *do* care."

An overwhelming urge to kick him in the balls consumed Julia. She'd never done that to a guy; it'd always seemed overly cruel. And, she'd never had a reason. Now, all she wanted to do was inflict pain on this person she once considered a friend. She lifted her right heel, then noticed everyone staring at her.

She lowered her foot and exhaled, settling her racing heart.

"If only you cared enough not to murder my husband." The words, dripping with hatred, seethed from Julia's mouth.

"¿Qué?" Lucia asked. She stared, dumbfounded, along with Hugo and Marcel.

A disturbed silence swept over the room. Julia smirked.

"Tell them, Carlo."

He glanced at the others, averting Julia's eyes. Then, looking at the floor, in a near-whisper, he said, "It's true."

Lucia gasped.

"I painted him," Carlo said.

"Into *Paradise*?" Marcel asked.

Finally, Carlo looked at Julia. Pain radiated in his eyes. His palpable regret took her aback. He spoke to the group. "No," he said. "I sentenced Nick to a *new* painting."

"Where he's all alone." Julia folded her arms, in part to restrain herself.

Again, he turned to her. Tears bubbled. "I did it for you. I wasn't thinking of Nick. It was Nick's body, but truly, I sentenced *Angelo*."

"They were the same!" Julia screamed.

"Angelo tried to kill you. I thought you were going to die. It was a miracle you didn't. Nick was my friend. I'd never do anything to hurt him. But Angelo didn't deserve retribution after attacking you."

His confession cascaded from his lips. But it wasn't a confession. It was an explanation—one Julia hadn't heard before.

"Two wrongs don't make a right," he added.

"Yet you added another wrong."

Carlo cleaved his hands through his messy hair. "I know. I'll do everything I can to correct it."

"Can you?" Fosca asked from the edge of her seat.

"I don't know." Carlo wiped his eyes and nose, then turned to Julia. "If possible, I will do it. I promise you."

She would never forgive him, but if he could somehow reverse the process or even put Nick in with Isabella, it would be something.

"Then I guess we need to figure out a way," she said.

Her tone possessed a compassionate softness that surprised her and lightened the room. The group nodded to each other. Carlo collapsed on the sofa as if he'd just completed a punishing hike. He reached for a slice of baguette, spread some hummus on it, and shoved the whole thing in his mouth. Julia hadn't noticed he looked as though he'd lost ten pounds since she punched him in the park.

Realizing her mouth was so dry she couldn't conjure enough saliva to moisten her lips, Julia reached for her tea and took a sip. It had cooled to the perfect temperature. The herbal remedy warmed her insides and pacified her irritability.

"So," Fosca said. "Are we good?"

"Hell no," Julia replied, scowling at the Order's Painter. She needed a stiffer drink after all, but she took a calming gulp of the tea. "We'll never be good. But... if Carlo can make things right, that will go a long way. Like you said, this is bigger than all of us."

"We can live with that," Fosca said.

The group nodded and voiced their agreement.

"Alright. So, Julia," Fosca said, "you were saying you know how to open the box?"

"You do?" Carlo asked. "I have information, too."

Julia nodded. "Maybe, but I need to double-check. It's *duality*. Tintoretto, the Order, they're about duality."

"Of course," Fosca said. "That could gel with the dials being on four sides."

"Yup," Julia replied. "There are *two* portraits of him. One has the word, 'IPSIUS' on it, but the Latin U is a V."

Carlo smacked his forehead. "How did I not think of that? It means 'himself.' It was his little joke. Or..." He grabbed a couple of almonds and tossed them in his mouth, nodding while he chewed. "It could also mean 'cannot be counted.'"

"Cannot be counted?" Fosca asked. "As in, he could not be counted on? Like, unreliable?"

"No." Carlo shook his head. "Too many to count."

Julia's jaw popped open. "*Uncountable*. As in the souls. That's gotta be it."

"You did it." Fosca cracked a smile.

Carlo typed into his phone. "Don't celebrate yet. There are two, no, three words on the portrait with six letters. This is the original inscription, most of which has been lost to time." He displayed the screen for all to see.

**JACOBVS TENTORETVS PICTOR VENETIVS IPSIVS. F**

"Jacopo Tintoretto, painter of Venice. Himself," Carlo said.

Julia squinted at the phone. "What does the F mean?"

"Facio or facies," Carlo replied. "Face. His face. You could translate it as 'made by myself.' He had a sense of humor, you know."

"Yeah, that joke isn't gonna fly on the standup circuit," Julia said. "Why would he abbreviate 'made?' It's a bit strange, isn't it? If *ipsivs* can be translated as uncountable, couldn't it be *uncountable faces*?"

A collective shiver passed through the trio.

"So," Carlo continued, "assuming the keyword is on this painting, we have *pictor*, *ipsivs*, and *facies*."

"Wait, I saw this portrait on my phone," Julia said. "Those other words aren't there. It's just *ipsivs*. What happened to the others?"

"At some point, they were removed. Who knows why? This painting has had many owners, even Marie Antoinette."

"Really? That's cool. I mean, besides the whole awful despot part."

Fosca perked up. "She helped establish the Order's Parisian chapter. Anyway, it's pretty safe to rule out *facies* since that's in the clue. *Pictor* is also part of the clue."

"You don't just rub off words from a painting," Julia said. "Especially the artist's name. Someone revealed the keyword to the world. *Ipsivs* has gotta be it."

"You're probably right, but there's more." Carlo chewed another almond. "I spoke with Quattrone."

"Who?" asked Marcel.

The name jogged Julia's memory. "You were having visions of his life. An old Venetian senator, right?"

"That and the Order's first Exalted Master," replied Carlo. "He was betrayed and sentenced to *Paradiso* in the Thyssen-Bornemisza. He's the only soul in there painted by Tintoretto."

"You can speak with him?" Hugo asked.

Carlo nodded. "It wasn't easy. I hear the other souls just as you do. But Quattrone is in my head. It was like trying to think with a thousand people screaming at you."

"Not *like*," Julia said. "It's exactly that." She paled, the memory of being locked in that room still fresh.

"I only had a moment," Carlo continued. "The Protectors were there. And Lobo."

"He saw you?" asked Fosca.

"He wasn't happy. When I got out, I sprinted the streets. Then waited at a bus stop until I thought it was safe to come here. Quattrone said it's the Painter's face and his *death*. Maybe the Vatican knew Tintoretto didn't die like a normal man. That could be the secret in the book."

"Wait," Julia said. "Sure, that's huge, but you think *that's* what all this is about? How could that knowledge bring della Porta unlimited power or destroy the Order? Nobody would even believe it."

"There must be something else," Carlo replied. "But—"

"But," Fosca joined in, "if the Church has definitively known about souls, past lives, and the power for extended life, yet they've been keeping it a secret? Think about what people would do if they knew. *There's no hell*, Julia."

Fosca paused, letting that notion sink in—and Julia got it. It would be enormous.

"Not just for Catholics," Fosca continued. "It would change everything for everyone. The Order has proof of many of the answers people have been pondering for millennia. Della Porta would have the Church over a barrel. We need to get that book before he does. Even if it doesn't have something that could ruin the Order, I'd rather keep those truths a secret than let him get that power."

Julia exchanged a knowing look with Carlo and Fosca. "Looks like we're going back to Venice."

"Good thing I never unpacked," Fosca said.

Julia chuckled. "The story of my life."

# XVIII

"**F**OR FOUR HUNDRED YEARS," said the elderly Spaniard, each word scorched with agitation, "the three chapters have been distinct from one another, with equal power, united by the singular Sun Crystal."

The man paced Vasquez's office, his cane tapping on the industrial carpet floor. His bushy eyebrows looked as if they were about to fly off his reddening face in an angry protest.

Della Porta watched from a guest chair with amusement that he hid behind a somber expression. The other three Spanish councilmembers also sat in guest chairs or the couch, though della Porta suspected they found no mirth in the situation. He considered bringing Bernardo or other Venetian councilmembers but decided that coming alone would be the most compelling display of power. With the Madrid council on the defensive, it had proven to be a wise decision.

"You come here," the senior Spaniard continued, "expecting to usurp power from us without so much as a vote? It's bad enough you threatened us in the Great Council Room. But *this*. This is beyond the pale."

The man paused to catch his breath. Della Porta shot up and balanced him with a supportive hand on his shoulder.

"Come, there's no need for such tension." Della Porta guided him back to his seat.

When the man had recovered, della Porta stood before the group and spoke calmly.

"You are quite right, señor." He crouched at his steel-shell roller suitcase, which he'd left behind Vasquez's desk. He pressed his thumb on the biometric scanner. The case clicked. He opened it and found an interior box mounted to the suitcase. He pressed his palm on the larger scanner on the box. That activated a screen, on which he entered a six-digit code only he knew. The box lock deactivated, and della Porta lifted the lid.

He'd seen the Sun Crystal countless times. Every time he laid eyes upon it, it was like witnessing a miracle. Perfectly spherical, crafted of a still unknown material, the crystal emanated shifting color light without any source.

He lifted it, cradling it like a newborn baby—but one far more valuable than any human.

The Spanish councilmembers gasped and cocked their heads.

"Why do you have the Sun Crystal here?" the eldest asked.

"As you said, señor, we are three distinct chapters, united by a singular work of art, our precious Sun Crystal." He displayed it for all to see. "We are also charged with a singular purpose—to rid the world of evil, are we not?"

The group nodded their heads. What choice did they have?

Della Porta continued. "I have no interest in taking over the Madrid chapter. My position as Exalted Master here will be temporary until you agree among yourselves who will be my replacement, something you have yet been able to do. You know—"

"But señor—" the elder started.

"You know my plans to expand through Veritism," della Porta said. "I cannot possibly run every chapter around the world, but this incessant bickering is holding us back. I shall relinquish my position as interim Exalted Master when the time is right. Similarly, we can no longer allow your *Paradise* to remain in its transitory state."

"We need a new Painter for that," said a woman sitting on the couch. Her dyed-brown hair cascaded over her late-sixties face.

"Precisely," replied della Porta. "We will pick up where Vasquez left off." He opened the office door while cradling the Sun Crystal with his other hand. "Lobo, come."

Diego Blanco-Romasanta wheeled a long cart into the room. He still walked with a slight limp, but he held his head high while he attempted to suppress a smug grin. He stood in the center of the room, like a model ready to be sketched. But he was a lump of clay about to be molded into something only four others in history had become.

The Spanish councilmembers gawked in astonishment, not only at Lobo's presence, but at what lay on the cart—a two-meter-long black vinyl bag.

"Please tell us," the elder Spaniard said with disgust infused in his wheezing voice, "that you have not dared to even think of defiling our most esteemed Painter by wheeling his corpse around the museum like it's a box meant for storage."

"We have taken utmost care," Lobo said.

"You," the man said to della Porta, "how dare you even think of installing a new Painter here, now, without a ceremony."

"We had the ceremony," Lobo replied, his high-pitched voice searing the old man.

"You cannot argue that," della Porta added.

"And *you*," the elder hissed at Lobo. "José Vasquez's funeral was only yesterday and here you are, conspiring with the man who seeks to seize power from all of us."

Lobo's face turned red. "Exalted Master Vasquez was like a father to me. Nobody in this room will mourn his death more than I. But that does not mean that everything should come to a grinding halt. We have a great deal of work to do." He glanced at della Porta. "Life goes on. The Order goes on."

The old Spaniard exhaled through his nose. His ascot cap tipped askew. "We are not even in front of *Paradise*. El Greco is dead. Will this work?"

"I'd rather not spend any more time with screaming souls," della Porta replied, tired of the man's relentless complaining. "*You're* already giving me a headache."

The elder narrowed his eyes.

Lobo chuckled.

"Besides," della Porta continued, "the Sun Crystal imbues the power. Not the painting. Bodies retain energy after they pass. Though, I admit we are in uncharted waters."

"Still," the elder pressed on. "This is unheard of. This is shameful to do it here, in this office." His colleagues voiced their agreement.

Della Porta clicked his tongue. "What do you know? Were you here when El Greco was given the power? No, of course not. Do not lecture me on what is unheard of, what has happened in the past, or the miraculous future you cannot comprehend. That we are allowing you to witness the transfer is a mere courtesy. Lobo, kneel."

"Courtesy?!" the eldest Spaniard yelled before Lobo moved. "How dare you! I will not take part in this. You are defiling a master *and* our rituals. This is a disgrace. You have my immediate resignation from the council." He sprang from his seat and stormed for the door, tapping his cane as loudly as possible with every step.

The others watched as he slammed the door behind him, but they made no effort to follow.

Della Porta shrugged. Good riddance. He shifted his attention back to the crystal and Lobo. He'd only done this process once before, with Carlo. That did not end as he intended. On the assumption they could do it away from the painting—and with a decaying Painter—Lobo would become della Porta's true protégé.

"Kneel, Lobo."

The Spanish artist did as instructed next to El Greco's body. Della Porta unzipped the bag, revealing a corpse that emitted a pungent odor of rotting pork with decaying fruit undertones. Holding his breath, della Porta knelt on the other side of El Greco.

With a gentle hand, he placed the Sun Crystal on the Renaissance master's body, worried the weight of it would crush the brittle ribs.

"Place your hands around the Sun Crystal. Support it," della Porta said.

Lobo did as he was told.

Della Porta then took El Greco's hands. Rigor mortis had set in, so it took some effort, but the body was so feeble, he adjusted the ancient Painter's hands and placed them on the crystal. He held his own hands over El Greco's to keep them in place.

"Et beatus est sol," della Porta said in Latin, releasing his grip so that only Lobo held the crystal with El Greco. "Blessed is the Sun. Lux in tenebris lucet. Light shines in darkness. Follow the sacred heart. There is nothing to fear."

The words started small. At first, nothing happened. Della Porta tried again, this time louder and with more energy. Again, no response. He signaled to the others to join in. Only the woman did as he repeated the words.

"Louder, everybody," he said.

Slowly, they all uttered the prayer in united harmony. Della Porta worried the process would fail as they said it five, six times. On the seventh intonation, as their collective volume rose, it began to work. Just as the words had with Carlo, they carried a power of their own, enveloping Lobo.

Della Porta grinned. Enough energy remained in the old body. He switched from Latin to a prayer in the ancient Tangut tongue.

Lobo tightened his clutch on the glowing Sun Crystal.

"You have been chosen," della Porta told Lobo in Latin. "This is your birthright. None shall hinder your path."

The crystal radiated hotter, and the light moved through Lobo's hands, beneath his shirt, and reappeared on his neck and face. Power and life suffused him. His body convulsed, trying to reject the light, and he jerked back, stunned by the impulse. His hands locked onto the crystal. Seconds later, his body relented. Visible energy coursed through him—his veins, his muscles, his bones, his soul.

Lobo smirked, basking in the power. He stood, still clutching the Sun Crystal.

Della Porta turned to the remaining Madrid councilmembers. Though moments prior they had expressed their disapproval, they now exhibited awe and pride.

While it was a massive leap for the young Spaniard from artist to Painter, for della Porta, it was another step closer to enacting Veritism. Nobody in the present day had known how to install a new Painter without transferring the power from a living Painter. He had figured it could be done since the original Painters needed to obtain their powers. He validated that theory and proved the process was straightforward. Before long, he would have dozens—no, hundreds—of Painters around the world.

All his life, Diego Blanco-Romasanta had excess energy. As a child, his parents often scolded him or made light, calling him *El Conejito Enérgico*—The Energizer Bunny. All children are energetic, but in his teens, when he'd be partying long after his friends had crashed, he realized his parents were right. He never sat still. He always had to keep himself busy; he always had to be moving. It was one reason why he loved painting—especially large-scale works. It enabled his body to be in motion without covering any distance.

Now, strutting through Madrid beneath streetlights that lit him as much as they did his path, it was as if he'd been recharged. No, *reborn*. The city's nighttime atmosphere surrounded him. Energy flowed through him, but not in the same way as merely being energetic. Previously, he'd felt impatient, always needing to do something, to move. The power coursing through his body made him more alive, tougher, healthier. This force healed his wounded leg; gone was any pain. Colors and sounds were more vibrant. He longed to paint, but first, he needed to celebrate.

After Lobo officially—and *finally*—became the Order's newest Painter, the remaining Madrid council was nothing but flattering. He wished for Vasquez, or even his parents, to be there. Della Porta was a worthy substitute for Vasquez. Perhaps a stronger one. Lobo had to admit that the deceased Spanish Exalted Master often lacked vision.

He appreciated that Della Porta reveled in the accomplishment. But it was just that—della Porta and the council were celebrating the outcome, not the man.

He envied Carlo in that regard. Carlo, too, had been selected out of necessity but was always the frontrunner. His ascension was all but inevitable. In Lobo's case, it was as if Vasquez had been his only supporter.

But there was no turning back.

After their brief celebration, the group visited *Paradise*, relieved that the souls had been returned to their two-dimensional state. Insisting on a return to normalcy, Della Porta instructed the council to bring the painting back to its usual position and for the museum to reopen as soon as possible.

El Greco's body, no longer needed, would be incinerated.

Riding an anti-climactic high, Lobo smiled and winked at an attractive redhead twice his age in a black skirt and leather jacket. To his surprise, she smiled back. She wasn't remotely his type, so he continued.

It didn't matter that none of the Madrid Council believed in him. He would prove to them he was the right choice—a far superior one to Carlo Zuccaro in every way. Lobo was a better artist and more suited for the role of warden of the souls. Carlo was weak. Based on his recent actions, growing weaker by the day.

Needing to rid his thoughts of Carlo, the best option was to drink and celebrate. A dozen meters from *Sentido Contrario*, his favorite dive bar, Lobo stopped in his tracks, wishing he'd brought a crutch.

The four Scots who'd threatened him the other night exited in roaring discord, arms draped over each other, beer bottles in their hands.

Without so much as a hint of caring, Tattoo Face whipped out his cock and pissed on the wall.

Never before had Lobo cared as much for Madrid as he did at that moment.

He stormed forth.

"Hey! You filthy tourist. You're desecrating my city."

All four Scots turned toward him, including Tattoo Face, who now soiled the sidewalk. After a moment of stupefaction vanished, the men erupted in laughter.

Curiously, Lobo also found amusement in the situation—though getting arrested wouldn't be that funny. He cupped his balls, gave them the finger, and cut down the alley adjacent to the bar. He longed for a fight, to release that pent-up energy, but it needed to be away from public eyes.

A stench of urine, spilled beer, and rotting trash from an overflowing dumpster wafted into his nostrils. Not everything about his heightened senses was enjoyable.

As he predicted, the four Scots followed him into the graffiti-covered alley.

"Och, if it isnae our wee Spanish puss," Tattoo Face said, leading his friends. "I kent ye had some balls on ye. Pity they're gonnae be buried deep inside yer minge."

Moving faster than expected, the man blitzed and shoved Lobo to the ground. Before he could get to his feet, the other three joined his friend, all four circling Lobo, taunting him.

The skinhead in the maroon shirt grabbed Lobo's long black hair with his free hand and dragged him backward. He raised the beer bottle, but Lobo twisted and sunk his teeth into the Scot's thigh. The man cried out and released Lobo, who jumped to his feet. He snatched the guy's bottle and smashed it into his assailant's cheekbone. Glass shattered into flesh and eye. The man went down, clutching his face.

"*That* is what a Spanish puss is willing to do." He beckoned them forth. "Who's next?"

Without hesitating, Tattoo Face released a growl and stormed Lobo. He swung, but Lobo ducked, causing the skinhead to lose his balance. Lobo straightened and launched into a roundhouse kick that connected with Tattoo Face's jaw, sending him to the ground.

Lobo's speed and strength shocked him. Never had he knocked anyone unconscious.

Now on offense and taking pride in his supremacy, he menaced toward Blue Shirt. Red Shirt took a step and punched. Again, Lobo ducked, quicker than his assailant. He grabbed a brick off the ground and walloped it into Blue Shirt's knee.

Screaming, the man collapsed to the street, dropping his beer bottle.

Lobo grabbed one of Blue Shirt's suspenders and wrapped it around the skinhead's throat. In a crouch, Lobo towed the pendejo backward, cognizant he could strangle him—and savored the thought.

A crack of shattering glass erupted on the top of Lobo's head. He released the suspenders and dropped to the ground. Blue Shirt sucked in air, rubbing his neck. Lobo compartmentalized the pain and turned to find Red Shirt holding the neck of a broken bottle, looming over him.

Lobo snatched Blue Shirt's bottle, smacked it on the concrete, and drove the broken shard into Red Shirt's calf and twisted. Lobo pulled out the bottle, sprang to his feet, and jammed the glass into his opponent's shoulder. Red Shirt cried out at the two lightning-fast injuries. He stumbled backward, landing on his ass.

Lobo set his sights on Blue Shirt. He hoisted him by the shoulders and drove his head into the dumpster.

Catching his breath, Lobo glared at the four men, out cold or writhing in pain at his feet. His martial arts skills were helpful, but pure rage was far better. If only his father could've seen him. He spat on Tattoo Face, then headed for *Sentido Contrario*.

More than ever, he was ready for a celebratory drink.

# XIX

JULIA CHUCKLED INWARDLY AT the insane absurdity as she walked the cobblestone-lined street of Murano with Carlo and Fosca. Had someone told her that her three-week vacation to Italy, which didn't have a planned visit to the island suburb of Venice, would include *two* trips there, she'd laugh it off. If that person suggested her second trip to Murano would be by boat without a stop in Venice, she'd wonder what that person was smoking.

After leaving Madrid, she, Fosca, and Carlo drove for two days to Trieste, where they rented a motorboat. Julia and Fosca took shifts behind the wheel since Carlo didn't know how to drive. While time-consuming, traversing Europe allowed her to see more of the continent while her body convalesced. She bought clothes—all on Fosca's tab, which was increasing exponentially. Pairs of black leggings and a few black tops met a dual purpose of comfort and inconspicuousness. With her black hair, she felt like she rocked a goth look, which strangely grew on her. Carlo also bought all-black clothes. Fosca wore an oversized, white button-down shirt, short jean shorts, and canvas wedges. Ironically, she blended in more with the tourists and locals.

Julia tuned out Carlo and Fosca's bickering as they walked. She needed a break.

Despite the outlandishness of the ordeal that led to a return to Murano, she loved being there. Like Venice, wheeled vehicles were prohibited, so the only way around was by boat or foot. Whereas millions of visitors traveled to Venice every year to marvel at the city's beauty, art and food, Murano received a tiny percentage of those people, most of whom came for the island's legendary glassmaking. Hardly anybody ventured from the restaurants, gift shops, and glass factory tours.

The late-July sun scorched the top of Julia's head, but the fresh sea air and garden-filled homes soothed her soul. If only she had her camera... and husband. She gazed at a seagull flying overheard and sighed, compartmentalizing her melancholia.

The trio headed toward the home of Isacco Uccello, the present owner of a lockbox in which his ancestor, Vito Uccello, hid a book that purportedly contained secrets so powerful, it could lift della Porta and his Order to new heights. Or destroy them all together. Provided that della Porta hadn't figured out the book's journey and beaten them to Isacco, Julia and the Guild were on their way to victory.

But della Porta was shrewd, and it had been over a week since Julia and her friends had visited Isacco.

"If it's not a big deal, then tell me," Carlo said to Fosca. "What did Marcel mean?"

Julia brought her attention back to her friends.

"I didn't say it's not a big deal," she replied. "I said it's none of your business. But it isn't a big deal anyway, so let it go."

"We're a team. I—we—have a right to know how you got the plans."

"What are you talking about?" Julia asked.

"I want to know how she got the plans to the Thyssen," Carlo responded. "Marcel said it was in a sneaky way."

Fosca threw her hands up in frustration. "Ugh. If you're going to judge me, Carlo, I don't care. I have different ideas about sex. I actually enjoy it."

"What? Wait, what?" he mumbled. "No, I—I enjoy it. I love it. Of course I enjoy it."

"Good to know," she replied. "Maybe we'll enjoy it together some day."

Amazement painted Carlo's face. "Really?"

Fosca jangled her head. "My God, you're predictable."

"So you slept with the Protector?" His olive complexion turned green.

"I got what I needed in more ways than one. It was honestly amazing, if you must know."

"I didn't want to know."

"Then you shouldn't have asked. Can we move on? Julia, do you want to move on?"

"Oh, yeah." Julia found the conversation amusing, but they had far more pressing concerns than Fosca's sex life and Carlo's jealousy.

"Good. Because we're here."

They stopped at the gate in front of a pale-yellow, two-story house with a tiled roof connected to a row of identical homes save their color.

"Remember," Fosca said, "Isacco seems to be on our side, but let's keep our knowledge from him at arm's length."

"How do you expect us to open the box without him there?" Julia asked.

Fosca waved her hand as if swatting the idea away. "I'm just saying let's not fill him in on everything we know, okay?"

The three nodded their agreement and followed Carlo, who opened the gate and approached the door. "That's new," he said, pointing to the camera doorbell.

"He's into tech," Julia said, recalling Isacco made a living reviewing products on YouTube, and had even done a video about her Nikon.

Carlo rang the doorbell.

Isacco's voice piped through the little speaker. "Buongiorno amici miei. Un momento."

After a few minutes, the door opened to reveal Isacco wearing blue-tinted, round glasses and a Phish T-shirt. With his scraggly, shoulder-length hair, he looked like the Italian neo-hippie Julia had remembered.

He beckoned them inside, speaking Italian a mile a minute.

"He apologizes for the wait and the mess," Carlo translated. "He was cooking."

Isacco waved his hands in frantic gestures and pointed to a closed door, which Julia assumed led to the kitchen. Why he was embarrassed about the kitchen was anybody's guess. His home was a pack rat's nest. Other than the dining table, two chairs, and an old couch, the living room was overtaken with boxes of electronics, catalogs, and magazines. Two monitors, two ring lights, and cameras mounted on tripods crowded a corner desk.

"It looks like he was expecting us," Fosca said in English, pointing to a box of diapers on the floor.

Isacco replied, and again Carlo translated. Julia knew Fosca understood but suspected she felt more comfortable speaking English.

"He said he took it out when he saw us on the camera," Carlo said. "He asked if we know how to open it. I told him we have an idea."

Isacco indicated for the group to sit on the floor of his worn green carpet around the box of diapers. He pulled out a few disheveled diapers and removed the brass lockbox. Julia again marveled at the intricate construction and symbolism. Isacco lifted the lid, but Julia placed a hand on his wrist. He smiled at her.

"One sec. Fosca, can you take a pic of the box?"

Julia wished she had her phone, though it was somewhat liberating to be off the grid. She often wondered if her and Nick's families and friends were freaking out. Then again, they were supposed to be on vacation, so while unusual they weren't posting on Instagram or contacting anybody, it was at least explainable.

The artistry of the box fascinated Julia. Dots in the yin-yang were amethyst and jade, valuable in their own right. Seven sunrays enveloped the yin-yang, and between the rays were other enigmatic symbols, mostly embossed into the brass. Four were made of copper, ivory, gold, and something green.

When Fosca finished snapping shots of the box, Isacco opened it and removed a perfectly square wooden container—the true lockbox.

"Prego," he said, handing it to Julia as if she were in charge.

She accepted it with trembling hands. So much was riding on the contents. For all they knew, it was empty. She examined it again. Though not as adorned as the outer box, it was more impressive in some respects. Four sides had identical wheel combination locks, and the other two had smaller versions of an engraved yin-yang symbol. The letters on two of the combination locks were inversed from the other two, so it was impossible to determine the top from the bottom. She couldn't even find a seam on the edges to know where it opened.

Isacco spoke in Italian to Carlo again.

This time, Fosca answered for him. She then spoke to Julia. "He asked if we know the code. I told him it could be *ipsius*, but I didn't tell him how we know."

Julia nodded without answering. She stared at the box, almost willing it to reveal its secrets. None came. She stilled her hand and rotated the wheels to spell out IPSIVS, remembering that the U in Latin was a V.

"The letters are all there. I don't think these wheels could hold 26 letters." She grinned. "I think this is it."

She rotated the dials on the other three sides, spelling out the word, then pressed her thumb on one of the latches, feeling the spring release, so close to pushing it in.

"What are you waiting for?" Carlo asked.

Julia lifted her hand. "Isacco said there's an acid inside, and if too many tries were attempted or the box was broken, the acid would destroy the contents. For all we know, we have one shot."

"For all we know," Fosca said, "the contents are already destroyed."

She was right. There was no point in delaying the inevitable.

Julia pressed one latch in, followed by the other three.

Nothing happened.

"Merda," Carlo said.

Julia's heart pounded. Did she screw up the spelling? She checked, but the dials were correct. She held the box to her ear. "I don't think anything happened on the inside."

"Great," Fosca said. "But how many more tries do we have? What the hell else *can* we try? We don't have a second guess."

Her words triggered a thought in Julia that had been bothering her.

"*Second* guess," she said. "Two. Duality. It's always about duality with Tintoretto and the Order."

"There are *four* sides," Carlo replied.

"Exactly," Julia said. "Two and two. Ipsius is it, but it's more. Why have four locks all with the same code? We only have two hands—" Her mouth popped open. "Of course. It requires two people to open it at the same time! That way, one person could never open it on their own. My God, that's brilliant." She turned to Isacco. "Care to do the honors with me?"

Carlo translated everything she said. Isacco nodded enthusiastically and held the box with Julia, intersecting sides with their hands.

"Wait," Fosca said. "What if you're wrong?"

"Anything we try can be wrong," Julia replied. She turned to Isacco. "On three, okay?"

"Okay." Isacco understood that much.

Julia grinned. "One... two... three."

They both pressed their latches simultaneously.

# XX

A GAIN, NOTHING HAPPENED. THE box remained perfectly intact.

"Fuck, fuck." Fosca said. "How's that for duality?"

"We're missing something," Julia said.

She took the box back from Isacco and examined it while the Italians discussed something with animated hands. The cube's simplistic mirroring made her head hurt. Even if someone knew the code, and you needed two people to open it, how would they know which locks to press?

There had to be something on the box that told them. Some sort of clue. She flipped the box over and over. Finally, she spotted it.

The yin-yangs.

They weren't identical. The darker dot, which is always on top, pointed to one side, and the lighter dot pointed to the other. She recalled what Lionel Benton had told her—Tintoretto and the Order were obsessed with the yin-yang. From what she knew, it represented the good and bad of nature. Opposite but interconnected forces. *Duality*.

Like a lock opening in her brain, it all clicked together. It was risky, but they didn't have another choice. On the sides to which the lighter dots pointed, she rotated the dials to spell out SVISPI—the inverse of IPSIVS. Maybe it wasn't a word, but if ipsius meant himself or uncountable...

"I think I got it," she said to the others. After explaining her thinking, she held the box with Isacco again so each person had an IPSIVS and SVISPI.

They nodded to each other.

"One," Julia whispered. "Two... three."

They pressed the latches. The two yin-yang sides fell off.

"Yes!" Fosca shouted.

A sheet of vellum slipped out and landed on the carpet.

Julia peered inside the box. Secured to the wood was a canister, presumably containing the rumored acid. Everyone exchanged dismayed looks.

"That's it?" Fosca asked. "One piece of paper is hardly a book."

Isacco picked up the vellum and read it. "È una poesia." He handed it to Carlo.

"It's a poem," Carlo said. He read through it, his eyes scanning across the page. "From Vito to someone named Paulina. It looks like a love poem." He turned to Isacco. "Sai chi è Paulina? C'era una Paulina Uccello?"

"Forse," Isacco said, glancing at the kitchen. "Non lo so."

"He doesn't know who she is," Carlo said. "I'll do my best to translate the rhymes," Carlo said. He read aloud:

> *Fair Paulina, jewel of my desire,*
> *Thy radiance outshines the sun's fire.*
> *Within thy heart, a secret lies concealed,*
> *Unlocking passions that time has sealed.*
>
> ~
>
> *Like a masterpiece in Mary's Garden,*
> *Thy beauty enchants, adorned without pardon.*
> *In Venice's heart, where we find our home,*
> *Our love shall bloom like ancient stone.*
>
> ~
>
> *Yet, in the realm where shadows abide,*
> *The Supreme Painter's deceit resides.*
> *His vibrant strokes, now frozen in time,*
> *Separate our hearts, our love sublime.*
>
> ~
>
> *As a precious gem lies hidden in earth,*
> *So does thy love, awaiting rebirth.*
> *Seek in the depths of thy gentle soul,*
> *The tender ardor that makes me whole.*
>
> ~

*For within the tapestry of thy heart,*
*Where love and art entwine from the start,*
*A desired tome that transcends the divine,*
*A timeless masterpiece, forever thine.*

~

*Fair Paulina, let our spirits entwine,*
*In passions deep, like sweet aged wine.*
*Together, we'll unlock love's grand design,*
*And let it flourish till the end of time.*

~

*Yours forever in every life,*
*Vito.*

Everyone let the words sink in for a few moments.

"He wasn't the world's greatest poet, was he?" Fosca said.

Julia agreed. She'd never studied poetry, but she knew it wasn't Shakespeare. Still, Vito wasn't trying to impress anybody but the woman in the poem—Paulina. "Can I see it?" she asked.

Carlo handed her the paper. The vellum was surprisingly smooth. A chill bubbled through her, knowing she held an ancient love poem. One that was so special, Vito locked it away. But why?

"Isacco has no idea who Paulina was?" Julia asked Carlo.

Again, Carlo asked Isacco, but Isacco merely shrugged. He stood and tapped his fingers together, unable to sit still. Julia pitied him. This was his ancestor's note—a letter tied to actions that had a rippling effect on his family for generations, all the way to the present—and she and her friends were picking it apart in a language he couldn't understand.

"Something's not right," Julia said. "Why lock this poem away, particularly in such a secure manner? Why not just give it to Paulina?"

"Maybe he couldn't," Carlo replied.

"Fair. Then why not give it to someone else to give to her?"

"Their love must've been secret," Fosca said, standing. "She must've been someone of note. A married woman. Or the daughter of someone prominent."

"Angelo thought Vito had a falling out with the doge," Carlo said.

Everyone turned to him.

"How do you know that?" Julia asked, her voice shaking.

Carlo's mouth popped open. He stared back at Julia, clearly realizing he just divulged a secret. He stood and turned away.

"You spoke to Angelo?" Julia asked, anger brimming her words. She also stood and forced Carlo to look at her, leveling her eyes with his. "When did this happen?"

The sad, puppy-dog look passed over his expression again. "A day or two after you woke from your coma. When I had my meeting with della Porta. I told you I went to the library, but I went to speak with Angelo. I did go to the library, but after that." He looked at Isacco. "It's how I knew to look for Isacco. Angelo told me the Bird Brothers would've taken the box." He turned back to Julia. "I'm sorry I lied, Julia. But I had to."

"Just tell me if you spoke to Nick."

"No. Angelo had taken over."

Julia sighed, growing numb to the anger she regularly felt. "And now that you're on the outs with della Porta, I'll never have the chance."

Fosca stepped over and rubbed her shoulder. "You will if we win. Right?"

She was right, of course. "Yeah," Julia said. She needed to focus. They needed to get back to business. "Okay, Carlo. So Angelo said Vito got on the Doge's bad side. It adds up. He was also betrayed and sentenced to *Paradise*."

"Paulina must've been his wife or daughter," Fosca said.

Julia stared at the poem again. "I'm thinking daughter, but that's inconsequential. Carlo, reread it."

She handed it back to him, and he did as requested. She let the poem absorb into her head. Certain words stuck out.

"This poem was for Paulina, but it's not just an expression of love. A desired tome? It's a riddle to find the book." She took the paper from Carlo again.

"Look at this," she continued, recalling Carlo's translation. "There are references to things hidden, locked, stone, art, and he went completely to the dark side in one stanza. What's the supreme Painter? Is that Tintoretto?"

"No," Fosca said. "It's God. Or what the Order calls God. The Supreme Painter is the creator, and like any artist, once he's done, the painting is left to the owners."

"Okay, poetic. I like it," Julia said. "What about the deceit part?"

"Vito was betrayed," Carlo answered. "He was angry."

Julia considered that for a moment. "To put it in a love letter?"

"Maybe Paulina was also sentenced to *Paradise*," Fosca added. She peered over Julia's shoulder. "They find their home in Venice's heart. Their love blooms like ancient stone, brush strokes frozen in time. That sure sounds like being imprisoned in a painting in the center of Venice to me. Especially back then. The Doge's Palace was unquestionably the heart of Venice."

Julia offered a half-hearted nod. That all made sense, but it still didn't feel right to her. "It adds up if he wrote this right before they were both sentenced. But then why lock it away? Wouldn't it have been the opposite? Wouldn't he have done anything to get the letter to her? No, there's something else. What about a gem hidden in the earth or where love and art entwine?"

The others shook their heads.

Needing a spark, Julia glanced around Isacco's mess of a home. A poster of Canaletto's famous *Grand Canal* painting hung on the wall in a cheap plastic frame. Then it hit Julia. "He's talking about Tintoretto. *He's* the deceit. Wouldn't they have been alive at the same time?"

Carlo snapped his fingers, picking up on Julia's thought process. He paced the room. "Yes, but Tintoretto died—no, he *never* died. Allora... he was supposed to have died *before* Vito. But..."

Julia finished his thought. "But Vito knew. *That's* the deceit. And Qua—"

With a loud throat clearing, Fosca shifted her eyes toward Isacco, who didn't seem to notice while he twiddled his thumbs. Possession of the box must've weighed on him for all these years. Julia imagined he wanted to rid himself of it and this mysterious love letter.

She returned the slightest nod to Fosca and internally admonished herself for nearly revealing that Carlo spoke with Quattrone and could hear the souls. She studied the letter again. Though she only comprehended a spattering of words, the poem's construct seemed more like music to her. A song. She read it to herself a few times, the words fitting into a melody. Some felt off-key.

As she did this, Carlo and Fosca discussed possibilities. Isacco nervously fidgeted.

"What does *orto* mean?" Julia asked.

The word must've meant something important, for Isacco perked up and finally stopped moving.

"Garden," Carlo replied.

"A garden could represent love," Julia said. "But why is it capitalized?"

Isacco peered at it over her shoulder, then smiled and snapped his fingers. "Madonna dell'Orto."

"Certo," Carlo said, beaming. He slapped Isacco's back. "Bravo, amico."

Julia and Fosca exchanged a shrug, both at a loss.

"Isacco solved it. Chiesa della Madonna dell'Orto. It is the church where Tintoretto is buried. Or, where he was supposed to have been buried."

The pieces fell into place for Julia. "It all circles back to him. The Painter's face *and* death. Anybody who knew the truth wouldn't think to look there. It must be in that empty coffin."

"It's gotta be," Fosca said.

"I bet you need a key to open it. I told you the key is a key that actually opens something," Julia said. "Speaking of which, where is our key?"

"In Venice," Fosca said. "In a safe in nonna-mère's home."

Julia frowned. "Where's this church?"

Carlo's enthusiasm switched to uneasiness. "Also in Venice."

Standing next to Bernardo and Dante, Della Porta listened until silence took over in the next room. He placed his hand on the doorknob, but it turned and opened. Della Porta and his men backed up as Isacco stepped into the kitchen.

Without a word, he went straight to the fridge, retrieved a Peroni, popped the cap, and chugged half of it.

"You should toast yourself," della Porta said in Venetian. "Well done, my friend."

Isacco's glare intended to cut through della Porta, but it merely bounced off. His plan went better than he could have ever expected. Not only did Carlo and his friends open the box, they cracked the riddle. He'd let them get the key from the countess's flat and allow them to find the book in Santa Maria dell'Orto. Then, he'd take it.

"And my family?" Isacco asked.

"Not to worry," della Porta replied. "All Uccellos are henceforth absolved of all sins against the Order and all debts owed to the Order. You have two witnesses here, and tomorrow I shall draft the paperwork."

A half-smile crossed Isacco's face. He nodded.

"Come, Bernardo and Dante. It's been a number of years since I've visited Tintoretto's grave."

He entered the living room and headed for the front door. Before he exited, he turned back to the Uccello descendant. "Oh, Isacco. You should join the Order. It's been too long since we had an Uccello."

# XXI

"**I** TOLD YOU, THIS is the best restaurant in Cannaregio," Carlo said, chomping into a salmon-topped bruschetta and chewing in time with the rocking of the boat.

With each succulent bite of bucatini mingling with tender mussels, Julia couldn't dispute his claim. Luxuriating in such superb fare from a takeout container on a boat was outright bizarre, especially in the company of a man she once thought of killing. Ironically, she shared a similar dish with Nick on one of their first nights in Venice—before everything went to hell. Dining on the canal beneath a copper-colored setting sun, drinking wine from plastic cups, she missed her husband more than ever.

Being moored one hundred feet from the building that could soon provide a means to avenge him—and potentially release him—was the only thing that prevented her from ripping her hair out. It was all too surreal.

After they left Isacco's, the trio spent a few hours in Murano. It turned out that the Madonna dell'Orto Church was on the edge of the Cannaregio district, the northernmost part of Venice, and only a thirty-minute trip. They needed to kill some time, which they used to strategize how to enter a church and dig up the body of one of the city's most famous residents. Armed with flashlights and a small crowbar they purchased at a tiny hardware store, they waited until the church closed for the night.

While Fosca went to her grandmother's, Julia got them dinner, and Carlo stayed in the boat. It was far too risky for him to be seen, and though Julia longed to see the countess's home, it was safer to split up.

Julia got a good look at the church when she went to pick up the food. Set back from a courtyard, the building was a magnificent example of Gothic architecture with Renaissance elements, showcasing a brickwork facade. The church was divided into three parts with sloping sides. Though scaffolding obscured the top of the nave, the roofs of the outer wings were adorned with six white statues, which she presumed were saints. An elegant bell tower, whose onion-shaped dome resembled an Islamic minaret, stood at the rear of the church. The main entrance had a beautiful rose window, while intricate Gothic tracery decorated mullioned windows on both sides.

Carlo wiped his mouth and took a drink of wine. "Tintoretto's house and studio is a block from here," he said. "He was quite religious and a member of this church. That's why he's buried here."

"Except he's *not* really buried here. And *wasn't* the devout Catholic everyone thought."

Carlo laughed. "Very true. He lived in a pink house if you can believe it."

"I'm assuming you've been there?"

"Certo. And to this church many times. It has fantastic art inside. Tintorettos, a Molinari, and more."

"So they need to protect it." Julia twirled some pasta on her fork and bit into it. White wine, parsley, and garlic blended perfectly with the homemade pasta. Thin strips of fried prosciutto balanced the salty, soft texture of the mussels. *This is takeout,* she thought, nearly losing sight of their mission.

"Of course."

Julia gazed back at the church, pondering how they would break in. She also wondered where Fosca was. She should've been back twenty minutes ago.

Carlo poured them more wine. The boat rocked as he shifted.

"When we first met," he said, "and you came over to my flat, one of the first things you asked was why I was getting involved. I didn't know you and Nick at the time. It was right for you to ask."

"So?" Julia searched the vicinity. No sign of Fosca. No sign of anyone in the sleepy neighborhood. It amazed her how the city quieted at night—at least out here. A raindrop landed in Julia's wine. She instinctively tilted her head skyward. It was cloudy, but the one drop was all that fell.

"Maybe I didn't know it then," Carlo continued, "but I always felt it. A part of me was incomplete. This is why I'm getting involved. To fight for justice."

"Why are you telling me this, Carlo?"

"Because I want you to know I will do the right thing."

Julia scoffed. "Yeah, well, I didn't trust you when I met you. Which turned out to be quite prescient, don't you think? Justice? You think you have the right to speak of justice? I can never trust you again."

Carlo looked down, not responding.

She couldn't trust him, but she needed him. As the Painter, even a banished one, he held more power than anyone. She thought back to that conversation Carlo had brought up.

"You said something else that day," she said. "That you wanted to discover what moves people, that you thought working broadly was a way to reach more people. But it's the opposite. You need to focus on the personal." Julia's words swam in her brain. She couldn't formulate the thought just yet but verbalized it anyway. "That's our ticket in. We need to convert one person."

"You started without me," came Fosca's voice as she walked the *fondamenta* to the boat. She boarded, swaying the vessel.

Wine splashed on Julia's hand. "Where have you been?"

"Mm, that looks good," Fosca replied, licking her lips at the takeout containers. "I took a shower. Speaking of which..." She eyed the starless sky with a frown.

Fosca had also changed clothes. She now wore black leggings, a black tank top, and black knit hat.

"We were worried about you," Carlo said.

"Yeah, you must've been panicking while eating and drinking wine. There was no rush. I figured I'd freshen up before breaking, entering, and disturbing the dead."

"Tintoretto's not actually buried in there," Julia said, wondering why she had to keep reminding these two of that fact.

"Good point," Fosca replied. "Either way, we're breaking and entering, so we need to look the part." She reached into her orange Fjällräven backpack and removed two black T-shirts and another black knit hat. She handed Julia a T-shirt and hat and Carlo the other shirt. "I couldn't find another hat to fit that big head of yours," she told Carlo. "Besides, your hair is dark enough."

Fosca grabbed a takeout container and dug in.

Julia pulled her hair into a ponytail, donned the T-shirt over her white tank, and put on the hat. "How do we know there aren't cameras inside?"

"Unlikely," Carlo replied. "They didn't have cameras last time I was here, and I doubt they have the budget for them now."

"Okay," Fosca said. "Curious as to how you know that, but more curious about the plan. Are you going to tell us or what?"

Carlo smiled and gazed sentimentally at the church. "Let's just say when you're a teenage artist in Venice, you and your friends find creative ways to entertain yourselves. Especially when your guardian—*supposed* guardian—was out most nights."

Julia glanced at Fosca with incredulity. "By what, breaking into churches?"

Carlo shrugged. "Museums have too much security."

Fosca just laughed. "You know he's serious. Keep in mind these churches used to be open twenty-four-seven. Some of them still are."

Julia couldn't believe she was okay with this. "That doesn't mean it's okay to break into them when they're closed."

"Don't worry," Carlo said, waving her off. "It's not like we stole or damaged anything. We'd sit on the floor with a bottle of wine, sketching the masterpieces."

"You could do that during the day," Julia said.

"Some degenerates, huh?" Fosca cracked up.

Julia shook her head. "I take you've allowed yourself entry into this one?"

"Of course." Carlo wiped his mouth after swallowing his octopus cicchetti. "More than once. It's Tintoretto's tomb. They don't lock the bell tower."

Julia craned her neck and felt the blood drain from her face. The tower had to be at least twelve stories tall. She tossed her remaining wine overboard, suddenly wishing she hadn't eaten—and definitely wishing she hadn't drunk any alcohol.

"You're kidding, right? You'd climb up there?"

"It's not as hard as it looks," Carlo said. "With the ornaments and statues, it's like climbing a ladder. Watch out for Simon the Zealot and Matthew, though. They were loose about ten years ago. I suspect it's why they have the scaffolding, which will make it a piece of pie."

Julia had to admit that the framework did make it seem easy. "But the scaffolding is on the opposite side of the bell tower."

"Don't worry," Carlo said. "We need to access the bell tower from the roof anyway. The bell tower is attached to the church. We'll be halfway to the top."

"So that's it?" she asked. "We traverse the roof, climb the tower, and sneak inside?"

Carlo smiled. "You sound ready."

"It's not going to rain, is it?" Julia asked. A drop hit her forehead.

"If we do this fast," Carlo replied, "it won't matter."

"No time like the present." Fosca planted her takeout containers on the bench and stood.

Carlo caught her hand to stop her. He glanced at his phone. "We need to wait fifteen minutes until the bell rings. We don't want to be up there when it starts."

More drops pelted Julia head. "Can we make it inside in fourteen minutes?" Climbing a tower in the rain seemed a far-worse option than an ear-splitting bell.

Carlo looked up at the clouds and tower. "If we leave now. Come on." He jumped onto the *fondamenta*.

Five minutes later, Julia again found herself checking her sanity. Climbing the scaffolding was a snap. She had no clue which statue was Simon or Matthew, so she steered clear of all of them. But when she pulled herself onto the wing's tiled sloping roof, a disorienting swirl of dizziness overtook her. Carlo grabbed her hand and helped her up. Throwing caution to the wind, she allowed him to assist her to the wall of the main section of the church, which had rough bricks that provided secure grips. She took a moment to regain her composure.

In silence, Carlo led the trio to the rear, where there was enough ornamentation that it seemed like climbing a ladder—one precariously perched three or four stories up. If she fell, she'd land on the tiled sloped side and topple off into the church courtyard. Additional drops hit Julia, as it started sprinkling in earnest.

"Don't worry," Carlo whispered. "You're almost there."

Cursing her decision to join them, Julia found a foothold on a brick and pulled herself up to the roof's center section, which was also tiled and sloped. She allowed herself to rest, fixing her feet on the tiny ledge while Fosca followed her.

"Did you know that over a third of the churches in Venice are now other things like museums and schools?" Carlo asked.

"Did you know you can shut up sometimes?" Fosca replied.

"Think of me as a tour guide." Carlo flashed a toothy grin. "Okay, this is the hardest part. Press your body against the tiles and shimmy up like a duck."

"A duck?" Julia asked.

"I don't know," Carlo said. "Like whatever animal does this. Just do what I do."

He flatted himself against the slope, and with his feet braced against the tiles on either side, he pushed himself up, looking like a slithering, waddling... duck with four feet.

There was no going back. Julia inhaled and followed Carlo, not releasing her air until she reached the top, thankful there was a flat three-foot wide gangway that ran the entire length of the church.

After catching her breath, she gasped. The view of Venice from this height was remarkable. A breeze rustled her hair, cooling her sweaty skin. She felt like a 16th-century assassin on a death-defying mission. The notion invigorated her. She pulled her hat lower.

"Whoa," Fosca said. In the diffused moonlight, her expression looked like she was thinking the same thing.

"Wait till you get to the top," Carlo said. He bounded about ten feet until he lined himself up with the center of the bell tower.

Julia joined him. "Now what?"

"I told you, the hardest part is done. Don't be scared. The tower is five meters wide. You can't miss it."

"What do you mean we can't miss it?" Fosca asked.

"Trust me," Carlo replied. "Piece of pie."

Before the women could respond, he sat atop the roof and slid twenty feet down the tiles. His feet hit the center of the tower, breaking his fall. He popped up with a smile. "I'm glad it's raining," he called with a loud whisper. "It makes it even more fun."

"This is a guy who's afraid of swimming," Fosca said. "After you."

There was no turning back. Julia placed her rear on the slope, held on to the flat part, and let go. Wind rushed through her hair. She fell too fast on the slick tiles. She'd miss it and plummet to her death. A second later, her feet collided with the tower bricks. Carlo helped her stand. He was right—it was kind of fun.

Fosca followed suit, releasing a whispered whoop and popping up with a grin.

"See?" Carlo said. "We're halfway there. Let's go."

Without another word, he climbed the narrowest ladder Julia had ever seen. The rusty bars were bolted to the bricks and looked at least one hundred years old. Only six inches wide, the rungs were spaced a foot apart—and wet.

She gazed up. Carlo moved at a brisk clip, nearly at the top.

"Remember when you wanted to kill this guy?" Fosca asked.

"Don't tempt me. Remind me why he couldn't have done this alone?"

"Because we're a pair of idiots?"

Fosca placed a hand on the ladder and climbed.

Julia shook her head. "We better be going out the front." Steeling her will, she gripped the metal, thankful it was cold. Her palms were already sweaty. She needed to wrap her hands completely around each wet rung to get any support.

"Don't look down, don't look down," she whispered.

The ladder was so narrow that it was like climbing a vertical tightrope—one that creaked with every step.

"Oh! Watch out!" Fosca called.

A half second later, her flashlight smacked Julia's head, then landed on the church roof. Julia cried out in pain. She wanted to rub her head but held fast to the ladder.

"Sorry," Fosca whispered.

A crack of thunder startled Julia. Her foot slipped. Lightning struck the sea. She blanched. She clung to what was essentially a lightning rod on the second-tallest structure in Venice.

"Oh, hell no."

She picked up the pace and reached an open-air window in the parapet, which Carlo pulled her through. A lit cigarette hung from his lips. She ducked away from the smoke and took in her surroundings. Three bells hung above them, all of which were large enough for Julia to fit in.

"We're going out the front." Julia's words came out in an angry hiss.

"Allora," Carlo started, "I don't know if—"

Julia jabbed a finger into his chest. "We. Are. Going. Out. The. Front."

"Okay, okay," Carlo said. "But first, we have a minute..."

He guided Julia and Fosca around to take in the view, which was nothing short of enchanting. From their vantage point, the city unveiled itself in a display of twinkling lights, gentle reflections, and the soft glow of streetlamps.

A rumble of thunder, followed by a lightning bolt that illuminated the scene like a camera flash, ended their sightseeing moment.

"Can we get inside already?" she asked.

"The hard part is over." Flicking his cigarette off the side, he took a few steps to the interior access door and tried the knob. It didn't turn. He pulled it harder but couldn't get it open.

"I thought you said they never lock it," Fosca said.

Carlo offered a sheepish look. "I guess that was before they mechanized the bells."

"Fuck, Carlo," Fosca said. "They're gonna start ringing any second."

"Good thing we have this," he replied, pulling the crowbar out from a beltloop. He pressed the tip of the crowbar between the door and the jamb and wrested the old door open. "See? Easy."

He tucked the crowbar away and switched on his flashlight. The door opened into a stone staircase that descended into the depths without a banister. They filed inside. Carlo shut the door. A booming gong resounded from outside.

Though Julia was anxious to be back on ground level, she dreaded slipping down the steps to get there. With her free hand pressed against the stone wall the entire way, she and Fosca followed Carlo down as eleven more gongs continued.

"Now be as quiet as you can," Carlo whispered. "There will be enough light through the windows." He shut off his light and indicated for Julia to do the same. He then pressed his finger against his lips, and, using the crowbar, pried the door open as noiselessly as he could. Poking his head out, he motioned that the coast was clear.

True to his word, moonlight streamed in through the upper windows. Julia wasn't religious, but she had to admit that seeing the cathedral in silence, with only slivers of muted light, created a holy effect. It felt as if they trespassed on hallowed ground and, on top of that, were about to desecrate it.

Carlo crossed the nave, walked through the pews, and led them to an apse chapel. The space was small and unremarkable, with unfinished concrete walls on the left and right. An altar stood at the rear beneath a painting of two saints.

Gooseflesh prickled Julia's skin. A bust of a man had been mounted to the right wall—a man she recognized from his self-portraits.

Jacopo Tintoretto.

On the center of the checkered stone floor was a five-foot-long marble ledger stone. Though the practice was not common in America, Julia had been to enough European churches to know that the most prominent members were often buried inside the building. It was the highest honor so the deceased could be as close to God as possible. The ledger stone was much like a gravestone but part of the floor instead of standing upright. Visitors had no choice but to traipse over them. This one was inscribed with quite a bit of Latin, but the largest words were unmistakable:

## IACOBI ROBVSTII TINCTORETTI

Jacopo Robusti Tintoretto.

Though she knew he was never truly buried here—never buried *anywhere*—seeing the tomb made her throat clam up. The man who was supposed to be in there had caused her so much anguish. She didn't feel so bad about desecrating it anymore.

Apparently, Carlo never had the thought at all.

Without a word, he used the crowbar to scrape away the mortar along the edges of the ledger stone. When enough was cleared away, he inserted the tool at the lip of the stone and hoisted it. He exerted effort but was able to lift it just enough so he could heave it off the side. Julia and Fosca knelt and helped him shove it over.

Ancient air engulfed them. Julia shined her light into the rectangular hole, revealing a rosewood coffin covered in dirt and dust.

Her heart galloped like she neared the finish line of a neck-and-neck marathon on a long, harrowing road. She never thought she'd be thrilled by the prospect of grave robbing, yet here she was, and it electrified her. It was as if they'd been on a scavenger hunt and were about to open the treasure box. In a sense, they were. Assuming the doge's book rested in the coffin—and assuming it contained the promised information—they could bring della Porta down, or at least prevent him from obtaining ultimate power.

Carlo and Fosca exchanged excited looks with her.

"Here we go," Carlo whispered.

He reached into the tomb and lifted the coffin lid.

# XXII

A CRACK OF THUNDER ricocheted through the church.

Julia jumped. Her light beam rested on a skeleton wrapped in a threadbare blanket.

"Who's that?" she asked.

"We'll never know," replied Carlo.

Brittle bones fell away as he lifted the blanket. And there it was, underneath the skeleton—a wooden box.

"Chiedo scusa," Carlo whispered to the deceased. Pressing his body prone to the floor, he reached in and retrieved the box from beneath the ribcage. Unlike the lockbox at Isacco's, this one had a simple design, about the size of a cigar box. Carlo sat with his legs crisscrossed, their salvation resting on his lap. He turned the box around to expose a keyhole.

Fosca produced the brass key from her pocket. She was about to insert it but stopped.

"You should do it." The key rested on her outstretched palm.

Julia accepted it.

She glanced at her two friends—her accomplices. They both nodded back.

They did it.

While Carlo gripped the box, Julia inserted the key and turned. The lid unlocked. Carlo opened it like a man would present an engagement ring. While Julia would always cherish the one time that happened to her, she had to admit this moment was more exhilarating.

Inside was something wrapped in leather—something that could only be a book. She removed the contents. Carlo put the box aside. Eyes wide in the darkened church, he and

Fosca gazed at the item in Julia's hand. She unwrapped the leather sheet to produce the bounty they'd sought.

Grins consumed their faces. Julia couldn't believe it.

Bound in black leather without an inscription, the book appeared to be a journal or diary. She unwrapped the leather bind and opened it to find at least fifty other notes, letters and envelopes stuffed inside.

Of course, it was all in Italian, Venetian, or Latin. She handed it to Carlo.

His eyes widened even more as he flipped through it.

"Porca vacca," he whispered. "Dio santo!" Mouth open, he gazed at Fosca and Julia, then back to the journal. "Unbelievable. Just the few pages I looked at. Incredible. The Vatican knew about the Order. They knew *everything*..." He paused on a particular letter. "Dio santo, dio santo, dio santo."

He turned the book around and handed it to Julia, displaying the letter to the women. He pointed to a red wax seal of two keys crossed beneath a crown that had been melted to the top of the paper. "This is the papal seal," he said with a giddy voice. "The Vatican... they owe the Order money. A *lot* of money."

The three of them gazed at each other, wide-eyed, all smiles. The ramifications didn't entirely compute for Julia, but she knew this could never fall into della Porta's hands.

"We need to make this public," Carlo said.

"Are you kidding?" Julia replied. "We talked about this. That's exactly what della Porta wants. If this is public, if the world knows, the Order wins. I'm not going to be one who brings Veritism to the world."

"What are we waiting for?" Fosca asked. "Let's burn it. No, there could be remnants. Let's throw it in the lagoon."

Slow clapping echoed off the church walls.

At first, Julia thought it was thunder. But the rhythm was unmistakable. As was the voice.

"Ah, indecision. The death of us all."

Della Porta.

Julia snapped the book closed.

He continued clapping as he approached the apse. To his sides stood Bernardo, Detective Lacasse, and Detective Fanella. Both cops wielded guns. In the dim light, Julia could make out three other hefty men, two of whom she recognized from when she was kidnapped. She recalled the one with the close-cropped beard and hair pulled into a tight ponytail was named Dante. Who knew how many waited outside? A brutal chill covered her body. She glanced behind her. The apse was completely sealed off. They were so close to winning. *So close.*

"Bravo, my friends," della Porta said. Euphoria filled his words. "Sincerely, I am impressed. I suppose I owe a thank you. So, grazie. Grazie mille. Now, if you don't mind, I'll take that book."

"The hell you will," Fosca snarled.

Carlo stepped in front of Julia protectively. Fosca positioned herself in front of him.

Della Porta adjusted his eyeglasses. "I must say, Fosca, you had me fooled for years. As we often find in life, the truth is disappointing. You disappoint me in many ways. Not the least of which is your strategic thinking. In the end, you were nothing but another termite. For how long did you think you could keep up this charade, that I wouldn't notice the little holes you left behind? Not to worry. It's over." He gestured to the solid stone walls behind them and his goons blocking any chance of an exit. "You have no way out. Though ironically, you're officially out of the Order. Here I thought you were loyal to your grandmother."

Even in the muted light, Julia saw Fosca's face turn bright red.

"You murdered her grandmother," Carlo yelled. His voice echoed through the sanctified building.

"Tsk, tsk," della Porta replied. "Your friend's husband killed her. And we know what happened to him, don't we? But we don't need to rehash old events. You should all be much more concerned with your future." He turned to Julia, his tone growing more serious. "Signora O'Connor, you have two options. Hand over the book without incident, and you can go home, all charges against you and your husband dropped. Or you can attempt to fight us, immediately lose, all three of you will be arrested, and we will get the book either way. It's your choice."

Fanella and Lacasse raised their guns.

The offer tempted Julia. She hated losing, but getting out of there unscathed, without getting arrested, could've been considered a win.

"What about Fosca and Carlo?" she asked.

"Julia, no," Fosca said, her voice quivering.

"As angry as I am with her, Fosca can go too." He spoke to her. "Of course, my dear, you are banished from the Order forevermore, as is the entire Baldesseri pedigree. I cannot say what your future holds, but every connection you've ever made because of the Order is now severed."

"And me?" Carlo asked.

Della Porta released an exhale of what sounded like genuine despondency. "You're the Painter, Carlo. You're coming with us. Alive, dead, or severely injured."

Carlo placed his left hand behind his back. He wiggled his fingers, motioning for the book. His right hand was also behind his back. In it, obscured by his leg, was the crowbar. Julia didn't like the idea of him going down in a kamikaze mission, but it was better than literally placing ultimate power in della Porta's palm. She gave the book to Carlo, then pressed his fingers around it.

"You promise," Carlo said, "in front of all these Protectors, that you'll let Fosca and Julia go?"

Della Porta bowed his head. "I promise."

"You swear on your ancestors—on the Order—that you'll let them go?"

"Sì, Carlo. I always keep my word. In truth, I do not need them."

"Julia," Carlo said without looking at her, "I am truly sorry about Nick. And Fosca, I apologize for getting jealous. I couldn't help it. I have no right to question or judge you."

"Why are you apologizing...?" Fosca let her words trail off. She knew the answer.

Carlo brought his hand to his front, revealing the journal.

"Go with them," he said to Fosca and Julia.

"What? No," Fosca cried out.

Julia approached della Porta. She glanced back at her friend. Tears glistened on her cheeks.

"Please, Fosca," Carlo said through gritted teeth.

Julia stepped to Bernardo, thinking he'd go the easiest on her, especially having only one arm.

Sniffing and doing her best not to start bawling, Fosca joined her.

"Now you, son," della Porta said.

Pale light crossed Carlo's face. In that shallow beam, Julia witnessed a silent rage like she'd never seen. Carlo's chest heaved. He clenched his jaw.

"E tu?" Carlo asked in a guttural growl. "What will become of *you*?"

Della Porta held out his palm. "Dammi il libro. Adesso."

Carlo smiled. "Va bene."

A blur of black in the monochrome light flew past Julia. Carlo whacked the crowbar into Lacasse's gun. The weapon discharged, releasing an ear-splitting boom that reverberated off the stone walls. Catching Fanella off guard, Carlo shouldered her to the floor. She cried out and managed to release another shot but also missed Carlo. The second shot was equally loud. Julia covered her ears, as did almost everyone else.

Dante swung his fist clumsily at Carlo. Carlo ducked under the punch and sprinted for the bell tower door.

"Fermalo!" della Porta called out, his voice as loud as the gunshots.

Lacasse and the three Protectors chased after Carlo.

"Take them outside," della Porta ordered Bernardo.

Bernardo gripped Julia's arm and shoved her forward. She winced from the squeeze. Fanella did the same to Fosca.

"You said you'd let us go," Julia pleaded.

"I don't have the book, do I?" della Porta said. He headed for the church door in a huff, ripped it open, and burst out into the rain. Bernardo pushed Julia out. Fanella was a few steps behind with Fosca.

Della Porta stepped into the center of the front courtyard. Bernardo and Fanella forced Julia and Fosca over to him.

The five of them stood in the square, watching the church.

"There," Bernardo said.

A shadowy figure traversed the roof. The supple, dexterous form had to be Carlo. Three Protectors lumbered after him.

Carlo reached the section of the church without a scaffolding. He shimmied over the side of the building, hanging onto one of the apostle statues ensconced in the wing. Dante followed, but Carlo shoved the statue from its position.

The stone apostle toppled to the ground, landing in a thunderous crash that sent pieces everywhere.

All were momentarily stunned by the action. Even Fosca gasped.

Dante dangled for a moment before pulling himself back up.

Carlo continued climbing over the remaining apostles like temporary stone dancing partners until he reached the edge of the building. Protectors stood on the roof above him, balancing themselves precariously on the sloped and slippery tiles, cautious about reaching down for him.

"Enough, Carlo," della Porta called out.

"You want the book, Salvatore?" Carlo yelled back. "Catch!"

While gripping the statue for support, Carlo heaved the book upward like an Olympic discus thrower.

As if in slow motion, Julia watched the book sail thirty feet over her head. She turned, along with everyone else, watching the trajectory of the small brown object soaring through the pelting rain, aiming for Carlo's target—the canal, at least fifty feet from his perch.

"No!" della Porta screamed.

Exhilaration again filled Julia. She couldn't breathe as she watched. She glanced at Fosca, whose face bloomed into a wide smile. Makeup streamed down her cheeks.

The book descended, flying toward a certain death in the water. It landed with a wet thud on the *fondamenta*, slid to the edge... and toppled off.

Julia couldn't contain her elation. He did it. Carlo *did* it. Even if someone dove to the bottom of the canal and fished out the book, there's no way the pages would be useful. She caught Fosca's expression; it matched hers. All smiles, Julia gazed up at Carlo. But he hung his head. She turned to della Porta, who smirked.

He casually walked to the canal.

Julia followed until she had della Porta's vantage point. A dinghy was moored right where the book had landed, obscured by the edge of the *fondamenta*.

Della Porta knelt and retrieved the book, wet but still in decent condition. The leather binding would've protected the pages. He removed a plastic bag from his pocket, and dropped the book into it, then tucked the package into his suit jacket.

Carlo had given it just enough strength and thrown it perfectly... if that boat hadn't been there.

Joy deflated from Julia for the final time.

"Grazie, Carlo," della Porta shouted.

Julia turned back to the church. Carlo and the Protectors stood still as if watching a movie.

"Get the Painter!" della Porta yelled.

The Protectors made a move. Two crouched for Carlo, and Dante shimmied down to the nearest statue. Carlo brought his body to the corner of the wing, scanning his exit routes. There were none. He glanced up, stepped on the statue's pedestal, braced his foot on the apostle's hand, and leaped, catching the lip of the eave above him. He swung his body onto the roof...

And slipped.

Fosca screamed.

Carlo caught the lip of the eave but couldn't hang on.

He fell.

"No," Julia said with a whimper, covering her mouth.

"Fool," della Porta said. "Recover him," he said to Fanella and Bernardo. "Broken leg or neck, bring him back to the Palazzo."

"And the girls?" Detective Fanella asked.

"I'm a man of my word, as you know, detective. I have the book. They can go. Good riddance. Without meeting their eyes, della Porta flicked his hand in Julia and Fosca's direction, then marched toward the rear courtyard where Carlo would've landed. Fanella and Bernardo followed.

"Oh, Fosca?" called della Porta.

She turned, along with Julia.

Della Porta stopped but spoke with his back to them. "Honoring my word once is honoring my word. Should you or Signora O'Connor return to Venice, it will be a direct trip to *Paradise*."

Fosca gripped Julia's arm. "Come on," she said. "Before he changes his mind."

Unable to process all that transpired, Julia allowed Fosca to lead her away. They picked up the pace as they hurried to the motorboat in silence.

Julia climbed in and sat on the bench. Rain showered her body, drenching her hair and clothes. It was a fitting scene for the worst possible scenario, for the worst possible finale.

Fosca untied the ropes and jumped in. She went to the engine and gripped the rip cord.

"Not yet," came a whisper from the water.

Julia peered over the side. Happiness—this time bittersweet—overcame her.

Carlo hung tight.

Fosca leaned over, breathing an exhale of relief.

He lugged himself along the gunwale until he was a safe distance from the motor. "Now," he said.

Voices shouted in the distance.

Fosca pulled the cord. The engine roared to life. She hustled over to the captain's seat and nudged the throttle forward. When she turned down the next canal, Carlo climbed aboard. Julia helped him. He collapsed in a heap on his back. Rain pelted his face.

When their boat reached the open waters of the Venetian Lagoon, Fosca pushed it to full throttle.

# XXIII

A FTER FIVE DAYS OF scrutinizing every word in the doge's journal, a realization hit della Porta: he was obsessed. It was far from the first time he felt it. He'd never been physically addicted to a substance, but he'd had passions throughout his life. Growing his father's business to advancing through the ranks of the Order, and even finding the very book that sat on his large oak desk, could be considered obsessions. He'd accomplished them all, improving his own life and those around him in the process.

Now, his fixation wasn't so much with the journal, but the contents within—contents that would enable him to achieve his vision of Veritism.

As the founder and head of the world's only verifiable religion—one that divulged truths and long-sought answers to humanity—he would become omnipotent. Of course, he wasn't vain enough to think he'd be a living god. No, he'd let others call him that if it were their decision to do so.

He ran his fingers around the book, framing his most prized possession.

The black leather binding was worse for wear from the night of Carlo's ultimate betrayal, and some of the edges of the interior pages had water stains. In any state, the journal would've been immensely valuable to a collector of historical artifacts, but to della Porta, the contents were priceless.

Carlo.

Another obsession, della Porta admitted to himself. Though, the doge's journal was helping him get over his life's biggest disappointment. Fosca, too, was a letdown, but one not of his doing. In fact, Fosca likely seduced Carlo, blinding him with her allure. What a foolish boy. For some cheap sex, he threw away greatness.

Carlo thought himself indispensable—another grievous error. As della Porta's network expanded, there'd be no place Carlo could hide. If he somehow managed to disappear, della Porta would make do. He needed Carlo for the Venetian *Paradise*, but that was it. In an ideal world, when revealing Veritism to the world, della Porta would initiate a power transfer from Carlo to another Painter, releasing the souls temporarily. He'd do this on live TV, numerous streaming platforms, and with a live audience of dozens of journalists from around the world. Many would dispute it as special effects, but he'd give them time to study the painting and the souls—if they could bear the deafening screams.

If he couldn't locate Carlo, he had Lobo or the French Painter. The *Paradises* in Madrid and Paris were smaller, but either would get the job done.

Following that, Carlo was useless. Now that della Porta had the doge's book, he didn't need to speak with any soul in *Paradise*. He'd prefer that nobody could, so perhaps it was a good thing that Carlo had vanished.

The journal proved to be more of a treasure trove than anybody had imagined. The secrets within were so valuable that he'd had additional biometric fireproof safes installed in his office and home. Only he and Bernardo had access. He had also tasked three Protectors to escort him everywhere he went. He couldn't take any chances.

His obsession was warranted. He wanted to know every page in the journal, backward and forward. Though much of the handwriting required him to squint until he could decipher it, it was worth it. With so much time spent locked in his office or home with it, he felt like he was living in the late 16th century.

He still wasn't sure why Vito Uccello had paid Angelo Mascari to steal it, but from hints in the doge's diary, it seemed Vito was having an affair with the doge's daughter, and Vito needed security. Why Renzo Scalfini had possession of the journal was another story, but della Porta suspected the doge couldn't trust those closest to him. The Guild had infiltrated the doge's inner circle. With Manuel's treason and now Carlo, Fosca, and potentially the countess, della Porta knew the feeling too well. He shuddered.

Nothing had changed in 450 years. The journal's contents were still too important to fall into the wrong hands.

He gingerly turned the pages with an uncontainable smile.

The journal confirmed everything. The Vatican had always known of the Order and its secrets. The Church knew about the afterlife, that there was no real hell, and multiple popes had been members. The Church could fight it, but seals and carbon dating would be indisputable.

The pope and three cardinals signed one letter that validated multiple secrets. Another thanked Senator Quattrone, then Exalted Master, for bringing them to Venice and showing them truths of this world. In writing, the pope and cardinals admitted that Quattrone had revealed the existence of God and his grand plan. But, the letter went on, they could not upset the delicate balance of the Church and its followers and mentioned the penalty for heresy.

To that end, the pope declared that should any member of the Ancient Order of the Seventh Sun be accused of heresy, he would pardon them unconditionally.

Della Porta turned the page to the most important document in the journal, if not the modern Christian world. A single sentence, written in Latin, would change everything:

**TO HONOR AND PRESERVE OUR SHARED COVENANT AND FAITH AND TO SAFEGUARD AND CONCEAL ALL MATTERS WHICH WE HOLD DEAR AND TRUE, THE HOLY SEE SHALL RENDER UNTO THE ANCIENT ORDER OF THE SEVENTH SUN AN ANNUAL TITHE OF 44,000 VENETIAN DUCATS.**

He reread the end of the pledge.

44,000 Venetian Ducats.

Della Porta had already read this contract over a dozen times, but a woozy sensation overtook on every occasion. His hand trembled. He had won the lottery. He had checked the Order's financial statements, and not one payment had been made—likely due to the disappearance of the contract.

No doubt the Vatican's attorneys would dispute the amount, and likely the claim itself, but it was common knowledge that a Venetian Ducat contained 3.545 grams of gold. The current price of gold valued the contract at the equivalent of nearly nine million euros... *annually*. The agreement was signed in March of 1588. Della Porta's entire body trembled.

435 years ago!

That brought the total owed to almost *four billion* euros. With interest!

Even with the Church's staggering wealth, this was not a paltry sum. On top of their debt was the written knowledge that they'd been withholding the secrets of life from their followers all this time.

Of course, della Porta had no intention of collecting a single euro. He didn't need their money. He needed their support. And, more importantly, their followers.

In short, the pope would have two choices: either reveal his belief in Veritism and instruct all Catholics to convert to it, or pay the Order and face the wrath of a billion people who'd been lied to for centuries.

A quick rap on the door provided an exclamation point to della Porta's thought.

"Enter," he said in Venetian.

Bernardo strode in.

"Lobo has arrived, sior," he said. "They're in the Great Council Room."

"Excellent, my friend."

Della Porta closed the doge's journal and wrapped the tie around the original black leather binding, then exited with Bernardo. Two Protectors who'd be stationed outside his office accompanied them to the Great Council Room.

With a smile, della Porta nodded to everyone present as he took his place on the dais. Along with Lobo, the councils from Venice, Madrid and Paris sat in folding chairs. Unfortunately, it was impossible for the Parisian Painter to make the journey—something della Porta would correct in due time. The lack of a Venetian Painter was a notable absence—something else that would be corrected. Hopefully sooner.

At the rear of the massive room stood one-hundred-fifty Protectors from all three countries, all sworn to the Order.

"Welcome, my friends," della Porta said in English. He gazed over the audience, making eye contact with as many as he could, even the Protectors. "Thank you for coming to La Serenissima. All of you know the nickname for Venice. *La Serenissima*. The Serene, short for the Serene Republic of Venice. But why serene? Why not great, united, or any other more typical adjectives? Venice was the greatest maritime empire on the planet for hundreds of years. We were hardly serene. Frequent wars. And more frequent parties."

He paused for dramatic effect while the room chuckled.

"In truth, nobody knows where the name comes from. It may come from the doge, who was referred to as Serenissima. Was the city nicknamed after him, or was he named after the city? The other theory, which I subscribe to, is that Venice has always been one of the most tolerant cities on Earth, embracing foreigners, religions, sexual identities, and more, far ahead of its time. This came about from our position between Europe and Asia, as well as the city's tremendous economy. Our citizens didn't care who they did business with, as long as they made money."

Again, the audience laughed, della Porta along with them.

"Because of this environment, there was a genuine climate of peace and serenity. People lived side by side in harmony. And cacophony. My friends, imagine if we applied that concept to *the world*."

He gazed out to those before him, letting the notion sink in. They eyeballed him, rapt. He raised the book, displaying it to the audience.

"While it may seem preposterous to say this, my hand holds the key to world peace." He released an involuntary scoff. "I am the first to say impossible. Human beings are too finicky. Yes, we will never have true world peace, but we will bring it as close as we've ever come—united through a single religion. The world's one verifiable religion. Veritism. You all know my plans, for you are all integral to it. As founding members, you will be richly rewarded."

A murmur rose through the audience.

"Friends, wheels are in motion, and they cannot be stopped. We will reveal Veritism to the world in just over five months... on Christmas Day."

The room ignited in applause.

Della Porta silently patted himself on his back.

# XXIV

COUNTLESS TIMES IN HER eleven years on this blessed Earth, Isabella Maria Leticia Stefanetti had crouched at the top of the stairs in their palazzo in San Polo, eavesdropping on her parents' conversations. Typically, they'd argue about her four older brothers; those discussions lulled her to sleep. When her father brought business partners or politicians home, she sat riveted, listening to the proceedings. She knew, as a girl, she could only dream of engaging in her family's shipping business. But dreams needed sustenance.

This night, however, had been unexpected. They had hosted a dinner for Uncle Pietro and his family. It had been a few weeks since she and her siblings had seen their cousins, and she had a joyful time playing with those her age. It was not unusual for her aunt and their servants to take the children home while Uncle Pietro stayed to chat with his brother, but their conversation was unlike any she'd heard. She knew she'd be scolded, if not belt-whipped if caught, yet she couldn't turn away.

"Certo, brother," her father said. "Their power has corrupted them. The Guild of Silvanus is virtuous, and its intentions admirable, but the breadth of the Order's dominion knows no bounds. The *doge* is a member."

"Satan is also powerful," Uncle Pietro replied. "Does that mean we stop fighting evil?"

Her father poured his brother another glass of grappa. "Ah, but God is mightier than Satan. He is omnipotent and has an army of angels on His side. Compared to the Order, we are nothing."

"You are right. We are but ants fighting an elephant."

"Exactly. Best not to get squashed."

Uncle Pietro consumed his drink and leaned back on the sofa as though contemplating. His face betrayed a hint of a conspiratorial shroud. Isabella had seen her parents wear the same expression when they surprised her on her last birthday with a trip to Carpenedo to ride horses.

"Allora. Let me ask you, brother," Uncle Pietro said, "if you were an ant, how would you defeat an elephant?"

Her father laughed. "It is impossible."

"Is it?"

"Sì. Unless I crawled into the beast's ear and gradually ate its brain…" Her father trailed his words as if comprehending the incomprehensible. "What are you suggesting?"

"Infiltration. At the highest level."

Isabella's father pursed his lips. "We embed one of our own on the Council?"

"Precisely. We shall need influence first. It may take years. But it can be done. Are you familiar with Renzo Scalfini?"

"Certo. He's the controlling partner of the wealthiest timber collegantia in the Republic."

"And…?" Uncle Pietro asked.

"And a Councilmember of the Order."

"As well as a confidante of the doge."

Her father leaned back as if letting ideas circle his head. "You have lost me, brother. If you're proposing we somehow recruit Renzo Scalfini, you must know far more about this game than I."

"Not recruit," Uncle Pietro replied. "*Infiltrate.* And influence. Like I said, it may take years. Nay, it *will* take years. Now is the time to build the foundation. Deep, concealed by the surface. You see, he recently became a widower."

"I was not aware of that."

"Terrible thing. No doubt he will seek to wed again. Perhaps to someone whose family can provide a generous dowery… and that family could benefit from a union with his timber business."

Isabella pondered her uncle's statement. She knew not of this Order, Guild, or Renzo Scalfini. She couldn't even guess why he'd be so prominent in Uncle Pietro's discussion. On the other hand, her father seemed to gather his brother's meaning. He shifted his gaze to Isabella's direction. She snapped her head back into the shadow, praying he didn't see her.

He turned back to Uncle Pietro and lowered his voice. "She's only eleven."

"Of age to be betrothed."

Her father steepled his fingers and rested his lips on his index fingers. He drew a contemplative breath. "There would be a multitude of benefits. Is Scalfini a decent man?"

Uncle Pietro smiled. "As decent as any soul we know."

Carlo's eyes popped open as the car hit a bump. He'd been in the passenger seat of the silver Peugeot 208 rental car for six hours, but it felt like six years. While the interior was comfortable, he still couldn't get used to sleeping in a car. He could barely get used to *riding* in a car. It bewildered him how non-Venetians spent so much time in these little boxes on wheels.

The revelation that Isabella's uncle conspired with her father so that she wed Renzo stunned him. Carlo wondered if her father and uncle had known of the man's brutality. Perhaps not. Though times were different back then, he recoiled at the thought of a father using his daughter as a living pawn in a dangerous and relentless game.

Nobody could have predicted the outcome of Renzo and Isabella's union—nor the chain of events it spurred.

Fosca turned the wheel and slowed down. Carlo didn't bother to look out the window. He had no interest if it wasn't the Adriatic or a Venetian canal. He snuck a glance at the back seat. Julia's head bobbed with the rough road. He brought his gaze back to Fosca, her attention squarely ahead. Every time he saw her, she was illuminated by new light, unveiling another layer to him.

"Are you gonna paint a portrait of me?" she asked.

"What?" The question bowled him over. "I could if you'd like. I'd be honored."

"Carlo," she said, irritation seeping into his name, "you're staring at me."

"Oh, sorry," he replied. He shifted his attention to the rustic, unpaved road.

For the last five days, the trio barely said anything other than small talk and formalities. It was as if they were in a collective depression, and why not? Della Porta had won. The only silver lining was they managed to escape alive and unhurt. How long would that last?

Carlo knew he had a neon target on his back. The Order wanted him alive to transfer his power and then kill him. The Guild wanted him dead as soon as possible. His proximity to Julia and Fosca put his friends in danger, and he needed to mitigate that risk.

After escaping Venice, they holed up in a hotel in Trieste with two beds. Fosca paid in cash. Carlo slept on the floor. They watched movies and ordered food. The hotel manager probably thought Carlo was the luckiest man alive. In reality, it was a miserable combination of boredom and despair.

They batted around ideas about how to steal the book back, but nothing was strategically viable. He pitied Julia. Trieste was close enough to Venice to taste. Her husband was there—Carlo's doing—and there was nothing any of them could do about it. If only he'd thrown the book with more strength.

On the third day, Fosca suggested they go to her family's farmhouse in Languedoc in southern France, not far from Carcassonne. She said they could hide out there as long as they needed.

Fosca said it was gorgeous, so it would help them recharge. Julia agreed without hesitation. When Carlo realized he had no place to be—that he had no place he *could* be, he also accepted the invitation.

The car came to a stop. Julia sprung her head forward and glanced around groggily.

"We're here," Fosca said, her voice raspy.

Carlo cracked his neck and opened the door. He got out and stretched but stopped halfway through, sheer awe interrupting his motion.

"Merda," he whispered to himself.

An estate stood before him on a sprawling vineyard. He knew the Baldesseris were wealthy. After all, the countess was one of Italy's biggest private art collectors. Carlo had hoped she would purchase his work—a dream that now felt like a distant memory. He was no stranger to wealth in Venice, but because of the size of the cramped city, nothing came close to what he saw at that moment. Towering oak trees spotlighted rolling hills covered in grapevines. He couldn't even see where the driveway reached the street. He had no idea how far the property extended, but it seemed it could fit all of Venice.

Joining him, Julia did the same double-take he'd done.

"Whoa," she said.

Carlo followed her gaze to the chateau. No, not a chateau—*a summer palace.*

"This is your family's farmhouse?" Julia's eyes were open as wide as her mouth. "How big is your family, the whole town? And you didn't say the farm is a friggin' vineyard. Wow."

Fosca shrugged. "This is nothing compared to other estates in the area."

Carlo marveled at the building, which was a sight to behold. He guessed it had been built in the mid-18th century but likely had multiple extensions over the years. Standing majestically amidst the lush landscape, it showcased a blend of architectural styles. Its façade featured intricate stonework and ornate detailing that spoke to its rich history and craftsmanship. Elegant windows opened out to the breathtaking countryside. An aroma of fresh lavender, grass, and pine invigorated his senses. Fosca was right. This place was just what they needed to recharge. It was timeless beauty.

A scruffy sheepdog raced out and greeted Fosca with a single bark. Reminiscent of a border collie in size and stature but with longer, straw-like hair, the dog stood on its hind legs to give Fosca a kiss, which she returned.

"Garfield," she said, giving him a vigorous rub. "It's been too long."

"You named your dog after a cat?" Julia asked.

"He's the family dog. Marcel's little sister came up with it, and we couldn't say no."

"Fucking finally," yelled a whiny French accent from the door.

"Speak of the devil," Fosca said.

A wiry figure appeared and approached them, all smiles. Carlo recognized that messy brown hair and pimpled face—Marcel, Fosca's cousin.

Though Carlo hadn't expected to see the twenty-year-old, it made sense since Marcel was part of the family. But then Lucia and Hugo, along with a man and woman in their late seventies, appeared behind them. Beaming, Lucia nudged Marcel out of the way and careered to Fosca with open arms.

"Mi mariposita," she said, giddy. "It's so good to see you." Lucia gave her a bear hug and kissed her all over, which Fosca allowed with a smile.

Carlo exchanged a glance with Julia, who raised an eyebrow. He suspected she wondered the same thing—did the whole Guild need to recharge? Before Carlo contemplated the answer, Lucia turned to him.

"Carlito!" She wrapped her arms around him and planted at least a dozen kisses on his face. "My sweet Julia," she said, doing the same to her.

Marcel and Hugo came over and greeted them—Hugo with hugs, Marcel with a fist bump, though he seemed like he wanted to hug Julia.

"Sucks what happened," Marcel said, "but glad you're not dead."

"Merci," Carlo said.

"Well," replied Marcel, "*you* may need to be dead soon."

Carlo shook his head, half-laughing because he knew Marcel was only half-kidding. "It's nice to see you too, Marcel."

"You told them what happened?" Julia asked Fosca.

"Of course," she replied. "I'm not going to hide something like that from the Guild. Come meet two of our dear family friends." She brought them over to the aging couple, both of whom wore beige gardening hats. The man was about Carlo's height and had tanned, leathery skin with deep-set, remarkably pale blue eyes. The woman's shoulder-length, wavy gray hair framed a tanned face that looked as if it had just been moisturized.

"Carlo, Julia," Fosca continued, "meet Georgette and Olivier."

The two rattled off words in rapid-fire French while shaking hands and giving Carlo and Julia kisses on each cheek, which they returned. Carlo picked out a few words, which he knew were greetings, but his French was grade-school level at best.

"They don't speak much English," Fosca said. "Don't worry. I'll translate. They're the property caretakers. Basically family."

"Ravi de vous rencontrer," Julia said.

"Ah, magnifique," Olivier exclaimed, flashing yellowed teeth. "Elle parle français."

"I studied it a few years and did a college semester in Paris," she told the group. "But," she said to Fosca, "it's probably best if you translate."

Julia's command of French was yet another thing that impressed Carlo. He hadn't known she'd studied abroad.

"Avec joie," replied Fosca. "Especially since our Spanish friends don't speak it."

"It's the language of barbarians," Hugo said.

Everyone laughed.

"Hilarious," Fosca said. "Let's take this inside. I'm starving. I'm guessing Carlo and Julia are too."

The interior of the chateau rivaled the exterior. Carlo lost track of the number of rooms but guessed there had to be twenty bedrooms, an expansive living room, breakfast room, formal dining room, library, billiards room, and enormous kitchen. The building had maintained its old-world architecture, but Fosca explained that almost all the rooms had recently been modernized. The décor seamlessly blended modern comfort with classic refinement. Every step on the tour cast an inviting ambiance. When she brought them to the theater, Carlo wished he could relax in one of the plush reclining chairs and spend the day there. That would've been enough to recharge, until she brought them through the sunroom and out to the pool at the rear of the chateau.

Carlo wiped his mouth from salivating. Ensconced beneath rolling hills and lined with ancient olive trees, the Olympic-size infinity pool had two dozen chaise lounges on the blue tile perimeter. All he needed was a pitcher of piña coladas, and he could recharge forever. He turned to Fosca and grinned. To his delight, she smiled back.

"Since we've been wearing the same clothes for five days, I asked Georgette to order outfits for the three of us, including swimsuits. They're in your rooms. If you don't like them, we can get more."

"Not sure what we did to deserve this five-star service," Julia said.

Marcel scoffed. "Are you kidding?"

"Come on," Fosca said, heading back to the chateau. "I saved the best for last."

"There's something better than this pool?" Carlo asked with genuine amazement.

She laughed and threw him a smile. "You can't even swim. I can teach you how, though."

He loved the way Fosca carried herself. She was obscenely wealthy but never flaunted it, even during a tour of what could've been a hotel. She acted the same with everyone, regardless of their background or socio-economic status.

"I have to say," Julia said while the group returned to the house, "I feel recharged already."

"Excellent," replied Fosca. "Mission accomplished."

The pool topped Carlo's list, but when Fosca said she saved the best for last, she wasn't kidding. Lucia, Hugo, Georgette, and Olivier headed to the kitchen to prepare lunch while Fosca brought the rest of the group to the wine cellar. No stranger to wine, Carlo's jaw hit the dirty ground when Fosca disarmed the alarm for the glass doors and flipped on the incandescent overhead lights that grazed his head. Hundreds, if not thousands, of dust-covered bottles of wine glinted at him in the amber light. An authentic cellar, the space was half underground to maintain an even temperature year-round. Bottles filled racks that were dug into the earth on both sides of the narrow, thirty-meter-long cave.

"I feel like an archeological vintner," Julia said. "What are we drinking tonight?"

"What do you want?" asked Marcel.

"How do you even know where to start?" she replied. "Are these wines organized?"

"Kind of," Fosca said. "The ones in the back are the oldest. Pick one. Honestly, you can't go wrong."

A bottle with what looked like a watercolor painting on the label caught Carlo's eye. He pulled it out. It was a 1970 Mouton Rothschild. "How about this one?"

Fosca leaned over and read the label. "Not a bad choice. We should decant it now, though. But first, I told you I saved the best for last."

"This isn't it?" Carlo asked with a mix of confusion and excitement. The only thing that could top what he'd seen so far was a time machine.

Fosca smiled and walked three-quarters of the way into the cellar. She counted some bottles on a rack from the top and chose three seemingly random bottles, all of which she rotated ninety degrees right or left. She then counted more bottles and stopped at a fourth, which she pushed in. A nearly inaudible click sounded from the rack. Marcel gave his cousin a hand as they pulled the entire rack section out, which was either on wheels or a track, revealing a secret passageway behind it.

Julia glanced at Carlo with an inquisitive eye. Then he asked, "What could be in there that's better than everything else you've shown us? Treasure? Gold coins we can swim through?"

Fosca giggled. "You'll see. Come on."

She entered the secret room and turned on a light. Marcel beckoned Julia to follow. When Carlo entered, he felt a little disappointed. Inside was a library. A nice one, to be sure, but still just a library and smaller than the one in the main section of the chateau. Three walls were lined with oak shelves—one wall filled with ancient books, the wall to her right containing modern books, and the rear wall overflowing with file folders and bankers' boxes. A large, decorative glass vase sat on the top of the rear bookshelf. A table stood in the middle with four comfortable-looking chairs, and two easy chairs, each with its own lamp, were positioned in the rear of the space.

"Another library?" Julia asked. "I take it all these books are super valuable?"

"*Invaluable* for us," Fosca replied. She gestured to the table. "Have a seat."

Marcel entered a moment later, carrying a bottle and four wineglasses. As Julia and Carlo took their seats, the skinny college kid popped the cork and poured four servings.

"It's a local Carignan. The best in Languedoc, in my humble opinion."

Carlo breathed in the aromatics before he took a sip. Notes of blackberry and rosemary caressed his nostrils. When he sipped, an earthy undertone balanced the fresh berry aroma for a full body palate. He'd always been partial to Italian wines but could get used to France.

After the four had consumed a few mouthfuls, Fosca stepped to a shelf and removed an oversized leather-bound tome, which she placed on the table.

She placed her hands on the book and faced Carlo and Julia with a look of solemn resoluteness.

"I truly brought you here to recharge. And recharge we will, in body, mind, and spirit. But remember that recharge has different meanings. It could also mean to boost, replenish, or even to... well, charge again."

Julia took a sip of her wine. "If that's a copy of the doge's journal, I will kill you."

Fosca laughed. "No, unfortunately not. While we were all wallowing in depression, thinking we'd lost, I realized we may have one last hope."

Enthusiasm surged through Carlo. While he had accepted a life of obscurity as his fate, he'd prayed there might be another way to stop della Porta. Naturally, it was Fosca who had the answer.

"What's your plan?" he asked.

"My grandmother—"

"*Our* grandmother," Marcel said.

"Our grandmother," continued Fosca, gesturing around her, "built this library to protect their books not so much for their monetary value—and they are valuable—but to keep them from the wrong hands. You're looking at the Guild's research on the Order from hundreds of years."

"Yeah," Julia said. "Hundreds of years of not being able to stop them."

"That's because they were going about it wrong," Fosca replied. "They were trying to stop the Exalted Masters and eliminate the Painters."

"For an unknown reason," Marcel said, "our nonna-mère thought it best to trust my"—he tapped his thumbs on his phone—"promiscuous cousin"—he did another search—"ah, to carry the torch."

Fosca leaned over to Julia and Carlo and spoke in a low voice. "Did I mention Marcel is AAF?"

"Ca c'était quoi?" Marcel asked.

"I said you're lucky we need your tech skills."

Carlo had no clue what AAF stood for. Maybe something Air Force? With the extent of Marcel's computer knowledge, he might have been studying something relevant, but

Carlo didn't know why that mattered. "So that's why you brought the Guild here. I'm guessing Georgette and Olivier aren't really caretakers?"

"They are," Fosca replied. "But they're also our two oldest—I mean longest-standing—members. I wasn't lying about them being like family. Our families go so far back that we think we're actually related."

"I bet they'd rather be the nobles than the serfs," Julia said.

"And pay bills and taxes instead of getting paid?" Fosca replied.

Julia replied with a shrug. Her fascination with the European class system and unbridled partiality toward justice and equality had always piqued Carlo's interest. He wondered if all her countrymen were like that. Whereas most Europeans lived with their situations—save a revolution here and there—it seemed as though all Americans thought they could become rich and reach their version of nobility: the nouveau riche. He'd been listening to their conversation, but his brain focused on Fosca's previous comment. Being one of the Order's Painters, he didn't love being talked about as if he were a thing.

He was all ears to any alternative. He turned to Fosca.

"You said the Guild was trying to defeat the Order in the wrong way. So what's the *right* way?"

A sly grin crossed her face.

"We're going to destroy the Sun Crystal."

Julia polished off her remaining wine. The one mouthful probably cost thirty euros. She let the wine settle on her tongue. She'd forgotten what she was drinking, but damn it was good. It tasted like history—a fitting flavor.

After swallowing and licking her lips, she tapped her knife on her glass, not to make a toast but to get the rambunctious crew to pipe down. She'd been eating dinner with everyone, and while the long wooden dining table sat twenty, the group was bunched together in the middle. Individual conversations had broken out. Excitement permeated the room beneath the classic chandelier. Not one person noticed her action.

1950s French jazz played through the speakers, the perfect soundtrack for the scene, though the conversations drowned out the music.

The food was as sublime as she'd come to expect. Georgette, Olivier, and Lucia had made coq au vin with asparagus and wild rice. Every bite melted in her mouth, but she'd realized she preferred Italian food. While French cuisine was about complex sauces, Italians focused on simple ingredients—and how to combine and mold them into their most divine form.

Everyone continued chatting enthusiastically. Inebriation loosened the atmosphere. Julia was on her fourth glass and couldn't recall how many bottles had been opened. It was as if she, Fosca, and Carlo were heroes of a fantasy, and their return reinvigorated the troops. Carlo had his arm on the back of Fosca's chair. She seemed uncharacteristically close to him. They laughed and clinked their glasses together.

Despite the food, the camaraderie, and the alcohol, she couldn't get how they could be so eager to pursue an impossible goal.

Carlo pulled his arm back and brought his hand under the table. Fosca's eyes brightened. She flashed him a seductive smile.

Julia didn't mind being the only person at the table lost in thought. Since they left Venice, she'd been in a contemplative state. Not so much melancholy or depressed, but perhaps shell-shocked. They were so damn close to getting the book. She wasn't convinced they'd be able to bring della Porta down, but at least they would've been able to prevent him from getting stronger. That also meant the prospect of saving Nick was one step—many leaps—farther away.

Maybe she should've taken della Porta's offer. He'd have the book either way, but at least she could've spoken with Nick one last time. Tears bubbled in her eyes. She grabbed her cloth napkin and dabbed them, pretending to blow her nose.

That damned della Porta. She hadn't discussed it with Fosca and Carlo, but della Porta's win had taken its toll on her spirit. Where did they go wrong? He or his lackeys could've thought that maybe the book was buried in Tintoretto's grave, but his language seemed to convey that he knew they'd solved the riddle. He *expected* it to be there. He let them dig it up, then took it. If that were the case, then Isacco must've told della Porta. *Shit.* The asshole was always one step ahead, if not more.

Now Fosca—and everyone else around the dining table—thought they could somehow destroy the Sun Crystal? Maybe Fosca knew where it was stored, but entering Venice would be challenging. Traveling through Europe had been nerve-wracking. Della Porta had local police, Interpol, all those Protectors...

*Absolutely impossible.*

The wine erased all inhibitions. She needed to be heard. She loudly cleared her throat and tapped her glass again, nearly cracking it. It worked, like she had turned the room's sound off.

Carlo brought his hand up to the table.

"How are we even going to get it?" she blurted out with unintentional exasperation.

Everyone rubbernecked her as if she'd just crashed a party—and ruined it.

A moment passed before anyone spoke.

"We'll find a way," Fosca said. "First, we need to figure out how to destroy it."

"You make it sound so easy," Julia replied. "You guys have been trying to do this forever. You have all that research in your secret library. Insiders highly embedded in the Order. You're Tintoretto's *descendant*. So now, what, we're going to mosey into the Palazzo, steal the Sun Crystal, and destroy it in some magical way so that the souls"—she choked up at the thought of Nick—"and my beloved husband could finally have peace?"

Fosca translated in a low voice to Georgette and Olivier.

Georgette spoke up first in slow, deliberate tones that seemed to rise from the woman's gut like smoky words.

"She said you are as wise as beautiful," Fosca interpreted. "She said she knows your pain. We've all suffered losses. The Order has betrayed our families. It's true the Guild has never been successful. That doesn't mean we should lay down our swords and let them win. It's more important than ever. We owe it to our ancestors. We owe to our children to at least try."

Julia offered a tearful smile to Georgette. "Merci," she said. She appreciated the woman's words but didn't feel the same conviction. "How many losses can we suffer? Sometimes, you gotta face facts. Della Porta beat us."

Other than Fosca translating, nobody uttered a word when she finished. Julia glanced around the table, making eye contact with everyone and ending with Carlo.

"It used to be killing the Painter," she continued. Her voice rose in agitation. She didn't care. She was sick of it all. "Yet he's sitting at this table, eating, drinking with us."

Again, Fosca translated, and again, nobody replied. Julia chugged the remainder of her wine. Marcel refilled her glass. The room was already wobbly. She reached for her water.

"You're right," Carlo said. "There are a lot of targets on my back. I'd be grateful if none of you sticks a knife in it. You are right, Julia. But so is Georgette. So is Fosca. It is worth one more chance. We're sitting around the table like it's our *last meal*. If we don't stop della Porta, nobody will. Let's determine how to destroy the Sun Crystal. If there's a way, I trust Fosca that it's somewhere in the library. Then we make a plan for how to reach it."

"You mean *steal* it," said Hugo.

Carlo took a healthy gulp of his wine and then turned to Julia. He spoke to her but loud enough for the whole table to hear.

"I made a promise to you," he said. "I will do whatever I can for Nick. I don't know what that is yet. None of us do. But whatever I can, whether it's reversing the process, freeing his soul, or uniting him with Isabella, I will try."

Julia swallowed at his words. She hated him for what he did, but at least he felt remorse. While Fosca translated, Carlo took another drink and wiped his mouth. He pulled out a cigarette. It trembled in his fingers.

"Oh, just light the fucking thing," Fosca said.

"Grazie," Carlo replied.

"Merci," said Georgette and Olivier simultaneously.

"Gracias," offered Hugo with a smile.

The four of them lit up, filling the place with putrid smoke. Julia glanced at the window, which was thankfully open.

Fosca shifted away from Carlo.

"I'm trying to quit," he said while exhaling. He snuffed the cigarette in an ashtray. "Della Porta wants me. He *needs* me. I am more than a target. I'm the keeper of the souls in the main *Paradiso*. So, Hugo, I do mean *reach* the Sun Crystal. I can surrender myself. I can pretend to want to be the Painter. Whether he plans to use me to sentence souls or more likely that he'll want to transfer my power to someone else, I'll need to be close to the Sun Crystal. I know how long it takes to do both. If there's a way to destroy it, I'll have time."

He nodded to Fosca, who spoke in French to Georgette and Olivier.

"And then..." Carlo continued, "one of you can take my life."

"What?" Fosca blurted out.

She interpreted with a shaky voice. Everyone but she and Julia raised their wineglasses and toasted Carlo. Olivier reached over and patted his back.

"No, no, no," Julia said.

Marcel grabbed a Rubik's Cube that was sitting on the table. He mixed it up, then solved it in less than ten seconds.

"You want to free your husband, don't you?" he asked.

"Of course, but I don't want Carlo to die. I don't want *anyone* else to die. There needs to be another way."

Tears welled in Fosca's eyes. "And if not?"

Julia didn't have an answer.

# XXV

D ELLA PORTA HAD NEVER considered himself paranoid, but the time had come to be precautionary. So, after securing a meeting with Cardinal Giovanni Diamante, Secretariat of State of the Holy See, della Porta chose to have Lacasse drive him the five-and-a-half-hour ride to Rome rather than fly. Given the distance to and from airports, even if he took a private plane and avoided security, the extra time on the road was negligible. The detective's Interpol-issued BMW also enabled them to travel above the speed limit on the highway. Lacasse always impressed della Porta, and his smooth driving did the same. Della Porta barely felt a bump in the back.

He had used the journey to continue reviewing the parts of the doge's journal relevant to the Church. The research team had painstakingly photographed the pages and printed them out; he had secured the actual copy in his home. He finished reading the promissory note for the countless time and gazed out the window. The heart of Rome rolled by. As with Venice, tourist season never ended, though he was thankful they were at least out of the summer peak. Trees in Borghese Park had begun to change to a crisp orange.

"How much longer?" he asked. They should've been only five minutes away but hit traffic.

"Twelve minutes," the detective replied.

Della Porta inhaled to settle his nerves. He wasn't worried about the meeting. No, he had the upper hand. Yet, he couldn't lie to himself—threatening the entire Catholic Church had him on edge. Even verbalizing the idea would've made his parents and grandparents recoil with horror and collapse from cardiac arrest. The gravity of his plan weighed heavily on his shoulders. His heart raced with anticipation. Within the hour, his life would change. Within months, the *world* would change. There'd be no turning back.

His phone buzzed to life. A video call from Bernardo.

Della Porta hit the 'accept' button, amazed by the countenance of the face on the screen. He had come to know all his friend's micro-expressions. The usually stone-faced chief Protector offered his version of a smile—pursed lips angled upward about one degree. It had to be optimistic news.

"Isn't your birthday in March, Bernardo? You look like you can barely control your excitement."

"I have good news on two fronts," Bernardo said. "Is Lacasse with you?"

Della Porta connected the call to the car's Bluetooth speakers.

"He is."

"Your friends at Interpol came through again, Detective," Bernardo said. "Carlo and the girls crashed in a flat in Trieste for five days. They had a car when they left, and cameras picked them up at petrol stations in Verona and Turino."

"They're heading west," said Lacasse. "Any idea where to?"

"Not yet, but I would guess France," replied Bernardo.

"It makes sense," della Porta said. "The Baldesseri family has property throughout France. Monte Carlo, too."

"My thinking, exactly," Bernardo replied. "I want to bring in Lobo on the call. He has more information."

A moment later, the Spanish Painter's gaunt mug appeared on della Porta's screen.

"Pleasant journey, Exalted Master?" he asked.

Ever since della Porta had elevated him to Painter, Lobo had been excessively subservient. He knew the kid was putting on a show, but della Porta figured the longer Lobo did it, the more it would become ingrained.

"It was fine, Lobo. What's going on? We're almost at our destination."

"I want to show you something, Exalted Master."

Lobo pivoted the camera to display a regal apartment dripping with opulence. He moved past gilded chairs set around a large oval dining table. Wallpaper depicting a hunting scene covered the walls. He entered a living area, where two plush violet sofas occupied the space next to a giant fireplace overshadowed by Monet and Gaugin landscapes on either side. Two Protectors jumped up from the couch.

An uncontrollable grin filled della Porta's face. He'd tasked Lobo with finding a way into the countess's home. Lobo was proving to be resourceful at every turn. Della Porta had never been inside the flat, something for which he'd always resented the old bag. He'd have to pay a visit on his return.

"Well done," della Porta said. "How'd you manage entry?"

"Gracias, Exalted Master. Let's say the maid needs a new employer now that her previous employer is deceased."

"Good thinking. Have you found anything useful?"

"Not yet, but we only just started."

The car pulled up to the entrance of the Apostolic Palace, home to the office of the Vatican's Secretary of State, as well as the pope's private apartment.

"We're here, monsieur," Lacasse said, stopping the car.

"Nice work, Lobo," della Porta said into the phone. "You too, Bernardo. Should either of you find any clue as to Carlo's whereabouts, or Fosca's for that matter, text me immediately."

Lacasse opened the rear door. Della Porta carefully tucked his papers into a steel briefcase before stepping out.

He released three quick exhalations, nodded to Lacasse, and headed for the building entrance. Pontifical Swiss Guards accepted his credentials and waved him through security. A plain-clothes guard escorted him to the third floor. Upon exiting the elevator, della Porta again marveled at the frescoed corridor leading to Diamante's office.

The guard relayed della Porta's arrival into his earpiece and opened the door for della Porta.

"Signor della Porta" said Diamante, greeting della Porta with an outstretched hand. "Welcome to Rome."

"Grazie, Cardinal," replied della Porta. He shook the secretary's hand with vigor, being sure to apply firmer pressure.

Diamante led della Porta to the sitting area adjacent to the man's desk. The thin red cushion on the 19th-century chair was far from comfortable, but della Porta appreciated the history—and how many regal asses had graced the fabric.

"On behalf of the Vatican and followers of Christ the world over," said Diamante with a bowed head, "I want to thank you for your generous donation."

Della Porta waved his hand dismissively. "A small token of appreciation."

"Others thought it was quite large. I saw articles about the tithe in a number of MediaStatuto publications."

"It seems they've taken a liking to me."

Diamante offered a thin smile. "How can I be of service to you today? Your secretary was unclear about the purpose of this meeting. Dare I think more charity is on the horizon?"

"In a manner of speaking." Della Porta placed the briefcase on the baroque table at his knees and opened it. He removed the promissory note from the file. "Off hand, do you recall when Sixtus the Fifth was pope?"

The cardinal cocked his head. "That question seems out of the blue."

"Humor me."

Diamante rubbed his chin as if presented with a worthy challenge. "There have been two-hundred-sixty-six popes. Nobody remembers the pontificate of all of them, but the cardinals like to quiz each other. Papal trivia is good fun for us. Sixtus the Fifth, you say?"

"Indeed."

"Well, if memory serves, he was the last pope to be called Sixtus. I'm going to say mid- or late-16th century."

"Bravo," della Porta said, genuinely impressed. He hadn't even heard the name until recently. "He was pope from 1585 to 1590. Quite important in his day, having completed major basilicas in Rome, limited the College of Cardinals to seventy, and doubled the number of curial congregations."

"His influence is felt to this day. Why are we speaking of this Holy Father?"

"How right you are, Cardinal Diamante. Earlier, you thanked me on behalf of followers of Christ. As we know, there are 1.3 billion Catholics in the world. But I'm getting ahead of myself. Let's get back to Pope Sixtus the Fifth. He was a member of two religious orders, the Conventual Franciscan Order and mine, the Ancient Order of the Seventh Sun."

Della Porta gazed deep into the cardinal's eyes. The man swallowed, not replying, but confirming della Porta's momentous statement.

Diamante cleared his throat. "My friend, is this really an epiphany? I am a member, as are other cardinals. We've always suspected that some popes were members."

"Ah, but this pope was an *active* member *while* he was pontiff."

"What are you saying?" Diamante shifted in his seat.

Della Porta opened his briefcase and removed the promissory note. "The influence of his Holy Father Sixtus the Fifth is far greater than you may realize."

He handed the letter to the cardinal.

"He made certain contracts, which you'll read in this promissory note," della Porta said. "A copy, of course, but the original is safe and verified as authentic. Contracts that were never fulfilled."

The two men locked eyes.

"Contracts," della Porta continued, "I intend to collect on now. With interest, of course."

Diamante released a half-cough, half chuckle, as if in disbelief. He returned his aston-ished vision to the note in his trembling hands.

"This... this cannot be real," he murmured.

"Oh, it is." A tight smile developed on della Porta's face.

"This would bankrupt the Vatican. We don't have this type of money. The biggest companies in the world wouldn't be able to afford this."

Della Porta shrugged. "Those companies didn't sign legal agreements four hundred years ago."

The cardinal tossed the note onto the table and stood with angry defiance.

"Are you blackmailing the Catholic Church?"

Della Porta motioned his hand in a calming manner. "Collecting a debt is hardly blackmail. Should the debtor be unable to pay, I'm open to negotiation."

"The Church and the Order have co-existed in harmony for centuries. This is an outrage!"

"So then you refuse?"

"As I stated and as you know, Signor della Porta, it is impossible."

Della Porta leaned back into his chair with an intentional air of victory. "Good. That was the answer I was hoping for."

Diamante raised an eyebrow.

"You see, Eminence," della Porta said, "if you don't pay, then it leaves me no choice but to make this public."

Blood emptied from the cardinal's face.

"Now you are beginning to understand," della Porta said with a buoyant smile. "What will the masses latch on to? That the Vatican has withheld truths? Or that they refuse to honor their obligations? Or that multiple pontiffs felt themselves so superior to their flock that they joined an order that would've been tried for heresy?" Della Porta extended his arms, exaggerating the motion. "What will it be? Does it matter? The media will cover this one for years."

Diamante's mouth trembled. "This will not be the first storm we've weathered," he said meekly.

"This is hardly a storm, and you know it. It's an *apocalypse*." Della Porta moderated his tone to a more friendly one. "You and I have been friends for years. You're a loyal member of the Order. Like I said, I am open to negotiation."

"What do you propose?"

Della Porta clapped his hands together. "An alliance. As you said, the Church and the Order have co-existed for years. I simply want to expand on that. There is no reason Veritism cannot be united with Catholicism. Tell the people that scrolls or even a new Bible has been found, or whatever you want. We merely introduce the indisputable truths of souls, reincarnation, and Heaven."

"No Hell? What will the people fear?"

They were the words della Porta had been hoping to hear. He grinned.

"Me."

The cardinal's eyes widened. He sucked in a gasp.

"See?" della Porta said. "It's already happening."

# XXVI

"I WISH I COULD," Lionel Benton said, his proper British accent coming through on the Zoom call. "I truly do, my dear, but I cannot be a part of this any longer."

Julia returned an empathetic nod. She had reached out to Benton hoping he or Maggie Yorn had information about della Porta's plans. Regardless of the purpose of her call, Julia enjoyed seeing the conspiracy-minded art critic again. His blue eyes shone brightly behind his round red eyeglasses. His slicked-back, blond hair and Botox injections still gave him the illusion of youth, despite the anxiety he'd been coping with.

"If you hear anything, please let me know. This is about much more than a black-market art ring," she said, recalling the theory he had shared with her months earlier.

"I'm afraid you're right, but I don't want to know what that megalomaniac is up to. I've received threats and I'm quite certain I'm being watched. Maggie Yorn has expressed similar concerns. I shouldn't even be having this call, Julia. I'm sure you understand."

"I get it, Lionel. Take care, okay?"

"You take more care, Julia."

She gave him a warm smile and ended the call before glancing around the dining room.

Julia and the rest of the crew had been staring at computers or the Guild's research for weeks straight. Though the Baldesseri Estate was glorious, cabin fever had set in. As a precaution, only Georgette and Olivier ever left, which they did every morning to replenish the food supply. At least Fosca had allowed the team to bring the files out of the hidden library. Anything that had been produced before 1850, however, had to remain in the cellar. When Julia initially saw the library, she was amazed, but after six hours the first day, she found it suffocating. The rest of the team agreed. Threatened with mutiny, Fosca relented.

Sitting at the dining table improved the team's spirits, but that only went so far.

Benton's reaction struck a chord within her, resonating like a somber note in the quiet room. She needed a reminder of home. Nobody paid her any attention, so she surreptitiously logged on to her Instagram account, feeling like she was cheating on a test. Her lips formed into a downcast smile. Images of friends and family, having fun at restaurants, events, and trips of their own, scrolled by in her feed.

Still wanting to remain off the grid, she resisted the urge to like a few posts, so instead, jumped over to her own profile. Her most recent pics were from the beginning of their trip to Venice, replete with plenty of likes and typical comments. She sneered at a dove on a rowboat, a shot taken shortly before her and Nick's dream vacation took a dark turn with unforeseeable consequences. She scrolled further down, lingering on images from what seemed like a different life: karaoke with Nick, brunch with friends, Valentine's Day on the Cape.

At this point, her family must've been freaking out. She wanted to send them a message, but didn't know what to say. She refrained from checking her email to avoid going down that road. A brief idea of letting Nick's boss know that they extended their trip hit her, but she thought better of it. Lying could land them in more trouble. Not to mention, any correspondence could alert the authorities—which meant Lacasse—to her whereabouts. It was best if everyone thought they disappeared, at least for the time being.

"Sacré bleu," said Marcel, shoveling a forkful of eggs benedict into his mouth while tapping on his laptop keyboard with his other hand.

Julia quickly signed out of her account and closed the program. "Please tell me it's not another article suggesting Nick killed your grandmother."

"No, those have died down." Marcel read from his computer screen. "MediaStatuto published another della Porta article. They have their noses so far up his ass they're like his personal bidet."

A cigarette-filled ashtray next to him made Julia gag. Despite Fosca's shared hatred of smoking, she allowed the team to do so in the dining room, though she strictly forbade it in the secret library.

"What now?" Georgette asked.

"Another puff piece. He made a sizeable donation to a fluff charity and he's prepping for a major event this Christmas at the Palazzo."

The news flustered Julia from the inside. She couldn't put her finger on it but sensed it would be more than a holiday party. Everything della Porta did was for his own benefit.

"What's the event?" she asked.

"It does not say."

Julia thought to herself. "I don't like it. We need to pick up the pace. This is what I was talking about. How are we supposed to figure out how to smash the crystal in a few months when the Guild had the same info for ages but never did?"

"What choice do we have?" asked Lucia.

"She has a choice, my dear," said Hugo.

Julia rubbed her bleary eyes. There it was. At least once a day, one of the team would remind her she could go home. "Do I really have a choice? You think I could live with myself if della Porta succeeds? I have a dog in this fight like all of you. My husband—"

"—is in *Paradise*," answered the table in unison.

"Oui, oui, we all know." Marcel stood. "Speaking of dogs... Garfield, viens ici." The dog followed him as he carried his plate to the kitchen.

Needing a pick-me-up, Julia tagged along for an iced tea. She found Marcel crouching, letting Garfield gobble up the rest of his eggs off his plate.

She poured herself a glass from a pitcher on the counter.

"We'll find a way to destroy it," Marcel said.

"Since when are you Mister Positivity?"

He shrugged and stood, putting the newly cleaned plate—glistening with canine saliva—back in the cupboard.

Julia rolled her eyes and laughed inside. She took a drink.

"I'm not Monsieur Positivity. But I know"—he shook his hand around like he was fishing for an invisible word—"Comment dit-on...? I don't know. *Things*. I know machines, inventions, tools, things. I know you don't make a weapon as powerful as the Sun Crystal without a way to destroy it. Or reverse it."

"Reverse it? You think..."

It wasn't the first time someone had mentioned the idea of reversing the process to Julia. More than anything, she hoped it was possible, but it seemed too far-fetched.

"What about the souls whose bodies were cremated? They're dust now. Where would they go?"

Marcel shrugged and gazed upward. "I suppose they'll be free."

"They'll go to Heaven?"

"If that's what you want to call it. Or maybe they'll be reborn."

"Did we miss breakfast?" Carlo asked, entering the kitchen. Fosca came in fifteen seconds later. It could've been Julia's imagination, but the two of them seemed a little close to each other... and they both wore glowing smiles.

"Where have you two been all morning?" Julia asked.

"Researching in the main library," Fosca replied.

"We figured we'd look there," added Carlo. He went to the cupboard and took the top plate. "How are the eggs?"

Julia glanced at Marcel, who winked knowingly at her.

"Delicious," she said.

Carlo scooped a generous helping of eggs from the pan. Fosca poured herself a coffee from the French press.

"Find anything? In the library?" Julia asked.

"Not yet," Fosca replied with a smile. She threw a glance at Carlo. "We'll look more later. Let's join the others." The two of them went to the dining room.

"You do that," Julia said. She took her iced tea and headed to the wine cellar, relieved to find the secret library door closed. She wasn't sure if anything had happened between Carlo and Fosca and was less sure why it bothered her if something did. Julia didn't care; they could do what they wanted. Either way, she needed time alone. As she unlocked the bottle rack and pulled it open, she realized why Fosca and Carlo's potential hookup—*why anyone else's intimacy*—bothered her.

Nick.

She missed his warmth, his voice, his scent. She missed being able to hold someone's hand or whisper thoughts as they lay in bed. She missed kissing, the sex, the love. Even though she'd been with her new friends, she felt alone. Of everyone there, she was the outsider. The only American. The only one not in the Order or the Guild. It had been so long since she'd felt like herself. So long since she'd been true to herself.

She flipped on the lights, shut the door behind her, and plopped down on the rug. She curled her knees into herself and let the tears flow, forgetting promises that she'd stop pitying herself. She just needed to cry. For minutes on end, she bawled, rocking back and forth—not thinking because they were the same old thoughts. She just needed to let it out.

Through glossy eyes and a stuffy nose, she gazed around the library, knowing that the end to her sadness—the end to the suffering of so many—was in that little room. The floor gave her a new vantage point. The team had nearly finished combing through the ancient books and the various files. Still, they'd ignored the bookcase filled with a hundred or so contemporary books—everything from secret societies to history books on Mongolia and the Tangut Kingdom to guidebooks for Venice and China.

Julia crawled over to the bottom shelf. A narrow, unlabeled file box sat next to a red book with Chinese characters on the spine. She twisted herself into a sitting position, pulled it out, and lifted the lid.

Her breath jumped in her chest.

Inside was a manuscript with about one hundred pages, bound by a vellum cover. It had to have been a few hundred years old. She rushed over to the table with it and donned cotton gloves, eager to dive in. As she carefully turned the pages, the book revealed nothing but text in handwritten Chinese. Most of the old books they'd found were written in Latin, French, Venetian, or Italian. Olivier had found one in German, which he nearly threw in the fire before Marcel talked some sense into him. This was the first they'd come across in Chinese, which explained why it was filed next to the other Chinese books, even though those were modern.

Without a clue to the meaning, she continued flipping through. She prayed this was her golden ticket and felt as desperate as poor little Charlie Bucket. Some of the pages had Latin scrawled in the margins. A quarter of the way through, she may as well have found gold foil. On the center of the page, with Chinese letters etched above and below, was a drawing of an orb—what could only be the Sun Crystal.

She turned the pages to find more drawings, including one that prompted a tear of joy. *The crystal was broken in two.*

Without a second thought, she grabbed the book and raced back to the team in the dining room.

"I found it." Her words came in quick spurts. "Look at this."

With an air of excitement, her friends gathered around as she opened the book to the drawings of the Sun Crystal, showing them all and stopping on the sketch of it broken.

"Oh, my fucking God," Fosca said. "You did find it!"

She kissed Julia on the lips and hugged her.

The action was so quick and so in the moment, Julia just took it. She needed that warmth and affection. She released her hold and wiped her wet eyes with the back of her hand.

"Does anyone here read Chinese?" Carlo asked, not as thrilled as the rest of them.

They all shook their heads.

"I know someone who does," said Fosca.

# 1805

RODRIGO RAMOS LED THE charge on horseback, flanked by his brothers. His Cordovan hat had fallen behind his neck, hanging for dear life by the strap. His leather coat flapped in the crisp autumn air. Dust kicked up as they approached the lone cottage nestled at the base of Sierra de Guardarrama, outside San Sebastián de los Reyes. The morning sun cast an orange reflection on the rocky mountain range.

They had left Madrid shortly after dawn, and he cursed their late departure. Their mother had begged them not to go and locked the stable, an action that only delayed the inevitable.

No matter what, he and his brothers would complete their purpose: vengeance.

As their horses' hooves pounded the ground, the cottage came into view. Smoke rose from the chimney. Two girls hauled water from the well. The mother, dressed in a conservative black dress, fixed clothes to the drying line. There was only one member of this family they cared about—Sancho, the teenage son who had wronged their sister. He had raped her on the eve of her wedding. By blood oath, all would pay.

The girls pointed in bewilderment at the oncoming stampede, but then Sancho and his father emerged, rifles in hand. The mother yelled to the two girls to run inside, but it was too late.

"Spread out," Rodrigo called to his brothers. The two did, drawing their pistols. Rodrigo didn't hesitate and fired at the mother, missing twice. His third bullet found its mark. The girls screamed. The father called to them. Rodrigo's brother shot the man in the chest. His other brother shot the eldest in the leg. The boy dropped his rifle and went down screaming. Rodrigo halted his horse just above Sancho.

Rodrigo and his brothers knew the consequences of their actions. They'd be hunted. If caught, they'd be jailed or executed. But Sancho's family knew of his atrocities, so they were all guilty. More so, should Rodrigo only take vengeance on Sancho, the rest of the family would seek them out in a never-ending pattern of violence. It needed to end *today*, with Rodrigo and his brothers victorious, if they could call it that. They had only one concern. There had been word that the family's patriarch, a prominent textile producer, had joined an Order with roots in Venice. This Order was already powerful and growing fast. If rumors were true, the Order's punishments against those who wronged their members or members' families were far worse than death.

To avenge his sister, he'd face any ramifications.

His brothers aimed their pistols at the two girls, neither older than ten.

"Do it. For our sister," he commanded.

They shot the girls, cold. Their fragile bodies crumpled to the ground, blood staining their dresses and coating the sand.

"Maricon," Sancho managed through dirt and tears. "We have no money. Why would you do this? My poor sisters!"

Rodrigo pulled his scarf from his mouth, revealing his face. "What of *our* sister?" he demanded through clenched teeth.

The boy gasped. He crawled backward.

"She..."

"She what?"

"She wanted it," he whispered with a lascivious grin.

Rodrigo raised his pistol. The bullet found Sancho's forehead.

# XXVIII

"I SAID, 'ARE WE boring you?'" della Porta asked in English.

Lobo shuddered his head, clearing the 19th-century vaqueros and slaughter from it. He'd never had a vision before, if that's what it was. And such a lucid mindfuck. More than the visuals, he felt Rodrigo's emotions. He *was* Rodrigo. Lobo wondered if he had a mental break, but at that moment, he needed to return to his present surroundings.

"Of course not, Exalted Master. It's this room, all of it"—Lobo gazed around, covering for his lapse—"it's awe-inspiring."

Along with della Porta, others from Venice, the Parisian Order contingent, and the president of the Louvre, he stood in the famed museum's Salle des Éstats, a room filled with many of the greatest Italian paintings in history. To their right hung the most famous in the world—*Le Portrait de Lisa Gherardini*, commonly known as *The Mona Lisa*. Directly ahead of him, about four meters up and enclosed by midnight-blue walls, hung the object of della Porta's attention—Tintoretto's second study for *Paradise*, entitled *The Coronation of the Virgin*.

Della Porta chuckled. Bernardo, Lacasse, and Dante shared their boss's reaction.

"So you *are* capable of humility," della Porta said with a smirk. "So? No thoughts then?"

"Forgive me, Exalted Master," Lobo said. "I was listening, but I didn't hear the question. Would you mind repeating it?"

Della Porta scoffed. He removed his glasses and pinched his nose. "That means you weren't listening. I asked if you thought there was anything unusual about this version of *Paradiso*?"

Lobo contemplated the artwork. Over three-and-a-half meters wide by one-and-a-half meters high, it was slightly smaller than the study in Madrid. It contained a different interpretation of Heaven from those in Madrid and Venice, but he was struck nonetheless by Tintoretto's vision of celestial splendor.

The painting portrayed a swirling composition of divine figures, angels, and saints arranged in a tiered formation that ascended upward like an inverted whirlpool. Where the versions in Madrid and Venice focused on the individuals, particularly Mary and Jesus, the setting was the subject of this one. The people got lost in it—in more ways than one. Lustrous gold and luminous blues dominated the vibrant color palette. Tintoretto's trademark use of light and shadow created a sense of depth and movement, transporting the viewer—and the imprisoned souls—into the celestial realm. Meticulous attention to individual figures showcased the artist's technical prowess. It was yet another testament to Tintoretto's ability to capture the sublime.

But Lobo knew della Porta wasn't asking about Tintoretto's craft or the painting's content. Since ascending to Painter, he'd learned El Greco had not only painted over Tintoretto's brushstrokes to capture the souls imprisoned in the work, but they had shrunk the souls using a prism, a technique that started in Venice when space soon became limited, even in the world's largest oil painting.

Della Porta had brought Lobo to Paris to meet his French counterpart, whose identity had yet to be revealed to him. He assumed that Painter used the same methods as El Greco—skills he'd soon acquire. If della Porta wasn't asking about craft, content, or technique, he had to be inferring something else.

When Lobo saw *Paradise*, it struck him that the painting hadn't been given as much prominence as its sister paintings had in the Palazzo Ducale and the Thyssen-Bornemisza. *Paradise* was the main attraction in both museums, hanging prominently by itself on an entire wall. In the Louvre, *Paradise* shared the spotlight with dozens of other master-works. One could say it didn't have a spotlight. Besides being adjacent to the world's most famous painting, it hung above Bassano's *Descent from the Cross*. The positioning forced a viewer to look at Bassano's work before raising their eyes to Tintoretto's.

"Does the Parisian chapter hold Convocations in this room?" Lobo asked. "Or do they move *Paradise*?"

"Why do you ask?" della Porta replied.

Lobo extended his arms. "*Paradise* is crammed here. If the Parisians have ceremonies, the painting should be in a different room, occupying its own wall."

"Excellent." Della Porta smiled. "They hold Convocations here, but they're largely ceremonial. The chapter is relatively inactive. They haven't sentenced a soul in over forty years."

"Forty-six," François said proudly.

Della Porta shot the elderly man a glare. "We're going to correct that."

François' smile faded.

"Come, Lobo," della Porta said. "It's time you met the last of the original Painters."

As Lobo followed the others to a rear stairwell that required a keypad for entry, his thoughts returned to the vision.

The sensation of riding on horseback seeking revenge thrilled him. He didn't know who Rodrigo was, but the man knew of the Order. It wasn't a leap to presume he had been captured and sentenced to *Paradise*. While he deserved his sentence, those they killed also deserved their fate. The vision had been so vivid, so lifelike, more like... *a memory.*

The pieces snapped into place in Lobo's head. Everything he witnessed occurred. Painters—even subsequent Painters—attained the memories of the souls they imprisoned. The knowledge blew him away.

He could only assume the other Painters—including Carlo—also had memories of the souls in their respective paintings. It made sense that Carlo had hid this information from della Porta. There was too much unknown. Would Lobo learn to control it? To seek out specific memories? Could he use that to his advantage to accumulate long-lost knowledge for wealth and power? The potential was limitless.

He hungered to learn more and to experience more visions.

The group descended into the bowels of the museum until they reached the medieval foundations. Though this was his first visit to the Louvre, Lobo knew it well. Before becoming a grand art gallery in 1793, the Louvre was a castle fortress with a moat dating back to the twelfth century.

Spotlights lit up what appeared to be former moat walls. They crossed under what would have been the bridge and stopped at a thick wooden door in the abutment, which would have served as the arsenal.

François inserted a key into the door's lock.

Lobo's heart rate spiked. He had expected to meet the French Painter in a manner similar to when he saw El Greco—in a grand procession, not locked away in a dungeon.

François opened the door and motioned for Lobo to enter. "Monsieur Blanco-Romasanta, s'il vous plaît."

Half worried they'd shove him in and slam the door behind him, Lobo glanced at della Porta, who nodded for him to proceed.

The space inside diffused a golden hue, lit by Edison bulbs in retro sconces. A softness pressed beneath his boots. He looked down to find a thick magenta rug lining the stone floor. A scent of citrus and jasmine wafted into his nose. The room was considerably more spacious than he'd expected, decorated with dozens of paintings, and richly appointed with comfortable furniture in a 1920s style.

A picture-tube TV on a table off to the side played a black-and-white movie without sound.

The center of the room drew his attention. His breath caught in his throat.

Lounging on a lime-green Turkish divan, was an ancient, emaciated woman in a red kimono. Thick black hair, which Lobo presumed to be a wig, draped over the woman's gaunt eyes and cheeks.

"Bonjour, jeune peintre," the woman said in a near-whisper. Her words sounded as if they trickled out of her mouth and turned to dust.

"Lobo," della Porta said, appearing beside him, "meet the goddess, Signora Artemisia Gentileschi."

Lobo couldn't believe his ears—or eyes. Without a word, he dropped to his knees, genuflecting before the master.

"I am not worthy to be in your presence," he muttered in Spanish.

While not a household name like many Renaissance masters, Artemisia Gentileschi was arguably the most influential female artist in history. Though not French, the Italian artist died in the mid-17th century and had spent time in Venice, so the timing fit perfectly for her to be selected in the Order's expansion. More importantly, her unrivaled skill and temperament made her a perfect choice for Painter. Artemisia had been considered a rebel of her day, rising to the top in a man's world. Another artist had raped her. While the man had been found guilty, she was tortured with the thumbscrews under the premise of verifying her claims, despite two witnesses. She never backed down. She never lost her grace or mettle.

Lobo had always felt an affinity toward Artemisia. Her most renowned painting, *Judith Slaying Holofernes*, was a groundbreaking work that depicted brutality with extreme detail and emotion.

Della Porta wrapped a hand under Lobo's armpit and helped him up. "Your humility shines like the sun tonight," he said, "but you are now colleagues. Granted, you will not be working together, per se, but you have the same job. Signora Gentileschi is eager to make her mark yet once again."

"Madame Gentileschi, I am humbled to be in your presence," Lobo said in English, continuing to bow his head.

She mumbled something unintelligible.

"You'll need to look at her," della Porta said. "She's as deaf as a doorknob. Worse. The door itself. She can read lips a bit, but it's best to write down what you want to say."

Della Porta removed a notepad and pen from his inner pocket and handed them over. Lobo snatched them like a toddler offered candy. He scribbled his statement on the paper, tore it off, and presented it to the living goddess.

She took it and smiled. "Comme tu devrais l'être," she said, her weak voice cracking.

Lobo only had a rudimentary knowledge of French, but he understood that phrase: *'As you should be.'*

He grinned at the ancient woman. Pure greatness sat before him. Holding the pen and paper, he ogled her, realizing he had so many questions, he didn't know where to begin. It was as if a window to the past had been opened. He didn't want to waste this opportunity, yet couldn't decide if he should ask her about the Renaissance, or focus on life as a Painter of the Order. Ultimately, he decided it was best to build a rapport.

He thought for a moment, then wrote in English: 'I have always loved your work. It rivals any man's.' He handed the notepad to della Porta.

The Exalted Master read it with a slight frown before clearing his throat.

"Forgive me, monsieur," Lacasse said, sidling up to them, mobile phone in hand. "I have an important update."

"Can it wait?" della Porta asked.

"I'm afraid not."

"Very well. Come, Lobo."

Lobo couldn't believe it. They were pulling him away from a miracle. "But we just started. We're in the middle of a conversation."

"One you can have later," della Porta said. "She's not going anywhere. You can be sure of that."

"No." Lobo didn't budge. They'd have to drag him away.

Della Porta crossed his arms and gazed at Lobo as if he were a petulant child. "Do you want to see Signora Gentileschi again? *Ever* again?"

The meaning was clear. Lobo relented. He bowed deeply to Artemisia and turned away with a forlorn tug in his gut.

The men exited the Painter's room. Lacasse handed della Porta his phone. Lobo hadn't seen any routers but assumed they were down there.

"The fugitives were spotted at a petrol station in Brussels," Lacasse said. "They were heading north."

"Carlo?" della Porta asked, reading the screen.

"Oui. Along with Fosca and Julia O'Connor."

Della Porta pursed his lips, then handed the device back to the Interpol detective. "Do you think they're going to Amsterdam?"

"There aren't too many other viable options in that direction," Lacasse replied.

"It's a big city," Bernardo said.

"With no shortage of cameras," Lacasse added.

"Go there," della Porta said. "Take Bernardo and Dante. And Lobo."

Lobo grinned. The prospect of apprehending Carlo fueled a surge of adrenaline in his veins. It was no substitute for speaking with Artemisia Gentileschi, but perhaps if he caught Carlo, he'd be rewarded with a private conversation.

# XXIX

"**I** STILL CAN'T BELIEVE neither of you have ever been here," Julia said.

"You've said that at least thirty times," replied Fosca.

"But it's *Amsterdam*."

"We know," said Carlo, with more than a hint of exasperation.

After Julia had found the Chinese book, everyone's mood lightened the moment Fosca had said there was a man in Amsterdam who worked with her grandmother on researching the Order's origins. Opting to play it safe, they drove twelve hours straight through France, Brussels, and the Netherlands, with Julia and Fosca taking turns driving.

Julia couldn't sleep when she was off duty, and it wasn't because of her European road trip. The closer they got to Amsterdam, the closer they got to destroying the Sun Crystal and freeing the souls. Still, she had to admit that much of her exhilaration came from the Dutch capital itself.

A wide smile crossed her face. "I'm finally leading the Europeans around."

Fosca shook her head. "You've also said that thirty times."

Julia guided her friends down Prinsengracht toward the world-famous Flower Market. When she did a semester abroad in Paris, she and her friends took a weekend excursion to Amsterdam. Beyond the nightlife and vices, the city left an indelible impression on her. As she trod the cobbled streets again, she was transported to a place where old-world beauty knew no bounds. Canals shimmered like ribbons, weaving a picturesque tapestry that captivated the soul.

Ironically, the only location where she'd felt a similar call was in that other renowned city of canals—Venice.

Like its Italian sister city, Amsterdam's architectural wonders, with their elegant gabled facades, stood as testaments to a rich past. Many of the homes were so skinny, with staircases so steep, furniture had to be hoisted up and pulled in through windows.

She fondly recalled evenings when dusk settled, after visiting the city's attractions. She and her friends dined on savory *bitterballen* followed by their fifth portion of *stroopwafels* that day. Their first night ended in a club called The Melkweg. She couldn't remember the Dutch punk band's name—and didn't enjoy the music—but danced her heart out, soaking her clothes with sweat. The only thing that could've improved the trip would have been if Nick—her boyfriend at the time—had been there.

Now, she found herself longing for the same thing. Passing a cheese shop brimming with dozens of types of Gouda, she vowed to herself that someday she'd rent an apartment, maybe even a houseboat, and spend a month in Amsterdam—hopefully with her husband.

They climbed a bridge as a tour boat motored beneath them. A steady stream of bicyclists rode over the bridge, pedaling to their destinations. While Fosca was all business, matching Julia's brisk pace, Carlo seemed lost in another dimension.

"Did you know there was another canal city?" Julia asked.

He laughed. "It's kind of weird. It feels familiar but in a different way. Almost like... wearing a new set of clothes."

"Sure you're not having another flashback?" asked Fosca.

"Could be," Carlo said, laughing again.

The Chinese book was secured in a metal briefcase, now gripped firmly in his right hand. His left brought a cigarette to his lips.

"Okay, it's just another block or two." Julia's excitement percolated in her voice. "Who are we meeting with again?"

"Jacob Hartog," replied Fosca. "He's one of the world's leading authorities on the Tangut Kingdom and apparently fluent in four Chinese dialects."

"Apparently?" Julia asked.

"I told you, I only met him for ten minutes once. Nonna-mère hired him as a consultant."

Julia pursed her lips. "I still don't get how she didn't know about this book."

"Maybe she did. Unfortunately, I can't ask her, can I?" Fosca's face darkened.

"Sorry," Julia said. "I didn't mean—"

"I know. Let's focus. We'll find Hartog, go somewhere safe, and have him translate."

"He'll be in the Flower Market?" asked Carlo. He flicked his cigarette butt into the street and stepped on it as they trod forward.

"He owns one of the shops," Fosca replied.

They rounded the corner, avoided an oncoming tram, and found themselves in the tightly-wound flower market, teeming with tourists and locals alike. Each open-air store invited pedestrians with a variety of foliage, but the star was the tulip, Holland's national flower. Hundreds of them filled the market, spread out like an urban technicolor meadow.

"It's called Singel Flower," Fosca said, craning her neck to read the names of the shops. "Wait, this is it," she said at the third.

The three smiled at each other. They were so close.

"Don't lose that." Julia motioned to the briefcase in Carlo's hand.

"Never in a million years," he said.

As she stepped over the shop's threshold, a fragrant symphony of delicate blossoms enveloped her. Fosca made a beeline for the cashier, then diverted her path to a small office in the back. Julia and Carlo were right behind her. A plump older woman with short, curly graying hair and bright green eyes sat at a tiny desk, handwriting invoices.

"Excuse me," Fosca said, "do you speak English?"

The woman laughed. "Can I help you?"

It always amazed Julia that the entire country of Holland was seemingly fluent in English. Many spoke the language with an American accent, often better than some Americans she knew.

"We're looking for Jacob Hartog," Fosca announced.

"He's not here today." The woman tore off an invoice and started another.

"Oh," replied Fosca. "I called him and let him know we're coming."

"He's still not here."

"Where is he?"

The woman placed her pen down and eyed them. "Are you picking up an order?"

"We're friends," Fosca replied. "Baldesseri is the name."

"Ah," said the woman, raising a finger. "I believe my son was hired by your grandmother."

"Jacob is your son?"

"He is. You'll find him in Westland."

"Westland?" asked Julia. "Where's that?"

"Near Den Haag," the woman replied. "About an hour's drive. It's our flower farm. Here." She ripped a blank invoice off a sales pad and scribbled an address on the back, then handed it to Fosca, who folded it and stuffed it in her jeans pocket.

"Bedankt," Julia said, amazed she remembered the Dutch word for thanks.

"Graag gedaan," the woman replied with an appreciative air.

Carlo and Fosca exchanged greetings with her, and the trio stepped out to the bustling Flower Market.

"Looks like we're seeing more of Holland," Fosca said, not hiding her disappointment.

"Fine by me." Julia slowed as they passed a tourist shop. A magnet caught her eye—a colorful city scene carved out of wood. She'd purchased the same one years earlier, and now it hung on her and Nick's fridge. An image of their apartment flashed in her head. All the plants must've been long dead. Maybe she should've contacted her friends and family, who were probably worried sick—at least Nick's brother. She made a mental note to tell him they went off the grid and to keep it secret. She didn't want to lie, but she also didn't want to worry anybody. What else could she do? When the time came, she'd reveal the truth.

The shop door opened, and a family of four stepped out. Julia briefly considered shouting to Carlo and Fosca that she'd catch up but gasped at the reflection in the glass door.

A man she never expected to see in Amsterdam made his way through the crowd: Interpol Detective Richard Lacasse, wearing his signature light-gray suit.

Without breathing, Julia filed between the family and caught up with Fosca and Carlo. She grabbed their elbows and picked up her pace through the tourists.

"Don't look back," she said.

Both of them veered their heads.

"I said, 'Don't look back.' It's Lacasse!"

"What?" they said in unison.

"How did he find us?" Carlo asked.

"It wouldn't be the first time," replied Julia.

Still clutching their arms, she was about to guide them around the corner but eyed what had become her hideout of choice—a McDonald's across the street.

"Come on." She released her hold. Dodging a bicyclist, she sprinted across the street between two oncoming trams from both directions, not turning around to see if Fosca and Carlo followed. She rushed into the McDonald's, relieved her friends were with her once they got inside. Crouching behind diners at a window counter, she ignored their unsettled looks and peered outside.

Three men followed Lacasse in the direction they would've gone had she not seen the Golden Arches.

"It's not just Lacasse. He's with Bernardo, Dante, and Lobo."

Pressing a finger to his ear, Lacasse gestured to the other men to follow him down the street.

Fosca pulled herself to full height and waved her hands around.

"What the hell are we going to do?" she asked, breathless.

Julia and Carlo also stood, giving the diners space.

"This is not good," Carlo said, looking equally perturbed.

"We have the upper hand," Julia said. "It's not a coincidence they're here, but Amsterdam is a big city. As much as I hate to leave, let's just get to Westland as fast as possible and find Hartog."

Fosca and Carlo nodded their agreement.

The restaurant was half the size of an average McDonald's in the States. Ten feet away, a uniformed worker in a blue Golden Arches baseball hat emptied a trash can. He tied up the bag and carried it toward the back.

"Follow me," Julia said.

The trio caught up to the worker, who punched a code into the door next to the cashier. As he opened it, Julia barged through. Fosca and Carlo joined her.

"Sorry. I need to use the bathroom," Julia said. "Emergency!"

"This is not the bathroom," the worker replied.

Unsure where to go, Julia hustled through the kitchen, Fosca and Carlo in tow. She aimed for the rear of the restaurant, hoping there'd be an exit. She was right. She shouldered the door open and burst into an area big enough to hold a pile of trash bags. A waft of rotting garbage accosted her nose. Cigarette butts paved the spot of ground beneath her feet.

Fosca and Carlo squeezed out of the restaurant.

"Wait!" Julia said, reaching for the door.

Too late. It slipped out of her grasp and shut behind them. There was no handle.

Fosca gagged.

Carlo held his nose. "The City of Venice could teach them how to take care of their trash."

"I gotta get outta here," Fosca said, ready to pound on the door.

"No." Julia grabbed her hand. "It'll draw attention to us."

Light peeked through a one-foot gap between the buildings. She climbed over a half-dozen trash bags and side-stepped through the claustrophobic crevice until she reached the street. Carlo and Fosca popped out a few moments later.

Fosca glanced around. "How do we get back to the car?"

"I'm pretty sure I know the way, but let me see your phone."

Fosca handed it over and Julia brought up Google Maps. She knew they'd parked on a side street near Leidseplein. Confirming her bearings, she took off in a different direction to circumvent the Order men.

The trio sprinted through quiet back streets and over footbridges until they found the silver Peugeot again.

"You drive," Fosca said, tossing the keys to Julia.

She caught them. "What?"

"You know Amsterdam better than any of us, and Carlo doesn't even know how to ride a bike."

Carlo got in the back, and Fosca in the passenger seat. With no time to argue, Julia took her place behind the wheel and started the car. She passed Fosca's phone back to her.

"Get directions to Westland."

Julia pulled out of the minuscule spot and drove down Prinsengracht, the narrow canal-side road that cars shared with bikes and scooters. She slammed on the brakes. Twenty feet in front of them were the Order goons. She locked eyes with Lacasse.

"Merda," Carlo exclaimed from the back seat.

"Back up, back up," Fosca yelled.

Lacasse mouthed something and pointed. The four men raced toward them, with Lobo taking the lead.

Julia threw the car into reverse and floored it. Using the rearview mirror, she exhaled a sigh of relief that no cars were behind her. But two bicyclists pedaled at a leisurely pace. She honked the horn.

"What the hell," Fosca screamed.

Julia looked back at the windshield. Lobo's hands smacked the hood.

Carlo jutted his body forward so he was practically in the front. He glared at Lobo. "They must have the license plate," he said.

"One problem at a time!"

She honked furiously. The oblivious bikers veered out of the way.

Gassing the car, Julia peeled away from Lobo. At the next street, she braked and jammed the shifter into drive. Lobo grabbed her door handle and pounded on her window. Julia opened the door and shoved it into him, knocking the Painter to the ground. She stomped the gas pedal, tires spinning and bouncing on the uneven cobblestones. She glanced in the rearview mirror. Lobo chased them like a maniac. She cut down another street.

"Turn right here," Fosca said, reading the map on the phone.

Julia did.

"Left up ahead."

Fosca barked out more directions, which Julia followed until they reached the highway. The trio caught their collective breaths.

"We need new wheels," Fosca said.

"One problem at a time." Julia focused on the road.

"They'll figure out we're going to Westland." Carlo sounded more angry than concerned. "Or our mobiles. They're tracking our phones. Turn them off."

"One problem at a time," Julia said again.

Carlo quickly powered his phone down.

"We'll get burner phones." Fosca scribbled the directions on her hand, then did the same.

Her friends were right. They needed to address those problems immediately. "Maybe they can track the car with cameras or something. They don't know exactly where we're going. They can only tail us, which gives us a lead until we can ditch the car. More importantly, they don't know *why* we're going."

# XXX

"**I**T DOESN'T MAKE SENSE," Fosca said, watching the expanse of grassy marshland speed past them. "I had tracking turned off in my phone. So did you."

"I told you," Carlo replied. "There are cameras everywhere. Facial recognition tech is so good that it can find people wearing masks. We must've been spotted with the car. Other cameras can read license plates."

"How do you know so much about this, anyway?" Fosca asked.

"Because I can read."

"Can you?"

"Fine," Carlo chuckled. "I watch a lot of YouTube."

Julia shared a look with Fosca.

"Either way," she said, "we need to be safe. No phones and a new car."

They'd had the same conversation for the last forty-five minutes, and she didn't have an answer but suspected Carlo was spot-on. The only other possibility was a mole in the Guild, but if that were the case why wait until Amsterdam? When Lacasse had picked up Nick and Julia in Milan, he admitted Interpol found them with facial recognition cameras. Nothing was stopping the international police organization from doing it again. Julia and her friends needed to stay out of sight.

As signs for Westland appeared, she scanned the area in wide-eyed wonder. The entire trip had been a flat landscape of farms and marshes, with the occasional windmill dotting the green countryside. Westland was another story. She had expected a quaint village where women in aprons with baskets picked tulips. Instead, it was unlike anything she'd ever seen. They passed enormous greenhouse after greenhouse. Some stretched for what had to be half a mile, topped with hundreds of solar panels. It was like farms from the future.

"Turn left at the next driveway," Fosca said, only glancing at her hand before gaping at the surreal surroundings again.

A colorful 'Singel Flower' sign announced their destination. Julia turned into the parking lot for one of the gargantuan glass structures.

"We shouldn't leave the car here," Carlo said. "They could be thirty minutes behind."

Julia parked and turned it off. "You're right, but they need cameras if they're tracking the license plate." She gestured to the parking lot.

"True," he replied.

"It's not like the car is bugged." Julia exchanged uneasy glances with her friends.

"Let's just be quick," Fosca said. "We'll tell Hartog to ditch this car and use his."

"Can we trust him?" asked Julia.

"With the fortune my grandmother paid him? We'd better be able to trust him."

Crisp air conditioning welcomed them as they entered the reception area, which was like a sterile office. A young-twenties girl with blonde braids greeted them with a toothy grin and said something in Dutch.

"Hi," Fosca said. "Do you speak English? Ou français?"

"Yes, of course," replied the receptionist, still smiling. "Et un peu de français. But English is better. How can I help you?"

"We're here to see Jacob Hartog," Fosca replied.

"Do you have an appointment?" The girl's mouth seemed to be in a permanent upward angle.

"Tell him Contessa Baldesseri's granddaughter is here."

With a polite nod, the girl picked up a walkie-talkie and spoke into it. A muffled voice said something back.

"He's excited to see you," the receptionist said and gestured to a glass door. "He's with the Rembrandts?"

"Rembrandts?" Carlo asked.

"Yes, next to the purples. You'll find it."

The trio opened the door to a type of airlock smelling of eucalyptus and lemongrass. As they entered, high-pressure air blew from nozzles in the ceiling, spraying Julia's hair all over her face.

The air stopped. A light switched from red to green.

"I think they're decontaminating us from insects," Fosca said.

Another automatic door opened, and the team stepped out. The greenhouse had to be the size of a dozen football fields. Color-coded rows of tulips in every pigment imaginable stretched to the glass-wall horizon. Workers in green uniforms tended to the flowers. The air was warm and humid but inviting, like the perfect temperature for human skin. And the aroma...

"Oh, my God." Julia exchanged a grin with Fosca.

The two of them breathed in deeply. An intoxicating perfume of millions of fresh flowers graced Julia's nose. It was as if she were a ladybug that had just entered a bouquet. A sudden urge to find a blanket and lie down filled her, but she shook it off.

"Can you smoke in here?" Carlo asked.

Fosca slugged him on the shoulder.

"Look," Carlo said, pointing to the ceiling, still chuckling.

Each row had a giant banner hanging from the ceiling with a different color, indicating the flower color beneath it. They found the purple one and headed for it. Next to that row were tulips that could only be described as Rembrandts. It was the only row they'd seen that had multi-color flowers. Some were red and appeared as though they were hand-painted with yellow stripes. Some were white with splashes of purple. Others were pink and magenta.

"Simply gorgeous," she said.

"Where's the Tintoretto flower?" Carlo asked.

Before Julia could respond, a stout, mid-forties man barreled toward them, his loose-fitting green uniform flapping in the wake of his breeze. With wide arms, he rushed Fosca and wrapped her in a bear hug. About Fosca's height, his mop of brown hair and unruly beard intermingled with her pink-tip-dyed blond bob, creating a hairy Rembrandt tulip.

Julia twirled her finger in her black hair, nearly forgetting her original color.

"I heard the news," Hartog said with a tender voice. "I'm so sorry for your loss."

Fosca released her hold. "Thank you, Mr. Hartog."

"The zakkenwasser." His tone turned gruff. "I'd kill him myself if I had the chance."

He traced the line of her face. His green eyes were so pale, they were almost yellow, balancing beautifully with his light-brown complexion. "I told you when we met to call me Jacob," he said, pronouncing his name 'ya-kob.' He turned to Carlo and Fosca. "Who are your friends?"

"Jacob Hartog," Fosca said, "meet Carlo Zuccaro and Julia O'Connor."

"O'Connor?" he replied, raising an eyebrow. He rubbed the hair on his chin and turned to Fosca. "Isn't that the name of the other zakkenwasser? The one who murdered your grandmother?"

"We have a lot to talk about, Jacob. But first…" Fosca glanced around and lowered her voice. "Is there a place where we can abandon a car?"

After tailing Hartog's red Porsche Macan for twenty minutes through open farmland, Julia followed as he turned down a street between two plots of land and pulled over. She got out of the Peugeot with Carlo and Fosca, grabbing their overnight bags and a metal suitcase containing the manuscript.

"It's a nice car, the Peugeot," Hartog said from the window of his car.

"It'll be a hefty bill," replied Fosca. "But c'est la vie."

The trio piled into the Macan, and Hartog took off as if being chased. He drove another twenty minutes to a suburb of Rotterdam until he stopped at a nondescript Dutch diner. The group ordered beers and pommes frites while Fosca recounted everything to Hartog—Nick's plight, Carlo becoming the new Painter, della Porta killing the countess, Lobo, Julia's incarceration, her breakout, della Porta's plan to rule the world through Veritism, finding the doge's book and della Porta's subsequent possession of it, and lastly, the Chinese book containing drawings of the Sun Crystal.

As the two conversed, sporadically asking Julia and Carlo questions, it became clear that Hartog was once a member of the Order and an on-and-off Guild member. Clearly, Fosca trusted him.

"The briefcase," she said to Carlo.

"You want to do this here?" Julia asked.

Blue-collar patrons, almost all bearded men, filled half the other tables. Nobody paid attention to them.

"Do you have a better place?" Carlo asked.

"A hotel?"

"We don't have time for that," Fosca said. "This place is safe enough."

Nodding his agreement, Carlo opened the briefcase and turned it around to display it to Hartog. His eyes enlarged. He pushed his plate far away from him before wiping his hands and using hand sanitizer from his pocket. He donned a pair of cotton gloves from the briefcase and gingerly opened the book, leaving it in the case.

"Incredible," he said. He skimmed the Chinese, running his finger down the lines of characters but not touching the paper. Audible huffs of wonder popped from his mouth every thirty seconds. Whenever he needed to turn a page, he seemed hesitant to do so and held each page with two hands as if handling the most delicate and valuable thing in the world.

Julia glanced at Fosca and Carlo, who exchanged guilty looks with her.

When he came across the Sun Crystal drawings, he asked, "Where did you find this?"

"In nonna-mère's private library," Fosca said.

"Why didn't she share it with me? She showed me everything. I spent months with her."

"I don't think she knew about it."

"What does it say?" Julia asked. She recalled when Nick had been impatient, and now she felt the same.

"It's the journal of Ludovico Barbo, a Benedictine Monk of the San Giorgio Monastery, who traveled to Western Xia in China, which was part of the Tangut Kingdom. He was a devout member of the Ancient Order of the Seventh Sun. Around 1588, he and other monks realized the Order their brethren had founded on faith was corrupt from the inside. The power-hungry were insatiable. The monks needed a recourse, a safety net."

"A way to destroy the Sun Crystal," Fosca said.

"Precisely." Hartog tapped the air over a sketch of a yin-yang surrounded by sunrays. "So they sent Barbo to find one. He lived there for seven years."

"What happened to him?" Carlo shoved a couple of fries in his mouth, followed by three gulps of beer.

"I don't know." Hartog waved his hand over the writing. "It's a long book. And this isn't Chinese."

"It's not?" Julia asked.

"It's Fan, the Tangut dialect. The Tanguts, or the Western Xia Dynasty, was annihilated by the zakkenwasser Mongols in 1227. Only a handful of people outside of China can read this."

"It's all Chinese to me," Carlo said with a wide smirk.

Julia and Hartog groaned.

"It was kind of funny," Fosca said, smiling at Carlo.

He flashed his eyebrows then turned to Hartog. "What's a zakkenwasser?"

The Dutchman chuckled. "What do you think? It's someone who washes your klootzak." He brought his attention back to the book. "I would imagine fewer people could read this outside of China when it was written, back when eighty percent of Europe was illiterate. Don't you think it odd that an Italian monk's journal is in the Tangut dialect?"

Nobody answered.

"Not a chance Barbo wrote this himself," Hartog continued. "It's too perfect. He must've had it transcribed to keep it safe. Which means..."

It hit Julia. "Which means he was working with the Tanguts."

"Right. They knew the Venetians had the Sun Crystal. They knew *everything*. There's another point of interest, which is that the Tanguts had survived. We knew this. There are plenty living today, but not to this extent for the time period."

"Interesting, I'll give you that." Fosca raised her hands in agreement. "But let's fast forward to the present, huh? Does it say how to release the souls?"

Hartog went back to the book. He turned the pages, scanning each. At one point, he shook his head and backtracked, landing on a page with an illustration of a towering pagoda that spanned the entire page. He exhaled and looked up at the group.

"Well?" Fosca asked.

"Good news and bad news," Hartog replied.

"Were you like this with nonna-mère?"

"She loved a good cliffhanger more than most."

Fosca looked like she was about to rip her hair out. "Moving on..."

"Unfortunately, it doesn't say how to destroy the crystal."

All the wind left the sails. Julia had been sure this book contained the answer.

"But," Hartog said, tracing his fingers over the characters, "it does mention the Keeper of Secrets."

"What's that?" Julia asked, her voice perkier than intended.

Hartog gulped his beer. "More of a *who*, I suspect."

"You're saying this person knows the answer?" Carlo asked. "I thought this book was supposed to hold all the secrets."

"A journey is not complete without struggle," Hartog said with a sly grin.

"We've had plenty of that." Julia jabbed her finger into the page. Her rope finally frayed. "This is the end of the road. This book is ancient. If such a person existed, they died with their secrets."

"Not necessarily," Hartog said.

Carlo perked his head. "He has the power of the Sun Crystal? Extended life?"

Hartog continued reading. "No. The secrets were entrusted to an individual and passed down through the generations."

Julia shook her head. None of this sounded right.

"The Tangut Kingdom was destroyed," Fosca said, on Julia's wavelength. "The last Keeper would've been killed."

"They were *not* completely annihilated," said Hartog. "Tangut culture and language survive to this day."

Julia exchanged a silent conversation with Fosca and Carlo. They agreed: they had one last shot.

"Assuming a Keeper is still alive, how do we find him?"

Hartog pointed to the illustration. "The Pagoda of Chengtian Temple."

Fosca flashed her eyebrows at Julia and Carlo. "I always wanted to visit China."

# XXXI

A WIDE GRIN CROSSED della Porta's face as he climbed the Giants' Staircase in the Palazzo Ducale. Three Protectors nodded to him as he passed. As it was after hours, the Palazzo was closed to tourists, but abuzz with activity nonetheless. He had put the growing Order to work, recruiting additional Protectors and finding potential Painters who della Porta could dispatch around the world as ambassadors—and wardens.

The days flew by. Christmas was only three months away, and he needed to be ready. He planned on closing the museum soon—perhaps permanently. His base of operations required space. The world would lose a jewel, but with everything it would gain from Veritism, it was a reasonable price.

He reached the *loggia's* open-air hallway and strode toward the Great Council Room.

With the Vatican on board and the Order reaching a record number of Protectors and members, he was ahead of schedule by the slimmest of margins. That comforted him, but he had to expect the unexpected. Most importantly, he needed his Painter. Others could paint new souls, but only Carlo had a connection to those in the main *Paradise*. Besides the practicalities of requiring a Painter in Venice, it would be an embarrassment if he didn't rein in Carlo before he brought Veritism to the world. It would be like throwing a *diciottesimo* with the birthday girl in absentia.

He had a backup plan. Lobo could paint a soul; he had a few candidates for that honor. But to show the world the power of the one verifiable religion, he needed to transfer Carlo's power to a new Painter. Then Carlo could have the honor of joining his father in *Paradiso*.

Carlo continued to be a serrated thorn in his side. He knew there were whispers in the different councils—if he couldn't control his Painter, a boy he raised, what could he control? In a sense, they were right. Those whispers needed to be quashed.

According to Lacasse, Lobo had nearly apprehended Carlo in Amsterdam. Though it was unfortunate they had to cut their trip to Paris short, it had proved to be the right decision. The Interpol detective assured della Porta it was just a question of time before the authorities picked up the interlopers. They had their car's license plate. Even if they changed vehicles, the three couldn't hide forever. They needed to eat. They needed to sleep.

But what were they doing in Amsterdam? Hiding out? It seemed like a poor choice, especially with Fosca's wealth.

He filed the question away as he entered the open door of the Great Council Room. An early-thirties Venetian with light-brown hair that cascaded to her lower back stood on the dais at a canvas. She held a brush and palette in her trembling hands.

Three councilmembers in folding chairs sat in front of the dais, watching her every move.

Though she'd come recommended by Mayor Giovanelli and was indeed the man's original choice for Painter, della Porta knew she wasn't a viable candidate. While an accomplished and capable artist, how could she paint souls before hundreds of members if she couldn't complete something basic in front of three people?

"Exalted Master," Davide Zotti said with a welcoming nod.

Della Porta returned the gesture and climbed the stairs. He approached the artist with a calm demeanor, but she gasped at his arrival.

"May I?" della Porta asked, referring to the canvas.

"Of course." The woman took two steps back.

The work was surprisingly impressive—a faithful reproduction of a *Paradiso* snippet depicting a Roman soldier and seven anguished souls. The artist had captured Tintoretto's use of sweeping brushstrokes, finishing in under an hour. While della Porta could practically feel the vibrations of the woman's nerves, she performed admirably. He changed his mind—of the dozen candidates, she was now at the top of his list.

"Excellent," he said. "Well done."

She lifted her gaze from her shoes. A flabbergasted smile crossed her face.

"Grazie, signore."

"I can see why you recommended her, Giovanni," della Porta said to the mayor.

He stroked his goatee and crossed his arms. "If only you had listened to me in the first place."

Della Porta's phone rang. He ignored the mayor's comment and pulled the device from his inner jacket pocket. Detective Lacasse's face filled the screen.

"We have a lead," he said.

"Talk to me," della Porta replied. "This has been going on for too long already."

"They used their passports."

"They left the E.U.? To where? England?"

Lacasse smirked. "China."

Della Porta inhaled sharply. They were going to the roots of the Order. There could've been any number of reasons why. Were they looking for a way to reverse Carlo as Painter? To release the souls? Whatever the reason, so long as he got Carlo, nothing else would matter.

"Follow them, Monsieur Lacasse. Take Bernardo, Lobo, and Dante. And this time, don't come back empty-handed."

# XXXII

JULIA CRACKED HER NECK and poured the remaining sesame crackers into her mouth. Air China's coach-class seats were roomier than those of any U.S.-based airline she'd flown, but her butt was soundly asleep. Hartog snored next to her, a space-themed eye mask covering his eyes. She looked across the aisle, but Carlo and Fosca weren't in their seats. Except for a few people working on their laptops or watching movies, every passenger slept in the plane's dimmed lights.

After hopping a puddle jumper from Rotterdam to London, the team boarded the Air China plane for the eleven-hour flight to Shanghai. She'd already slept for four hours, ate two meals, and watched an Adam Sandler comedy, and they still had another three hours to go. They had four hours in Shanghai before catching another three-hour flight to Yinchuan, the location of the mysterious Tangut pagoda that housed the Keeper of the Secrets.

Though she didn't put much faith in this so-called secret keeper, and questioned if he still existed, the worst-case scenario was a trip to China.

The situation was ludicrous. In what seemed like a lifetime ago, she and her husband had left for a three-week trip to Italy. They never saw a city on their list other than Venice.

Instead, she'd been to Spain, France, Holland, and now China.

Fosca generously paid for their tickets in cash but said she was running low and needed to book coach. Given that the tickets were $2500 each, she had to go to a bank in Rotterdam before buying them through the only remaining travel agent in the city. Fosca assured Julia there was enough money to fund the Guild until the end, which was hopefully soon.

What concerned Fosca—and all of them—were the 5-by-3.5-inch booklets they carried for identification. Passports. They contemplated finding fake passports, but nobody had a lead on a forger. If they found one, it could've taken too long, and there was the additional risk of getting busted with counterfeit documents. Though it was clear Lacasse had used his Interpol resources to find them, they didn't think there was a warrant for any of their arrests. They chose to play the odds, and that gamble paid off.

That said, they didn't know the inner workings of the International Police Organization. Though they were allowed to leave the country, their passports could have been flagged, and Lacasse would've been alerted. Which means della Porta would know they headed to Shanghai.

Hartog had the brilliant idea to buy their Yinchuan tickets in the Shanghai airport. That gave them a good head start and few breadcrumbs for the Order to follow.

Needing to stretch her legs and use the restroom, Julia unbuckled her seatbelt and headed for the back of the plane. Regrettably, the two lavatories on her side of the Airbus A330 were occupied. She was about to cross over to the other aisle but ducked behind the partition. Emerging from one of the bathrooms on the opposite side were Fosca and Carlo, their giggling hardly concealing their lack of discretion.

He zipped up his fly and grabbed Fosca's waist. She turned around with her finger over her laughing mouth.

Julia's suspicions were confirmed. Now she had to deal with it.

In their distraction, she hustled to the back of the dimly lit aircraft. She reached the rear lavatories and spied the two of them returning to their seats, where they'd likely be unable to control their desires beneath one of the thin red blankets. Grateful for the solace, she slipped into a vacant restroom, locked the door, and pressed her head against the mirror.

The tears flowed uncontrollably.

She didn't want to leave until the plane landed.

She missed Nick so damn much.

# 1614

T HE RHYTHM OF CANAL water lapping against the *fondamenta* brought a nostalgic smile to Angelo Mascari's lips. It had been twenty-five years since he was forced to flee Venice. Twenty-five years since he had traversed Europe and the ocean. Twenty-five years since he had seen unimaginable wonders in the New World. All while being pursued by the Order.

He stood in the unsteady gondola with three of his newfound friends and compatriots. Though he'd known the men only four months, he trusted them with his life. Like them, Angelo had taken an oath to protect each other in their pursuit of destroying the Ancient Order of the Seventh Sun.

A late January breeze cut through him. He welcomed the cold, as it helped to still his nerves. A crescent moon scantily lit their surroundings. They had snuffed their lanterns upon arrival.

He wished he could've seen more of his city, that he could see his long-lost family, taste the food he so craved, and even lay eyes on his beloved Isabella in *Paradise*. Sadly, his death warrant rendered his wishes impossibilities. Even being on the edge of the city under cover of darkness was of great risk.

He had chosen the Rio di San Girolamo because it was the last place he'd seen when he left all those years ago. Though that moment was brief and also at night, he recalled every potential hiding spot, should they be ambushed. More importantly, they had a means of escape to the Venetian Lagoon.

"They're late." Ludo Stefanetti whispered the words in his throaty voice.

"They'll come. The temptation is too great for Quattrone." Angelo kept his eyes fixed on the canal corner, though he shared his friend's concern.

Their plan was rife with danger but had the potential for them to reap the reward they pursued. Senator Marco Quattrone, Exalted Master of the Order, had agreed to meet under the banner of a temporary truce. Not unexpected, for the Guild had been a deepening dagger in Quattrone's side—ever since Angelo joined.

Upon his return to the Veneto, he had sought out Ludo, knowing the man's father had been a member of the Guild of Silvanus. Angelo promptly joined the cause, swearing allegiance. With his knowledge of the New World and Quattrone's schemes, he had conceived a plan to negotiate the release of high-value prisoners of *Paradise*.

Another memory from a quarter-century prior graced Angelo's mind, one he didn't wish to disclose to his new friend. Around the corner from where their gondola now bobbed, Ludo's father—his identity then unknown—was murdered when he aided Angelo's escape.

That nobleman, Pietro Stefanetti—Isabella's uncle—gave his life to the cause. He had instructed Angelo to go to the New World until it was safe to return to free Isabella and the others. Angelo never imagined it would take twenty-five years. In that time, Tintoretto imprisoned hundreds of other souls and Quattrone had his sights on far greater designs. Angelo would give the man whatever he wanted, if only he could free Isabella.

"There," one of the two Guild soldiers whispered. He pointed to the canal corner.

The glow of a dim lantern hanging on a gondola's bow appeared.

Angelo and his men readied their crossbows. They had two-dozen bolts prepared at their feet and each had a sheathed rapier. Though Angelo's prowess with a blade was unmatched, he knew the Order's methods. They, too, would carry swords, but no doubt would use the crossbows as initial weapons. The unprepared never won battles.

The gondola made its silent approach.

"Who goes there?" Ludo asked. "Quattrone, is that you?"

"Keep your voice down," came an angry whisper.

The gondolier steered their craft broadside to the Guild's.

Four men stood in the boat in the muted light. As expected, three of them—Protectors—wielded crossbows. Mongolian short swords hung at their hips. A bearded man, about sixty-five years of age, positioned himself in the center of the gondola.

"Which one of you is Angelo Mascari?" he asked. His voice was deep and he spoke with confidence.

"Are you Quattrone?" Angelo replied.

"You shall address me as Exalted Master."

Angelo narrowed his eyes. "I shall do no such thing."

"Very well," Quattrone replied. "Then 'Senator' will suffice. You are still a Venetian, are you not?"

"I have always been and will always be. I left only because I was forced to leave. By your hand."

"Your hand turned the dials of fate."

"I was thrust into a machination not of my making."

"Yet you embraced it wholeheartedly."

Unable to control his temper, Angelo raised his crossbow. Quattrone's Protectors matched his stance. Angelo's forefinger rested on the metal trigger; how he longed to squeeze it and release a bolt into Quattrone's throat. If he did, the same would happen to him. He had no fear of death, but it would accomplish nothing—the Order would instate a new Exalted Master and all the souls would remain in *Paradise*.

"With all due respect, Senator," Ludo said. "Did we come out here at this time of night to discuss Angelo's history or our proposal? Do you agree to our terms?"

Quattrone nodded at his men to lower their weapons. They did as instructed. Angelo relaxed his grip and lowered his. Ludo and their compatriots followed suit.

"Tell me about Vito Uccello," Quattrone said.

"You already know him," Angelo replied. "He's your man."

"You were in the New World with him. Things changed between the two of you. Why?"

Angelo exhaled through his nose. He had no desire to rehash past events and less interest in providing the senator with any information outside of their terms.

"Will you release Isabella and the others we requested?" He phrased the statement as a question but uttered it as a demand.

"Provide me with the information and maps of the New World you claim to have," Quattrone replied, "and they shall be released immediately."

"Release them first. I need to witness. Then, and only then, shall I provide you with the promised items."

Quattrone raised an eyebrow. "Very well. It will happen by week's end. We will make arrangements with your envoy."

Angelo glanced at Ludo. He nodded back.

"Then we have an agreement," Angelo said to Quattrone.

He indicated to one of his compatriots to depart. Still holding his crossbow, with his free hand, the man lifted the gondola pole and pushed off.

Angelo never moved his eyes from his enemies.

"If you don't honor your word," he said, "the Guild will never cease fighting the Order. We shall release all the souls and banish the Order to hell."

"I'd like to see you try," replied Quattrone, his voice carrying across the water.

# XXXIV

O F ALL THE REGRESSIONS that Carlo experienced, those to Angelo Mascari always unnerved him the most. In part, it was a reminder that he had sentenced Nick's soul. In doing so, he obtained Nick's memories and those of all his past lives, including Angelo. More importantly, it always amazed Carlo that events from over four-hundred years prior had lasting effects that rippled in a circle of violence to the present day.

Quattrone never lived up to his end of the bargain. No souls were ever released. Was it because Quattrone himself had been betrayed by the Order and sentenced to the Spanish *Paradise*? Or perhaps there was something else, such as a societal or political incident, that prevented him from doing so. More likely, it was because Quattrone was well aware he needed an artifact to perform the task—an artifact that Carlo and his friends had traveled halfway across the world to find.

His thoughts scattered, like the images of the enormous city flying by his window of the small rental car. Fosca sat in the back with Julia while Hartog drove. They rode in silence, exhausted from the trip.

He glanced back at Fosca, throwing a quick smile her way. He couldn't believe how quickly their bond flourished. Their physical connection was undeniable. They were two pieces of the same puzzle; their bodies fit together perfectly. Moreover, their spirits seemed to meld. They did their best to hide their relationship from Julia, but when they were alone, they were in sync, with their personalities balancing each other out. Gone were his feelings for Julia, replaced by Fosca. He felt awkward, which was strange since he knew it was for the best. Real guilt came from finding happiness when Julia was so distraught over losing Nick—an action he caused by his own hand. Hopefully, they were driving to the remedy for that situation.

Knowing they were so close to finding a way to end della Porta and the Order and freeing Nick and the other souls, Carlo indulged in contemplations of the impending future—a month cocooned in Fosca's embrace. Needing to focus on accomplishing that goal, he concentrated on the city zipping by.

He had read about Yinchuan on the plane. Located in Western China in the Ningxia Hui Autonomous Region, the city sat in the Gobi Desert outside the Great Wall. But since the Yellow River snaked through the ancient metropolis, the land was much more fertile than he had expected.

For a place he'd never heard of, he was shocked to learn it had a population of 2.3 million. The city was founded in the year 678 CE and had been a stop on the Silk Road. That, of course, made sense, given Venice was the final destination of Silk Road traders for centuries. The Order's origins traced back to Marco Polo, who had visited the area in his travels.

They were in the right place.

Yinchuan's cleanliness and open layout was also a surprise. He had expected the metropolis to be cramped and serpentine, much like Venice, Rome, and other ancient cities, but it was the opposite.

The architecture showcased a harmonious blend of traditional and modern elements, with ornate pagodas and mosques standing alongside sleek high-rise buildings. Contrasting styles created an intriguing skyline that exposed the city's cultural diversity and embrace of the present.

The warmth and friendly nature of the people touched Carlo. From people in the airport to the car rental agency, locals offered kind smiles and helpful gestures, making the team feel welcome and at ease in this new environment. He suspected much of their disposition came from Hartog's fluency in Mandarin. Carlo had experienced the same in Venice countless times. Though he spoke fluent English and was conversant in other languages—and was before gaining new knowledge as Painter—if a non-Italian tourist made an effort to speak the language, he'd automatically respond more favorably.

Hartog pulled off a city street and entered a park, passing a sign in Chinese and English welcoming visitors to Haibao Park, a beautiful green space nestled next to a lake. They took an arched bridge over a slow-moving river with rocky outcrops and arrived at the parking lot for the Haibao Temple.

Stepping out of the car, Carlo joined the women as they took in their surroundings. The dry autumn air had a floral scent mixed with a woodsy essence that felt contradictory to the arid geography.

"Gorgeous," Julia said with a smile.

Ahead of them was the Haibao Temple grounds, a walled area within the park. The entrance, which Carlo assumed was a gatehouse, had a sloping Chinese-style roof, beneath which was colorfully decorated wood and banners with Chinese characters. Two stone Asian lions flanked the gatehouse. Though they couldn't yet see the other structures inside the temple complex due to the perimeter wall and trees, one building dominated the skyline before them—the Haibao Pagoda Temple.

The eleven-story structure reminded Carlo of a narrow apartment building. About half the height of St. Mark's Campanile in Venice and made of ashen-colored stone, each floor had three faux arched windows, one jutting out and two set back. Though he could only see two sides of the building from his vantage point, since they were identical, he assumed all four were symmetrical. A large, green onion bulb adorned a pyramidal top.

"That's it," Hartog said, joining them. "Shall we?"

He led the way through the gatehouse, followed by Fosca and Julia with Carlo at the end.

The complex felt like a village, with dozens of buildings, incense wells, and shrines. Besides the pagoda, the three main structures were Buddhist halls of varying design and style. Two stood across from each other in a diametric position. Tourists snapping pictures on their phones strolled about the complex while monks in orange robes and shaved heads went about their business. There were also additional workers, all wearing olive-green uniforms, raking, tending to the buildings, or standing in front of the various other smaller buildings dotting the campus, which appeared to be dorms, classrooms, kitchens, and other infrastructure. A sundry shop had a rack of chips and a bucket of water bottles outside. A kiosk close to them sold incense sticks. A robed man wheeled a cart by them with beaded necklaces for sale.

"We're in the right place," Julia said, pointing to the two halls. "Duality."

Wooden wind chimes sang a gentle song in the distance.

"Exactly," Hartog said. "Those are the Hall of the Jade Buddha and the Hall of the Four Heavenly Kings. But we're here for the pagoda. Come."

As they walked the park-like setting, all motor traffic dissipated, creating a sanctuary of peace and harmony that captured Carlo. He released a contented sigh. Though he'd never been there, he felt... settled, like he had returned home.

"Is the Keeper of the Secrets at the top of the pagoda?" Fosca asked, looking up at the imposing structure.

"Of course," Hartog said with a straight face. "She—or he—will throw down their hair."

"You're kidding, right?" Julia asked. She tied her hair up in a ponytail using a hairband on her wrist.

Hartog chuckled and scratched his beard. "We'll find out. Pagodas are typically empty inside. Some have stairs, like this one, but there aren't any rooms. You can just go up there and take in the view. I suspect our Keeper will be somewhere in the complex, but we may as well start at the pagoda."

"So if they're empty," Fosca said, "what are pagodas for?"

"Not all are empty," Hartog replied. "Some contain relics. They're used for places of prayer, meditation, and paying respects to the Buddha." He gazed upward at the tower. "They symbolize enlightenment. Unlike Christianity, they're not used as places of congregational worship but are more focused on personal spiritual practice."

"They're pretty cool architecturally," Carlo said.

As he lifted his head, a mouthwatering aroma wafted into his nose, tantalizing his growling stomach. They hadn't eaten anything since their flight from Shanghai. The congee—rice porridge with pork—wasn't half bad, and three cups of coffee helped, but now he needed something more substantial. He turned his nose toward the source of the scent and spied three wooden food stalls that beckoned him.

"How about we eat something first?" Carlo asked. "We don't want to meet the Keeper of Secrets on an empty stomach."

"We also don't want to miss an opportunity because we're dillydallying," Hartog replied. "The food will be there when we're done."

Continuing toward the pagoda, they passed additional incense wells. A new scent hit Carlo—a fragrant blend of burnt earth that filled the air with a serene ambiance. An older Asian couple stood at the well, with three sticks of lit incense pressed between their hands. They bowed in unison toward the well.

They continued, passing shrines filled with various dedications to the Buddha, as well as what Carlo could only describe as an open-air bookshop or mini library with three bookshelves. He guessed the books had to do with Buddhism and were for the monks. A woman in her mid-eighties with shriveled tan skin sat cross-legged on the floor, her back pressed against one of the bookshelves. A long, thin silver pipe was nestled in her palm. Trails of light gray smoke that matched the color of her stringy hair rose from the pipe's bowl.

Besides the odd vignette, Carlo was taken aback by the woman's stark gaze. She stared directly at him. Or, really, more like *into* him. Unsettled, he caught up to the others.

As the pagoda came into complete view, he realized it sat on a two-level pedestal that raised the tower's height by another six or seven meters. A broad staircase led to the tower door—a weathered, red-arched door that was shut, with a sign on it.

"Strontballen." Hartog threw his hands up in frustration.

"What's wrong?" Fosca asked.

The group climbed the pedestal to the door. Hartog read it, but Carlo didn't need to understand Chinese to know what it meant.

"It's closed," Hartog said. He turned to a young couple and exchanged words in Chinese. When they finished the conversation, he spoke to the group. "It's been closed for two years for renovations. They don't know when it'll be open again."

"I guess we really will be climbing someone's hair," Julia said, looking upward. "I hope they washed it."

The group released a collective sigh of dismay. They'd come all this way to be stymied yet again.

"What now?" asked Carlo.

Hartog rubbed his beard. "Like I said, I wasn't expecting the Keeper to be in the tower." He began walking the pedestal's square veranda that wrapped around the tower.

The additional six or seven meters gave them a bird's-eye view of the temple grounds but didn't offer anything new.

"Why don't we split up and ask people?" Julia asked. "Hopefully some speak English."

Fosca nodded. "I like that idea."

"Same." Carlo smiled. "I'll ask the food vendors."

"Be subtle," said Hartog. "We don't want to spook anyone and lose our one shot."

The group continued back toward the stairs.

"Why would we spook them?" Julia asked.

Fosca and Hartog exchanged a glance. "There are thoughts," she said, "that there could've been a rift between the Order and the Tanguts."

The information rocked Carlo. None of his regressions had alluded to such a thing. "You're just telling us this now?"

"We don't know for sure," Hartog replied as he descended the flight. "If it happened at all, it was after Ludovico Barbo visited. There may have been a second emissary. Some zakkenwasser who had less than reasonable demands."

"That was hundreds of years ago," Julia said.

"Grudges don't die here," said Hartog.

They reached the bottom of the stairs.

"And the second emissary? Where did he die?" asked Carlo.

"Nobody living even knows his name," replied Hartog. "Like I said, there have only been whispers about this. Hints in different texts."

Hartog's answer explained why Carlo hadn't seen anything about it. Maybe Quattrone didn't even know. Then again, Carlo only saw snippets of memories. He hoped the Order hadn't wronged the Tanguts—the creators of the Sun Crystal—on top of all their other crimes. Either way, he needed to focus on their present mission.

"I'll go that way," he said, staking his claim for the food vendors.

"Don't mention anything about the Keeper of the Secrets or the Order," Hartog said. "Just say you're on a research trip and would like to speak with the person most knowledgeable of the temple's history."

Carlo chuckled. "My Chinese is a little rusty, but I'll do my best."

"Right," said Hartog. "If you find someone, come get me, and I'll speak to them."

Carlo raised his hand in a wave as he wandered off. He'd been growing tired of chasing kites in a storm, especially one that could lead to his death. If he was going to do this, he needed dumplings in his stomach.

Heading back to the food stalls, he passed the library stand. Again, the peculiar elderly woman stared at him. She removed the pipe from her cracked lips.

"We've been waiting a long time, Latin," she said.

Carlo cocked his head, amazed at the words. And even more amazed that she had uttered them in Fan, the Tangut language. It was a tonal language, predominantly mono-syllabic... *and he understood every word.*

That he knew Fan meant only one thing—a Tangut was sentenced to *Paradise.* Hartog was right. The Order *did* betray them. How did this woman know who he was? Was she the Keeper of the Secrets?

She flapped her aged-spotted hand, gesturing for him to come closer.

As he did, she packed more tobacco into her pipe. He longed for a cigarette, but he'd been refraining as much as possible for Fosca. He had only smoked one in the last twenty-four hours, at the Shanghai airport.

The woman whispered something, but he couldn't make out the words.

"What?" he asked in Fan.

She mumbled and beckoned him forth.

"I'm sorry, I can't hear you," he said in English.

She motioned him to come closer.

Carlo did. He crouched to her, now eye to eye, so close he could touch her. The woman's face bore a tapestry of wrinkles, each crease a testament to the wisdom that had woven the intricate history of her years. She put her lips to the pipe, angled it down, and blew into it. A puff of smoke rose from the bowl, consuming Carlo's face.

Carlo blinked his eyes half open. Groggy and in a daze, he didn't know how long he was out or where he was. An eerie, greenish light lit the darkened room. He felt weightless and disoriented, unsure which way was up, down, or even left or right.

A disturbing sensation he wasn't alone overcame him.

Trying to turn, his heart skipped a beat.

He looked at his feet and gasped. Weightlessness wasn't a sensation—he was in the air. Worse, he couldn't see a floor. The depths beneath him extended forever.

He checked his hands and body for ropes or chains, but nothing suspended him.

His brain quickly shifted to a greater concern. As his eyes and ears adjusted, they confirmed his suspicion: he was *not* alone. Far from it.

People—or beings—surrounded him. Above, beneath, to his sides. A foot kicked his head.

Carlo cried out.

The murmurs began.

First, as a slow drone, as if waking from a deep slumber. Then they grew disturbed, some screaming in pain.

Carlo twisted his body one-hundred-eighty degrees.

He realized where he was.

*Paradise.*

Before him was an impossible vision: the Great Council Room. As if looking through a transparent fabric, he saw everything. People bustled about. Della Porta stood on the dais with Davide Zotti, pointing at the walls and ceiling as if explaining something. Sounds from the room seeped through the fabric, but the cries of the souls drowned them out.

*How did the woman send me here?*

The screams increased—the voices of the damned, their anger directed at him, the Painter. Like him, they could only move their limbs and twist their bodies, suspended in painted positions.

Panic set in. He had to get out of there. If the volume were anything like he'd heard from the other side, it would be exponentially unbearable from within the painting.

The old woman from the temple complex climbed to the dais in the Great Council Room. She walked through della Porta and approached the painting.

"Why are you here, Latin?" she asked, her voice clear through the cacophony.

Carlo struggled in his confined position. He was desperate to be free.

"To learn how to destroy the Sun Crystal," he blurted out.

Carlo blinked his eyes half open. Groggy and in a daze, he realized he was back in the park, sitting before the old woman. He offered a half smile, relieved he said the correct answer.

"Wrong," the woman said in Fan.

She blew into the pipe. A cloud of smoke engulfed Carlo.

Carlo blinked his eyes half open. Groggy and in a daze, he recognized his surroundings immediately. He was back in *Paradise*. The souls were awake. The moment he appeared, they began their furious screams. He could make out the words of those closest.

They demanded freedom.

He had questioned if even the evil souls deserved it. He'd also questioned if eternity was too great a punishment. Now, he knew the answer.

He shifted his body to face the canvas. The old woman stood next to della Porta, who continued speaking with Zotti as if only a second had ticked by.

"Why are you here, Latin?" she asked.

Knowing his previous answer was wrong, Carlo didn't respond. Adjacent souls jostled him. Every muscle in his body tightened—a soul about his age reached for his throat.

"To free the souls," Carlo shouted, though he now thought maybe some *did* deserve their sentences.

Carlo blinked his eyes half open. Groggy and dazed, he sat before the woman again, praying he said the right thing.

"Wrong."

She blew into the pipe. A cloud of smoke engulfed Carlo.

Carlo blinked his eyes half open.

As if expecting him, the souls shouted at him when he appeared. They twisted their bodies, their arms outstretched for him. It wasn't his imagination—they were getting closer.

He searched for his father amidst the horde, but it was a futile attempt with so many souls surrounding him.

"Why are you here, Latin?" the woman demanded.

Carlo didn't know what to say.

"I... I don't know."

Carlo blinked his eyes half open.

"Wrong."

A cloud of smoke engulfed him.

Carlo blinked his eyes half open.

He lost track of how many times he'd been transported back to the painting. She'd asked him the same question over and over. Maybe hundreds of times. Was it hours? Days? An eternity?

Was he doomed to suffer like Tantalus, always tasting freedom but never obtaining it? Could his friends save him?

He didn't know how the woman could work this magic. And he didn't care. He just needed to get out.

The souls continued their relentless screeches, commanding him for freedom, ordering him to reverse the wrongs laid on them.

"Why are you here, Latin?" the woman asked.

The souls' hands draped over him—ripping his clothes, in his hair, pulling his limbs. Fingers jabbed into his chest, squeezing for his heart. Other hands gripped his face. Teeth bore down on him.

This was it.

He couldn't breathe. He couldn't speak even if he knew the answer.

He had one last chance.

"To right wrongs," he said with decrepit fingers in his mouth. "To right the wrongs of hundreds of people over hundreds of years." A long-lost thought tickled his brain. He stared deep into the woman's eyes. "Including you and your people."

Fragments of images flashed before Carlo: two Venetian men shouting at a group of Tanguts... one of the Venetians driving a sword into an elderly man's heart... Tanguts wailing and mourning... a Tangut man chained to a chair in the Great Council Room.

The woman flashed a toothless smile.

She clapped her hands together and bowed.

The souls snapped back to their positions, leaving Carlo dangling in the ether in silence. Chest heaving, he wished he was on the other side, but thankful the souls stopped their clawing and screaming.

"If that is true, Latin," the woman said in Fan, "you must make the ultimate sacrifice. All three Painters are tethered to the Sun Crystal."

"I know," Carlo replied. "Can the souls be put back in their bodies? Is that possible?"

"As steam escapes from the kettle, it is no longer water."

"Then how can I right wrongs?"

"You do not listen. Steam continues to rise unless blocked. The souls wish to ascend. You and your brethren have caused them great pain and suffering."

"I want to end it. I do. I am ready."

The woman closed her eyes briefly and bowed her head.

"There are one hundred and eight pagodas," she said. "Find a bowl. Only this bowl can destroy the Sun Crystal."

The Keeper brought her hands together, ready to clap.

"Wait," Carlo said. "How can I help you and the Tanguts?"

She only smirked and clapped her hands together.

Carlo blinked his eyes half open. Groggy but aware he was back in the park, he needed an answer.

"Please," he said. "I want to help."

The smoke cleared. The woman was gone. He sat on the ground, his back against a bookcase.

Bittersweet emotions roared through him. Finally, he learned how to destroy the Sun Crystal. He knew he had to go with it and didn't worry about his life, but how could he right all the wrongs if the Tanguts weren't avenged?

"What are you doing?" asked the sweet voice he'd grown so fond of.

He gazed up to find Fosca, the sun breaking through the clouds, haloing her head. She truly was a beauty, inside and out.

"You okay, babe? Why are you sitting there?"

Carlo smiled. "Why don't you join me?"

"Come on, get up."

"Thanks for coming back for me. How long has it been?"

Fosca gawked at him quizzically. "Are you smoking this incense or something? What are you talking about?"

Carlo pulled himself to his feet. Earlier emotions of dread and dismay lifted. A great peace enveloped him. He gazed at the temple complex, taking in its splendor. He hadn't appreciated it before, but the structures worked harmoniously with the nature surrounding it.

"I've been gone for days," he said. "Perhaps years."

Fosca screwed up her face. "Now you're really freaking me out. It's been like six or seven minutes. I only came back to see if you wanted to grab a bite."

Carlo smiled. "I am hungry," he said thoughtfully. Her revelation that it had only been a few minutes settled much of his mind.

"Hey," Julia said, approaching with Hartog. "You guys find anything?"

"Ask Carlo," Fosca said. "Seems like shrooms or something found him."

Hartog looked into Carlo's eyes and scratched his beard. "Did you find the Keeper?"

"I believe I did," Carlo said, beginning to feel like his old self. "But it doesn't make any sense. She said there are one hundred and eight pagodas."

Hartog slapped his thigh. "Of course. I'm such a dumb zakkenwasser. How could I not think of that? It makes perfect sense. The 108 Pagodas is a place. It was part of a Buddhist temple constructed by the Tanguts in the eleventh century."

Carlo looked back up at the Haibao Pagoda, the setting sun casting a cinnamon hue over the area. "There's a place with 108 of those? That's what she meant?"

"They're not quite as tall..." Hartog rubbed the beard around his open mouth as if he'd stumbled upon a long-lost architectural find. "The pagodas represent a fusion of Chinese, Tibetan, and Central Asian influences. This region was a crossroads of diverse cultures and religions. Sound familiar?"

He made for the exit.

"Fuck," Fosca said in a loud whisper. She pulled the three others behind a shrine. "You've gotta be kidding me."

"What?" Carlo asked. A pang of fear shot through him. Was the woman back?

"Keep your voice down," she said, pulling everyone into a crouching position behind the shrine. She motioned her head toward the Hall of the Jade Buddha.

Carlo couldn't believe it. Speaking—or trying to converse—with the Keeper of Secrets was none other than Lobo. Behind him stood Bernardo, Dante and Lacasse. The old woman sat stoically while Lobo used pronounced body language.

Carlo exchanged a worried look with his friends. Besides the potential ramifications of Lobo recognizing the Keeper of Secrets or having a similar experience in *Paradise*, the Order was far too close for comfort.

Hartog tugged on his shirt and pointed toward the gatehouse. They made a mad break for it.

# XXXV

"**Y**OUR PHONE IS OFF, right?" Fosca asked. She threw an accusatory look at Carlo, who sat in the passenger seat.

"Yes," he replied. "I'm more concerned with how Lobo knew that was the Keeper."

Julia sat next to Fosca in the back while Hartog drove to the site of the 108 Pagodas. How those goons had found them—and continued to find them—was a mystery. Did Interpol's reach extend this far? Using facial recognition cameras in the airport was one thing, but at an ancient temple?

"Maybe they're just on the same track," she said.

"They want Carlo," Fosca said.

"Yes," agreed Hartog. "If the zakkenwassers knew we came to China, they'd make a logical connection that he'd be here. Carlo, how did *you* know that was the Keeper?"

"I didn't, really. I just felt a connection."

"Well, there you go," Hartog replied. "Maybe Lobo also felt it."

"Except if there's anything that can destroy the Sun Crystal," Carlo added, "they'll want that too."

"Does it matter?" Julia asked. "How the hell are we gonna get away from them?"

"We're a step ahead," Fosca replied. "We can do this."

Julia let out a weary sigh. She had thought they'd be able to find the artifact in peace. Besides the Order on their tail, Carlo related his experience with the woman sending him to *Paradise*. A strange, disconcerting sense of comfort settled over her. She wished the woman had sent him to Nick's painting. The knowledge that the souls existed in the ether, no matter how painful, proved that a part of Nick lived on. They were that much closer to freeing him. Whether she could see or speak to him again—let alone touch him—was another story entirely.

"You know, Carlo," she said. "I don't think that woman transported you to *Paradise*. You have a connection to the souls. She tapped your mind. Maybe from the perspective of a soul in there, just like you can get their memories and speak their language."

The group drove in silence for a moment, contemplating her statement.

"I think you're right," Carlo said. "It makes sense."

Julia switched her attention to the window. As they followed a road alongside the Yellow River, the terrain shifted from urban to fertile to desert. She yearned for her camera. The golden hour light was stunning, causing the sandy mountains to glow a crisp orange. Four tan, deer-like animals with long, spiraled horns grazed on the sparse vegetation. Despite the scenery, they'd been driving for an hour, and she was getting antsy.

"It seems unlikely she'd tell Lobo and his guys about the 108 Pagodas," she said, "but we can't take any chances."

"Maybe she'll send Lobo to the abyss permanently," Carlo said.

"Let's hope she had her pipe." Hartog pulled off the road and entered a vacant parking lot.

"This place better not be closed," Fosca said.

Hartog turned the car off. Everyone got out.

"I don't believe it ever closes." He pointed to the sun. "But you don't want to be out here at night. And don't expect mobile service."

A shiver scurried over Julia. A little sunlight remained, and the temperature had dropped ten or more degrees. While she was glad they were alone there so they could examine the pagodas without interference, Hartog's comment worried her. Jeans were fine, but her black T-shirt wouldn't suffice.

As they left the parking lot, Carlo pressed on Julia's arm, slowing her down while Hartog and Fosca forged ahead.

"I'd like you to do something for me." His voice was low and infused with desperation.

"What?" After everything, Julia couldn't imagine what he'd want from her, let alone what she'd do.

"If it comes to it, you need to kill me."

Julia swallowed. Killing the Painter had come up, and, of course, she'd thought about doing it out of revenge, but Carlo had never made the request. It was one thing to frivolously say or think about it in passing. Actually ending another person's life was another story.

He picked up on her thoughts.

"I'll be immortalized," he said, as if that were consolation. "It's every artist's dream."

"It is?"

"Well, typically after a long, natural life, but yes."

Fosca turned back to find them lagging. "Come on, you two. Let's go."

Julia had killed El Greco, but the man wasn't supposed to have been alive. Then again, they needed to liberate the souls and stop della Porta. That was the goal of this whole mission—if they could destroy the Sun Crystal, the Painter needed to go with it. There was no way around that fact.

"Okay," Julia whispered. "I'll do it."

Carlo offered a sad smile. "Thank you."

Hartog brought everyone into a wide, paved space that was the inverse of the Haibao Temple complex. Where that one felt lush and mysterious, this place was cold and dead. Two small shrines stood opposite one another on a paved floor.

She followed Hartog's gaze; he stared upward appreciatively.

Built into the sandy mountainside that abutted the area were 108 bell-shaped stone pagodas arranged in a pyramidal formation, with the largest pagoda at the top. Another shrine was further up the hill.

With the sun inching behind the mountain, the pagodas cast long shadows that toppled into each other, creating an even more dramatic effect.

"When Genghis Khan sacked the Tangut Kingdom," Hartog said, "the Tangut emperor offered vast riches as terms of surrender, but nothing appeased the Great Khan."

"He was after power." Carlo winked at Hartog. "The zakkenwasser."

"A mystical power," Hartog replied. "But he never got it. Genghis was the biggest zakkenwasser of all. On his death bed, he ordered the complete obliteration of the Tanguts, which they nearly did. There are very few living descendants. Kublai Khan, Genghis's grandson, discovered a cache of treasures in a monastery, but were unable to tap the Tanguts' power. That cache included the Sun Crystal, which was gifted to Marco Polo, who then brought it to Venice. If Kublai knew of its power, he never would've given it away."

"Now we have Salvatore della Porta," Carlo said.

"Whoa," Fosca said, still eyeing the pagodas. "The tool that will destroy the Sun Crystal is in one of those? And the woman didn't tell you which?"

Carlo shook his head. Hartog massaged his beard.

Fosca wasn't kidding. Julia backed up for a better view. The thought of checking all 108 pagodas was intimidating. Even trying to isolate a single one felt dizzying. Still, there had to be a way to narrow it down. The Order often obsessed with numbers, especially seven. She counted twenty pagodas on the bottom row before calculating that 108 wasn't divisible by seven. Then she realized it didn't matter—there were seven rows climbing up the mountain.

And the seventh row had seven pagodas.

She hustled for one of the two flanking staircases. "I got it. Come on. We don't have much daylight left."

Her friends quickly caught up.

As they neared the pagodas, Julia realized they were bulkier than she'd thought from the ground. Each one was about ten feet tall and reminded her of a dinner bell, with a base roughly four feet in diameter. Rather than stone, they were constructed of bricks set on octagonal pedestals. The pagodas were capped with metal discs or octagonal shapes and topped with balls or gourd-like shapes.

"Did the Tanguts capture souls?" Julia asked.

"There's no indication they did," Hartog replied. "It's possible they sent souls directly into the ether, but that's theory. Nobody knows and nobody ever will."

The wind picked up as they ascended the stairs. The Yellow River snaked through the desert below. At the seventh level, Julia turned into the row of seven pagodas. Each was unique, with different carvings of animals, designs, or Chinese characters.

The group stopped at the fourth pagoda, the center of the row.

Julia's breath caught in her throat. "Look at the designs. This is it."

One half of a yin-yang was alternately carved into each of the four sides of the pagoda, indicating they were in the right place, but the bricks were packed with mortar. There was no clue that any could be removed, let alone that something was hidden inside it. From what she could tell, all the pagodas were of solid construction.

"I thought you said pagodas are hollow," she said to Hartog.

"These are more like statues. And over a thousand years old."

"Did your lady friend say how to open it?" Fosca asked Carlo. "Or what we're even looking for?"

"My lady friend?" Carlo replied with a chuckle. "No, she didn't bother to mention that after she cast me into the infinite abyss."

Looking for differences, Julia examined the pagoda next to them, then went back and forth to the center one. Whereas their target pagoda had the four half-yin-yang symbols, the one next to them had a geometric design. She looked up. The first stars poked through the darkening desert sky. The center pagoda's cap caught her eye.

"Jacob, hand me your cell phone," she said to Fosca. "I need the light."

He handed over the device, and Julia activated the flashlight. She propped herself on the pedestal and shine the light on the cap. She was right—it was a little different. Chinese characters were faintly embossed on the sides. She climbed around the pagoda and found four of them.

"Check this out," she said, jumping down.

Hartog joined her and took the flashlight. "Remarkable. These are the Xia characters for north, east, west, and south." He paused and viewed the river, puzzled. "They're facing the wrong directions."

Almost simultaneously, Julia exchanged an excited glance with Carlo and Fosca.

"Turn it to the right direction," she said.

Hartog tried, but it didn't budge. He passed the cell phone back to Julia. Carlo stepped onto the pedestal and joined him. They tried together, but nothing.

"Wait," Hartog said. "Turn it counter-clockwise."

"It's moving," Carlo said.

Together, they turned it ninety degrees.

"That should do it," Hartog said. "East is now pointing toward the river."

Julia pursed her lips and circumnavigated the pagoda. "Nothing happened—"

She cut herself off, realizing what she was looking at. Each half of the yin-yang carvings had a small dot embedded within the swirled teardrop. She rubbed her finger over the circle. It was indented, like an inverted button. "Guys, jump down."

They did.

"This is like Tintoretto's box." She pointed to the shapes. "Four sides, diametrically opposed to each other. It's the yin-yang. Duality. These circles sure look like buttons to me." She stretched her arms out. She was able to reach two. "Just like the box, it would require two people to open. There are four of us. Shall we?"

Everyone placed their finger on a dot.

"On three. One... two... now."

They pressed their buttons. The slightest swish sound resonated around Julia's knees. She crouched for a closer look. A set of seven bricks had popped out about an inch, all mortared together.

"Holy..."

Her friends gathered around her. Excitement brimmed in all of them. Could this be it? After so long, after so many disappointments, she didn't want to look. She couldn't take another failure.

"What are you waiting for?" asked Hartog.

Julia took a deep breath. She gripped the sides of the brick set and tugged it out. It was heavier than she expected, and it slipped. Carlo caught it in a flash before it landed on her foot.

"Thanks," she said.

"Anytime."

She shined the flashlight into the hole. Reaching in, she retrieved a yellow velvet bag cinched at the top. There was something bulky inside, but it wasn't heavy. She grinned at her friends and handed the light to Hartog.

She opened the bag and removed a bowl and pestle.

In the light beam, it looked like the bowl was made of brass or bronze and the pestle was made of jade or green marble. A pattern of indentions circled the exterior.

"A taijitu," Hartog said, pointing to an etching of a yin-yang surrounded by seven sunrays on the inner bottom.

"What the hell are we supposed to do with that?" Fosca asked.

"Buonasera, Carlo!"

The high-pitched voice came from the ground. Its echo ricocheted between the pagodas. Julia's heart dropped. She had never met its owner, but she knew the voice.

Lobo.

She peered around the pagoda with her friends. The Spanish Painter stood at the base of the 108 pagodas with Lacasse, Bernardo, Dante—and the Keeper of Secrets. Lobo gripped her arm.

Carlo gritted his teeth. "I'm going to murder him."

"It's time to come home, Carlo," Bernardo yelled. "We only want you to return to Venice with us. Everyone else can go."

"You can't go with them," Fosca whispered. "They'll kill you."

"No, grazie," Carlo called back.

Lobo shoved the woman forward. "This woman's life hangs in the balance. Come with us, and you can spare her. Your friends' lives too."

Carlo rubbed his jaw. "How does he know who she is?"

Julia shrugged. "There could be a Tangut in the Spanish *Paradise*."

"I don't think so."

"Maybe he saw you talking to her," Julia offered. "Feel him out."

After a moment, Carlo called down, "Why would I care about that old woman?"

"Because she's a living, breathing person," Lobo shouted. "Or do you want me to change that?"

"How about you go fuck yourself?" Fosca yelled.

"Perra inútil," Lobo said. "You don't have a choice, Carlo. Get down here now."

"Come up and get me," Carlo called. "We can have a rematch."

"You're right, maricon. I don't care about her." Lobo shoved the woman away. She tripped and collapsed to the ground.

Lacasse and Bernardo moved to aid the Keeper, but Lobo pounced on Lacasse.

He reached into the detective's jacket and stole his gun. He aimed it at the group and fired. A bullet ricocheted off the pagoda in front of them, sending shards of brick into the air. Julia screamed. They all ducked behind the pagodas.

"Lobo!" said Bernardo. "What are you doing?" He helped the Keeper to her feet.

"I'm losing my patience," he shouted. "I'm losing my patience with *all* of you. How about I kill your friends, Carlo, and you come with us anyway?" He seized the Keeper from Bernardo and jammed the muzzle into her head. "I'll start with her. I know you, Carlo. You say you don't care? I know you care. But I don't. So don't test me."

He pulled the woman closer, then planted the gun squarely in the back of her head.

"I'll do it, Carlo. Or you can save her life. Your choice."

The Keeper whimpered and covered her face in fear.

"He's right," Carlo whispered to Fosca and Julia. "The Tanguts have suffered enough. I can't let him shoot her. Even if she weren't the Keeper, I could never live with myself."

"There's another way," Fosca exclaimed. "We can fight them."

"He has a gun, mi amor." He gestured up the mountain. "There's nothing but desert behind us."

Carlo stood with his hands raised. "Let her go," he called. "I'm coming."

Lobo did as requested. The woman hurried away.

Carlo turned back to the group. "They don't know about the bowl. Keep it that way." He grabbed Fosca and kissed her lips, then he looked at Julia. "Destroy them. Free the souls. Do whatever is necessary."

"No," Fosca said, her voice cracking. Tears filled her eyes.

Julia had never seen her so emotional. She knew exactly why—there was only one way to end the Order. And it didn't mesh with Carlo's life.

With his arms raised, Carlo descended the steps until he reached the Order goons. Lobo grabbed him and pressed the gun into his back as they marched away.

"Stay up there," Lobo called.

Julia longed to race after them but restrained herself. The moment the assholes were out of view, the three of them raced down the stairs.

"Go," Fosca said, rushing to help the Keeper.

Julia and Hartog sprinted to the parking lot, but the lone remaining car was theirs.

"We can catch them," Hartog said, jumping in.

"What about Fosca and the Keeper?" Julia asked.

"We'll come back for them. Let's go!"

Julia bolted to the passenger side and climbed in. Hartog started the car. He revved the engine and threw it into reverse.

Ka-thump!

Julia's head wobbled. It felt like they drove into a giant pothole.

She got out of the car. Dismay hit her all over again.

Both rear tires had been slashed.

# XXXVI

"THE PRODIGAL SON RETURNS," della Porta said in Venetian. Beaming from ear to ear, he extended his hands wide, as he walked the hallway that led to the Great Council Room, his heels clicking on the marble floor.

Carlo had never seen such a display of pure bullshit. If he wasn't held by Bernardo and Dante, he would've clocked his one-time father figure in the teeth.

Instead, his captors allowed the head of the Order—the man responsible for so much evil—to wrap his arms around him. Carlo wanted to vomit. His stomach roiled at the man's touch.

His proximity to *Paradiso* served to heighten Carlo's nausea. The painting had already taken on a sinister form for him, but after being inside it, he could never be near it again. He forced a wad of bile down, though part of him wanted to hurl it onto della Porta's face.

The man released his hold and smiled at Carlo.

"Welcome home, son."

Hatred fumed within Carlo. He considered breaking free from the clutches of Bernardo and Dante, fantasizing about wrapping his hands around della Porta's throat. Knowing that both Protectors were armed, with concealed guns and swords beneath their tailored jackets, the odds of Carlo incapacitating both swiftly enough to snuff the life from della Porta was slim. Plus, they weren't alone. Protectors and staff filed in and out of the Great Council Room, striding past them.

"Well," della Porta said, "aren't you going to say something? Could the famous Carlo Zuccaro, our present-day Casanova who could sweet talk any woman in Venice, be at a loss for words?"

Carlo narrowed his eyes. "It's been a long two days."

That was putting it lightly. After being abducted in China, Lacasse faked an international arrest, forcing Carlo to fly wearing handcuffs. He didn't know what happened to Fosca, Julia, Hartog, or the Keeper, but he was thankful his team had the bowl. Of course, the bowl's function, or how they'd use it with the Sun Crystal, was anybody's guess. That's where the Order had made their biggest mistake.

Carlo was now closer to the Sun Crystal than they'd ever expected.

Lobo and Lacasse left immediately after bringing Carlo to the Palazzo Ducale. He didn't know where they went, but without them, it would be two fewer people he'd need to deal with. Not to mention, he couldn't stand being next to Lobo for another moment. The Spanish Painter had turned the trip into a living hell. At times, Carlo wished he was back in the abyss.

"Come, Carlo," della Porta said, "I want to show you the changes we've made. We have big things in store."

He took Carlo's arm but paused when he saw he wasn't restrained.

"Bernardo, let's not take any precautions."

The chief Protector raised an eyebrow. "It's *Carlo*."

"Precisely."

"Certo, Exalted Master." Bernardo retrieved a zip tie from his pocket and wrapped it around Carlo's wrists.

"You understand," della Porta said to Carlo. Then leaned into his ear and whispered, "Don't you, son?"

Though the word infuriated Carlo, it was tempered by della Porta revealing his hand. All of his congeniality was for show. For whose show, Carlo didn't know, but it confirmed everything he had suspected—the man was full of shit. He needed to be taken down.

Bernardo and Dante guided Carlo to the Great Council Room, but Carlo halted at the threshold. Though the souls were relatively quiet, their voices penetrated his mind in a sickening moan.

"I'm not going in there," he said.

Della Porta turned, confusion segueing into a faux smile of understanding. "Ah, of course. Well, just come to the doorframe. We can see from here."

Curious, Carlo took another step, making sure to stay out of view of *Paradiso*. At least four dozen people buzzed about the room, performing various tasks. Workers assembled scaffoldings on the sides and back of the room. Hundreds of seats filled the center.

Della Porta gestured to the scene.

"We've invited politicians, journalists, academics, scientists, philosophers, authors, clergy of all faiths, even celebrities from around the world. Five hundred people will be in this room just over two months from today. We want everyone to witness the glory that is *Paradise* and the Ancient Order of the Seventh Sun in person. It will be the dawn of Veritism. Right here."

He pointed to the scaffoldings.

"Twelve networks and streaming services will televise the event. Sure, people will think it's special effects, a Las Vegas show. But unlike magicians, we *will* show our cards. We'll empty our top hats and roll up our sleeves. We'll let everyone examine everything. The Order has kept truths of this world hidden for too long. I'll let you in on a little secret." He lowered his voice. "Four patriarchs of the Catholic Church will be here to witness everything. Emissaries of his Holiness himself."

Unease crept through Carlo. He tried to swallow but couldn't get it down. It seemed impossible that della Porta could convert Catholics to Veritism. But... if the Church supported the new religion—or worse, embraced it—della Porta could achieve his vision. The massive room's walls appeared to be moving in on him. His stomach lurched. He couldn't control it any longer. Puke erupted from his mouth and landed on the floor, splattering on Dante's shoes.

The three men recoiled in disgust.

"Carlo," della Porta said, "are you ill?"

Carlo wished he could wipe his mouth. "I need a bathroom."

"Allora," della Porta said. "This isn't good. You're the star of the whole show."

"What?" Carlo said, aghast. He spat out a morsel of vomit.

"There's plenty of time to discuss. Bernardo, be a good friend and take Carlo to his room."

# XXXVII

J ULIA'S DAD LOVED QUOTING Yogi Berra. Until she was in her early twenties, she didn't even know he was a baseball player. She thought her dad was saying "Yogi Bear" in a funny way since she was a little girl.

It was Nick who told her Yogi was a real person. At first, she didn't believe it. Who names their kid Yogi? Besides that, how could her dad not tell her? It was a double whammy of disbelief. The wool had been pulled from her eyes, only for her to learn she was wearing a sweater backward her whole life.

Julia's favorite Yogi quote blazed in her brain as their taxi rolled up the long driveway to Fosca's chateau.

*It was déjà vu all over again.*

They had worked so hard. They had traveled so far. Again, it all came crashing down in a few minutes.

She had the bowl safely in her carry-on, sitting on her lap, but they didn't even know how to use it. Hartog had ideas, and they figured the Sun Crystal needed to be placed in the bowl. But how could they access the crystal? Della Porta would have it guarded twenty-four-seven.

And he had Carlo. Even if they managed to accomplish the impossible, it seemed too late.

Della Porta wanted Carlo for one reason—to transfer his power to a new Painter who'd be fiercely loyal, just like Lobo. He'd probably transfer the power to another sadist if he hadn't already. Between spending a freezing night in the 108 Pagodas parking lot in their rental car, getting the tires fixed, bringing the Keeper of the Secrets back to Haibao Park, dealing with an angry rental car company, and missing their flight, they were three days behind the Order.

Three crucial days in which della Porta could've secured victory.

Fosca had called the rest of the team to see if there was anything they could do, but she could only connect with Marcel, who had already returned to Paris for his fall semester.

The taxi stopped in front of the Baldesseri estate. Julia stepped out into moist, chilly air that penetrated her thin jacket. There was no fanfare or greeting like the last time they arrived. What was there to welcome? They had failed miserably.

The driver peeled out, leaving her, Fosca, and Hartog in a cloud of dust.

Garfield trotted toward them, head down, tail barely swinging, as if obligated to say hello. He even whimpered a bit.

Fosca crouched and gave him a warm hug and pat on the head.

"I know, my sweet," she said. "I know."

Releasing more despondent whines, he scampered back to the house.

Julia exchanged concerned glances with Fosca and Hartog. Dogs were empathetic creatures but not psychic. This was over the top.

Without a word, Fosca hurried to the house. Julia followed her with Hartog.

"Hello?" Fosca called out as she opened the door. "Anybody here?"

A strange sense of foreboding filled Julia. "Where is everyone?"

"Maybe at the pool?" Hartog asked.

"Not much of a swim day," Julia said.

Fosca remained silent, her swift stride leading her through the living room to the back patio door but stopped in her tracks. So did Julia. They all heard it—a weak cough coming from the sofa, but nobody sat on it.

They hurried over. A collective gasp escaped their lips.

Hugo sat on the floor, his back against the couch. Garfield lay next to him, tenderly licking his hand.

A vivid crimson stained Hugo's shirt, his eyes shut in evident pain.

The trio rushed to his side.

Fosca knelt beside him, her voice trembling. "Oh, my God," she said, gripping his hand. "What happened?"

He didn't respond.

Desperation surged in Fosca as she touched his chest, her uncertainty palpable.

Tears filled Julia's eyes; this nightmare couldn't possibly be unfolding. Her eyes darted across the space, searching for their missing companions.

With a gentle tap on Hugo's cheek, Fosca roused him. He opened his eyes. A faint whisper escaped his lips.

"Mariposita," Hugo wheezed.

The unexpected word caused Fosca to choke up. She bit her hand.

"Did... did you destroy the crystal?" Hugo asked.

"What happened?" Fosca asked with a broken voice. "Where's everyone else?"

A sudden expression of shock and remembrance crossed Hugo's face. With great effort and pain, he rotated his head, scanning the room. "Where... where is mi corazón? Where is Lucia?"

Tears streamed out of Fosca's eyes, coating Hugo's hand. "I don't know, Hugo. She's not here. What happened? Please!"

Hugo coughed. Blood dribbled from his mouth. "The Order. They came. They... shot... me."

Fosca covered her mouth. She gazed back at Julia, who watched the scene in horror and disbelief.

"I... I fought back," Hugo continued. "Della... Porta." He coughed and hacked up blood. "Lucia... Mi corazón ..."

His eyes stared straight ahead. His head tipped to the side. Fosca tried to revive him, but it was far too late.

"Do something," she screamed at Hartog and Julia. "Get help!"

# XXXVIII

E YES SHUT, CARLO LAY on the same filthy cot that Tintoretto had used for God knows how long. It'd been six days since he'd been locked up. With nothing to do but paint and think, the frequency of uncontrolled regressions intensified. He'd had so many that he lost count.

Some seemed timely and relevant to the situation, as if locked away in his brain and banging on his skull to escape, but most were random vignettes of people's lives. He enjoyed getting to know them. Others were decidedly random. Some souls got the eternal purgatory they deserved. Others had been betrayed by the Order, like his father.

He concentrated on deep inhales through his nose and longer exhales through his mouth. He'd been using the technique daily, trying to will his mind to travel to his father's memories. Though he'd yet to command a full regression, the method seemed to work. Blurry visions and snippets of conversations drifted into his mind's eye. Della Porta featured prominently, along with Paganelli and Bernardo, the latter's presence surprising Carlo. His father's emotions came forth, as well. An acute knowledge of della Porta's true nature. Along with treachery. Disappointment. Regret.

Through the haze, an image presented itself. His father's workshop. Being led outside under false pretense. The smell of gas. Held back while the workshop burned. In the window's reflection, a glimpse of the perpetrators who committed the crime.

Tintoretto's wicked grin. Inconceivable terror.

Carlo opened his eyes slowly and stared at the ceiling of the Painter's room—or prison cell, which would be a better description.

Though he didn't visualize the complete picture, he *felt* it. He *knew* the unequivocal truth.

Della Porta sentenced his father and covered it, ruining Carlo's life.

Bernardo was there, though reluctantly and unsettled by the situation. But he could've stopped it. Della Porta was right. Bernardo was an accessory. It was no wonder he stuck by della Porta's side all this time.

Profound desolation saturated Carlo's being. He rubbed his forearms.

Needing to relieve himself, he slipped off the bed and stepped over to the chamber pot by the door. He still wasn't used to his living conditions, and the pot was arguably the worst. He couldn't fathom how Tintoretto—or anyone who lived before flush toilets—could keep those things under their beds. The persistent stench of his body's waste made him gag.

At least della Porta was kind enough to have his men carve a section out of the bottom of the door through which they could pass food and the chamber pot. They also carved a little slot at eye level, which visitors could open on their side. If someone came in, they passed handcuffs through and ordered him to cuff himself to an immovable bar affixed to the wall within arm's reach of the door. The slot was large enough to slide the cuffs or key through, but not a hand.

The moment they threw him into his new residence, he had checked for an escape. The hatch that led to the *pozzi* was sealed shut. The door was impossible to break down, even with his strength. He knew he couldn't chisel away at the stone walls, for they went nowhere. The Order had also removed anything that could be a weapon. Three plastic LED lights had been installed in barred ceiling fixtures. They left him paint, canvases, and paintbrushes. Except for the bed, the writing desk and a chair, the room was barren. He considered using the paintbrush and fighting back, but to what end? He knew where he was. Nobody came to him alone. If he overpowered one or even four men as Tintoretto had done, he wouldn't get far after that.

Carlo didn't know for how long he would be imprisoned, but he sensed della Porta wasn't planning on an eternity. He'd yet to force Carlo to sentence anyone to *Paradiso*.

With nothing to do but think and paint, Carlo did just that. No clock. No indication of time. He lay on the bed for hours, regressing into other people's lives. When he woke, he often didn't realize where he was—or when he was—especially since he had nothing modern in the cell. He spent the rest of his time painting. At first, he resisted the act, thinking it was what della Porta wanted him to do. Before long, the lure of painting in Tintoretto's home was too great to defy. The man was a monster but also a giant of the

Renaissance. Carlo stood in Tintoretto's literal footsteps. For all he knew, he was using Tintoretto's original paintbrushes.

Paintings of Fosca covered every part of the room he could place them on. He even managed to fasten two canvases to the rough-hewn rock walls. He stepped behind his easel. Besides the images of Fosca, only one thing in his cell comforted him—an ancient bullet, lodged in the wall. He had discovered the relic on his first day. Amazed Tintoretto never removed it, Carlo rubbed the lead ball. Perhaps the previous Painter kept it as a reminder of his mortality—or his superiority. To Carlo, the bullet shone as a symbol that he wasn't alone in this fight. Emanuele Quattrone and dozens of other good people had died for the cause. Carlo prayed he'd be able to end the Order—and that the next bullet wouldn't be for him.

The door slot slid open.

"Carlo," said the thick voice that could only belong to Bernardo. "You know the routine," he said in Venetian.

Bernardo passed the handcuffs through the slot. Carlo took them and secured one wrist to the holding bar.

Four locks disengaged. The door opened. At least three Protectors stood behind Bernardo, but his former friend entered alone. He closed the door behind him.

Bernardo inspected the room with a somber countenance and a long exhale.

"This was not my choice, Carlo," he said. "Please know that. I fought della Porta on putting you in here."

"You could've fought him on many things, Bernardo." He rattled his handcuff against the bar for emphasis. "Things going back years."

The chief Protector cocked his head as if trying to gather the statement's meaning.

Carlo allowed him a moment. After it was evident that either Bernardo didn't understand and wouldn't be forthcoming, Carlo said, "I know. I know you were there the night my father was taken. The night you burned down my life."

A glimmer of remorse broke through Bernardo's poker face.

"I know the part you played," Carlo continued. "How you lied to me—and my mother—every day thereafter."

Deep sorrow emanated from Bernardo, cutting through Carlo's core. He was expecting to confront the man, not console him. Bernardo sat at the desk, seemingly weak at the knees.

"You don't know how heavy this burden has been on me," he said.

"Not as heavy as it's been on my father. Or me. Or my mother."

Bernardo pinched the bridge of his nose. "You are right. Of course. This isn't about me. I have no defense, Carlo. Della Porta has held this over my head since then. And now, much worse."

Carlo rubbed his shackled wrist with his free hand. "Is it any worse than the consequences of truth?"

Bernardo raised his head and leveled his gaze at him. "I'm not concerned about my own fate, Carlo. I'm concerned about what Salvatore would do if I weren't there to keep him in check."

The statement took Carlo aback. "Keep him in check? How exactly are you doing that? He's running wild, and you're right there with him. I don't recall Salvatore in China."

"No, but Lobo was there."

"So you answer to him now, too?"

Shame filled Bernardo's face. He looked away. "I'm in too deep."

"After I became Painter, do you remember meeting me in the Great Council Room? Just the two of us?"

Bernardo nodded. "Sì, certo."

"You asked me about my initiation. When I was asked what kind of man I wished to be."

"You said, 'A good man.'"

"That initiation ceremony hasn't changed since it was first written, right?"

"Slight modifications, I believe. But in general, no. It's the same."

"It can be traced back to when the Order was a force for good."

"It's *still* a force for good, Carlo."

"Come on."

"I admit some have lost their way—"

"Bernardo, hundreds, maybe thousands, of souls don't belong in *Paradiso*. Including my father. Now this whole Veritism thing?"

"Allora," Bernardo said, his hands raised defensively. "I admit we've... *detoured* a bit."

Carlo offered the man a warm smile. "What was *your* answer when you were initiated?"

Bernardo swallowed. "That I wanted to be a good man."

The chief Protector checked his stainless steel Brega watch. "It was nice to have this chat, Carlo." He headed for the door. "I do hope we can continue it."

"We are not punished *for* our sins," Carlo said, "but *by* them."

Bernardo paused at the words he knew so well. Then he left the room.

# XXXIX

"**H**EY," JULIA SAID.

She placed a cup of coffee on the side table next to the sofa, where Fosca had slept for the third night in a row. Garfield lay curled up at her feet. Blood stained the carpet and couch next to them.

Grimacing at the discoloration, Julia sat on the adjacent sofa. She sipped her own coffee.

The last seventy-two hours had been so surreal.

Knowing Interpol was after them, they couldn't file missing persons reports with the police. The chateau had no cameras, so they had no clue who carried out the crime. It could've been any of della Porta's men. Still, Hugo's family deserved peace. If they buried him and Lucia went missing, it would've been an unsolved case for years that would've driven the family mad.

Hartog agreed to take one of the estate's trucks and drive the body to Madrid, where he'd deposit it somewhere. He didn't know where yet, which was a risk, but eventually, the body would be found. That, too, would be an unsolved case, but at least the body would give the family some closure.

"Then I'm done with this zakkenwasser life," Hartog said before driving off.

Julia couldn't blame him. He had a family too. There was too much danger all around. To the best of their knowledge, Hartog was in the clear. Julia and Fosca agreed to keep it that way.

They had to assume the Order took the rest of their friends, but for what reason, they could only guess. Leverage was the most probable motive, but it was just a hypothesis until the Order contacted them. For all they knew, the others were dead.

Though it was a psychological nightmare, Fosca and Julia decided to take a cue from the Order's playbook and stay at the estate. It was the last place anybody would think to look for them. To cover their tracks, Fosca told a few people she was on a family boat in Monte Carlo and that Julia had returned to America.

Julia took another drink of her coffee and stared at Fosca. Her friend had been through so much and for so long. Not just the recent events, but her grandmother and her family—even before she was born. She'd been texting Marcel the news. He took it hard and offered to come to the chateau, but Fosca insisted he stay in Paris.

"I should've turned myself in," she mumbled into the couch arm.

"What?"

"To Lobo and Lacasse. In China. It would've given Carlo time to get away."

"Get away where? There was nothing but desert. Carlo did the right thing. And who knows what they would've done to you."

Fosca raised her eyes. "What are you doing here?"

Julia cocked her head, pleased her friend was having a conversation but unsure of the question.

"What do you mean?"

"Why haven't you gone home?"

"Della Porta will find me."

Fosca shook her head. "If he's even looking for you. If he is, then go to Brazil or Argentina. Or Iceland. Or Mars. Disappear. We lost, Julia. Go home."

Julia picked at her fingernails. She'd asked herself the question a thousand times. She could've gone home months ago. Instead, she embroiled herself in an adventure with disastrous results. A glimmer of hope that she could free Nick spurred her on, but now, with so many gone and the mountain growing impossibly high, all seemed lost.

In her heart, she knew the answer. She leveled her gaze at Fosca.

"Do you remember the first time we met?" Julia asked.

"On the boat to Murano."

"Did you know I wanted to punch you and throw you off that boat?"

Fosca took the mug and wrapped her hands around it. "I had a feeling. Like I told you then, we had no idea what would happen to Nick when we gave him Isabella's urn."

"Remember that time in the park in Madrid? Outside the hotel?"

"Arguing with the creepy bum watching us? How could I forget?"

Julia laughed. "I wanted to punch you then, too, for not telling me that Carlo had painted Nick into a new canvas."

Fosca drank her coffee and met Julia's eyes. "So why didn't you?"

"Because of your conviction. I saw it in you. I knew nothing you did was malicious toward me. You and I share a simple belief: justice is always worth it."

A trifling smile graced Fosca's lips.

"This has always been about so much more than Nick or me," Julia continued. "You've always been fighting for others. Fighting the good fight. Riding into battle, guns blazing with no concern for your own safety. Spending money like there's no tomorrow, I should add."

Fosca laughed. "For real about that last part. Good thing I still have my childhood piggy bank."

Julia shared the moment of levity. "So why haven't I left? How could I? Justice is always worth it, Fosca. I can't abandon you now. Or Carlo. I couldn't live with myself if I did."

"It's quite the turnaround."

"Tell me about it. I wanted to clock him in the face, too."

"You wanted to do more than that."

"Too true."

"I'm glad you didn't." Fosca took another drink. "I have a confession to make."

"You and Carlo hooked up?"

Her friend spat some coffee out. "You knew?"

"You're good at keeping lots of secrets, Fosca. Not about who you're sleeping with."

"You're not mad?"

The question took Julia aback. She tilted her head and squinted her eyes. "Why in the world would I be mad?"

Fosca raised her hand in defense. "I'm not saying you're jealous—"

"I'm definitely not."

"I know, I know. It's just, you know, we're a team. We don't want to make you feel uncomfortable."

"Well, it looks like you and I will be in the same boat anyway."

Tears flooded Fosca's eyes, which puzzled Julia. She didn't want Carlo dead or who-knows-what would happen to him, but there was more to Fosca's reaction. Perhaps her relationship with Carlo was about more than just sex. If that were the case, she was happy for her. For both of them. She sat beside Fosca and gently held her hand.

"There's another reason why I haven't left," Julia said. She shook her head, amazed by the thoughts that entered. "The truth is, I have nothing to go back to. Not without Nick."

Fosca wiped her eyes and squeezed Julia's hand. "I can't believe I'm saying this, but I feel the same about Carlo."

Contagious tears came to Julia. "If there's even the slightest hope that we can save Carlo and our friends and maybe free Nick and the souls and bring down the Order... we *have* to try."

"As they say in America," said a familiar nasally French voice, "'Ain't that the truth.'"

"Marcel," Fosca exclaimed.

She hurried over to him and gave him a massive bear hug, which he reciprocated. Julia watched the tender exchange. Despite their differences and teasing, their familial bond couldn't be broken.

Finally, Fosca released him. Julia stood. She couldn't resist and gave Marcel a hug of equal strength but a quarter of the length of time.

"I could use one of those," he said, pointing to Julia's coffee mug.

"There's a fresh pot in the kitchen," she replied.

The three of them moved to the kitchen, where Julia and Fosca sat at the counter while Marcel poured himself a cup from the French press. It wasn't hot, and he drank the entire thing in two gulps. He spied a loaf of bread and tore off a slice, which he shoved into his mouth.

"Hungry?" Fosca asked.

"Julia," he replied with a full mouth, "what's the American expression about chasing and cutting?"

"Chasing and cutting?"

"Oui, when you don't want to... what's the American expression about a bush and beating?"

Fosca and Julia cracked up.

"Beating around the bush," Fosca said after she recovered. "It means when you're not talking about the subject you *should* be talking about."

Marcel snapped his fingers. "Exactement. So what is the opposite?"

Julia slapped the table with satisfaction. "When you cut to the chase. Which I think you can do by now."

Marcel snapped his fingers again, ending in a point at Julia. "Oui. I shall cut to the chase." He removed his backpack and plopped it on the counter. He pulled his laptop out, powered it on, and typed into it. Then he spun it around to show Julia and Fosca before ripping off another hunk of bread.

There were five different windows open on the screen. Four contained code, and one was a camera view of what looked like pavement. A few people hurried by.

"Are we supposed to know what we're looking at?" Fosca asked.

"Je m'excuse," he replied. "Let me explain. I hacked into different accounts, including the Palazzo Ducale email server and *one* security camera."

Julia shared an enthusiastic look with Fosca. That news was unexpected.

"Okay, I'm impressed," Fosca said. "Are you gonna cut to the chase or what?"

Marcel raised his hands as if indicating his audience to quiet down. Julia was getting frustrated, but she waited for him to speak.

"First, the rest of the team is alive."

"Oh, thank God," Fosca said.

Equal relief washed over Julia.

"For now," Marcel continued. "Della Porta has something planned for them. It will be when he announces Veritism to the world... on Christmas Day."

"Shit," Fosca said. "That's around the corner."

"Right," Marcel continued. "He has invited hundreds of people to the Palazzo to witness everything in person. Camera crews too. He will reveal everything. He has new Painters."

"What do you mean?" Julia asked. "Is Carlo dead?"

"I don't think so. Della Porta has given the power to new Painters. He must have something planned for Carlo since he controls *Paradise* in Venice. The new Painters are for new paintings all over the world." He polished off his remaining coffee and looked Fosca and Julia in their eyes. "He wants both of you, too. He doesn't know you're here, but Protectors are coming to check it out again."

Julia's mouth popped open. "What? You could have led with that!"

"We have time," Marcel said nonchalantly. "It's okay."

"How much time?" Fosca asked.

Marcel checked the time on his cell phone. "Maybe six or seven hours. At least five."

"What? You asshole," Fosca said. "Why didn't you say something? We need to go *now*."

Julia rubbed the bridge of her nose. "So much for della Porta being a man of his word."

Fosca paced the room. "Jesus. We need to go. We gotta pack and call a taxi."

"We have time," Marcel said. "I borrowed my roommate's parents' car. We can take it, and you both can stay with me in my flat. We'll bring Garfield to the neighbors. But first, I want to see the bowl you found."

With a huff, Fosca just shook her head and stormed off. "Come on. We need to get it anyway."

After Fosca grabbed a duffel bag, the three went to the secret library in the wine cellar, which the Order hadn't discovered. Fosca immediately began packing various books.

"You know nonna-mère would kill you if she saw how you're handling those," Marcel said. He placed four bottles of wine he nabbed from the rack on the table.

"She'd kill you if she knew you didn't bother to say people are coming to kill *us*! Meanwhile, you're pilfering the family's wine."

"Who knows when we'll be back? We should take a case."

Julia went to the back of the room. She opened a box to retrieve the bowl and pestle, which she set on the table. It had been days since they'd examined it. When she first found it in the dim light of the Gobi Desert, she had thought the outside was a design pattern, but it was covered in a dialect of Chinese characters that Hartog couldn't translate.

About ten inches in diameter and six inches deep, the bowl was the perfect size for the Sun Crystal. The bowl was two-tone, with the characters carved into a darker, rougher brass. The characters were individually polished, so they shone against the darker background. A one-inch, highly polished strip that glinted in the light circled the top of the bowl. The yin-yang, surrounded by seven lines indicating sunlight, had been lightly etched into the bottom. The pestle was also a work of art. Hartog had identified it as jade. It was a deep, intoxicating shade of green with natural white veins. Additional characters were carved into it.

Marcel's eyes widened. "Mon Dieu," he said with his jaw agape. "You girls don't know what this is?"

Julia and Fosca exchanged glances, clearly on the same wavelength and not loving his condescending tone.

"It's a mortar and pestle," Julia said.

"Yeah," Fosca said with an equally annoyed voice. "You grind up herbs and stuff. We're thinking you put the Sun Crystal in there and somehow smash it."

Marcel shook his head. "It's a *singing bowl*."

"A what?" Fosca asked. She checked her watch. "Can we talk in the car?"

Ignoring her, he picked up the pestle. He opened his mouth to speak but put it down. Muttering to himself, he tapped on his cell phone. "Ah," he said, lifting it again. "In English, this is called a striker."

With his hand held out flat, Marcel balanced the bowl on his palm and tapped it with the striker. It released a melodic hum that echoed off the stone walls.

"It's used for Buddhist ceremonies and relaxation. Neither of you have ever seen one of these?"

Julia shrugged. She hadn't but wasn't surprised it was used for relaxation. The tone sent pleasant waves through her, calming her growing anxiety about needing to leave.

He tapped the bowl's rim. This time, the pitch was higher but still beautiful. It brought an involuntary smile to her face.

"But *this* is why it's called a singing bowl." In a deliberate, constant motion, Marcel ran the top of the striker around the bowl's rim.

It was aptly named. The bowl released one of the most exquisite and harmonious sounds Julia had ever heard. It really did sound like it was singing. It even sounded like a chorus. She stared at the bowl, captivated by the music it produced.

She glanced at her friends, who also seemed to be in near-trancelike states.

The tone drew her in. The world turned fuzzy, as if her vision blurred, but she didn't mind it. She craved more of the bowl's song. It was as if it sang to *her*. Everything else around her dimmed to the background as she stared at the relic. Distant voices whispered to her, telling her of her past, present, and future—and they were the same. All time blended together.

In her mind's eye, her life zipped back to the day she was born. She cried, distraught, unaware of this new world filled with light and air. As her mother cradled her against her chest, an indescribable warmth filled her core and emanated across her skin, radiating tender shivers everywhere.

Time sped forward to the present. The bowl hovered in midair. It was only Julia with it, somewhere in space, somewhere in time. The bronze oscillated and warped. Stars twinkled around her. So many stars. Brilliant and maternal, each one providing life to the universe.

She blinked—or thought she blinked—and time rocketed forward, but only to a few seconds in the future. That future was a blank wall, like a giant piece of paper, but solid, made of unknown material. The wall stood on all sides, above and below her. And it was fracturing.

Her mind was sucked back into the present.

Everything was blurry, but she was cognizant of Marcel continuing to roll the striker around the bowl. He stared at it, as did Fosca.

A strange crackling sound cut through Julia's ecstasy. The volume grew. She didn't want to look away from the bowl but turned her head slightly—

A huge crash detonated.

Marcel stopped the motion.

They all whipped their heads to the noise's source.

Light returned. Julia's vision sharpened.

The decorative vase had shattered into thousands of tiny colorful pieces, blanketing the floor and bookcase.

After taking in what happened, they gazed at each other with open mouths.

"Whoa," Julia said. "Did you guys..."

The two of them nodded.

"That was trippy," Fosca said. She turned to Marcel. "You didn't roofie us, did you?"

"I don't know what that is." Marcel gaped at the bowl and striker in his hands.

"Holy shit, you little dweeb," Fosca said. "You figured out how to shatter the Sun Crystal."

"I also do not know this word 'dweeb,'" Marcel replied wryly. "It must mean genius?"

"Something like that," Julia answered. She stared at the wine bottles. "But why didn't *they* break?"

They pondered the question for a few moments before Fosca answered.

"Who knows? Can we talk about it in the car?"

"That's probably a good idea," Marcel said.

They grabbed the bowl, striker, books, and wine.

# XL

C ARLO TUMBLED TO THE floor in the corridor outside his cell. Stone met shoulder and knee, sending ripples of sharp pain into his bones. By sheer reflex he managed to twist his body and avoid landing on his face.

His hands and feet were both cuffed. Lobo had shoved him down, not because della Porta asked him to, but because the man was a sadist.

Carlo grimaced and twisted his body around. He glanced at della Porta and Bernardo. The hall was lit only by sporadic bare bulbs in yellow plastic cages, but the expression on their faces was clear—neither was pleased with the Spanish Painter's action.

"Pick him up," Bernardo said.

"He can pick himself up," Lobo replied. He nudged Carlo's gut with this foot. "Do it."

Carlo crawled to his knees and stood. He tried to rise with dignity, but between sleeping on an ancient cot that was hard as wood and being cuffed at the feet and hands, it was pointless. The chain between his feet was long enough to allow him to walk with short steps, but he couldn't run.

The three men had taken him from the cell a few moments prior without explanation. It was the first time he'd been taken out of his room since his confinement. With no window or clock, he had lost track of the time and date. He knew it was mid- or late-December, so he figured this was it. Whatever della Porta had planned, he'd find out soon enough.

To Carlo's relief, they did not take the corridor that led to the Great Council Room. They traversed a different hallway until they reached a narrow stone spiral stairwell.

"Up," Lobo said.

Carlo climbed the steps. At the top, Lobo pushed him through a panel that led to one of the main hallways within the museum. The three men escorted him to the Chamber of the Scrutinio, the second-largest room in the Palazzo. Originally a library, this chamber ultimately became used solely for elections.

Lobo shoved him inside. Carlo's eyes went wide with horror.

Beneath a glorious ceiling of artwork in gilded frames, ten people stood in front of three sculptures, lined up shoulder-to-shoulder, their backs to the door. Their hands were bound behind them, and they wore something on their heads—either blindfolds or gags. Or both. A pair of Protectors stood on either side of the line.

"Keep going," Lobo said, prodding him forward.

"No," della Porta said, entering the room, followed by Bernardo. "I want him here for now."

A sickening weight dropped to Carlo's stomach. Now he knew what della Porta wanted. Whoever these people were, they would be the next victims in *Paradise*.

"I won't do it," Carlo said.

Della Porta raised an eyebrow. "Won't do what?"

Carlo gazed at the prisoners. "Your dirty work. Paint them yourself."

Della Porta smiled, as if he were hiding something. "Do you remember the mayor's party, the night you met the Countess Baldesseri?"

"Before you murdered her?"

"You can make all the false accusations you want, Carlo. It won't change the truth that, in all likelihood, your friend committed that heinous crime. But moving on. I presume you remember that night?"

How could Carlo forget? It was a night that should've propelled his art career into the stratosphere. Instead, somehow along the way, his career trajectory landed on being an executioner living in a windowless cesspit.

Reading Carlo's expression, della Porta continued.

"That night, I said you were an integral piece of a picture still being sketched. I must admit. When I said the words, I injected them with hyperbole to excite you about the future."

Della Porta gazed at the open door. "If only we could've had this conversation in the Great Council Room. You'd be impressed with our progress." He turned back to Carlo. "Honestly, I didn't put much thought into the words I said that night. Yet it turns out they couldn't have been more accurate. That picture will soon be complete."

"Not by my hand, it won't," Carlo said.

Lobo snickered. "We'll save the world from seeing more of your crap."

Bernardo narrowed his eyes at the Spanish Painter. He clenched his jaw.

"You're observant, Carlo," della Porta said. "You always have been. It's what makes you a *true* artist." He threw a glance at Lobo, who recoiled at the words. "Your talent is undeniable. It's that ability to observe the world, absorb emotion, and then empty it onto the canvas that sets you in the upper echelon of the world's greats. It's not just your natural skill and technique, or even your original ideas and content. The passion that translates from the brush puts you on a par with Tintoretto. You were always the perfect replacement."

The unexpected shower of accolades left Carlo both appreciative and perceptive. He sensed a genuine admiration from della Porta but couldn't shake the suspicion that this was another instance of the man's buttery words, a familiar tune from their history. Nevertheless, no amount of flattery could sway him into accepting the role of the Order's Painter.

"What you fail to see," della Porta said, "is that our methods aren't any different from religions past, including the one we were born into. Do I need to remind you of the millions who've died in the name of religion? If anything, Veritism is far more humane and civilized. This job does not require the world's greatest artists. It requires people with vision, with the right temperament—those who are willing to do what it takes to make the world a better place. You want me to paint them myself? Maybe I will." He rubbed his jaw. "I have some skill and know the basic techniques. Admittedly, not like you, but again, it doesn't matter. It doesn't need to be a masterpiece."

This comment shocked Carlo. "You'd deface *Paradiso*?" he asked.

Della Porta jutted his head back. "Of course not." Then he chuckled. "You thought I was talking about *Il Paradiso*? If there's one thing you and I see eye-to-eye on"—he swept his hand out at the art covering the walls like a game show host—"is *Paradiso* is a groundbreaking masterwork. No, no, no." He clapped his hands. "Bring them out."

One of the Protectors opened a door on the far side. A fifth suited Protector escorted ten men and women into the room. They all had varying hair and clothing styles, but being one of them, Carlo could tell instantly—*these were artists*. The Protectors lined them up to the side of the prisoners.

"Carlo, take a good look at the future. At your *successors*."

Waves of horror rolled through Carlo. Ten Painters? Plus Lobo and the French Painter? Would all twelve work on *Paradiso*?

"But how?" he asked.

With a grin, della Porta stepped toward the prisoners. Lobo prodded Carlo to follow, which he did. He wondered who the prisoners were but fixed his eyes on della Porta. The Exalted Master walked the line of artists, patting their shoulders and shaking their hands.

"For years, I wondered how the Order gave the first Painter his power." Della Porta spoke to the room but directed his words at Carlo. "Then the next two. I combed through texts. It was you, or really, your access to Angelo, that made me realize I was digging far too deep."

Della Porta approached Carlo.

"Do you know how they did it, *son*?"

Carlo inhaled a slow, burning breath through his nose but remained silent.

"You think you don't," della Porta continued, "but ironically, you were the first to witness the process."

This piqued Carlo's curiosity. "You transferred the power from Tintoretto to me."

Della Porta smirked. "Or so we thought. In reality, the man was dying. We imbued you with the Sun Crystal's energy." He gestured to Lobo. "As I did with Lobo. We had El Greco in the room, but it wasn't necessary." He swept his hand out to the ten artists. "Just as I did with your new ten colleagues."

Shock registered in Carlo. He had expected disturbing news. Not this.

"Impossible," he said.

A cocky laugh erupted from della Porta's mouth. "Oh, it's more than possible. It's done. Our new Painters will begin their own masterpieces in the Great Council Room in one short week. Then, a squadron of Protectors will escort them to their new homes around the world. But I have one more surprise for you—the first subjects of their paintings. Prisoners, turn around."

None of them moved.

"Fuckers," Lobo said. He stormed over to the line and forced a middle-aged woman around. She tripped and toppled to the floor.

Bernardo hustled over and helped her up, revealing her face to Carlo: Lucia.

A weight in his gut impelled vomit up his throat, which he couldn't control. He puked on the floor.

"Carlo!" della Porta said. "Show some control."

"It's why he always fails," Lobo said. "No control."

Della Porta grabbed Carlo's face and forced him to look at the prisoners.

"Turn around," Lobo screamed. "All of you."

Reluctantly, the prisoners did as instructed.

Savage wrath billowed in Carlo, supplanting his queasiness. Lined up, with their hands and mouths bound, blindfolded, were Lucia, Georgette, Olivier, Karim, Hartog, and five other people he didn't recognize. He was shocked to see one man was quite old, at least eighty, with bushy eyebrows and a bald head except for wisps of white hair on the top of his nape.

Hugo and Marcel must've gotten away. He said a silent prayer of thanks that Fosca and Julia weren't in the lineup.

"This is my gift to you, Carlo," della Porta said. "You see? You're not needed. You're quite expendable."

Carlo spat a morsel of vomit onto della Porta's shoe. He still held a card or two.

"I'm the warden of the primary *Paradise*," he said through clenched teeth. "If you kill me, then nobody will control them. Maybe you can create new Painters, but Tintoretto's power *did* transfer to me. I know *everything*."

Della Porta stared at Carlo with haunting eyes.

"I expected so much more from you. Such a shame." He snapped his fingers at Bernardo. "Take him back to his cell."

The chief Protector stepped over and grabbed Carlo's arm.

"How are you letting this happen?" Carlo whispered to the Protector as he marched them away.

"Oh, Carlo," della Porta called after him. "I forgot to mention something. These ten Painters? They're just the beginning. Soon, we'll have *hundreds*. The Venetian *Paradise* is already inconsequential. As are its prisoners."

# XLI

WITH NOISE-CANCELING HEADPHONES SECURELY over her ears, Julia started the stopwatch on Marcel's burner phone and ran the jade striker around the rim of the singing bowl.

It was just as Marcel had done, except the bowl rested on a donut-shaped green cushion.

Five drinking glasses of different shapes and thicknesses sat on the table next to the bowl. She couldn't hear the beautiful tone—and strangely yearned for it—but continued rotating the striker, simultaneously watching the glasses and the clock.

She stopped at three minutes and forty-seven seconds. Nothing. She noted the time—and additional failure—in a notebook.

It had been three weeks of experimentation in Marcel's flat, and they were no closer to figuring out the bowl. Additional glasses were all over his small kitchen, wrapped in towels to absorb the vibrations. Everything that was glass in the flat, other than the windows, had been wrapped in towels or plastic. But it didn't matter. Fosca and Marcel agreed—either it only worked on certain density glass, or they were doing it wrong. They tried different speeds and lengths of time, held it, put it on the cushion, and even had Marcel buy some crystal sculptures. They'd yet to replicate their experience in the secret library at Fosca's chateau.

Still, Julia persisted. What else could she do? She'd been couped up in the old apartment, as she and Fosca were too worried about a camera spotting them.

The window caught her eye. That glass didn't break, either.

She poured herself another coffee and went over to the wide window nook. Taking a seat on it, she wrapped her hands around the mug. A half-eaten bowl of Corn Flakes she'd made for herself sat next to her.

Gazing out to the Porte de Clignancourt neighborhood from the fourth floor, her eyes tracked the snowflakes that dusted the trees. People below, mostly Sorbonne students, hurried by. She longed to see the city, but they deemed it too risky and found being inside comforting. It brought her back to her days in college when she had studied in Paris for a semester, cramming for tests, pulling all-nighters writing papers, or just drinking with friends. Of course, back then, she wasn't sleeping on a couch and planning how to bring down an ancient religious order.

But the college vibe was ending.

Marcel had finished finals two days prior. His roommate had left that day, giving Fosca his room.

Since then, it had been all business.

That suited Julia just fine, as well.

Despite the worldwide adventure and seeing things that should've been impossible, she was ready for it to end. She didn't necessarily want to go home—what did she have to go back to? There was just way too much to explain to people. She was tired. She had enough energy to drive a stake through della Porta's heart. After that, she wanted to sleep. For a month. And maybe—*just maybe*—Nick could be there with her. She wasn't holding her breath.

She had to focus on the present. They still had work to do.

The door to Marcel's roommate's room opened. Wearing pajamas, Fosca yawned, glanced at Julia, and yelped, covering her heart.

"Damn, I'm still not used to that," Fosca said, catching her bearings.

"It's like looking in a mirror," Julia replied.

She adjusted her focus in the window to study herself, though she could've just looked at Fosca.

The two of them had cut their hair to a short bob and dyed it matching red.

"I always wanted a sister," Fosca said, joining Julia at the window.

They looked like twins, and Marcel said that was the point.

"I have two," Julia said. "I miss them."

Fosca rubbed her back. "You'll see them soon." She gazed around the flat. "Speaking of relations, I assume mine is still sleeping?" She went to the fridge and pulled out a can of Coke, which she cracked open.

As if on cue, Marcel entered the flat carrying a plastic bag. "Bonjour mes demoiselles." He placed the bag on the dining table and retrieved three pairs of sunglasses from it.

"Check these out," he said.

Julia and Fosca joined him and studied the shades.

They looked like rectangular aviators. The lenses had a blueish, semi-reflective tint. The frames were rainbow camouflage. Julia tried them on and looked at herself in the microwave. Between the funky sunglasses and her short red hair, she had no idea who she was looking at.

"Pretty cool," she said, taking them off. "Why did you buy us these?"

"These aren't just sunglasses. They trick facial recognition cameras. That's the theory."

His statement piqued Fosca's curiosity. She examined the glasses and tried them on. If she and Julia were next to each other, they may've been mistaken for Oompa-Loompas.

"My friend said they fool facial recognition by 20%," Marcel said.

"That's not much," Julia replied. "It would be nice to be able to leave this flat."

"And get into Venice undetected," Fosca added.

"The tough thing is your actual face." Marcel rubbed his cheeks. "The distance between your eyes, your nose, your mouth. The angle of them all. The best facial recognition detects differences by the micron. So, you can wear Covid masks. You'll look like weird bank robbers, but it should do the trick. I bought an extra pair, just in case."

"You learn this stuff in the Air Force Academy?" Julia asked, aware she had been subconsciously touching her face.

Marcel scrunched his eyes and cocked his head. He turned to Fosca for help, but she shrugged with an equally inquisitive expression.

"Why would you think I'm in the Air Force?" he asked. "I'm studying engineering."

"Fosca said you're AAF."

Fosca spat out her Coke. She burst into laughter so hard that soda bubbled out of her nose. She choked and wiped her face, barely able to control herself.

Marcel narrowed his eyes at her, as if knowing his cousin had played a joke, but she was the only one in on it.

She recovered and said, "Oh, man. That's rich. Priceless. I need to use that in the future. No, Julia, Marcel is not in the Air Force. The first A stands for 'annoying.' AF stands for 'as fuck.'"

Julia couldn't help but laugh. Marcel bared his teeth and growled at his cousin.

"You have to admit," Fosca said. "It's true."

"Boucle-la." Marcel grabbed a Rubik's Cube from the kitchen counter and started rotating the sections in one hand. "Petite crétine."

"See what I mean?" Fosca said, still laughing.

When they calmed down, Julia returned her attention to the sunglasses. "I suppose there's no way of testing it, is there?"

"No," Marcel said. "There's too much risk."

"We only have four days to get everything together before della Porta's coming out party," Fosca said.

Julia shook her head and threw her arms up. "The hair, these sunglasses, they're great, but we still don't have a plan." Once again, it all seemed impossible. "Four days? We also need to drive there. How long does that take?"

"About 12 hours," Fosca said with a frown. "We have another cousin outside of Geneva. We can stay there overnight."

Julia laughed. "So, three days. We need a plan, people." She tapped the table for emphasis, though she knew full well she was preaching to the choir. Hell, Fosca and Marcel weren't the choir. They were children of the church's founding members.

Julia slid the bowl over to her. "We still don't even know how this thing works."

"We're aware," Fosca said with equal disappointment.

"We've yet to replicate breaking glass," Julia said, "no matter how many objects we try, no matter how long we do it for."

She worked the striker around the edge of the bowl. Again, it made the most serene melody.

Finding herself becoming entranced, Julia placed the striker on the table and pinched the edge of the bowl to dampen the sound. She flicked the wineglass with her fingers, producing a soft bell sound. "Still perfectly fine." She pointed to the windows, the TV, the cupboards. "Everything, totally fine."

"We know," Fosca said.

"So then what?" Julia knew they were just as exasperated, but she had to vocalize it. "We drive to the Palazzo, knock on the front door, and hope for the best?"

Fosca raised her hands in defeat. "Do you have a better idea?"

Julia didn't. But she knew one thing. "I need to get some air." She shoved her chair back and stood. "And something French to eat! We're in Paris, eating goddamned Corn Flakes!"

"It's not worth the risk, Julia," Marcel said. "I can get you anything you want."

Julia snatched a pair of sunglasses. "Merci, Marcel." She headed for the door. "If Interpol is monitoring every bakery in Paris, then it's fate I get arrested stuffing a croissant into my mouth."

"I still think it's the best option," Marcel said, chomping into his croissant like it was a Twinkie. "Della Porta has invited over one hundred people. We'll show up as invitees and sneak in."

Julia delicately tore off a piece of her flaky pastry, careful not to lose a crumb. They'd bypassed two bakeries to reach Marcel's favorite in the neighborhood. Wow, was he right. The croissant defined perfection. The light, airy texture balanced the rich, buttery flavor that melted on her tongue. It was almost like eating cotton candy, yet it was bread.

"I can find some members of the press who owe our family a favor," Fosca said, finishing up her brasillé. "Mm. Damn, that's good. Maybe they can get us in."

Until a few moments prior, their conversation had grazed the edge of Julia's subconscious. But she realized what they were talking about and needed to bring them down to Earth, just as she needed to do for herself from French baked goods heaven. She glanced around. Amidst the gentle cascade of snowflakes outside, the bakery exuded warmth and comfort. A symphony of butter and almond-scented pastries danced in the air, mingling with the rich aroma of freshly brewed coffee. Customers, mostly clad in black coats, found solace in the café's cozy interior against the winter's chill.

It was a painting-like setting in which Julia could've lost herself. But now was not the time.

"And then what?" she asked.

"We use the bowl as quickly as possible," Marcel said. "The moment we see the Sun Crystal."

"I'm sure security won't be checking backpacks." Julia didn't hide her sarcasm.

"Okay, I'll tuck into my shirt. Pretend I'm pregnant."

Julia conceded that one. "Not bad. But who knows how close we need to be, which increases our chances of getting caught."

Fosca wiped her mouth with a napkin, then spoke to Julia. "You're right. We need redundancy. If one of us is caught, another person takes the bowl and does the job."

Julia scoffed while finishing her croissant. "Two pregnant girls with orange hair. That won't attract attention. What are we going to do, put the bowl on the floor with everyone there and start running the striker around it? We don't even know how long we need to do it for."

"Then we go to plan B. Brute force," Fosca said. "We snatch the Sun Crystal and throw it into the lagoon."

"Sure," Julia said. "I'll pass it to you right after I'm shot. Or stabbed with a sword."

She rubbed the scar on her abdomen. The pain had long subsided, but the memory would never dissipate. Both plans were suicide missions, and they knew it. There was only *one* answer. Julia glanced at Marcel, who nodded to indicate he thought the same thing.

Julia took Fosca's hand. "Plan B is the *Painters*," she said with a supportive voice.

Fosca yanked her hand away. Her eyes shimmered. "I know what you're implying. No. We agreed there's another way."

"You said it's like two-factor authentication—"

Fosca pounded the table. "We can't kill Carlo, Julia. I won't let you." She covered her face with her hands, sobbing into them.

"Then Nick and all the souls will be lost in the abyss forever."

A deep exhale escaped Julia. She knew in her heart if it came down to it... Carlo needed to die. She was prepared to do it.

Silence descended over their table.

"Maybe we can get a message to Carlo," Fosca said, wiping her eyes.

"How?" Julia asked. "By sending a rat with a little secret message tied to its paw?"

Fosca scowled at Julia.

Julia picked at the crumbs of her croissant. She felt bad about causing Fosca grief, but her husband was in a worse predicament. "That's if we're not caught," She twirled her finger in her hair. "I like the idea of nobody suspecting two redhead twins, but we also stand out."

"It's too bad we can't use the bowl remotely," Fosca said. "Can you hack into a video feed?"

Marcel shot his head up. "I don't think we need to. Why can't we do it remotely?"

"What do you mean?" Fosca asked.

"A microphone and speakers," Marcel replied. "We can amplify the bowl's song. We can reach the Sun Crystal. Reach the *people*. *Everyone* will hear it. When we destroy the crystal, they'll see della Porta is a fraud."

As her French friends discussed that ridiculous idea, something Marcel said triggered a forgotten thought in Julia's head.

*Reach the people.*

"Carlo and I were talking on the boat. Outside the Madonna dell'Orto church," she said. "One of the first times I met him, we talked about art and how to reach people. Is it the subject? The colors? At one time in our careers, we both thought the answer was to work broadly."

"It's the opposite," Fosca said.

Julia nodded. "People react to personal things. Things that *connect* with them."

"So what's your point?" Marcel asked.

"My point," Julia said, "is that we're thinking too broadly. Our way in isn't storming the gates or setting up concert speakers outside the Palazzo. The answer is just one person. If we can sway one person—the *right* person—that person can get us in. And get us close."

Marcel and Fosca nodded.

"Easier said than done," Fosca said. "Humoring you for a second, who do you have in mind? Lacasse? He always seems conflicted with his tie to the law."

Marcel tapped the table. "If he were so conflicted, he'd follow the law."

"Exactly," Julia said. "He's had plenty of chances to do the right thing. Hell, he was there in China, using Interpol to abduct Carlo."

"Point taken," Fosca said. "Then who?"

"What's your relationship like with Bernardo?"

Fosca and Marcel exchanged glances. He rolled his eyes and looked away.

"I've known him since I was a kid," Fosca replied. "Marcel knows him too. But he also killed Uncle Enzo."

"I've seen how he acts," Julia said. "I've seen that look in his eyes when della Porta does or says something stupid. Bernardo isn't on board."

"He's della Porta's right-hand man." Fosca was clearly incredulous. "He was in China, too, remember?"

"Maybe he was forced to be there." Julia sipped her latte.

Fosca shook her head. "I admit the guy is level-headed. He sees the pros and cons of everything, but if there's one person who's entrenched with della Porta, it's Bernardo."

Julia placed her coffee mug on the table. "That's why he's the guy. He's level-headed *and* entrenched. He can't possibly be okay with this. In all the times I've seen him, he's always looked pained and unhappy."

"That's because he's a pained and unhappy dude!"

"This is different," Julia said. "It's like he's forced to follow della Porta's commands."

"So what are you proposing?" Fosca asked.

"Reach out to him. Say we want to meet. Someplace private and safe. Let's feel him out."

"What if he comes with an army of Protectors?" Marcel asked. "We could be setting our own trap."

"Is that any different from plan A?" Julia replied. "You can set up your concert in St. Mark's Square if it doesn't work."

"That's plan C," Marcel said.

Julia laughed. "So now we have a new plan A. If it doesn't work, we go straight to plan C."

He cocked his head. "Doesn't that mean plan C is now plan B?"

"What was the original plan B?" Fosca threw her hands up.

"I have no idea," Julia replied. "Does it matter?"

The three chuckled, then sat in contemplative silence for a moment.

"C'est bon," Marcel finally said. "Like you said, what's the difference?"

Fosca tapped her fingers on the table, then exhaled. "Okay. I'll text him."

"Do it from the burner phone," Marcel said. "Block your number."

"Got it," Fosca replied.

Julia watched over Fosca's shoulder as her friend found Bernardo's number in her contacts and sent him a simple text: *'It's Fosca. Are you willing to talk? In person. In private.'* She quickly added another: *'Outside of Venice.'*

"Do you think he'll go for that?" Julia asked.

"Looks like we're about to find out," Fosca replied.

She angled the phone to them. It showed three bouncing dots, indicating Bernardo was typing. Then the dots vanished. A moment later, they started bouncing again. They stopped again. The friends gazed at each other and shrugged. The Protector was either conflicted or trying to get his words right. Or both. The dots bounced again, and a half second later, the message appeared:

*'Bene. I know a place.'*

"He's in," Fosca exclaimed with an astounded smile.

Marcel wagged his finger. "Très bien. We need to dictate the location."

"Agreed," Fosca said.

She wrote back: *'I know a better place. I'll text you.'*

# XLII

AN HOUR'S DRIVE NORTH of Venice, Castello di Conegliano was a medieval castle in the heart of the region's wine country. Fosca had explained the castle was a thousand years old but now a tourist destination, with a small museum and a restaurant.

Perched atop a knoll in the town of Conegliano, home of prosecco, the castle offered sweeping views at the base. From the top of the tower, the panorama took Julia's breath away. She had her fill of towers but this one was child's play—in daylight, with guardrails, and a dozen tourists snapping pictures of the scene with their cell phones.

A sanctuary of winter beauty stretched out beyond them. Terracotta roofs, rows of dormant vineyards, barren trees, and evergreens were framed by undulating hills in the distance. Like many of the views she'd seen, it painted a tapestry of heritage that she imagined looked much the same in Isabella and Angelo's time.

Marcel waited in the castle restaurant, connected to Fosca's and Julia's earpieces. The devices weren't exactly CIA-quality, but their hair obscured their ears enough. Even if Bernardo saw the earpieces, it was preferable to an ambush. If that happened, Marcel would call the police. Fosca chose this site because she didn't think the Order had a foothold in this town.

"Remember what I said." Marcel's voice seeped into Julia's ear with startling clarity. "If something smells funny, don't engage. Tell me immediately, and you get down here."

"We get it boss," Fosca replied. She pointed to the roof's edge. "There."

Julia followed Fosca's line of vision and found a man with a buzzcut gazing out at the sweeping vista. He wore his trademark navy-blue suit, with one sleeve pinned where his missing arm would've been. His one arm rested on the battlement.

They headed over and stopped about five feet away to keep their distance.

"Thank you for meeting us, Bernardo," Fosca said.

The chief Protector turned. He remained silent, forcing Fosca to speak first.

"Why did you come?" she asked.

"Do you think those ridiculous sunglasses and your dyed hair disguise your appearance? You look like clowns."

Fosca pursed her lips and threw a quick glance at Julia. "Are you a fashion critic now?" she asked. "You came, we thanked you. Answer my question."

Bernardo squinted at Fosca's face, then Julia's. "Who's on the other end of those?" he asked, indicating their earpieces.

"Don't worry about it."

"No," Julia said. "He should worry about it." She spoke to Bernardo. "We have an entire army of police listening to this conversation. Try one thing funny, and they'll be swarming the tower. I've already told them about your crimes."

It was the first time Julia had ever seen the man smile.

"I'm impressed, Signora O'Connor," he said. "You've come a long way from the first time we met. But you're not any better at lying. Someone is listening, but it's not the police. What makes you think I won't rip those earpieces out of your ears, throw them over the side, and bring the two of you back to Venice?"

Chuckling nervously, Julia and Fosca took a step back.

"With one good arm?" Julia asked.

"The same arm used to subdue your husband," he replied.

She swallowed. Hard. His words hit home, renewing painful memories, and crushing her spirit. Maybe contacting Bernardo wasn't such a good idea after all.

"Fosca," Bernardo said. "You asked why I came. Nick O'Connor is but one reason." He looked Julia in the eye. "What happened to him, what happened to you, is most regretful. That is not who the Order is. It's not what Veritism is."

"Yet you're a loyal servant of both," Fosca said. "You've even adopted della Porta's name for this ludicrous so-called religion."

"It's not a bad name. There's legitimacy in it. Yes, I'm a believer. You may not agree with the Order's methods, but you know the truths. So do you, Signora O'Connor. How could one not accept Veritism? As della Porta says, it's the one veritable religion. This is indisputable."

Julia couldn't refute this. "You're right," she said. "I've seen things I never would have believed. Things my husband swore were true, and I didn't trust him until I saw them with my own eyes. When I did, I realized everything he said was real. But that doesn't mean that millions of people's souls should be incarcerated for eternity, with one man in charge, dictating who is sentenced."

Bernardo nodded. "This is why I came. He's going too far—"

"He's *already* gone too far," Fosca yelled. Tears filled her eyes.

Three middle-aged women, bundled in coats and scarves, made a bee line for the other side of the roof.

"You know he killed my grandmother," Fosca continued. "And Manuel."

Bernardo gave her a mournful look. "I supposed as much. I don't have proof, but there are no other suspects in my mind. It was certainly not Nick O'Connor."

"So why haven't you stopped it?" Fosca asked. "Why didn't you help Uncle Enzo?"

The chief Protector dropped his gaze as he pondered her question. "Again, Fosca. This is why I'm willing to talk."

"How's Carlo?" she asked.

"Alive."

Fosca exhaled a sigh of relief. "What does della Porta plan on doing with him?"

"What do you think? He's the Venetian Painter. He's going to transfer Carlo's power to someone loyal."

"Will that kill him?" Julia asked.

"Truthfully, nobody knows," Bernardo replied. "Della Porta is hoping it doesn't. He wants to make an example out of Carlo."

Julia exchanged a worried glance with Fosca.

"He'll paint him into *Paradise*?" Julia asked.

"Precisely," Bernardo replied. "I hate to say it, but that's the least of it. Veritism is getting worse before it's even started." Sorrow unsettled his words. "Lobo is a sadistic disgrace. If we send hundreds of Painters of his ilk around the world, evil will spread like a cancer, and there will be no turning back."

"Then join us," Fosca said. "Help us put an end to all this."

Bernardo rubbed his jaw with his one hand. He gazed out to the distant hills, then looked back at Fosca. "I took an oath."

"So did I. I'm a member of the Order, too." Fosca placed her hands on her hips. "That oath didn't include subservience to a person trying to take over the world. Breaking your oath won't destroy the world. Keeping it might."

Bernardo exhaled through his nose. He offered the slightest of nods. "What do you want me to do?"

"Is shooting him in the back of the head too much?" Julia asked.

Fosca and Bernardo snapped their heads at her, shocked she'd say such a thing.

"What?" Julia asked. "Isn't that the easiest solution?"

"This was a mistake," Bernardo said. He headed for the stairwell door.

"Bernardo, wait," Fosca called. "We're not asking you to kill him."

He stopped and turned. "Then what?"

"Get us into the Great Council Room on della Porta's big night," Fosca said. "Front and center. That's all you have to do."

Bernardo pursed his lips. "What will *you* do?"

# XLIII

C ARLO BLENDED DROPLETS OF yellow light hansa, pyrrole orange, and iridescent white into the quinacridone crimson on his palette and brushed a minuscule amount of the new tone onto Fosca's cheekbones. He stepped back and admired his creation.

He painted the portrait entirely from memory. It was a dramatic departure from his typical artwork. Fosca was shrouded in black from the neck up, much like Tintoretto's self-portraits. But while the master had rendered somber depictions, this visage of Fosca embodied life.

It was the best work Carlo had ever produced—for the best thing that had ever happened to him.

Tears welled in his eyes.

He'd never see her again. He'd never be able to press his lips against hers or hear her laugh, her spry sense of humor, or feel her undying energy.

The door to his cell opened, adding salt to his wounds. He couldn't even mourn in peace. He didn't turn around, yet he knew it was time. He wanted to stand there and stare at Fosca for as long as possible. If he was going to die, he wanted the image of her face branded on his brain.

"Buon Natale," said a voice he'd learned to loathe.

There he was, Salvatore della Porta, a man Carlo once considered a father figure, who now was his abductor and destroying his life, wishing him a happy Christmas. The only thing happy about the day was that Carlo knew his suffering would soon end.

"I want you to know," della Porta said in Venetian, "I wish things could've been different. I think you know that."

Carlo gritted his teeth. He refused to turn.

Instead, della Porta joined him at his side. "I say this with genuine, sad irony, Carlo. You were born to be the Order's Painter. This work, it's... it's astounding. You captured her spirit."

Carlo closed his eyes. Della Porta's compliment was a double-edged sword, the words cutting to the bone. A realization set in—what if they'd kidnapped Fosca like they did the others and would force him to paint her soul? No. He wouldn't do it. He'd kill himself before he let that happen.

A sudden urge to destroy the painting—to protect her—overwhelmed him. He reached for the canvas but couldn't bring himself to harm Fosca. Della Porta was right—Carlo had captured her spirit. A single blemish would be sacrilege.

"I have a gift for you," della Porta said.

"My freedom?"

Della Porta replied with a snicker.

"Is that funny?" Carlo asked.

"Ironic, really. You were—still are—in a unique position to liberate everyone."

Carlo raised an eyebrow.

"You of all people should know this," della Porta said.

"Know what?"

"Truth, Carlo. A quest for truth. And once that truth is found, to make sure everyone knows it. This is about the entire human race. Correcting it to a truth. Imagine if everyone knows what we know. How many wars, acts of terror, and crimes will be avoided in the future? Humanity can finally unite."

Della Porta grew gleeful as he expressed his vision.

"With you in charge." Carlo shuddered at the thought.

"Someone needs to be."

"And if people don't like your ways?"

"The means are nothing new, Carlo. The end—a glorious end, which is a new beginning for humanity—*that's* new. Come with me. You'll appreciate this."

The man's delusions of grandeur knew no bounds. Worse, Carlo thought, he actually believed what he was saying. Della Porta opened the door and extended his palm.

Since he didn't have a choice, Carlo said a silent goodbye to Fosca and followed della Porta and four Protectors—all holding pistols—out of the cell. After securing his hands with handcuffs and ankles with a chain, they escorted Carlo down the corridor and up the stairs that deposited them in the *Sala delle Quattro Porte,* the Four Doors Room.

Carlo dreaded della Porta's supposed "gift," expecting it to be additional friends he would soon imprison. At first, Carlo thought the room was empty, save four additional armed Protectors guarding each door.

A faint feminine voice emanated from the walls: "He's here. He's here. He's here."

It couldn't be. Della Porta couldn't be that cruel. In the moment, that voice—that sweet, melodic voice—was at once panacea and sheer horror.

He stepped further into the room. A full picture came into view behind the nearest Protector—a woman in a black dress sat on one of the side red-oak benches, rocking as she uttered her mantra.

Despite his mother's mental failings, her lovely oval face exuded health. Her dark hair grayed at its roots.

Tears came to Carlo's eyes. That della Porta would do this, to paint his mother into the Abyss, after he did the same to his father, was the most unforgivable act anyone could ever perform.

Two desires ambushed Carlo's brain—to hug his mother or to rush della Porta, wrap his hands around the man's neck, and choke the life out of him.

He chose the latter.

Even with the chain between his feet, Carlo used his blazing speed to storm della Porta, his hands extended for the man's throat. He got within half a meter before a searing pain jolted his ankles and shot through his body. He dropped to the floor, convulsing.

His mother screamed.

Through the hazy agony, Carlo saw della Porta standing over him, wielding a small black box with an antenna.

Finally, Della Porta released the button in his hand.

The pain subsided. Carlo breathed deep, but electricity still coursed through him.

"They're called stun cuffs," della Porta said.

He admired the remote control. "80,000 volts. Can you believe that? It looks like it hurts."

Carlo got to his knees and spat on the floor. "Haven't you done enough? I'd kill myself before painting my mother's soul."

"Carlo, no," his mother cried. She tried to stand, but the Protector pressed his hand on her shoulder to keep her down.

"Tsk, tsk, Carlo," della Porta said. "Do you think me a barbarian? I told you I had a *gift* for you. A chance to say goodbye to your dear mother."

"Goodbye?" his mother whispered.

"Mamma," Carlo said. "Do not listen to him. He's a liar and a murderer."

"Again, with the insults," della Porta said. "You've known me since you were a boy, Carlo. I raised you in your formative years. We may have had our differences recently, but I am a man of my word. I do what I say, whether you agree with it or not."

"You won't paint her in?"

"Of course not."

Relief washed over Carlo. "And the others? Those you brought to this room?"

"Those people are criminals." He smiled warmly—almost longingly—at Carlo's mother. "Your mother is a saint."

Carlo gazed at his mamma. At least he and della Porta agreed on one thing.

"Have your time with her," della Porta said. "Then she can watch your big night."

Compartmentalizing what della Porta had in store for him, Carlo sat beside his mamma. He took one hand between his cuffed two. She touched the chain and sniffed.

"It's not too late," della Porta said.

He eyed Carlo expectantly as if waiting for an apology or vow of allegiance. Carlo blocked the man out and turned to his attention to his mother.

"Very well." Della Porta snapped his fingers and exited with two Protectors. Six remained to guard Carlo.

Snowflakes drifted onto Julia's cloaked head. The gondola floated down the canal as a tuxedo-clad Bernardo steered them toward the Bridge of Sighs. She sat next to Fosca, both wearing black cloaks over evening gowns.

Their hands were cuffed on their laps.

Julia's hands rested on her belly, which looked five-months pregnant. The metal bowl pressed into her stomach, requiring her to shift her position every minute. She glanced at Fosca, who maintained her composure. They had abandoned the redundancy idea since it would've been more suspicious if they were both expecting, and it made sense for Julia to be the pregnant one. Bernardo hadn't noticed the bulge or her fidgeting. Or maybe he thought she was on edge—which was definitely true.

She gazed up toward the night sky, allowing the snow to land on her skin. The Palazzo Ducale loomed over her on her right. Other buildings stood on the left. Unlike other canals, this one had the decided feeling of cruising down a flooded street in lower Manhattan.

On their second day in Venice, she and Nick had taken the Secret Itineraries tour of the Palazzo. The jovial tour guide explained the Bridge of Sighs. The 425-year-old bridge was made of stone and enclosed, with just two small, barred windows. Guards escorted prisoners from the interrogation chambers in the Palazzo to the new prison that stood ominously over her left shoulder. The bridge got its name because prisoners would sigh when they reached the window—their last view of Venice before being taken to the prison cells.

Julia knew those interrogation rooms all too well.

A strange irony set the scene of attempting to sneak *into* the Palazzo as prisoners.

"Remember," Bernardo whispered. "Just press the button, and the cuffs will release."

A simple enough instruction but only one part of their plan. Julia shivered in the cold Christmas air. Her rapid breathing created little clouds. Should any fragment of their plan fail, it would be the end—for everyone.

"Marcel," Fosca whispered. "Are you ready?"

"Not exactly," said Marcel, his voice tinny in Julia and Fosca's earpieces.

"What do you mean, 'Not exactly?'" Fosca asked.

"The place is crawling with cops and guards."

Fosca shot Julia a worried look. So much for plan B. Or was that plan F? Julia couldn't keep them straight.

"I'll figure something out," Marcel said. "Worry about yourselves. Remember, if shit goes down, like my Irish friend says, get out of there before the devil knows you're dead."

"Don't worry," Julia replied. "He knows."

"Stop talking," Bernardo said.

"Remember what my nonna-mère used to tell me," Fosca whispered to Julia. "Own it."

*Own it*, Julia repeated in her head.

If she didn't, she'd soon be dead.

The gondola glided under the Bridge of Sighs. Bernardo pulled the craft over a few feet away at a dock attached to the Palazzo. Lacasse and two Protectors stood in front of an open door, which Julia assumed was used for deliveries. One Protector knelt and moored the bow of the boat. Bernardo jumped out and tied the stern.

Lacasse held out his hand to Fosca.

"Looking sharp, detective," she said.

Julia had to admit that Lacasse filled out his tuxedo nicely. Unlike Bernardo's standard black bowtie, the Interpol detective's gray straight tie complemented his gray hair and features and accentuated his eyes, even in the muted light.

"Good evening, Fosca." He nodded to Julia. "Madame O'Connor."

Fosca took his hand with her cuffed ones and allowed him to help her onto the dock. Julia did the same.

"We have plenty of questions," Lacasse said. "Let's get out of the cold—"

He cut himself off and eyed Julia's face. Then she realized he wasn't looking at her face—he was scrutinizing the side of her head. He pulled her hood off, brushed her hair back, and smirked at her ear.

"Nice hair," he said of her red bob. "And nice try. I'll take these." Lacasse removed Julia and Fosca's earpieces, which he held in a closed fist. "In case these are microphones..."

He removed both of their earrings and necklaces.

"Bulgari doesn't make spy gear," Fosca said.

"I suspect not," replied Lacasse.

"I want those back." Fosca glared at the detective.

"It is unlikely you'll ever wear them again. We'll donate them to charity."

He spoke into the items in his palm. "Whoever is listening, say goodbye. And know that we will find you."

The detective wrapped everything in a handkerchief, which he handed to a Protector. The Protector shoved the small package into his pocket and left.

Julia swallowed hard. She exchanged a glance with Fosca, who wore the same "we're fucked" expression Julia felt. Even if Marcel could get situated for plan F, without communication, it would be impossible to pull off. That meant zero margin of error for plan A.

Lacasse turned to Bernardo. "It's high-tech, but you should've caught those."

"A careless oversight, signor," Bernardo replied. "I frisked them thoroughly. They're otherwise clean."

"We can never be too thorough," Lacasse said. "We'll do it inside. Come."

Ever the polite Frenchman, Lacasse motioned for Julia and Fosca to enter the building, which they did. The men followed.

Lacasse led the group through an unimpressive storeroom lit by bare bulbs.

"Remove your cloaks," he said.

"That would be a neat trick," Julia replied. "Unlock us, and no problem." She raised her hands to display the handcuffs. They'd need to be unfastened for her to get her arms through the cloak's sleeves. She wasn't sure if the guards would notice the fake cuffs, but at the moment, it seemed like a calculated risk; requesting the cuffs be opened reinforced the idea that they were real.

Lacasse chuckled. "I am not a magician, but I will be gentle."

He lifted the bottom of Fosca's cloak and pulled it over her head, draping it over her cuffed hands. Lacasse sucked in air and raised his eyebrows. Fosca wore a form-fitting, one-shoulder black evening gown with pinprick-size sparkles. In the ancient storeroom with incandescent lights that grazed their heads in the low ceiling, her dress looked as if it were cut from the fabric of space.

She shook her body. "It's freezing in here."

Ignoring her, the detective did a perfunctory frisk. Seeing the skin-tight dress, he clearly knew there was no way she could be hiding a weapon.

Fosca flashed him a flirty smile. "Are you gonna buy me dinner later?"

Not saying a word, Lacasse moved to Julia. He pulled her cloak off in a similar fashion. The room's frigid air bristled her skin.

Lacasse gasped and took a half step back. Bernardo was also audibly startled. Julia wore a spaghetti-strap black gown that flattered her figure, but the men were eyeing her belly.

Lacasse reached his hand out but stopped himself.

"How far along are you?" he asked.

"Well," Julia said, glaring at him, "considering the last time I was intimate with my husband before you assholes took him from me, that would be six months."

The Interpol detective raised an eyebrow and cocked his head. Julia mentally crossed her fingers, hoping he wouldn't question the size of a six-month baby bump.

Relief came quickly. Lacasse gave her a quick pat down, avoiding her stomach. Even if he ran her hand over it, she was confident he wouldn't feel the bowl. The prior day, when they were selecting their outfits, Fosca, Julia, and Marcel had debated on how best to conceal the bowl and striker. Strangely, it was Marcel who suggested Spanx. The strapless cupped mid-thigh bodysuit was perfect. It held the bowl in place with the striker tucked inside and smoothed over the metal edge. It would've been firm to the touch, but she didn't think Lacasse would knock on it.

Of course, getting the uncomfortable slab of metal *out* of the Spanx and her dress was another story, but she'd tackle that challenge when the time came.

Satisfied, the detective pulled the cloak back onto Julia and instructed them to continue.

They reached a stairwell that led to the inside of the Palazzo. Even under the circumstances, Julia found the architecture and art glorious. They took another stairwell she'd never been in and walked down the hall, stopping at a wooden door.

Lacasse knocked on it.

"Venire," said a voice from behind it.

One of the Protectors opened the door for the group. Again, Lacasse motioned for the women to go before him.

Julia entered first to find herself in a spacious office filled with antiques. Detective Fanella reclined on a couch, her legs crossed beneath her black cloak. Adjacent to her was a desk at which Salvatore della Porta sat. He typed on his computer keyboard, without looking at them.

"I never thought you were the suicidal type, Fosca," he said.

"And I always thought you were a gentleman. Why didn't you have *her* do the pat-down?" Fosca pointed her thumb at Detective Fanella.

Della Porta exchanged shrugs with Fanella and Lacasse.

"Fair point," della Porta said, standing. "She should have, and I apologize for that oversight. Forgive me if I'm brusque, but as you know, I have a pressing engagement. Your surrender to Bernardo was a surprise—one worth exploring. A welcome surprise, but more than a hint suspicious, despite your... condition." He motioned to Julia's belly. "So, ladies, tell me why you're here. You were given fair warning about what would happen if you returned to Venice."

They'd rehearsed this scenario, but Julia looked to Fosca for guidance anyway. Her friend nodded to her.

"We have information you'll like," Julia said. "But I want to speak to Nick first." She rubbed her belly. Genuine tears welled in her eyes. No longer was she acting, knowing that unless a miracle happened, she would never have a child with the man she loved. "He... deserves to know."

Della Porta stepped to the front of his desk and sat on the edge. He adjusted his cufflinks and bowtie. "Okay, I'll bite. What information?"

"You heard her terms," Fosca said.

Della Porta cocked his head. "Right you are, Fosca."

"I want to speak with Nick now." Julia wiped her eyes. "I'll tell you the information *after* your little party."

"How do you expect to speak to your husband?"

Julia managed a smile. "Through Carlo."

Della Porta nodded with an appreciative air. He checked his watch. "We're starting soon."

"That's why we got here early," Fosca said.

With a grin, della Porta slid off the desk. "And *you*, Fosca? Why are you here?"

"You need to let us go," she replied. "*Really* let us go. For good."

"Why would I do that after all your sins against the Order?"

Fosca gazed at Bernardo and the Protectors before giving della Porta a smug smile. "Imagine... two Baldesseris missing, with you being the last to see them? Everyone knows you murdered my grandmother."

"Not true," della Porta interjected. He cleared his throat.

"You're right," Fosca continued. "I guess not *everyone* knows it. How would your growing flock—especially the Madrid and Paris chapters—react if you murdered two prominent members?" She craned her neck to speak to the others in the room. "Does that sit well with you, boys? Who's next? Do you really feel secure, Bernardo?"

Bernardo remained silent but swallowed.

Della Porta released a long exhale through his nose. "I am sure you have an ulterior motive or plan that will undoubtedly fail. You've piqued my curiosity, though." He turned to his chief Protector. "Bernardo, escort Signora O'Connor to Carlo. Have the portrait of Nick O'Connor brought there. I'll meet you shortly."

"Va bene," Bernardo replied. He took Julia's arm and began taking her away.

Julia shot a worried look at Fosca.

"What about me?" Fosca asked.

"Did Signor O'Connor impregnate you?" della Porta asked. He raised an eyebrow. "Or perhaps Carlo did?"

Fosca's eyes reddened. She didn't answer.

"I didn't think so." Della Porta nodded to Bernardo and Fanella, who guided Julia out.

She gazed back at Fosca, hoping she'd see her friend again.

In Bernardo and Fanella's custody, the men brought Julia to a room with four doors and glorious masterworks on the walls and ceiling.

"Julia," cried Carlo.

He sprang from one of the benches, but the two Protectors flanking him shoved him down. Each held a pistol.

"Carlo," Julia responded with equal emotion. She moved to rush to him, but Bernardo kept her back.

"Are you okay?" Carlo asked. "Are you hurt?"

"I'm fine," she responded. "What about you?"

He raised his shackled hands. "I've been better. I thought I'd never see you again. Where's Fosca?"

"She's okay too. We turned ourselves in."

"What?! Why would you do such a thing?"

Julia sniffed. She brought her gaze and hands to her belly and caressed the bowl. "I need to speak to the father of my child."

She glanced at Carlo again. His mouth popped open.

A moment later, two Protectors, each wearing white cotton gloves, carried in a stunning portrait of her husband. In addition to the impressive technique, Carlo had captured Nick's essence perfectly. His eyes expressed warmth, humor, and strength. Then Julia realized why—she *was* looking at Nick. Repressed fury boiled within her. His killer—her supposed friend—sat ten feet away. Like some sick court-ordered punishment, she now needed to communicate with the victim through the victim's murderer.

She almost puked but swallowed it.

For the first time, it occurred to Julia that she, too, was about to commit an atrocity. Nick would think she's pregnant. He'd know he wasn't the father.

"Ah, we're all here," della Porta said, parading into the room. He checked his watch. "Let's get started, shall we? Signora O'Connor, please say what you wish. Carlo, you will act as an intermediary."

Floodgates released in Julia's eyes. Uncontrollable tears washed out of her. She couldn't believe she was doing this. This was a mistake. She collapsed to her knees and covered her face. In the worst of life's vicious ironies, Julia *had* been pregnant. But Angelo Mascari—the man who shared a soul with Nick—killed the baby when he stabbed her.

That thought gave her a strange drop of relief. If Nick did the math, he'd know he could be the father. At least he wouldn't think she cheated on him.

"Abbi pietà," Carlo said to the painting. He gestured to Julia. "Nick ti lascerebbe parlare con Isabella."

His words snaked into her ears through her sobbing. This would be her only chance to speak with Nick. She needed to use it wisely, not on the floor in a defeated wreck. Composing herself, she dabbed her eyes with her sleeve to preserve her makeup. She rose and straightened her cloak, pausing for what she hoped was an imperceptible amount of time. She knew all eyes were on her. In that moment, she realized the cloak obscured the bowl. If she chose the right words, she wouldn't need to lie to Nick about the baby.

Carlo turned to Julia. "Angelo tends to dominate the soul. I implored him to let Nick speak with you." He jerked his head back to the painting. He smiled and, after a moment, spoke to Julia again. "He says he misses you more than life itself."

"I miss—" she turned to Carlo. "He can hear me, right?"

"Every word." Carlo nodded with red eyes and genuine remorse.

"Nick... honey," she said to his portrait, gazing into his visage, "you are constantly in my thoughts. You will be forever. There's... there's so much I want to say. So much I want to tell you. So much has happened. I wish we had more time. You—"

"Speaking of which." Della Porta tapped his watch. "What's this alleged information?"

Julia threw him a vengeful glare. "I told you. *After* your event."

"Then I suppose we'll need to reconvene."

He snapped his fingers and nodded to the Protectors holding Nick's portrait. The men lifted it and carried it away.

"No, wait," Julia screamed. "Nick!" Frantic, she turned to della Porta. "What are you doing? You said I could speak to him!"

Della Porta clasped his hands in front of him. "You just did, signora. Please, you do not want to become agitated in your state."

Steaming-hot blood rose to Julia's face. She puffed in and out through her nose like a bull. "Agitated?" she said through gritted teeth. "I'll show you agitated!" She raised her manacled hands and charged for his throat.

She took one step before Bernardo and Fanella grabbed her and held her back.

Della Porta raised an eyebrow. He pointed his finger at Julia and Carlo. "My, you two are quite the pair. Carlo required extra restraints. Is that something *you* need Signora O'Connor?"

Julia shot a glance at Carlo, who whiffled his head. She breathed in, calming herself. "No," she said.

"Va bene," della Porta replied. "You shall have your time with your husband. *After* the ceremony." He raised a finger. "Ah, I almost forgot..."

He removed a folded piece of paper from his inner jacket pocket and waved it.

"You'll recall your husband wrote you a letter before he escaped from prison."

Julia nodded her head. She eyed the handwritten blue ink. Though she just had a moment to speak with him, she desperately wanted that letter. At the time, della Porta's price was too high.

"I am a man of my word, signora," della Porta said. "I had asked if you knew Fosca's whereabouts, and you delivered beyond my expectations."

"What are you talking—" Julia's heart shriveled. She had hand-delivered Fosca to the Order.

Della Porta opened his free palm as if welcoming her to a game she didn't realize she was playing. He handed the letter to Bernardo, who tucked it into his inner jacket pocket.

"Remove her cloak," he said to Fanella. "She's not a member. Fosca's, too." He spoke to Julia. "You shall also have the letter at the end of the night. Tomorrow, you'll be escorted home, first class. We have no more quarrel with you, Julia."

Della Porta turned on his heel and headed for one of the four doors.

"What about my friends?" Julia asked. "Fosca? Carlo? The others?"

The bastard exited through the door without another word.

# XLIV

THE GREAT COUNCIL ROOM looked to Julia like it had been set up for a political rally. Hundreds of folding chairs filled the space. Crews had erected scaffoldings on the sides and rear for television cameras and spotlights and worked the gear. Three projection screens were set up—two in front of the doors and one on the stage in front of the council seats, but carefully positioned so they didn't block *Paradise*. The stage had been widened and expanded outward. Black curtains had been placed behind the two monitors in front of the doors. A lectern with three microphones was situated at the front center of the dais. Two presidential-style, transparent teleprompters flanked the podium. Loudspeakers were positioned next to the screens, as well as on the sides and rear of the room. She counted a dozen of them.

Dante and another Protector brought her to the red-oak bench that lined the room and sat her down at the front end. Dante stood next to her, his arms folded over a bulge in his suit jacket, which Julia assumed was formed by his Mongolian short sword.

When the Protectors took her from the Four Doors Room, they left Carlo with his guards. She had no clue where Fosca was, but a scuffle from behind the far black curtain soon gave her an answer.

Two additional Protectors led Fosca out, relieved of her cloak. She was still cuffed, but, in typical fashion, caused a commotion. The Protectors forced her down on the bench on the other side.

Julia caught her attention, and the two made eye contact, though seventy-five feet separated them. Their sole redemption was being positioned in front of the first row of chairs. Had the Protectors seated one of them just a few feet toward the room's rear, they wouldn't have been able to see each other through the seats, let alone once people filled them.

Despite the metal chafing her wrists, Julia realized she was subconsciously rubbing the bowl as if it were her baby. She brought her hands up but continued doing it to keep up the charade. It also helped calm her. The experience with Nick and della Porta left her frazzled, but it distracted her from what was to come.

The last time she was in a similar situation, in Madrid, her hands weren't bound, she had a knife in her purse, and she was wasted. Now, stone-cold sober with no weapon, her body shook like a weather vane in a hurricane.

She needed to control her emotions. She closed her eyes and breathed. Her cuffs were *fake*. She could get out of them in seconds. And she had a weapon—the bowl.

Voices rose from the rear of the room. Julia opened her eyes and straightened her back. People were arriving. She looked over at Fosca, who nodded to her.

*Be ready.*

It took nearly an hour for everyone to take their seats. Julia lost count early on but estimated at least five hundred people arrived. At first, people entered quietly as if joining a somber gathering. But that ambiance was short-lived. A hubbub buzzed the space as excitement took over. She eavesdropped on some conversations. While people were dismayed to be there on Christmas night, most felt it was worth it—as though they were part of a select few about to witness history.

The front rows—over one hundred people—wore cloaks. Julia assumed these were members of the Order. Behind them sat various people dressed in black tie and clergy of all religions and denominations.

It was quite a sight to behold. Julia had to hand it to della Porta—the man knew how to create a spectacle.

A cloaked Order member approached the front. She recognized that goofy beard and those little round glasses—Isacco. He saw her and quickly twisted his head, before shuffling deep into the sea of black robes. He should've been ashamed. Now she knew how della Porta found them at the Madonna dell'Orto Church.

She had more important things to think about.

When the last people took their seats, dozens of black-suit-clad Protectors filed into the room after them. The men and women stood, flanking the audience. Julia estimated there had to be an additional two hundred Protectors. Dante remained next to her in silence.

The turmoil of five hundred people speaking was so loud that it soon became impossible for Julia to home in on any one conversation.

Fanella and Lacasse entered from the rear and walked down either side of the audience. Upon reaching their respective corners of the stage, they faced the room, providing additional security.

Julia glared at Fanella, who was closer to her.

"I entered as a pilgrim. I charge forth a shepherd." The voice rang through the loudspeakers.

Simultaneously, every Protector in the room clapped their hands in a single clap. The move frightened Julia and everybody else—into silence.

Julia brought her attention to the dais. Della Porta stood in front of the microphones, hands raised for silence. All three screens showed his face. Lights in the room dimmed. A spotlight lit della Porta from above. He milked the moment until every eye was on him, then gripped the lectern's sides.

"I entered as a pilgrim," he said again in his impeccable English. "I charge forth a shepherd. We *all* have entered here as pilgrims tonight. I promise each and every one of you, we shall charge forth as shepherds. I want to thank you all for coming. So many have joined us." He gestured to those before him. "We have politicians, members of the press, clergy of all faiths, atheists, scientists and engineers, law enforcement, doctors, attorneys, celebrities, social media influencers, and so many more from all over the world, watching on the internet, and of course, members of our esteemed Ancient Order of the Seventh Sun. I thank you all. I am well aware it's Christmas night. You took time from your friends and families. Even those of you not of the Christian faith traveled far and wide." He smiled. "Though I suppose an all-expense paid trip to Venice had something to do with it."

The audience chuckled.

*All expenses paid?* Julia thought. *They must've spent a fortune.*

"That is far from the only gift you'll receive tonight."

He strolled the dais, admiring the paintings, with his eyes landing on *Paradise*.

"Many of you have been to this palace, to this room," della Porta said, his voice amplified by his lapel mic. "I suspect most of you are familiar with the Venetian Republic. At one point, we were the most powerful maritime empire in the world. Wealth flowed into this city like an untapped firehose." He gestured to *Paradise*, looming over him. "Many of you are intimately familiar with this glorious masterwork, *Il Paradiso*, created by one of history's greatest artists, Venice's own Jacopo Tintoretto. For many of you, it is undoubtedly the first time you are beholding this masterpiece, the largest oil painting in the world. Only a few of you are aware that those are real people up there."

Audience members cocked their heads, seemingly unsure if he meant the portraits were modeled on real people or if they were *actually real people*. A part of Julia wished she didn't know the truth.

Della Porta pivoted and motioned to the whole room. "The founders of Venice had lofty ambitions. This building was inspired by King Solomon's Palace, which was designed by the architect Hiram of Tyre. Those who know our Order know our beliefs can be traced back to the greatest religions and civilizations the world has ever known."

He stepped back to the podium.

"You must be wondering why I mention any of this. You're probably also wondering for how long I'll be speaking."

Again, the audience laughed.

"Not to worry," della Porta said. "I won't drag out the main event. We promised great things tonight. Maybe you expect a Christmas gift like you used to get when you were children. Just as we all thought Christmas was magical when we were kids, perhaps you'll feel that way tonight. What you will see is special, but not special effects. Fantastic, but not fantasy. And yes, magical but not magic."

He took another dramatic pause. Julia gazed at the audience. Every eye in the room watched della Porta.

"It's no secret that Italians revere history. Why wouldn't we? From the Holy Roman Empire to the Renaissance to Gucci, Ferrari, and tiramisu"—he let the audience laugh again—"we've been in the thick of it. There have been monumental moments in recorded human history. Epochs. The birth of Jesus—whether you believe or not—is an indisputable epoch. The moment changed humanity as we know it. The same can be said for the founding of all the major religions. As well as for the printing press, electricity, the automobile, the moon landing, and soon, a landing on Mars. Think of it. People walking on another planet."

Again, della Porta took a dramatic pause, letting the audience soak in his words. Julia's heartbeat quickened. He was winning over the crowd, and the Sun Crystal hadn't even been brought out.

"Tonight, my friends"—the word echoed across the room–"tonight, you will witness an epoch. A monumental moment in recorded human history of which only a few have so far been aware. Whether you are religious or a scientist, our lives and our world revolve around faith—faith in a higher power, faith in yourself, faith in the world around us. The laws of physics and nature."

Numerous heads bobbed in agreement. Julia wiped the sweat from her brow. She felt his big pitch was coming. By all accounts, everyone in the room was eager to hear it.

"Now," della Porta continued, "the world's religions—and there are nearly four thousand—differ in many ways, but share a singular commonality... faith. No matter how firm your convictions are, if you dig deep, it's all faith. That is why people from all faiths are present tonight."

Again, della Porta paused, this time longer than the last.

"Tonight, my friends, we introduce you to Veritism... the world's one *veritable* religion."

Gasps rose from the audience. After a moment, the response morphed into guffaws and laughter. The front rows of Order members sat in complete silence.

Julia whistled through her teeth. Maybe della Porta wasn't as charismatic as she'd thought.

"Christianity is verifiable," someone called out from the audience. "Just look at the miracles all around us."

Numerous people joined in with that person, shouting at della Porta. Some rose from their seats. They waved their hands as if fed up with this charlatan on the stage. Julia shifted in her seat, concerned violence might break out.

"I entered as a pilgrim," della Porta said boldly and loudly into the microphone. "I charge forth a shepherd."

All at once, every Protector brought their hands together in a single clap and foot stomp. The sound of two hundred people doing this in a cavernous room was like a thunderclap, resulting in immediate silence.

The audience members who'd been riled up gazed at the Protectors lining the room, staring them down. They got the message. They took their seats.

Julia got the message, too. If violence were to break out, it would be *against* the audience, not by them. One way or another, della Porta would persuade these people to follow Veritism. She didn't know when she'd be able to use the bowl or how much time she'd need, but the minutes marched on.

"There are three people I'd like you to meet," della Porta said.

He nodded to Bernardo, who went behind the screen on Fosca's side of the room and disappeared through the curtain. A moment later, he brought out Lobo, who sprang onto the dais with one leap. He tossed his long, greasy black hair over his shoulder with a pompous grin that contradicted the symbolic innocence of his white cotton robe.

Della Porta offered him a half-smile at the action, then gestured for Lobo to join him at the podium.

"Ladies and gentlemen," della Porta said, "meet Diego Blanco-Romasanta, our Spanish Painter. Those familiar with art will recognize him by his moniker, El Lobo Blanco. When I first heard his self-imposed sobriquet, I found it arrogant and juvenile."

Lobo offered the audience an innocent shrug that appeared larger than life on the projection screens.

"But, I must admit, through his actions and demeanor, he has earned the epithet. He embraces the role of Painter wholeheartedly and has the disposition and temperament for the role. Just like his predecessor... El Greco. His *immediate* predecessor. Whom he just replaced."

Amused chuckles rose from the audience as if unsure if they'd heard della Porta correctly. Or if they had, they hadn't understood.

Della Porta laughed along with them. Julia gazed around the room. Other people nervously did the same. Each Protector remained as stoic as ever. Della Porta raised his hands for silence, which the audience gave him.

"I expected that response," he said.

The screen across the room switched to a view Julia knew all too well.

Della Porta continued. "You are looking at a live feed of Tintoretto's study for *Paradise*, located in the Thyssen-Bornemisza Museum in Madrid."

To the casual observer, it was just a shot of a painting. A different picture began forming in Julia's mind.

"This is Lobo's domain. Literally and figuratively."

The screen closest to Julia switched to another feed of a painting she'd only seen online.

"Here," della Porta said, "is a live feed of Tintoretto's other study for *Paradise*, located in the Louvre. It is the domain of our oldest living Painter. In fact, the oldest living person in the world. And Italian, of course. Ladies and gentlemen, please meet the esteemed Artemisia Gentileschi."

Another Protector came from behind the screen closest to Julia, wheeling a frail woman in a scarlet kimono, who appeared on the main screen behind della Porta. Ebony locks cascaded over the lady's sunken gaze and pallid cheeks. The Protector wheeled her up the ramp to the stage next to della Porta, who kissed her hand.

"You expect us to believe that?" a voice shouted from the crowd.

"I got all dressed up to see an old bag in makeup," said an American woman sitting two rows behind the Order members. She rose and shuffled for the exit.

Multiple people voiced their displeasure and stood.

From all that she'd seen, Julia knew the truth. Yet she still couldn't believe it. She'd studied Artemisia Gentileschi in college. As one of the few major female artists of the Renaissance, Artemisia was a legend. Apparently, a *living* legend. It made perfect sense the Order recruited her. Besides her raw talent as a portraitist, she was an effervescent personality—defiant in her personal and professional life.

"I entered as a pilgrim," della Porta called into the microphone, louder than ever. "I charge forth a shepherd."

"I charge forth a shepherd," all the Order members said in unison.

Again, the Protectors did a single clap, but this time, they took a menacing step toward the audience.

The effect chilled Julia. She wasn't the only one. Those who had stood stopped mid-stride, as if caught in a time-stilled dance. They gazed at the Protectors, who stared straight ahead. They eyed the hundred-plus Order members, who remained sitting stock-still with their hoods on. Fear restored, the dissenters took their seats.

"Friends, friends," della Porta said. "When I first heard these claims, I also thought them fabricated and outlandish. How could one not? But there is more. The figures in *Paradise* above me are real. The same is true for those in the *Paradises* in Paris and Madrid. I do not say that figuratively nor do I imply they are based on real people from history. In fact, each and every one of them is a soul, confined to the painting, put there for their sins. And I can prove it."

Della Porta nodded to Artemisia's Protector. He wheeled her down the ramp. Dante took the wheelchair and parked her a few feet from Julia. Up close, the ancient woman was a sight to behold. It could've been her imagination, but Julia swore she got a whiff of death.

A ruckus came from behind the curtain nearest them. Two Protectors brought a man out, each holding an arm. The man's hands were restrained, and a gag had been stuffed in his mouth. He struggled as they dragged him toward the dais.

Julia recognized that disheveled blond hair and bright blue eyes, filled with fear. Lionel Benton. The London *Times* art critic who was the first person to tell Julia about the Ancient Order of the Seventh Sun. Her first ally. And a massive nuisance for della Porta.

Many of the audience members stiffened at the sight. A rock hit Julia's gut as she realized what would happen to her friend. She yearned to run up there and help him. But she held her place.

"You will learn truths tonight," della Porta said into the mic, as the Protectors dragged Benton onto the stage. "Indisputable and *verifiable* truths. Earth is hell."

Two more Protectors emerged from the curtain, dragging another bound victim—a woman Julia didn't recognize.

"Our corporal bodies are vessels for a single soul," della Porta continued. "This *one* soul, which we all have, passes through seven bodies until it is judged by Him."

Additional Protectors came out with new prisoners—Hartog, Lucia, Georgette, Olivier, Karim and three others, including an octogenarian man whose legs buckled with each step. One by one, they were brought out for the crime of simply disagreeing with the Order's policies. Her friends' presence confirmed Marcel's intel, but it also proved they were destined for a fate worse than death.

"Upon judgment," della Porta said, "your soul either ascends to Heaven or is extinguished. Unless, of course, your soul is put elsewhere. Somewhere it will remain... for eternity."

The main screen switched to a view of the nine Prisoners lined up on the side of stage. Unbridled fear exploded in their expressions. They glanced around, desperate for help. Hartog spotted Julia.

With her eyes welling, she shook her head. She had to do *something*, but the time wasn't right. She prayed that it wouldn't be too late when the time came.

"Observe." Della Porta's word echoed through the cavernous room as everyone watched in stunned silence.

Two Protectors appeared from the far curtain near Fosca, carrying a five-foot-tall golden candleholder with three wrought lion's feet, which they carefully positioned in the center of the stage.

All the cloaked Order members began chanting in a low rhythmic voice. Artemisia seamlessly joined in, mumbling their sacred mantra.

A teenage girl in a green cloak stepped onto the stage carrying a black cushion. Julia's heart quickened. Sitting on that cushion was the Sun Crystal, casting a spray of light despite any visible power source. Della Porta kissed her head and took the Sun Crystal from her before she left.

Julia uncrossed her legs and straightened her back, positioning herself to remove the bowl.

Dante placed a hand on her shoulder. Julia jumped at the motion. She gazed upward and met his watchful eyes, quashing any hope of using the bowl at that moment.

Members continued their chant, raising their volume. Cradling the sun crystal in both hands, Della Porta carried it to the candleholder and inserted it into a swirling mount. A thick black and red braided candle was positioned below the Sun Crystal.

Two painted slats in the ceiling slid open, and two devices on chains began to lower.

Additional Protectors brought out a rack and a wooden chair.

Benton's captors dragged him over to the center of the stage. He struggled to no avail. They forced him into the chair and strapped his hands and feet. Two other Protectors placed the blank canvas in the rack.

The devices lowered. Closer to Benton was a two-foot, rectangular wooden box with a small hole pointing at him. Behind the box hung a multi-faceted glass prism. It was an object she'd only heard about—from Carlo. His father had crafted that prism... and died for it.

Julia choked up. She gazed at *Paradise*. The poor man's soul watched the entire procession.

Protectors raised chains from concealed panels in the dais and secured the prism and wooden box so that they were fastened from the top and bottom behind Benton. The candleholder stood in front of him.

Della Porta removed a long lighter from his inner pocket, which he used to light the candle. It instantly flared and rose to an unnaturally intense flame.

The seated members swayed, their chant growing more fervent.

The flame's heat bathed the crystal, which glowed an orange hue. Della Porta cocked his head at it, then turned to Lobo and nodded to him.

Carrying a palette and box of paints, Lobo strode over to Benton. The screen zoomed in on the Spanish Painter's wicked grin. The camera then focused on the Sun Crystal.

The orange brilliance expanded, seeping beyond its confines.

Benton freaked, tugging and pulling at his binds. Julia's gaze darted around. The audience watched, raptured. She turned back to the grim spectacle unfolding before hundreds of onlookers.

The light spread from the crystal and condensed into a beam. It spiraled into itself and back out again. Lavender blended into the orange, punctuated by yellow and green, creating a mesmerizing spectral display, like long fingers interlocking and releasing.

The chant's volume and tempo escalated to a fevered pitch. Della Porta joined in. The potency of the Order's words compelled the light to do their bidding.

The light engulfed Benton, obscuring his features and infiltrating his body. Even through the gag, he screamed in agony.

Julia watched in horror. She needed to act. With the distraction, she was sure she could remove the bowl without being seen, but the chanting drowned out any hope of hearing the bowl's resonance.

Through the spectrum of light, Benton's features muddled, and his face aged. It withered and took on a leathery pallor with deep creases. His head arched back, his neck straining in anguish.

The once-distinguished art critic was unrecognizable. His skin had lost its color. He ceased his struggle, hands falling limp.

The light broadened and engulfed his body.

The chanting reached a deafening crescendo. Members rocked back and forth, feeling the ceremony, guiding it forth with their voices.

Benton's torso contorted at an unnatural angle.

A white, amorphous form ascended from his body as if vacuumed out by the light, hovering like a small cloud.

The shape elongated into a recognizable image.

After everything Julia had heard and witnessed, she couldn't believe what unfolded before her eyes.

Benton's soul was being extracted from his body.

Edges of his skin flowed freely as if in a breeze. His soul's arms extended, useless. A luminous tether tailed from his body like an intangible umbilical cord.

The soul slinked toward the rectangular box, drawn into the hole. It exited the opposite end, inverted. It then became more compressed, like a beam.

The chant continued in a disturbing, unified roar.

Benton's body shriveled. The tether began to fade.

His soul's light intensified as it floated toward the prism. It absorbed him and blazed the color of a blinding sunset, fueled by the energy of the soul within it. Passing through the prism, the light refracted to a corrected position, landing on the blank canvas.

The tether to Benton's body vanished. His life was gone.

Slumped in the chair was a corpse that looked like it had died months earlier.

Uncontrollable sorrow crushed Julia's spirit. Tears waterfalled from her eyes. Her grief was not solely for Benton, though that was a tragic loss. No, she now grasped something far more horrific...

*The same thing happened to Nick.*

He was dead. His soul was gone. She bawled so hard, through blurred vision, that she noticed Artemisia glancing at her with hollow eyes, seemingly concerned.

There would be no returning Nick's soul to his body.

Despite all the conjecture, the process *could not* be reversed.

Julia wiped her eyes and attempted to focus.

Lobo was already painting by the time she saw what was happening. He worked fast, capturing each characteristic of Benton's soul, fixing it permanently to the canvas.

Maybe it was because Lobo was a fast painter, or perhaps he was tracing over an image, but he finished within minutes.

He stepped back to admire his work. While not as good as Carlo's portrait of Nick, it was a stunning reproduction. No, not a reproduction. It *was* Benton.

The chanting ceased.

An unnerving silence overtook the room. Every audience member, every Order member, every Protector stared at what just happened.

All but della Porta.

The man scrutinized the room, smiling. He extended his arms, welcoming those who would unquestionably join the fold.

Julia failed. Fosca failed. The Guild failed.

She rubbed the bowl hidden in her dress as if it were a real baby, consoling it.

The world would never be the same.

Protectors pulled two men and one woman from the audience and brought them to the stage.

"In case there is any doubt you witnessed special effects," della Porta said into the podium mics, "I have invited three doctors from three countries to examine the body."

The Protectors ushered the unwitting volunteers to Benton. Another Protector brought them stethoscopes. The physicians stared in bewilderment at the corpse.

"Take them," della Porta said. "Do a thorough examination."

After some pensiveness, they took the devices. One inserted the earpieces and placed the bell against Benton's quiet chest. She only listened for a moment, as it was obvious to everyone watching the stage and screen.

"You..." the doctor said with a thick Texan drawl, "you... *murdered* him."

The mics picked up the words, broadcasting them through the speakers. A low murmur of shock and agreement rose from the crowd.

"Nonsense," della Porta said into the pulpit mics. "He got the sentence he deserved."

"What... what did he do?" asked the doctor.

"He was an enemy of the Ancient Order of the Seventh Sun," della Porta responded. "As you saw with your own eyes, he was judged by the Sun Crystal. His soul has been preserved so that his evil will not be reborn onto this Earth. We have nine other prisoners to sentence tonight. And soon, to *Paradises* all over the world." He turned to the doctors. "Take your seats."

The Protectors brought them back.

Ten men and women of different ages were led from behind the curtain nearest Fosca. The camera panned over them, displaying them on the center screen as they lined up on the side of the dais. All ten wore white robes. They carried a paintbrush in one hand and a palette in the other.

Julia scanned the audience. Fear plastered every person's face. Many eyed the Protectors surrounding them.

"Veritism," della Porta said, "is the world's one veritable religion. Indisputably. The Creator is the Supreme Painter of the Universe. The Artist has the power to create, change... or destroy. He has the power of forgiveness. Not us. Those who are believers—no, not *believers*, those of us who *know*—bear the burden of corporal judgment. The Order can see demons for who they truly are."

Della Porta turned to the Sun Crystal and *Paradise* behind it. He nodded his head at them solemnly. He snapped his fingers at a Protector who stood by the far curtain, then turned back to the audience.

"Demons walk the entire Earth," della Porta said.

The Protector emerged from behind the curtain carrying a sheet-covered canvas smaller than the others. He brought it onto the stage and propped it on the far council seat.

"Nobody will be safe from judgment." Della Porta yanked the sheet off the canvas. "Or conviction."

Julia covered her mouth. Nick's portrait watched the vast audience in frozen contemplation.

"This American sought to destroy us. He murdered our seniormost councilmember. Nearly burned down this room. He learned his lesson."

Many in the audience cleared their throats and shifted in their seats.

"We have been in existence since the year 1350," della Porta continued. "The Sun Crystal is hundreds, perhaps thousands, of years older. All this time, we have been in the shadows, preventing future crimes and saving your world from evil. Now"—he swept his gaze over the crowd—"you have a choice. Join us. Or dissent."

Julia couldn't swallow the lump in her throat. There it was—the ultimatum. Join or be imprisoned for eternity. This was della Porta's grand plan. He had collected influential people from around the world and from all aspects of life—people who would not only endorse Veritism, many would help enforce it. With a choice like the one della Porta presented, of course they would join him. He'd have *hundreds* of Pauls spreading the word, not by traveling great distances and proselytizing, but through modern communication. Julia's skin grew ice cold at the daunting thought of della Porta running what would become the world's biggest—and most fascistic—religion.

A man dressed like a rabbi in the middle of the group stood. "And give up our faith?" he asked.

Della Porta smiled. "No. You can merge the two, as many in the Order have done. In time, a short time, you will see there are singular truths in this universe, as Veritism just revealed to you. We have more in store for you tonight. I'd like to introduce you to another prominent member of our illustrious Order."

Swells of chanting, yelling, and della Porta's voice seeped into the dark stone corridor, heightening Carlo's anxiety. He'd puke again if he had anything in his stomach. The spiral staircase above him led to the secret door beneath *Paradiso...* and to his destiny.

Once again, his hands and feet were cuffed. Four armed Protectors guarded any chance of escape, with two in front of him and two guarding his rear path. One behind him planted a pistol in the small of his back.

When the audience's voices rose or the Order members chanted, Carlo felt like he waited to enter a Roman arena—to be fed to lions. And from the sound of it, in front of an enthusiastic audience.

It wasn't so much the crowd or the Protectors that petrified him. No, his true source of dread came from two-dimensional spirits. They would be more incensed than ever with whatever was going on up there. Their screams always brought excruciating pain, like skewers driving through his ears, straight into his cerebral cortex.

It had been quiet for a while, save a muffled amplified voice, which he could tell from its cadence was della Porta.

The Protector in front of him touched an earpiece. He nodded to the fourth, who produced a pair of wireless earbuds, which he inserted into Carlo's ears. He then tapped his phone. Techno filled Carlo's aural spectrum. The same man placed a pair of airport-style, noise-canceling headphones over Carlo's head.

He appreciated the effort, though he knew it was only because della Porta needed his Painter to be conscious for whatever he had in store. It didn't matter anyway. The music was a distraction, and the headphones were useless. Carlo heard the voices in his *head*, not his ears.

The men nodded to each other. The one with the gun nudged it farther, indicating for Carlo to follow the two men climbing the stairs. It was the same path Tintoretto had trod hundreds of times—the same route Nick had taken that fateful night he ended Tintoretto's unnatural life.

Every step was an ascent toward his inevitable torture, before what would surely be either an agonizing death or imprisonment in the abyss. They could lock him away in his cell, but they couldn't force him to paint. Yet, if he didn't, they'd replace him with someone like Lobo.

He considered reaching up and yanking the feet of the Protector in front of him. It would cause that man to fall, leading to a domino effect with Carlo and the two Protectors beneath him. Carlo was sure he had the time and strength to pull it off, but he wasn't faster than a man pulling a trigger. He'd be shot in the back, though it could be worth it. He'd likely suffer a traumatic injury toppling down the stairs, but he'd take out a couple of Protectors.

He stretched up.

The Protector with the gun grabbed his shoulder and pulled him back.

In just two steps, the man in front of him climbed the rounded staircase out of his reach.

Carlo exhaled. He missed his chance. The man behind him prodded him forward. They climbed until Carlo arrived at the secret door. He poked his head through to find the other two Protectors waiting, guns out.

The man behind him shoved him through. With his ankles bound, Carlo stumbled onto the stage. The scene in the Great Council Room astounded him—hundreds of people, television cameras, giant screens. It was too much to process. His only saving grace was his position. Since he stood directly beneath *Paradiso*, perhaps with the distractions, only a handful of souls had noticed him. Though they were loud, he realized he could handle the dozen or so yelling at him.

"Ah, here he is," della Porta said into microphones on a lectern. "Our Venetian Painter."

Lobo stood next to the candleholder, which housed the Sun Crystal, pulsating from within. A group of shackled people, including many of Carlo's Guild friends, cowered in fear on the far side of the stage.

"Walk," said the Protector behind him.

Carlo didn't budge and instead scanned the room. To his right, on the edge of the bench that lined the room, sat Julia, wearing a stunning evening gown, her hands clasped on her belly. Next to her sat an elderly woman in a wheelchair. He couldn't pinpoint her but felt a strange sense of recognition—and connection.

His heart leaped upon searching the left side of the room. On the opposite wooden bench was his beloved Fosca, gorgeous in a black sequined dress. His sweet mother sat a few people away. At least he had a chance to rest his eyes on them again. He smiled at Fosca. Her eyes lit up on seeing him, before she broke down in sobs.

The Protector thrust his hands into Carlo's back.

He tripped and landed on his knees. Pain ricocheted up his thighs. The Protector yanked Carlo up, inadvertently turning him toward the painting.

The souls awoke in a fury.

All those voices, screaming at him, blaming him for their unjust incarceration, lashed at his mind, slicing through his thoughts, his hearing, and his field of vision. Angrier than ever, they accosted him. He yearned to free them, but they didn't know that.

The pain was too intense.

"Tintoretto's replacement," della Porta said. "He can hear the souls."

Carlo gazed up at his father, silently pleading for help.

None arrived.

He slumped over in a heap. His head whacked the wooden stage floor.

The world went black.

# 1591

I NCONGRUITY HAD BEEN TEARING Jacopo Tintoretto apart as if two versions of himself were painted on opposite sides of a single canvas. Since he accepted the role of Painter, for three years, he struggled ratifying his convictions. As a devout Catholic, the word of Christ infused his very being. He strove to live by His word. But as a member of the Order, he'd been exposed to truths—truths he needed to serve.

To serve, he needed to be able to perform his duties. To do so meant an assault on the senses no one could imagine.

The Order knew he could hear the souls. Initially, it wasn't a problem. With each soul added, the volume intensified. At the last Convocation, his 259$^{th}$ prisoner had been the tipping point. He had stormed off the dais and sprinted back to his room. He hadn't stepped foot in the Great Council Room since.

Jacopo Tintoretto was anything but a coward. He always faced his fears and life's obstacles head-on, with enthusiasm, even. But 259 individuals screaming in his head, demanding release, was too much to bear. It was too much for any mortal to bear. He wondered how God was able to hear so many prayers from people around the world.

Standing at his easel, he focused on a portrait of his beloved wife, Faustina. She died six years prior, and he missed her with every passing day. He'd painted dozens of portraits of her and their children, all from memory. The one on the easel captured the first time he had laid eyes upon Faustina, her hair a sunset copper, her skin glowing with youthful energy.

A knock rapped on the door.

"Enter," Tintoretto said in Venetian.

The door opened. "Merci," said a gravelly voice.

The French reply caused Tintoretto to pause his brushstroke. He turned and gaped, immediately placing his artist's tools on the table beside him. He dropped to one knee, genuflecting before the man at his door.

Tintoretto was not worthy to be in the presence of Cardinal Philippe de Lénoncourt. He had met the man on a visit to the Vatican, introduced by His Holiness himself. Besides being one of the Church's most prominent cardinals, de Lénoncourt was preceptor of the Order of the Holy Spirit, appointed personally by King Henri III. He was also a strictly undisclosed member of the Ancient Order of the Seventh Sun.

"Rise, good Painter," the cardinal said, switching to Latin.

Tintoretto dared look up. Dressed in full scarlet attire, de Lénoncourt's gray hair poked out from beneath his biretta. Bright brown eyes were nestled in youthful, vibrant skin.

"Please, sir," he said, "I am not here on official business."

Tintoretto rose. "To what do I owe this honor, your Eminence?"

"May I?" The cardinal gestured to Tintoretto's desk chair. "It has been a long journey."

"Of course."

Tintoretto rushed over to help the cardinal sit, but the man waved him off.

"Would you care for a glass of pinot grigio or some bussoli? I have a meager stock, but the servants replenish it every morning."

"The wine would be nice, thank you," said the cardinal as he settled into his seat. "I have heard of... an issue, shall we say, that prevents you from performing your painterly duties."

Tintoretto poured two glasses of white wine from his jug and placed one in front of de Lénoncourt. The cardinal nodded his thanks and took an appreciative sip. Tintoretto sat in his guest chair.

"You are referring to the souls," he said. "Yes, I can hear all of them. Simultaneously. It is driving me mad."

The cardinal observed Tintoretto's ears. Ashamed, Tintoretto brushed his long white hair in front of them.

"A fruitless attempt at drowning them out," said Tintoretto. He had scratched his ears until they bled. The action did nothing.

"As you are well aware," the cardinal said, "you perform a function that is critical to humanity. Many in the Church would disagree with me, which is why I, and others, must operate in secret. We—you and I—and all the members of the Order know the truth. What we do is for the betterment of the Christian world. The Lord forgives, but in my view, and that of His Holiness, some sins are unforgivable. If we can prevent those sins from happening, it is our responsibility to do so. It is you, your hand, that removes sin."

Tintoretto nodded. "It is a great burden, your Eminence. One I embrace with all my heart."

"We—nay, the world—thanks you for that." The cardinal took a healthy drink of his wine. "I believe you know I serve as royal counselor to His Most Christian Majesty, King Henri III."

"I do."

"You are unlikely aware that his Highness suffers from... a lack of focus."

Tintoretto raised an eyebrow. He had not heard that of the French king. He'd thought him quite the opposite.

"You are correct, Eminence," he said. "I did not know that. Is that why you grace me with your presence? To help me... focus?"

"Most astute, good Painter."

Tintoretto inhaled, pondering the offer. His situation was quite different from the king's—from anybody's—but he'd take any suggestion, especially from a man like Cardinal de Lénoncourt.

He bowed his head in gratitude.

"Thank you for gracing me with this honor, Eminence. One of which I am indubitably unworthy."

"You are most worthy, Monsieur Tintoretto. You have proved yourself a dozen times over."

Tintoretto smiled at the compliment. "So, how do we begin?"

"With one soul at a time."

# XLVI

U NRELENTING SCREAMS MOLESTED CARLO'S head.

He forced open his eyes. He focused on a single grain of wood inches from his face.

The regression to Tintoretto's memories with Lénoncourt remained fresh in his head, not only those moments in the Painter's cell but for months following that meeting. Lénoncourt had dutifully trained Tintoretto on the art of focus. Every day, the cardinal brought the Painter to the Great Council Room, teaching him to sharpen his concentration on a single pinpoint. Tintoretto learned how to control his mind, so he could shield it from the mass assault on his senses. Ultimately, he was able to isolate individual souls and converse with them. Though he never overcame his habit of scratching his ear canals.

Carlo had seen it all unfolding in real-time. In the present day, it may have been minutes, even seconds.

Sounds of the room drifted in through the souls' screams; his earbuds and noise-canceling headphones must've fallen off when he crashed to the floor.

Hands hooked beneath his armpits and hoisted him to his feet.

Carlo targeted his focus onto the feeling of those hands. While still present, the souls drifted to a recess of his brain, enabling him to take in his surroundings.

Nothing had changed. Protectors on either side of him gripped his arms. Della Porta stood at the pulpit observing Carlo. The audience viewed the proceedings in silence. Lobo stood ten feet from the candleholder, looking as smug as ever, with a victorious grin. Fosca watched from her seat, her face plastered with apprehension.

Carlo zeroed in on her, tuning out the souls and whatever della Porta was droning on about. He lingered on his love for only a moment; he needed to bring his focus elsewhere.

He shimmied out of the Protectors' grips and gazed up at *Paradiso*, identifying a single soul in the upper right of the painting.

"Papà," Carlo called to his father.

*"My son,"* his father replied in Venetian. *"It has been so long."* The voice that only Carlo could hear cracked with sadness.

The souls continued screaming at Carlo. He was vaguely aware of della Porta or someone in the audience saying something, but he shut them all out. Time was not on his side. Della Porta wouldn't allow this conversation for long.

"I know what happened," Carlo said. "I know the truth."

*"My murderer stands behind you. You must stop him. Do it now, before his power is too great. Do it, son. Do it now!"*

The father-son reunion was short-lived. Carlo owed his father—and his mother—vengeance. He was the only one who could stop della Porta. But he needed a weapon. The cuff chain was too short to choke him. He glanced around. His eyes landed on the candleholder. Nick O'Connor had successfully used it to kill Tintoretto and disable multiple Protectors.

With a singular focus, he twisted free of the Protectors' grasps. He bolted for the candleholder, reaching out, ready to grab it and swing it into della Porta's head.

Knuckles slammed into Carlo's jaw. The punch snapped his head back. He stumbled on his feet to find Lobo standing in front of the candleholder.

"Not this time, pendejo," Lobo said with gritted teeth.

Carlo tongued the blood in his inner cheek. He glanced behind him. Protectors approached.

"He's mine," Lobo shouted.

Fists raised, he swung for Carlo.

Carlo blocked the first punch, but Lobo landed a swift jab to his ribs that shot pain into his chest. He shoved Lobo away and took two steps back to regain his footing.

An agonizing electric charge gripped Carlo's ankles. He collapsed to the floor. As before, the shock rippled through his body, causing uncontrollable convulsions.

Through the agony, a now-familiar sight came into view: della Porta stood over him, the remote control in his hand.

"We don't have time for this," he said.

The moment the fight broke out on stage, Julia exchanged eye contact with Fosca, who returned the slightest nod. This was it. Now or never.

*Own it. Do it.*

A glance at Dante confirmed the Protector was sufficiently distracted. He had stepped a few feet away and watched the fight, his hand tucked into his suit jacket. Julia stuck a finger into her mouth and retrieved a wad of wax she and Fosca had hidden behind their molars.

She broke the moistened wax into two pieces and pressed half into each ear.

Across the room, Fosca did the same.

Then Julia went to work. She pressed the button on her cuffs, releasing them. With her hands freed, she reached into the Spanx beneath her dress and retrieved the bowl and striker.

Placing the bowl on her flattened left palm, she ran the striker around its rim in a practiced rhythm. Just like in Paris, she couldn't hear the music, so she didn't know if it was effective. In that small apartment, they had played back recordings to confirm it worked. She knew it would cause a trance but affecting the Sun Crystal was another story. Additional uncertainty gnawed at her: was it loud enough?

She looked up at Dante. The man swayed, as if in a daze. The people nearest her mirrored his motion. Conversations dwindled into silence, quelled by the bowl's serenade. Like a ripple in a calm pond, the song spread, captivating all who heard it.

The melodic tone reached the stage. The Protectors nearest her, followed by Fanella, della Porta, Lobo, Lacasse, the prisoners, and even Carlo soon succumbed to its allure. They lifted their heads, as if hearing something wondrously peculiar and extraordinary that had ensnared their senses.

Julia watched Carlo turn to Fosca with an inquisitive expression.

"Headphones," Fosca mouthed.

Carlo shook his head, not comprehending.

"Headphones," she yelled. She cupped her ears in a pantomime.

As if drunk, Carlo wobbled over to his noise-canceling headphones. He scooped them up and put them on. He visibly snapped out of his trance.

Julia continued circling the bowl with the striker, concentrating on an even, constant rotation.

She refocused her attention on the stage. Carlo removed an entranced Protector's gun from its holster. He strode over to della Porta, who was also spellbound by the singing bowl, and snatched the remote control, which he tossed to Fosca.

He then set his sights on the Sun Crystal.

The crystal pulsated in rhythm with each rotation Julia made on the bowl.

*This is it*, she thought.

Her heart rate increased with her excitement, but she continued the steady motion.

Carlo pocketed the pistol and removed the Sun Crystal from its mount. He held it high, displaying it to the souls in *Paradise*. The crystal's pulses increased. It started vibrating.

*Paradise*, too, shimmered as the painted souls animated. The same happened on the screens televising the paintings in France and Spain.

Crack!

A sharp pain engulfed the top of Julia's head. The wax popped out of one ear.

The bowl slipped from her hand. It landed on the marble floor with a clatter that echoed throughout the room.

The Sun Crystal's light returned to a solid state. Carlo brought it down and stared at it quizzically.

Julia turned to find Artemisia standing beside her, a cane clenched in her leathery hands, threatening to whack Julia again. She couldn't believe it. A one-time hero of hers—a woman who'd been persecuted for her own rape—had foiled the freedom of hundreds. Whether wittingly or not, Artemisia would bring ultimate power to Salvatore della Porta.

Those farthest from Julia regained their awareness first. Then, like a slow-moving reverse wave, one after another, everyone returned from their sublime states.

Julia got to the floor and crawled for the bowl. Her fingers glanced the edge. Cold, sharp metal pressed into the back of her neck. She twisted to find Dante's short sword pointing down at her. With his free hand, Dante retrieved the Tangut treasure. Artemisia returned to her wheelchair, exhausted.

Julia raised a hand in surrender. She got to her knees as Dante allowed her to stand. His sword remained leveled squarely at her neck.

From her vantage point, she watched the scene unfolding on the stage.

Lobo tackled Carlo. The two tumbled to the floor.

The Sun Crystal escaped Carlo's grip. It bounced to the stage and rolled straight into della Porta's waiting hands.

"No," Julia screamed.

"Subdue him," della Porta yelled to the Protectors nearest Carlo.

Four moved for a scuffle. Along with Lobo, they held Carlo down, who writhed and twisted. He managed to free a hand. He found the gun in his pocket and brought it out against the resistance of the man holding his arm. Slowly, he forced the barrel up to his chin.

"Carlo, no!" Fosca shouted. She charged for him.

The gun fired, echoing across the cavernous room.

The bullet slammed into the floor, an inch from Carlo's face. A Protector gripped the gun and ripped it from Carlo's hand.

The gunshot reawakened those who'd yet to snap out of it.

Audience members screamed at the noise. Many jumped up and raced for the doors in a panic, overtaking the outnumbered Protectors, who stopped those they could. Even some Order members, unnerved by the gunfire, moved for the exit. Fanella and Lacasse attempted to quell the agitated crowd.

"Everyone, sit down," della Porta snapped into his lapel mic. "Now!"

Many ignored him, but far more rushed back to their seats in terror.

"That won't happen again," della Porta said.

Gripping the Sun Crystal, he marched over to Carlo.

"His hands," he ordered the Protectors. "Put them on the crystal. Keep them there."

Against Carlo's will, two Protectors forced his hands on the crystal while the other two held him down.

"Get that bowl," della Porta said to Lobo.

With his and Carlo's hands wrapped around the Sun Crystal, della Porta began a low chant amid the pandemonium engulfing the room.

Julia caught Bernardo's attention, who stood off to the side as if conflicted.

"Help," she mouthed.

He remained motionless.

"Et beatus est sol," della Porta said in Latin, gripping the Sun Crystal with Carlo. "Blessed is the Sun. Lux in tenebris lucet. Light shines in darkness. Follow the sacred heart. There is nothing to fear."

Della Porta switched to a mantric chant that sounded like Chinese, if not the Tangut dialect. The Order members joined him, their collective voices growing ever more passionate.

The Sun Crystal glowed. Carlo's body arched. His pupils clouded.

"I have been chosen," della Porta said in English. "This is my birthright. None shall hinder my path."

The crystal radiated a bright yellow.

Della Porta's body jerked back, but his hands remained locked on the crystal. He absorbed the power, and it seemed as though his body glowed.

At last, he relaxed. He pulled the Sun Crystal from Carlo's grip and stood triumphant.

"Everyone," he called out, his voice booming. "Back to your seats. Now!"

Some in the crowd stopped, but others quickened their exodus.

Julia looked for Fosca, but she was nowhere to be seen. Then she spotted her friend sprinting to the back, dodging people and Protectors. She reached the media scaffolding and climbed to the center TV camera.

Her face filled the main screen.

"Now, Marcel," Fosca yelled. "Do it!"

Nothing happened.

"Stop her," della Porta shouted.

Fanella, Lacasse, and Protectors rushed for Fosca.

Lobo appeared at Dante's side. He snatched the bowl and scowled at Julia, then headed back to the stage.

"Marcel, now!" Fosca called again, hanging on for dear life.

Julia glanced at Dante. He alternated his attention between the screen and the live action at the back of the room.

In his distraction, Julia contorted her body away from Dante's sword.

She grabbed the hilt, ripped it from his hands, and in one motion, spun—and sliced the blade across Artemisia's throat.

The ancient Painter's mouth popped open. Blood poured out from the laceration. The last hint of life in her eyes fixed on Julia.

"Look!" called a woman near Julia. She pointed at the screen displaying *Paradise* at the Louvre.

Just as in Madrid when Julia killed El Greco, the painting came alive. This time, everyone in the room—everyone watching around the world—bore witness. Those around her and on the stage, again like a wave across the room, stopped to watch the incredible scene.

Angry souls escaped from the painting, but they remained tethered.

The Sun Crystal needed to be destroyed.

Lobo spun to Julia, his face smoldering with rage.

"Puta," he said. "What have you done?" Furious, he spewed a torrent of Spanish.

"Marcel, do it!" Fosca shouted, still hanging on the scaffolding.

Lobo charged for Julia.

She feebly swung the sword at him. He backed away and grabbed the hilt, ripping it from her hands.

She tripped and fell.

He raised the sword, ready to strike.

She scrambled backward and covered her eyes.

Another earsplitting gunshot rang out.

Blood, bone, and brain matter sprayed Julia.

Lobo landed on top of her. The sword scraped the floor next to her.

She screamed at the bloody exit wound in his forehead. She shoved the Spanish Painter off to find Bernardo standing before her. Smoke drifted from the barrel of the gun in his hand.

Suppressing her nausea, she exhaled a sigh of relief.

Panic erupted around her. Audience members scattered from the violence, running every which way.

"Bernardo!" della Porta called into his mic. "Traditore! Prottetori, arrestatelo!"

Julia didn't need to speak Italian to know della Porta called for Bernardo to be seized. Dante was the first to move for him. Bernardo held his gun out in defense.

"Don't make me shoot, Dante," he said. "Signora, behind me."

She clambered to her feet and did as he instructed. The two backed against the wall. Multiple Protectors moved for them.

"Look," someone called. "The other painting!"

Julia checked out the screen displaying *Paradise* in Madrid. With Lobo dead, the souls burst free, again desperate for ascension but still confined to their purgatory.

"Marcel!!" Fosca screamed into the camera, her face still on the main screen. "Now!"

Fanella and Lacasse climbed up for her. She kicked, but they grabbed her feet and dragged her down.

Julia couldn't see what happened to her friend from her vantage point but prayed she was okay. She also prayed that Marcel got the message and had a chance to set his speakers up—and that they'd be loud enough.

The moment she heard the tone, she felt like a toddler swaddled in her mother's arms.

The sound didn't come from outside, but from all the speakers della Porta had set up within the Great Council Room. The bowl's transcendent melody filled the space, entrancing every individual there.

Marcel had done it, Julia thought. He didn't need his outdoor speakers. He hacked the system and played one of the recordings they'd made.

The volume rose.

The music bathed Julia, coaxing her into a state of serenity. Still conscious, perhaps because she knew what to expect, she watched as everyone else fell into the bowl's trance.

But she didn't care about them.

She fixed her gaze on della Porta. He stood on the stage, front-center. He also seemed to slip into a hypnotic state, but he was aware, as he, too, watched the Sun Crystal in his hands.

It pulsated, but he held fast, not releasing his grip. He brought it into his body, cradling it to dampen the vibrations, but it had the opposite effect. His body quivered. He pulled in a long, uncontrollable breath.

The Sun Crystal's throbbing intensified until it glowed a solid bright white.

Then it transitioned to black. A shimmering black.

For a moment, it stilled... along with the world.

Then shattered.

The Sun Crystal exploded into a million pieces, spraying out and ripping through della Porta like buckshot.

The song stopped.

Della Porta's body tipped back and landed with a thud.

Julia came to, snapping out of her trance. She nudged Bernardo aside and dashed up to the stage.

Crystal fragments lay all around, shimmering like diamonds, refracting light rays that streamed across the Great Council Room.

Carlo crawled over to his once-father figure. Dozens of tiny crystals were embedded in della Porta's face. Blood seeped out of other holes in his body, soaking his tuxedo shirt. His hands had been shredded to flaps of skin on exposed bone.

"We are not... punished *for* our sins," della Porta whispered with feeble breaths, "but... but *by* them." His head tipped to the side.

Carlo closed his eyes.

It could've been Julia's beleaguered vision, but she could've sworn a dark haze engulfed della Porta's body, then faded into oblivion.

A serene hum brought Julia's attention upward.

*Paradise* glowed.

She glanced back for a moment. The entire room watched in awe and wonder.

The souls expanded and pulled from the painting. One by one, they departed from their long purgatory. The same happened in Madrid and Paris.

Hundreds of bright, translucent souls swirled around the room and headed for the ceiling, where they disappeared. Iridescent masses were everywhere, pure exultation on their diaphanous faces. Benton escaped the confines of his painting. The glimmering soul of a man with dark eyes flew to Carlo, then to Carlo's mother, where he circled her before rising to the sky.

Amid the phenomenon, Julia focused on the only soul she truly cared for. Nick's portrait, propped against the wall, lit up like the others.

His soul exited and soared to her, swirling around her. His essence wrapped her like a warm blanket of uncompromising love. He stopped in front of her and smiled. He reached out, and she touched his intangible hand, like bringing her fingers through a ray of sparkling light. His radiance melded with her being. For a moment of divine bliss, they were one again. He captured her gaze, then floated up to an auburn-haired woman waiting for him.

Isabella.

When the two souls connected, Nick's features morphed into those of his first life—Angelo.

Angelo nodded to Julia sympathetically, apologetically, and filled with gratitude.

The last to go, Isabella and Angelo intertwined in a mesmerizing array of luminescence... and locked together, spiraled upward to Heaven.

Uncontrollable tears streamed down Julia's cheeks.

"Goodbye, my love," she whispered.

The room fell silent.

The painting was nothing more, nothing less. Paint on canvas. But truths had been exposed to the world. Nothing would ever be the same.

Fosca raced onto the stage, making a beeline for Carlo. She threw her arms around him and kissed him all over.

Bernardo joined her a moment later. He uncuffed Carlo's wrists and ankles. Carlo nodded his thanks and embraced Fosca.

"Well done," Bernardo said to Julia.

Julia wiped her tears. She couldn't help but laugh. The chief Protector joined in. The two of them looked around the room. Nobody moved, still amazed by everything that happened.

A shimmer on the floor caught Julia's eye. She crouched and scooped up some shards from the Sun Crystal.

*It couldn't be.*

"They look like diamonds," she said to Bernardo. "Is that what they are?"

He picked one out of her hand and held it to the light.

"If they are," he said, "I think you're entitled to a handful or two. And this." He reached into his inner suit pocket and pulled out Nick's letter.

She took the paper and admired her husband's portrait. With a bittersweet smile, she gazed upward.

# Epilogo I

TURQUOISE WAVES KISSED JULIA's kayak as it skidded to a stop on golden-white sand. Niran, her Thai helper, had been waiting faithfully, as he always did. He handed Julia a towel and towed the craft ashore.

"Kop kun khrap, Niran," she said.

"You are welcome, Miss Julia."

Gripping the Nikon SLR strapped to her neck, she jogged up the beach to her private cabana to check out her latest batch of photos of the tropical scenery.

It had been over a year since all that transpired.

After three long weeks of interrogation in Italy, the U.S. State Department negotiated her extradition. They asked her questions for another three days before she was allowed to return to Boston. It turned out della Porta hadn't disposed of Nick's body, so she had it flown home and arranged a funeral the day it arrived. She felt bad that not all of his friends and family could make it, but she needed immediate closure. Following that, she wrapped up Nick's loose ends, sold nearly all their belongings, and vacated their apartment—which had stunk of stale air and rotting plants.

Because the events at the Palazzo had been streamed, it was hard to find a person who hadn't watched them by the time she returned home. She recoiled at the word 'celebrity,' but everybody recognized her. Even the customs agent couldn't stop staring at her when he stamped her passport. Every media outlet in America wanted to interview her. She turned them all down.

Della Porta didn't succeed at becoming the head of the world's singular religion, but there was no question his actions changed everything. Skeptics existed, and their voices were growing louder, claiming the whole thing was special effects and a conspiracy, but more than enough people knew the truth. Millions who didn't witness it believed it, and that's what mattered—concrete evidence of the existence of souls and the afterlife. Unlimited questions persisted. Scholars, scientists, and clergy researched, debated, and pondered. For now, that's all they could do, with the most significant question being:

*Will people live differently?*

The lasting effects of Veritism were still to be seen, but either way, Julia wanted none of it. She needed to go. She needed to relax. She needed to *sleep*.

Her friends and family were concerned for her well-being and thought she was flippant when she left just days after Nick's funeral.

Their protests didn't stop her.

It turned out the Sun Crystal really was a giant diamond. When she left the Palazzo, she carried off two handfuls of the gems. They were even more valuable because people were willing to pay a fortune for a piece of the Sun Crystal. Between those and Nick's life insurance, she was set for life and then some, able to live out her dream of traveling the world taking photos.

She started in Australia and New Zealand, then found herself in Southeast Asia. It had been a month already on Ko Pha Ngan, a flawless island in the Gulf of Thailand, and she felt she could spend the rest of her life there. There was a strange irony that she ended up in actual paradise.

She brushed aside the drapery of her cabana.

Her phone buzzed on the table. She plopped down on the chaise and answered with a smile.

Fosca's smiling face appeared beneath her still-red bob. Julia had dyed her hair to its natural blond, matching the growing roots.

"My God, Julia," Fosca said, "have you moved into that cabana? When are you getting your Thai citizenship?"

Julia grinned. "What can I say? I like it here. When are you going to visit?"

"Oh, man. You know I'd love to. Carlo is so jealous of you."

"Then come. I miss you so much. I'll have a jet pick you up tomorrow."

Fosca laughed. "How about I get *my* jet to fly you to Venice?"

"Not in this lifetime."

"You know that expression has a new meaning now, right?"

"Very true. Either way, I'll leave Venice to you and Carlo."

Fosca glanced behind her, then lowered her voice. "You know it would've meant the world to him if you were here."

All day long, Julia had a sensation of forgetting something. "Shit. It's tonight, isn't it?"

"Yeah, we're starting in like five minutes."

"Tell him I said knock 'em dead or break a leg or whatever you're supposed to say." She paused on Fosca's forlorn expression. "And... that I wish I could've been there. Maybe... maybe another time."

"I get it. We *are* talking about visiting you, wherever you'll be. We miss you. We just have so much going on here. It's hard to get away. Speaking of which, I better go. Love you."

"Hey, Fosca."

"Yeah?"

"Don't let time become your master. Make time for yourself."

Fosca thought to herself for a moment, then nodded. "Well said, oh wise one."

"I mean it. Love you too."

Julia ended the call and exhaled with a satisfied smile. She was truly happy for her friends and wished them all the best. The thought brought her attention to the other side of the cabana. Propped against the pole was a possession she brought with her everywhere—the portrait of Nick. With a forlorn exhale, she blew him a kiss, then gazed through the cabana opening out to the shimmering ocean.

She knew in her heart... she'd find happiness again.

# Epilogo II

C ARLO EYED FOSCA END the call with Julia. He had heard half of it, and though he wished Julia could've been there, he completely understood. Being in the Palazzo Ducale was hard enough for him and Fosca.

She strode over, straightened his black tie, and planted a kiss on his lips, which he eagerly returned. He massaged his stubble. All his life, he had never needed to shave. Strangely, days after della Porta used the Sun Crystal to siphon the power from him, he began seeing some facial hair. A few gray hairs also appeared in his sideburns.

"I should've shaved," he said.

"It makes you look distinguished. I love it. Don't worry, you're going to kill them out there. In a manner of speaking."

He smirked. Fosca's humor, spirit, and beauty consistently overwhelmed him. She'd become the rock he never knew he needed—the missing piece in his life. Well, maybe he knew, but he had never admitted it before.

"Amore mio," he said.

"My love," she replied.

There was no way to confirm his suspicions, but he knew. Fosca knew. They were soul mates.

Fosca brushed the shoulders on his black suit jacket though they were spotless.

"Ready?" she asked.

He opened his mouth, but no words came out. He nodded.

The two of them stepped to threshold of the Great Council Room. Bernardo greeted them with a warm smile. He opened the door.

Carlo steadied his nerves and entered the cavernous room.

Like spontaneous combustion, five hundred people erupted into thunderous cheers. He had never experienced anything like it. The audience rose to their feet, applauding as if he'd saved all of them.

Maybe he did. But he was just one small part of a team. So many did their part. So many paid dearly for it.

Tears welled in his eyes, but he fought them back.

After one last glance at Fosca, who wore a massive smile as tears of joy streamed through her mascara, he climbed the dais, and approached the podium.

He gestured to Fosca and Bernardo so the applause would target them, as they so richly deserved, then raised his hands for silence. The audience abided. His mother sat in the front row, beaming.

"Stand tall, Carlo," she mouthed, just like she would say when he was a boy.

His Guild friends were in the same row, all glowing with pride.

He drew in a deep breath.

The teleprompters before him displayed a painstakingly prepared speech, but the lines felt off.

Every person in the room was fixated on him. They waited for him to speak, to hear—and follow—every word. This was an opportunity unlike any other—an opportunity not for him but for the world.

"When I was a boy," he said into the mics, "I had learned that people—that *everything*—came from stardust." He glanced at his mother. "My mamma does not know this, but one night, I snuck out of my room and went to the roof of our house. I lay on my back and gazed at the sky for hours with one thought. If we are made of stardust, does that not make us stars?"

He let the room ponder the thought for a moment.

"When I was a teenager," he continued, "I found solace in art and music. I lost myself in images and lyrics. I've always loved Bob Marley. For hours, I listened to the genius of his words. Lately, there is one particular line from his masterpiece, *No Woman No Cry*, that I can't stop thinking about. 'In this great future, you can't forget your past.'"

The tune played in his head as he uttered the words.

"My relationship with Salvatore della Porta is no secret. I will never justify what that man did, nor will I defend his actions. But the strength of Veritism cannot be denied. He lifted a curtain. Some believe special effects were used, but most of us know the truth. Truths of this universe. In the scheme of a grand design we cannot begin to comprehend, we are nothing but microscopic specks. But each of those specks is stardust. We are the light in the dark. Our lives have purpose. *We* matter. Our *actions* matter. Our actions have reactions that can reverberate across the centuries. There are still evil souls in the world. There always will be." He sighed with an unexpected sense of regret. "We, all of us, every person alive, now stands in front of two doors."

He glanced back at Fosca. She covered her mouth with her hand, unable to contain her emotions, but he knew she beamed with pride. Bernardo stood beside her, his one arm wrapped warmly around her shoulder. An irrepressible grin enveloped his once-stoic face.

"One door," Carlo continued, turning back to the audience, "opens to the same path humanity has walked since the dawn of time. One filled with selfishness, greed, and wars. The other door leads to a *new* path. A path paved with the knowledge that *actions matter*." He pointed to the rear of the room. "A path that leads to a great future."

*finito*

# THANK YOU!

Thank you for reading MASTER OF THE ABYSS. If you enjoyed it, please consider leaving a review on your platform of purchase, Amazon, Goodreads, and/or BookBub. Nothing helps an author more. Your review will encourage readers to pick up a copy of this and other books by Rob Samborn.

# Follow Rob on Social Media

**www.robsamborn.com**
(sign up for the newsletter to be informed of events and new books)
**Goodreads**: https://www.goodreads.com/author/show/21829341.Rob_Samborn
**BookBub**: https://www.bookbub.com/authors/rob-samborn
**Facebook**: https://www.facebook.com/RobSambornAuthor
**Instagram**: https://www.instagram.com/robsamborn/
**Twitter**: https://twitter.com/RobSamborn
**TikTok**: https://www.tiktok.com/@robsamborn

# Time Has No End

The story has ended in the present day, but you'll recall the opening scene in *The Prisoner of Paradise* is Angelo escaping Venice under cover of darkness while the Order pursues him. All the flashbacks in the books that involve Angelo happen *before* that scene until he returns twenty-five years later. We know Angelo isn't the type of guy to just give up, especially after what happened to his beloved Isabella. Want to know what happened to Angelo? Read about his journey in *The Swordsman of Venice*.

*The Swordsman of Venice Part I* is currently available as an e-book exclusively on Amazon. Part II and the combined book will be released in 2024 as an e-book and paperback, available everywhere.

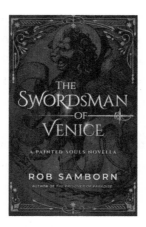

# ACKNOWLEDGEMENTS

Writing these acknowledgements is immensely bittersweet for me. Not because of the gratitude I have for so many people, but because the series has concluded (in the present day, at least). Those who know me well will be surprised to learn that I wrote the epilogues with tears in my eyes. I wasn't sad, though. Quite the opposite. These were tears of joy. They were tears of pride for Julia, Carlo, and Fosca. Yes, I was sad for Julia and Nick, but Julia rose to the occasion to defeat della Porta against impossible odds. In *Painter of the Damned*, she realized this was much bigger than her or releasing Nick. Once she did, she never backed down. Similarly, Carlo started as a self-absorbed player, chasing his art career and girls, not taking anything seriously. He, too, rose to the occasion, willing to make the ultimate sacrifice.

It's no secret that I first wrote *The Prisoner of Paradise* as a standalone screenplay. During the adaptation process, the story grew organically, and I knew it was destined to be a trilogy. I had ideas on where it was headed, but I didn't have a clue as to how the heroes were going to win the day. Writers know that characters take on lives of their own as the story unfolds. I created these characters and wrote the words, but in a sense, I dropped them into a maze and let them figure it out. They did in spades.

I think we all wonder what we'd do in extreme circumstances. Hopefully none of us will ever find ourselves in such situations, but if we do, I hope we all rise to the occasion and do the right thing.

There are so many people to whom I owe my thanks, not only for their support with *Master of the Abyss*, but the entire Painted Souls series.

First and foremost, I need to thank my incredible wife and daughter for their support and understanding. I'm well aware of the hours I lost being with my family to write this book. I do believe that in the end it will all be worth it, just as it was for the characters in the story.

The year in which I wrote *Master of the Abyss* was a challenging one, to say the least. My son was born just under 10 months before the release of this book about 4 months after the release of *Painter of the Damned*. I love him more than words can say and his and my daughter's birth are two of my greatest joys in life. But any parent knows the challenges presented by a newborn.

I also have a demanding day job that requires a degree of travel. You might be wondering how I found the time to write a 300-page book. I wonder that myself. Let's just say if a vampire bit me, they'd be wired on caffeine for a week.

On top of a new baby and demanding day job, I also left my previous publisher after a tumultuous and to date, still ongoing, experience. My new publisher, Lost Meridian Press, has been phenomenal and I want to thank everyone involved with LMP. Needless to say, republishing two books while writing a third was a wee bit stressful. But enough about challenges. Life is about overcoming them, right?

I also want to thank my agents at Brower Literary & Management, Aimee Ashcraft and Kimberly Brower. Their undying support through thick and thin has been nothing short of extraordinary. From my initial query letter, which I think I sent a century ago, to the release of *Master of the Abyss*, it's been a long road, and they've been with me for the whole journey. Thank you both.

Thank you to everyone at Tantor Media for believing in my work and bringing voice to *The Prisoner of Paradise, Painter of the Damned,* and soon *Master of the Abyss*. Special thanks goes to Zac Aleman, whose narration still bowls me over. It's no easy task to narrate a book that contains dozens of characters from multiple countries and centuries, but he brought each one to life perfectly. Did I add some new nationalities to *Master of the Abyss* just to see if Zac can pull off the accent? I'll never tell. ;-)

Thank you to my incomparable editor, L.A. Mitchell, for catching all my mistakes and making me an infinitely better writer. Only she knows how crappy the first draft of this book was. Fortunately, she's sworn to secrecy, under penalty of her soul being banished to an eternal (yet artistic) purgatory.

Thank you to David Ter-Avanesyan at Ter33Design for creating yet another brilliant cover that looks like it's leaping off the page and into readers' hands.

The writing community at large is nothing short of a global phenomenon. For all of social media's downsides and amid a time of worldwide upheaval, I have connected with and befriended dozens of writers from around the world, from people working on their first manuscript to million-copy bestselling authors with 30+ books out. Without exaggeration, every one of these people has been incredible. The writing community isn't just limited to writers. It also includes reviewers, bloggers, people in publishing, and so many more.

Many of these people have taken time from their busy schedules to read and review my books, providing invaluable blurbs. The list of who I want to thank is long and I'm sure I'll miss people. If your name isn't on this list, please know that it's a mere oversight. So, in no particular order... thank you, Jayne Ann Krentz, Gary McAvoy, Kiersten Modglin, Ellen Meister, Shanessa Gluhm, Ty Keenum, Bruce Leonard, Karen Kile-Carr, Alex Blevens, Mike Krentz, David L. Robbins, Avanti Centrae, Mary Kubica, EJ Mellow, Yasmin Angoe, Jane Thornley, Andrew Clawson, Damyanti Biswas, Laura Kemp, Terry Shepherd, C. D'Angelo, Robert Gwaltney, Jeff Gordon from Writers Boot Camp (where I wrote the original script), Kevin Willmering and Frank Gladstone (who optioned the original script), all the friends I made through TPP, those in the Rabble Writers group, 2021 Debuts, 2022 Debuts, the TradAuthorHive group, all my writing groups in L.A., and my current writing group in Denver, the Mile High Writers Workshop.

Many people in MHWW read and critiqued a portion of at least one of my books and their support has been undying. Again, I'm sure I'm missing people here, so please don't take it personally. The list includes Jennifer Duggins, Johnny Rad, Jared, Henry, Maddie, John K., Karen, Brenna, Andre, Lorraine, Michael G., Sidney, Ray, Sam D., Mike L., Brennan, Ian, Shawn, Ed, Matt, Brian, Grace, Kate, Rick, Yvegenii, Aaron, Anthony N., Jenna, Liz, John S., Grant, Tracy, Robert L., Johnny Red, Jamie G., Anthony M., Ben, J.R., and everybody else.

The phenomenal artist Andrea Marin also provided insight into Venetian culture, as well as the Palazzo Ducale. He, the other artist members of "Prisoners of Art," and all emerging artists, are my true inspiration.

Everybody who worked with me on the ongoing marketing of the Painted Souls series. You may not be named here, but you're in my head and my heart. Thank you.

Again, I want to thank all of you who reviewed, shared, and championed my work. The list is long. You know who you are.

Of course, incredible gratitude goes to my parents, brother, extended family, and friends—you all provided everlasting support. You're not named here but you know who you are. I am forever grateful.

Finally, I want to express my undying gratitude to <u>you</u>, the reader. I like to think of myself as a storyteller more than a writer. Without readers, a book is just words in an author's head. To be able to share my stories with you is one of my greatest and most fulfilling rewards in life, outside of my family. I have hundreds of tales in my head, and I can't wait to share the next stories with you, including a whole new series on the horizon.

Thank you all!

Printed in the USA
CPSIA information can be obtained
at www.ICGtesting.com
LVHW090346081223
765818LV00058B/1466